SURPRISE
PACKAGES

THE COMPANY OF GOOD WOMEN

THE COMPANY OF GOOD WOMEN

SURPRISE PACKAGES

a novel by

NANCY ANDERSON • LAEL LITTKE
CARROLL HOFELING MORRIS

DESERET
BOOK

SALT LAKE CITY, UTAH

Visit us at deseretbook.com

Library of Congress Cataloging-in-Publication Data

Anderson, Nancy.
Surprise packages / Nancy Anderson, Lael Littke, and Carroll Hofeling Morris.
    p. cm. — (The company of good women ; 3)
  Sequel to: Three tickets to Peoria.
  ISBN-13: 978-1-59038-908-9 (pbk.)
   1. Female friendship—Fiction.   2. Mormon women—Religious
life—Fiction.   3. Domestic fiction. I. Littke, Lael. II. Morris,
Carroll Hofeling.   III. Title.
  PS3601.N5444S87 2008
  813'.6—dc22   2007053016

Printed in the United States of America
Worzalla Publishing Co., Stevens Point, WI

10 9 8 7 6 5 4 3 2 1

*To the teachers and mentors who taught us
to get to the heart of the matter in life and in writing,
especially Helen Hinckley Jones, in memoriam*

Acknowledgments

To Suzanne Brady, whose gentle encouragement and keen insight have made all the books in this series better; Dr. William Keig for information on treatment of fractures and osteomyelitis; Lt. Col. David Hofeling, Ret., for insights into the life of a career officer in the Air Force; Keri Anderson Hughes, Erin Langely, and Christy Astorga for making life in Gainesville, Florida, come alive; Jewel Adams for her candor regarding growing up black in the South; Clark Coberly for legal consultation; Walter Hofmann, M.D., ret., and Susan Hill, M.S.L.P., for answers to psychological questions; Roger Allen for ideas on how to talk to young people about sealings; Joel Gyllenskog for information on computer consulting businesses; Kara Palmer and Amy Christensen for passing along the word *Lovence*. Special thanks to Tiffany Witkin and her daughter, Jesse, for sharing the real-life choir experience and giving us permission to use it; the ladies in the Country Brook Ward, who really do have fleece blankets in Relief Society when the air conditioning is too cold; Tiffney Gibson Anderson for her brilliant plot idea; Jim Anderson, Gary Morris, Lunch Bunch, and other family members and friends for their support, especially when the deadline was looming.

Prologue

2004

The three women sitting at a table in a pizza parlor in Moab, Utah, eyed an assortment of colorful brochures on the table.

The redhead put aside the brochure for the trail ride they'd taken that morning, and they pored over the ones remaining, selecting those with activities they were interested in. Then the blonde picked up a copy of the local paper included with their information packet and flipped through it.

Pointing at a photo above an obituary, she said, "This woman reminds me of Gabby. Listen to her obit."

When she finished reading, the dark-haired one said, "You're right. She was a genuine Crusty Old Broad, like Gabby."

"I wonder if she wrote her own obituary," said the blonde. "That's what I plan to do when the time comes. That way, I'll know it's the way I want it."

"How are we supposed to know when the time comes?" the redhead asked.

The blonde looked thoughtful. "We might not. We should write them now. That way, they'd be done, and we could see how close we are to becoming Crusty Old Broads."

The blonde and the redhead fell into a contest to see who could come up with the silliest obituary lines. Neither seemed to notice that their friend wasn't taking part in the fun.

Chapter 1

1996

JUNEAU

On February 1 Juneau decided to make an inventory, not of her cup-
boards and closets but of her life. She set up two columns on her computer screen, one titled *The Good* and the other *The Bad*. After gazing at
those headings for a while, she deleted them and typed *Positive* and
Negative. Still not satisfied, she deleted again and sat thinking. *How do
you assess a life on paper?* Finally, at the top of the first column she wrote
Got and across from it *Not*. As number one on the *Not* side, she typed
Gideon.

Today was Gideon's eighth birthday. He'd been on her mind all day,
as he had been every day since Misty had wrenched him away on
Christmas. How could she not think about him? For almost eight years
he'd been like her son, hers and Greg's. Misty, their flighty, restless daughter, was his biological mother, but she'd skipped out on him when he was
three months old. Juneau and Greg had been the ones who kissed his
boo-boos better and explained the intricacies of tying shoes. They should
be the ones watching him blow out the eight candles on his cake and
sharing his excitement about being baptized. But the guardianship papers
they'd drawn up when Misty left Gideon with them as a baby turned out
to have been inadequately prepared and, as their lawyer friend Vance
said, too flimsy to stand up in court.

It was her fault, what had happened. Not only had she done nothing
to stop Misty from whisking Gideon off to Idaho but she'd actually kept
Greg and Trace and Ira from physically preventing Misty from going. At
the time, she'd been afraid of how it would affect Gideon to see them
fighting over him like dogs over a bone. Now she regretted that decision,
fearing he was more devastated by their letting him go than he would
have been by their efforts to keep him.

Staring at his name on her inventory, Juneau wondered what she
could put on the *Got* side that would even begin to balance out the loss of

Gideon. She couldn't think of anything, but perhaps time might change her mind. As a writer, she knew the nature of stories. There were always many twists and turns and surprises before the resolution. As she'd told her friends Deenie and Erin when they'd been together in Hawaii in January, Gideon's story wasn't over yet.

She closed the file, assigning it the name *GotNot*. Then she checked her e-mail. There was a message from Trace, Gideon's birth father. "Juneau and Greg," Trace wrote, "an e-mail birthday greeting has been delivered to Gideon from all of us! I did it through Cath's mom, who 'just happened' to be at Gideon's school in Preston this morning when Misty dropped him off. Misty was ticked big time, Cath's mom said, but Gideon glowed when she handed him the printout. He knows we haven't forgotten him."

The e-mail was signed, "Trace, the Triumphant."

Juneau leaned back and smiled. It raised her spirits immeasurably to know that Trace had gotten a greeting to Gideon. Misty hadn't allowed any of them to be in touch with him, claiming it would be easier for him to adjust if she cut off all contact when she took him to Idaho.

"Good for you, Cath," Juneau said aloud. She suspected that the wily Cath had engineered the whole thing—her family home in Mink Creek wasn't that far from Preston—and she thanked heaven that the girl had come from Idaho to work in California. She was a distant cousin and had become a member of the group that Juneau and Greg counted as their family. And she'd become close friends with Trace.

Juneau was petting Gideon's cat, Numbtail, asleep on top of her computer, when she heard Greg's car in the driveway. She checked her desk clock: 2:10. Since Greg had quit his teaching job at Cal State Los Angeles and he and Arnie Gilbert had started Smoketree Systems, a computer consulting business, he never came home until well into the evening. Why would he be here at this hour?

Anxiously she hurried to the door and flung it open. Greg stood there, grinning. "Good news, Juney."

She put a hand to her throat. "Gideon?"

His grin faltered. "No, but it's still good. We got a contract we needed. A *big* contract. Smoketree Systems is going to fly yet."

Greg grabbed her and did a swing-around, as Giddy called it, with her feet off the floor. "Let's celebrate," he said. "Dancing? Sailing? Dinner atop the Hilton? How about driving up Angeles Crest and stopping somewhere to neck?"

Juneau laughed. "All of the above, but how about dancing? I heard there's a square dance group starting up tonight."

"Well, doll yourself up, little darlin'. I'll be home again by six." After planting a resounding kiss on her lips, Greg said, "Gotta get back to the office. I just wanted to tell you the news in person." He sprinted to his car, pausing long enough to leap into the air and click his heels.

Watching him, Juneau laughed aloud. Was this boyish leaper really her fifty-one-year old husband? Her faithful, dependable, always-there-like-the-furniture Greg?

Hurrying back to her computer, she brought up the *GotNot* file. After glancing fondly at GIDEON on the *Not* side, she shifted the cursor to *Got* and underneath it typed GREG.

There was more than one story that wasn't over yet.

ERIN

Caitlin was up to something. Erin saw it the minute her sister swept into the house on a blast of April rain, an extravagantly wrapped present held protectively inside her jacket and a wide grin on her face. Erin knew that expression. It announced better than words that Caitlin was hatching a plan centered on eligible men. *Again.*

"Happy birthday." Caitlin thrust the present into Erin's hands and hung up her jacket.

"Thanks." Erin led Caitlin into the great room, where she put the package on a table. "What's with that grin?"

Caitlin's eyes widened innocently. "Me? Grinning?"

"You're planning something, I can tell."

"Maybe." Caitlin greeted ten-year-old Mark, who was absorbed in Super Mario, and kissed her toddler niece, Hannah, who dozed on the couch, thumb in mouth. At Hannah's feet lay the family's golden Labrador, Rascal.

"Where's Kayla?" Caitlin asked.

"Where else but the ice rink? She's been on fire ever since she did so well at the McCandless Competition last month." The McCandless was a yearly competition held at Kayla's home rink in Edina.

They settled on the living room couch to wait for the rest of the family to arrive. And the food, which Erin's father, Andrew, was picking up at a favorite restaurant. Her mother was bringing carrot cake, Erin's favorite.

"So how does it feel to be thirty-eight?"

Erin huffed. "Same as thirty-seven felt yesterday."

"Tell the truth," Caitlin prodded.

"Honestly? I hate birthdays. They bring up too many memories."

"About your life B.C. and A.C.?"

"Before Cory and After Cory? Very funny. But yes. I never imagined I'd end up divorced."

"You never imagined Cory was gay."

"Thanks for reminding me." Chagrin replaced Erin's sarcasm. "I still feel stupid about that. But he's been great with the kids, and when I need advice, he's always there."

"Honestly, sis, you're too close to him. You need a life of your own."

"Single mothers don't have a life of their own."

Erin had started to give a rundown on the kids when she noticed Caitlin's mischievous grin was back. She couldn't help but return it. "Okay. Spit it out."

"Hold onto your hat. I've got us set up for a double date." Caitlin laughed at Erin's expression. "You'll like Ben. He's the twin of Alex, the doctor I'm seeing."

Erin hooted. "Twins dating twins?" Caitlin was younger and shorter than Erin, but the two were often mistaken for twins because of their hard-to-tame red hair, straight eyebrows above blue eyes, and strong jaws.

"Why not? They're good-looking, funny, and smart. Alex is an internist. Ben's a dermatologist."

Erin wrinkled her nose. "What do you say to someone who looks at itchy skin all day long?"

"Give him a chance. You'll never find a man if you don't go out."

"I can't see that your catch-and-release dating has helped you narrow the field down."

"But it's fun." Caitlin gave Erin a playful nudge. "How about it?"

Erin surrendered. "Why not? But they better not be wearing matching outfits."

The door flew open and thirteen-year-old Kayla bounded inside, skate bag in hand. She was followed by Erin's mother, Joanna, and her husband, Jake, who'd provided taxi service. After that, everything was a whirl as the rest of the extended family arrived: Cory, whom Erin had divorced before Hannah was born, his parents and widowed grandfather, and Erin's and Caitlin's father, Andrew, and his wife.

The house was full of conversation and laughter as everyone assembled around the big table in the dining room. Partway through dinner Andrew stood with a glass of sparkling grape juice in hand. "To Erin. A talented woman, loving mother, and wonderful daughter. Happy birthday. And to Kayla. When you were too young to care about old family history, you claimed me as your Grandpa Andy and insisted Lottie and I be invited to family gatherings. If you hadn't, we wouldn't be here today."

After everyone had toasted Erin and her birthday cake was being served, Andrew said, "Lottie and I have news. We've decided to downsize, and we've bought a new house."

He was inundated with questions, but Erin hardly listened to the answers. Their leaving the stately house in St. Paul could mean only one thing: Lottie's multiple sclerosis was getting worse.

"I've got news, too," Caitlin said. "I've talked Erin into double-dating with me."

"Hallelujah!" Joanna said. Kayla added, "You go, Mom."

But the reaction wasn't universally positive. Mark grimaced, and Cory's parents, Skipp and Linda Johnson, attempted to look pleased but failed. Erin knew they still harbored the hope that she and Cory might get back together.

As for Cory, when he caught her eye, he gave her a grin and a thumbs-up.

It was after eleven before Erin climbed the stairs to her bedroom, the happiness of the evening dampened now by the longing for someone with whom to share it. Most of the time she kept herself too busy to feel lonely, but at times like this, she missed the emotional intimacy and partnership that had been the best part of her marriage to Cory.

She hated admitting that because it made her feel vulnerable to her longing. She didn't want to risk falling in love again. Going out with the dermatologist wouldn't pose that kind of risk. The men Caitlin knew were more interested in a pleasant evening than in a serious relationship.

With a sigh, Erin changed into her long flannel nightgown—April nights in Minnesota could still be cold—and climbed into her bed. It was a long time before she fell asleep.

E-mail, April 22, 1996
Dear COBs,

I let Caitlin talk me into going on a double date. With twins! I hate to admit it, but I really liked my twin, Ben. (Think Tom Cruise but taller.) I let him know right from the first that I was a mother and a Mormon—and he still asked me out again. I said yes. What was I thinking?

Your Erin

WILLADENE

Deenie closed the folder that lay on the kitchen table in front of her with a sigh of relief. All the tasks itemized under *Unplugging Community Connections* were complete.

"Now that's the face of a happy woman," Roger teased as he entered the room.

"I do like to see a project satisfactorily concluded," Deenie admitted with a smile.

"You just like checking off the items on your list."

"That, too." Deenie tilted up her face for Roger's kiss.

"So are we unplugged?"

Deenie knew Roger was referring to the advice Sally Greenwood, her former therapist and longtime friend, had given her: "You have to unplug your energy from life in Wellsville so you'll have a fair chance to plug into life in Gainesville."

"Yes," she said. "Bear and I have officially resigned from Search and Rescue, and we've visited both nursing homes and the senior center to say our farewells."

"That must have been hard."

"Not as hard as refraining from writing copious instructions for Carl and Paul on keeping up the house while we're not here. I'm glad they're living in it while they're going to Utah State University in Logan, but I don't want them to turn it into a bachelor pad."

"But you still refrained, didn't you?"

Deenie grinned. "Yes, but I had to chew on leather to keep from doing it."

"How about lists for Liz?" Roger asked.

"Lizzy told me she didn't need any motherly reminders. She said Addie Spencer will keep such a tight leash on her while they travel that even I would be satisfied." Deenie frowned. She was still having problems accepting that instead of coming with them to Florida, her oldest daughter would be spending the next year traveling Europe as companion to and student of Miss Addie Spencer. And she was irked by the idea that anyone else could take as good care of Lizzy as she could.

"I settled for packing a box of envelopes in her suitcase addressed to reach us at our new place," Deenie continued. "It felt odd writing The Rasmussens, Gobb Hill, c/o The Academy America, Gainesville, Florida. I can't imagine living in an apartment again after all these years in our own home. It's too bad Gobb Hill was under renovation while we were there last year. I would like to have seen the inside."

"I know," Roger agreed. "But I'm glad they offered it until we decide where we want to live. It's convenient, fully furnished, and free. What more could we ask?"

"A kennel for Bear?" Deenie said.

"Marsha Warrington—remember the academy president's secretary?— said she'd take care of that," Roger assured her.

"I'll have to thank her for that and for sending us old photos of the place. Too bad they don't give me any idea what it's going to be like living there."

"We'll find out soo—"

Lizzy rushed into the kitchen carrying a garment bag, stopping Roger mid-sentence. She was followed by her best friend, Danny.

"Mom, wait 'til you see what Danny's given me," Lizzy said excitedly. She took a dark blue wool jacket and slacks out of the garment bag. "Danny's grandma made these for her, but the jacket's too short-waisted, so she's giving the outfit to me. It fits me like a dream."

"How nice of you, Danny," Roger said.

Danny's eyes twinkled. "Say my name with an *i*, please," she said. "If Beth gets to be Liz, then I get to be Dani with an *i*. Danny with a *y* isn't a name for a grown woman." Giggling, the girls shoved each other back and forth as they left the room.

"Grown women, my eye," Deenie said.

Roger leaned over Deenie's shoulder and thumbed through a still open notebook labeled *Unplugging Church*. "What's left on this list?" he asked.

"Once you deliver the gift baskets to your home teaching families, we'll have unplugged there, too." Deenie pointed to the four lovingly filled baskets that contained jams and jellies from her own pantry, a loaf of homemade bread, and a bunch of spring flowers from the garden. "That's the last thing on this list. And I'll even let you check it off. Then there'll be only four more folders to go."

JUNEAU

Juneau was grousing over the construction of a paragraph in her new book one Saturday afternoon in late April when Trace and Cath knocked at the door. "I hope we're not interrupting the great American novel," Trace said when she invited them in, gazing admiringly at these two good-looking people, both tall and slender, both blond. They looked like a set.

"I'm happy for the interruption," Juneau said. "My brain won't start up today."

Cath glanced at the monitor with only a page number and "Chapter Seven" showing on it. "How *do* you get started? It must be a challenge to face that blank page each day."

Juneau snorted. "Most mornings I'd rather scrub floors."

Trace and Cath laughed. Then Cath asked, "How's your writing class going? Are you enjoying being the teacher rather than a student?"

"Very much. It's a great class." Juneau led them into the living room. "Sit down so we can talk." Because they were holding hands, she half expected them to announce the engagement she'd been hoping for ever since Cath had moved to California.

Trace and Cath sat on the couch. Juneau sat opposite them. "Is Greg here?" Trace asked.

"No. Smoketree Systems is taking off, which means long hours and Saturdays."

"Well, we'll tell him later." Trace cleared his throat. "Uh . . . Cath and I have been talking with Vance, that lawyer friend of yours. We're going to make a bid to get custody of Gideon."

Juneau straightened. "Do you think it's possible?"

"He says I'd have a good chance."

"Oh! It would be so wonderful to have Gideon here at home again."

There was a small silence. Trace looked down at Cath's hand, which he still held. "Juneau, if I get custody, he won't be living here with you."

Juneau felt as if she'd been kicked in the stomach. "Of course."

"I'm sorry." Trace's expression was pained. "But it may be our only chance to get him back to California, what with that lawyer guy Whitford Morgan in Idaho on Misty's side."

"I know." Juneau managed to keep her voice even. "So what does Vance advise?"

"DNA testing, for starters." Trace smiled wryly. "I guess that's the one good thing that came out of the O. J. Simpson trial. It brought DNA to public attention. It would prove I'm Gideon's father."

"Misty doesn't dispute that," Juneau said.

"We need legal proof."

They talked for a while longer. Juneau offered them lunch, but when they said they had to go, she didn't try to detain them. She needed time to think about this new situation. *Gideon would not be returning to this house.*

After Trace and Cath left, she went back to her computer. She needed to write to Deenie and Erin. She wouldn't mention what Trace and Cath had told her, though. Seeing it on the screen would make it too real.

E-mail, April 27, 1996
Dear Willadene and Erin,

I'm certain the relationship between Trace and Cath is heating up. They just left here, stopping long enough to play kissy face under my liquidambar tree. I expect an engagement announcement very soon!

Other news: Beto is counting the days until Nicole gets home from her mission in Mexico. I don't know what to hope for when she arrives. I love Beto, but there's that looming question of the difference of religion.

No romance in Ira's life that I know of. He's still mourning Misty and the way she dumped him. He's doing another pickle commercial as well as working on his Ph.D. in English at UCLA.

Misty? Nothing new.

Juneau paused, her fingers poised over the keyboard. She'd been about to tell them the latest about her writing class and the man named Clyde, but she knew they didn't approve of her relationship with him.

She hated feeling guilty about something that was so innocent. Clyde was an important part of her life but only as a friend. Since taking over teaching Mrs. Jarvis's writing class, she'd stopped meeting with him afterwards at the cafe across the street. No, she wouldn't mention him. With a sigh, Juneau closed the e-mail and hit the send button.

Chapter 2

ERIN

Erin stood before her bathroom mirror putting on makeup while Kayla watched.

"Where are you and Ben going?" Kayla asked.

"A performance of A *Prairie Home Companion* at the Fitzgerald Theater." Erin turned to check herself out in the mirror. She was going casual: dress jeans, silk T-shirt, and a leather jacket that was the perfect weight for an early May evening.

"How come Ben never comes over to visit us kids? He only says hi and bye when he picks you up."

"Because we're not serious. I don't want you to get attached to someone who's not going to be around."

"Then why are you going out with him?"

Erin paused in putting on her ankle dress boots. "It makes me feel like a woman again."

Kayla looked doubtful. "I guess that's good."

"Your dad will be here soon to pick you and Hannah and Mark up. Are you ready to go?"

"Mom? Do you like Ben better than Daddy?"

Kayla's question pierced the firewall Erin had built to hold back the complicated feelings associated with Cory—love, betrayal, grief, and loss of cherished dreams. Despite her effort to move past the turmoil of the last two years, her emotions still had power to throw her off balance. She took a steadying breath. "I like him in a different way."

JUNEAU

E-mail, May 7, 1996
Dear Erin and Deenie,

Nicole will be home from her mission a week from Friday! We're thrilled, but Beto is beside himself with uncertainty.

Apparently their correspondence while she's been gone hasn't done anything toward resolving their religious differences.

Still more good news!! Greg and Arnie offered Trace a job in Smoketree Systems (he graduates next month). They've landed still another contract and need to take on employees, and Greg says Trace has all the right stuff. Cath thinks so, too. I'm hoping for an engagement announcement momentarily.

Love,
Juneau

P.S. Deenie, we haven't heard from you in ages. I know you're getting ready for your move to Florida, but please let us know you're out there!

On the ninth of May, Juneau was surprised to receive an e-mail from Misty's address. Misty had avoided any contact whatsoever since she had whisked Gideon away in December.

But when Juneau opened the message, she saw that it wasn't from Misty at all. It was from Gideon.

"Dear Mama and Daddy," it said. "I will be babtized next Saturday. Can you come? Will you take me home? My other mama dunno I am writing to you. Don't tell her. Your friend, Gideon."

The unexpectedness of the e-mail and its implications made Juneau wail aloud. "Oh, Giddy," she cried. "I'm so sorry."

When she reread the e-mail, she realized that Misty had scheduled the overdue baptism for this particular Saturday precisely because Nicole would be arriving home the day before. Misty knew Juneau and Greg would want to be at the airport to welcome her home. There wasn't much chance they'd skip out on that to attend Giddy's baptism in Idaho.

Furious, Juneau called Greg. When she finished reading Gideon's message, he said, "What do you think we should do, Juney?"

"We should be there for Gideon. We could fly to Salt Lake Friday night after Nicole gets here and then drive to Preston. Nicole would understand."

There was silence except for Greg's breathing. Finally he said, "If we go, he will expect to come home with us."

The thought of Gideon feeling abandoned again was more than

Juneau could bear. And the fear of what Misty might do in retaliation if they showed up unannounced. But they had to do something. "I'll ask Cath's mother to tell Giddy how much we love him and why we can't come," she said. "We don't want Misty to find out he's written to us."

Greg sighed. "I guess that's the best we can do right now."

When Trace found out about Gideon's note, he immediately made airline reservations for him and Cath. "It'll work out," he told Juneau over the phone. "We'll be able to see Nicole briefly before boarding our flight to Salt Lake."

"But Misty will . . ."

"We won't let her know that Gideon wrote to you. We'll tell her we came to make arrangements for our wedding and found out about the baptism after we got there."

Juneau gasped, "Did you say *wedding?*"

"Cath has agreed to marry me! Can you believe it?"

On Friday they rode with Juneau and Greg to the airport, along with Marisol, Beto's mother and Juneau's best friend and neighbor. Trace and Cath chattered about their engagement and how happy they were to go to Gideon's baptism. And to welcome Nicole home. The only downer of the day was that Beto couldn't make it to the airport.

"I hope Nicole won't be too disappointed," Marisol said, "but he's swamped at the end of his first year of medical school."

Juneau wondered if that was only an excuse. Maybe Beto had decided that they'd better cool things. And maybe that was for the best.

They sat for a long time in the foreign arrival terminal waiting for Nicole to get through customs. All the while Trace and Cath talked excitedly about their plans. Juneau couldn't help but contrast their happiness with how Nicole was going to feel when she saw Beto wasn't there.

Nicole finally appeared in the arrivals passageway moments before Trace and Cath had to leave to catch their plane to Salt Lake City. She smiled widely as she approached, but Juneau saw how her glance went from person to person and then back through the whole crowd again. Her face crumpled.

Then, amazingly, she lit up with enough wattage to light the terminal.

Following her gaze, Juneau saw Beto running through the waiting crowd. Nicole dropped her purse and carry-on and ran toward him. People grinned and moved out of the way, obviously expecting a romantic reunion.

But two steps from Beto, Nicole skidded to a stop and held out her hand. "I'm still a missionary, you know," she said. But her flushed face and glowing eyes told him what Juneau knew she couldn't say until she was officially released.

Marisol and Juneau stood together, watching their children. "What do you think?" Marisol whispered.

For a moment Juneau let herself believe in happily ever after.

WILLADENE

Deenie woke up early to the kind of June day she'd always thought of as perfect. She sat alone in her kitchen, breathing in the fresh mountain air. *I can't believe we're leaving today,* she thought. In a few hours, she would be leaving her family, the house she had worked on long and hard to turn into a home, the gardens and orchards that were her place of peace, the community, her ward, easy access to the Logan temple—all the things she loved about living in Wellsville, Utah.

There would be no more quiet afternoons next to Sunny's grave, feeling the dear presence of her younger sister, who had passed away in 1993. There would be no more dusty autumn days on the farm with Roger's parents, Wilford and NeVae, nor adventures at the shooting range with her father, John. No more shared lunches at the Bluebird with her mother, Margaret, and Aunt Stella filled with lively conversation and ready affection.

How am I going to survive? Deenie wondered, trying to hold her panic in check. *If I unplug from everything in Cache Valley that makes me who I am, will there be anything left to plug into life in Gainesville?*

On top of that, Lizzy was leaving that morning as well. After breakfast and cleanup, Deenie joined everyone gathering on the front porch around Lizzy, who stood next to her suitcases ready to embark on her year abroad with Addie Spencer. For the first time since the plans had been finalized, Deenie could see how nervous her daughter was. She repeatedly checked her purse for her passport, smoothed the wrinkles in her slacks, and ran her fingers over the nosegay of plump red roses pinned to her jacket.

The nosegay was all that remained of a spectacular arrangement of long-stemmed roses that had arrived for Lizzy on her graduation day. They were a gift from Brad Donaldson, longtime family friend and, prior to her death, Sunny's sweetheart. Deenie had been disturbed that a man nearly eleven years Lizzy's senior would be sending her such a gift, but Lizzy said he was only fulfilling a promise he'd made to her when she was small and had wished aloud that someone would send her roses when she grew up—the way he'd sent them to Sunny.

Deenie had been so busy with plans for the move to Florida that she had accepted the explanation with relief. But now as she watched how tenderly Lizzy stroked the roses, she wondered what more was going on in her daughter's mind.

In short order, the extended families on both sides arrived for the big sendoff.

"I'm so glad you're here," Deenie exclaimed as she hugged Roger's parents.

"I couldn't miss seeing Liz off on her big adventure and you off on yours," NeVae said. She scanned the group. "Where are my grandsons?"

"Carl offered to drive Addie and Lizzy to the airport in Salt Lake City. He's picking up Addie now," Roger explained.

"And Paul and Dani are taking Bear for a run to wear him out before he has to get into the truck," Deenie added.

"So you really are taking that monster dog with you?" Aunt Stella asked with one of her hallmark snorts.

"Where Deenie goes, Bear goes," said Roger. "The Academy is even building him a kennel."

As the minutes ticked by, everyone moved closer together, talking in quiet tones of inconsequential things, giving a touch here, a kiss there. Deenie made the rounds of Roger's family, accepting hugs that were heartfelt and filled with "I'll miss you" and "I'm sad you're going." Until she came to Roger's sister-in-law Jenny, who was smiling as if she'd won the lottery. They'd never been good friends, but Deenie was shocked to see Jenny's delight that they would soon be three thousand miles apart.

Besides Jenny, only Evvy, Deenie's eight-year-old bundle of energy, seemed completely comfortable with the move. She was convinced that living in Florida was going to be an endless adventure. She flitted from person to person, admonishing them to cheer up. "This is going to be so fun!" she repeated over and over.

Deenie knew Evvy's faith that whatever came next would be fine came from knowing everyone in Wellsville loved her, from believing that they would continue to love her while she was gone, and would be glad to see her when she returned. So she had no reason to imagine that people in Florida wouldn't love her as well. Deenie wished she had a chunk of that same self-assurance as she watched Evvy jump down the stairs and run to the end of the block.

"They're here," Evvy squealed as Carl's blue Blazer turned the corner and pulled up in front of the gray house. Carl stepped out and helped Miss Addie to the curb. Then everything seemed to happen at once. Liz's luggage was stowed away, and final hugs were given, along with advice and promises to write. Paul, Dani, and Bear loped into the yard barely in time for a final farewell.

Then Carl, Miss Addie and Lizzy were gone, and it was time for Deenie and her family to leave as well. "Come on, sweethearts," Roger said, taking her by the one hand and Evvy by the other. "Cowgirl up! It's time to ride."

JUNEAU

E-mail, June 4, 1996
Dear COBs,

Sorry I haven't been writing much lately. I've been dealing with the annual writer's conference that's part of taking over Mrs. Jarvis's job. But I have news about Gideon.

Trace and Cath said they arrived early for Gideon's baptism in Idaho and waited in the church parking lot to greet him. Gideon dashed into Trace's arms and wouldn't let go. Misty started shrieking about them undoing all the progress she'd made in weaning him away from anything California (meaning us, of course). The mighty Whitford Morgan (ptu, ptu—a bad taste) apparently got everyone calmed down enough to go into the church and get Giddy baptized—by Whitford (ptu, ptu).

Afterward, Trace and Cath gave Gideon the card and letter from Greg and me (with a picture of Numbtail enclosed) and the cards from Nicole and Beto and Ira. What breaks my heart is that he sent back his favorite T-shirt for us to bury under the pomegranate tree beside Max's Christmas stocking, Rhiannan's scarf, and Philip Atwater's ashes. So we won't forget him, he said. As if!

Misty told Trace and Cath to stay out of their lives and threatened to disappear with Gideon if Trace interferes again. Now Trace is afraid to do anything. We sent a letter to Misty, but it came back unopened.

Your weepy Juneau

P.S. Trace and Cath have chosen August 4 as their wedding date.

ERIN
E-mail, June 11, 1996
Dear COBs,

Family relationships can certainly get tangled, can't they? But have hope, Juneau. You never know what might happen. Case in point: the housewarming for Andrew and Lottie's new place. (Main level with handicap-accessible features, view of the Mississippi, and suites on the lower level for Theresa, their live-in housekeeper, and Caitlin.)

That was an afternoon I'll never forget! Andrew used the occasion to bring the kids and me together with his parents, Sean and Margaret McGee, the elegant octogenarians who are pillars of the St. Paul diocese and supporters of the arts. (Deenie, did you realize your mother and my grandmother have the same name?)

It was a risky thing to do. The McGees have never acknowledged me as their granddaughter—I was born on the wrong side of the blanket—or shown any interest in my children, who are their only great-grandchildren. But you should have seen them shift gears when that clever Andrew put them in a situation where they couldn't disavow our kinship! They managed to make the kids feel loved and accepted, as if some huge misunderstanding had kept them apart all these years.

Not so for me. I don't know how Margaret managed to look down her nose at me when I'm at least five inches taller, but she did, saying, "You have the McGee stamp."

Ben and I are still going out, mostly on weekends when Cory has the kids. It's a nice change from using those weekends to catch up on sleep. I've been running on adrenaline for the last two years, and I'm tired all the time. My mom and Jake (The Jays), Cory's mom, and Caitlin have been helping out a lot by driving Kayla to the rink, watching Hannah, and otherwise bailing me out, but I can't expect them to keep on doing that. Something's got to give.

I think it's the Big Barn Sale. It hurts even to write that, but in addition to private clients, I recently got a big job decorating the models at a new Dwyer Homes development in Maple Grove. It'll be the real money-maker for me this year, so it's got to come first.

I can't leave Colleen in the lurch, though, so I've contracted with another person to make the buying trips I don't have time for these days. Naieem, who used to work for Jake at Finishing Touches, has a great eye and a tendency to be a workaholic. Just what we need! Hopefully, she'll become a permanent fixture. I'd hate to have to sell my part of the Sale.

Juneau, in answer to your e-mail question about whether Ben's a good kisser, I'd say he's *too* good!

Your Erin

Chapter 3

WILLADENE

The trip from Wellsville to Gainesville was grueling. After the first day, Evvy's enthusiasm for the trip waned. The small trailer Roger hauled behind the sedan, which held family treasures and the pioneer oil painting Deenie had inherited from Gabby, required repacking after every tenth pothole. And Bear, riding in the truck with Deenie, developed motion sickness.

To keep Bear from throwing up, Deenie had to drive with the windows down for him and the air conditioning cranked up all the way for her. Having the air conditioning on gobbled gas at an alarming rate, which meant she had to make more stops than Roger to fill up the tank.

After five days of miserable cross-country driving and in the middle of a downpour, the caravan pulled through the gates of Academy America and came to a stop on a winding road behind the administration building. Feeling enormously relieved, Deenie did her best to finger-comb her hair and straighten the wrinkles on her shirt, hoping that by tucking it in she could hide the pop spill and dog drool along the hem. She clicked Bear's leash onto his collar, grabbed an umbrella, and got out of the cab to join Evvy and Roger, who stood at the foot of a gentle rise where a wrought iron sign was posted that read, *Welcome to Gobb Hill.*

"Wow! Would you look at that?" Evvy said in awe.

"Yeah," Roger echoed. "I don't remember it being that big."

Deenie tipped back her umbrella and looked through the rain past the low stacked-rock wall, the vast lawn, and the formal garden beds to the house.

"Tara?" she asked weakly.

"Ah think so, Miss Scarlett," Roger replied in a corny Southern drawl.

As they stood staring at the house on Gobb Hill, a silver Lincoln Town Car pulled alongside Deenie's truck. The window rolled down and through the rain a hearty voice said, "Welcome to Florida. The garages are on the other side of Gobb Hill. Follow the road around the curve. Delia and I will meet you at the back door to show you around the place. Marsha will be along later to help you settle in."

Even though it had been almost a year since Deenie had met him, she recognized the voice immediately as belonging to Ferris Tucker, president of the board of directors of Academy America and acting head of the school. She cringed at the idea of him and his wife seeing her family at their worst—wet, wrinkled, and tired.

When Ferris helped Delia out of his car at the columned back porch of the mansion, Deenie felt even worse. A dainty woman, Delia had perfectly coiffed hair and wore what looked to be designer yellow capri pants and sleeveless top. Deenie shuddered to think how she must look in comparison.

After introductions, Ferris ushered the Rasmussens through the back hall into a state-of-the-art commercial kitchen, complete with a walk-in fridge. Delia arched her brows as Bear followed behind.

"We use this kitchen when we're entertaining in the public rooms of the house," Delia explained, maneuvering so that either her husband or Roger was always between her and Bear.

"Public rooms?" Deenie asked. She sent a querying glance toward Roger. He shrugged and shook his head.

"You'll be in charge during events held here. As Ferris's secretary, Marsha, surely informed you. And on the three mornings a week when the house is open for tours."

"She didn't," Deenie sputtered.

"Hmm. We can go over the details later." Delia led them onward. "That door leads to the butler's pantry and the formal dining room. This door leads to the entry hall, reception rooms, and library."

The butler's pantry? Deenie thought, dazed.

"After we see the rest of the downstairs, you can get settled in your apartment," Ferris said.

During the tour of the remaining rooms on the main floor, Deenie was hard pressed to keep Evvy's eager fingers and the swipe of Bear's atomic tail from destroying the fine china figurines and cut-glass works that covered every possible surface. She was relieved when Delia and Ferris led them up the wide double staircase to the second floor.

"There are four guest suites for visiting dignitaries and your after-hours office in the wing on the right, Roger," Ferris said. "The residential apartment is in the wing on the left, through these double doors." He opened the doors and invited Deenie to go in first. Handing Bear's leash to Roger, Deenie stepped inside her new home. It was like walking into a spread from *Country Living,* with every nook and cranny filled with precious bits of historic paraphernalia. Deenie took one look around and stopped dumbfounded in front of a giant oil still life that hung over the fireplace mantle.

"That's the work of one of our famous Floridian artists," Delia said with pride. "Look at the details in the magnolia blossoms."

"Look at that huge dead goose and that great chunk of moldy cheese," Deenie responded with astounded awe.

"Well, we certainly don't want to force our Southern tastes on any unwilling subject," Delia said lightly, but Deenie could hear the steel in her voice. "Marsha will be here soon with an inventory of the apartment. You can mark on it anything you want removed to make more room, and the movers will come and pack it and haul it up to the attic."

"That's so thoughtful," Deenie said, backpedaling as fast as she could to regain lost ground. She knew at Delia's condescending smile that she had failed.

Only a short walk through of the apartment remained before the Tuckers left Deenie and her family alone in their new home. Deenie pulled a thick white cotton towel from the bathroom closet and placed it in the armchair in the master suite. Then she sat down and tried to get her bearings. *How am I ever going to manage being a mansion hostess,* she wondered, thinking of all the new responsibilities Delia had listed. *And how is Dead-Eye Deenie ever going to live in a place like this? What will Juneau and Erin say?*

On the Sunday following their arrival in Gainesville the Rasmussens attended their new ward for the first time. When they pulled into the church parking lot, Evvy pointed at a trio of preteens walking nearby. "I want a pair of shorts like those."

"Not in this lifetime!" Deenie said. The girls were wearing the shortest shorts she had ever seen, slung low at the waist and not quite covering their backsides.

"But, Mom, it's so hot!"

"Modesty is modesty, no matter what the climate," Roger said as he exited the car.

Deenie agreed with him—before she stepped into the hot, humid chapel. She sang the hymns with pleasure and tried to listen intently to the messages that were being given. But as the minutes ticked by the temperature in the chapel rose, and the air began to smell of warm bodies, aftershave, and perfume. Evvy tried to cool herself with a paper fan Grandma Rasmussen had sent, using exaggerated sweeps of her arm as if to tell the world, "I'm melting here!"

Distracted, Deenie quit listening and started looking. In every direction she saw sisters dressed in flyweight cotton skirts and tops or scoop-necked dresses. Most were bare-toed in flip-flops or sandals. *Am I the only one suffering in a suit and pantyhose?* she wondered.

Sunday School, held in the still, humid air of the gym, was hotter than sacrament meeting. As soon as the closing prayer was said, Deenie grabbed Roger's hand and headed for the cooler air of the foyer, where they'd promised to meet Evvy.

She was waiting at the appointed place, leaning over the air conditioning vent and chatting happily with a group of girls her age. As Roger and Deenie reached her, they were intercepted by their new bishop, Shurl Nunn.

"Welcome to Gainesville," he said when they'd introduced themselves. "We're mighty glad all y'all could make it this Sunday." Urging them into the foyer, he introduced them to another sister.

"This is Sister Luvy McSwain, our Relief Society president. Luvy, these good folks are the Rasmussens—Roger, Willadene, and Evangeline." They all shook hands, and then he said, "If you'll see that Sister Rasmussen gets to Relief Society, I'll take Roger to priesthood and Miss Evangeline to Primary Sharing Time."

With a smile, Luvy McSwain ushered Deenie down the hallway, greeting everyone they passed. In a flash Luvy had introduced her to a Colette, a Claudette, a Paulette, and a Claire. "We're an interesting mix of folks in this ward," she explained. "Members born and raised in Florida, like me, and transplants, like you and your family."

She stepped back and motioned Deenie to precede her into the class-room. Deenie gasped as a blast of cold air raised goose bumps on her arms.

"Welcome! I'm Cleo Kenady," the greeter at the door said. "Y'all might need one of these." She handed Deenie a fringed lap robe of light blue fleece covered with yellow ducklings. "This is the only room in the building where the air conditioning really works. We can't turn it down, so we make do."

"Cleo has a daughter, Christiana, who's Evvy's age," Luvy McSwain said as she followed Deenie into the room. "I'm certain they'll be good friends." She motioned Deenie to an empty seat and made her way to the front of the Relief Society room.

Bundling up in her ducky fleece, Deenie pondered her quick and easy introduction to Cleo Kenady, the first black Relief Society sister she'd ever met. She listened to the women chatting before the opening exercises began, wondering if any of them would turn out to be Crusty Old Broads in the making. Which one would be her visiting teacher, or become a special friend like Pat Fenton or Lark Donovan? Perhaps there was even an Aunt Stella or Grandma Streeter in one of those lightweight dresses, someone with a Southern drawl and a different color of skin, who would be her new friend.

"Here." Cleo handed Deenie a hymnbook and sat down beside her. The pianist played the first chords of the opening hymn, "There Is Sunshine in My Soul Today." Feeling the words of the song like a hug from Sunny, Deenie relaxed into her fleece duckies and joined in the singing.

Chapter 4

JUNEAU

In July Shannon Beldon (married, one child, new in the ward) was added to Juneau's visiting teaching list. Her companion couldn't go with her, so Juneau went alone to welcome the family to Pasadena. She needed a distraction to keep from dwelling on the situation with Gideon.

Her knock on the door was answered by a small blonde woman wearing jeans, a long-sleeved green shirt, and a pair of large dark glasses. "Oh, hi," she said. "You must be Sister Caldwell."

"Call me Juneau."

Sister Beldon smiled. "If you'll call me Shan. Come in."

The first thing Juneau noticed was an open suitcase on the floor with a little girl, probably six, standing beside it.

"I'm sorry," Juneau said. "I see you're busy packing."

Shan motioned for her to sit on a chair by the big front window. "It's Serenity who's packing. She's running away."

"She's what?"

"She wants to find a home where french fries are on the menu every night," Shan said.

Juneau looked at the girl, who stared boldly back. "And a TV all for myself," Serenity said. "What do *you* think I should take with me?"

"What do you have already packed?" Juneau countered.

"My video of *The Little Mermaid*." Serenity looked into her suitcase. "A jar of peanut butter. My piggy bank. I've got $2.97 in it."

"I think that's about all she needs, don't you, Juneau?" Shan said.

Juneau knew Shan's eyes must be smiling behind those dark glasses. "Well," she said, "I'd take my pillow, if I were running away."

Serenity shrugged. "When I find new parents, they'll have pillows."

Shan nodded. "Okay, then. I guess you're all packed."

Serenity closed her suitcase, picked it up, and went out of the door. "Let us know where to send your mail," Shan called after her.

Juneau had a twitch of alarm. How much of this was for real? She and Shan watched Serenity lug the big suitcase down the walk. The child paused when she got to the front gate.

"That's as far as she'll go," Shan said.

Juneau was reassured. "So she's done this before."

Shan nodded. "About once a month."

She didn't offer any more, so Juneau said, "Are you enjoying Pasadena so far?"

"Love it," Shan said. "So does Dexter. He's my husband."

"Is there anything I can tell you about the city?" Juneau offered.

"Do you know if the college offers a good writing class?"

Juneau grinned. "I teach one, and I think it's good."

"Wow!" Shan said. "I guess that old saying is true—'When the student is ready, the teacher will come.' Where do I sign up?"

Before Juneau could reply, Serenity dragged the suitcase back into the house. "There's a cloud," she said. "I guess I won't go today."

"Okay," Shan said. "Go unpack your suitcase, and I'll fix ice cream for the three of us."

Juneau left twenty minutes later, delighted with her new assignment and pleased that she'd have Shan in her writing class. But she was uneasy. Was it Serenity's repeated running away? Or was it that Shan had not removed the dark glasses in all the time Juneau was there and she hadn't offered an explanation for them?

ERIN

On the sultry July day before Erin's children were to start their two weeks with their father, Erin was deadheading flowers in the front yard while Hannah sat on the grass nearby, examining everything that crawled. Suddenly, a car screeched to a halt in front of the house. Kayla's friend Megan leapt from it, crying, "Mrs. Johnson, come quick. Kayla's hurt, and the ambulance took her to the hospital."

Head buzzing, Erin thrust Hannah into Megan's arms and dashed into the house. She scribbled a note for Mark, who was due home soon from a Cub Scout activity, grabbed the cell phone she'd purchased for business use, and ran back to the car.

Megan was buckling Hannah into a child seat in the back when Erin climbed into the front passenger seat. Megan's father took off before Erin had completely shut the door.

"How bad is it?" she asked him.

"Her leg's badly broken, from the sound of it," he said. "I'm so sorry."

Erin turned to Megan. "What happened?"

Megan sniffed, tears streaming down her cheeks. "We were roller blading—"

"What? Kayla promised her coaches she wouldn't do that! She doesn't even own a pair of in-line skates."

"She used my sister's."

Megan hurried to tell Erin how careful they'd been, skating on neighborhood sidewalks until they'd reached the bicycle path around Lake Harriet. "It wasn't our fault. Some boys were showing off, doing wheelies with their bikes. They crossed right in front of us, and Kayla couldn't stop."

"They took off before anyone could find out their names," Megan's father added.

A whirlwind of anger and fear made it hard for Erin to think. She whispered a prayer and began making calls on her cell phone. As they neared the hospital, she turned to Megan's father. "Cory and my mom are on their way. Would you take care of Hannah until they get here?"

"Of course. Anything you need . . ."

Cory arrived at Fairview Southdale Emergency as Erin was signing the form authorizing treatment. She clutched his arm as the two of them followed a nurse to the cubicle where Kayla lay hooked up to IV drips. Her eyes were closed, her face colorless. Gauze covered her lower right leg where the injury was.

A short, balding man in scrubs introduced himself as Dr. Spicer and explained that Kayla had a severe compound fracture of the tibia right above the ankle. "She needs surgery to get the wound cleaned. Dr. Mancuso—he's the surgeon—usually leaves breaks like this open for a few days so he can excise whatever dead tissue shows up. Then he'll put in a rod and stitch her up."

Erin tried to stifle a gasp. Dr. Spicer touched her shoulder briefly.

"She's in good hands. Now take a moment with her before she goes up to OR."

Kayla was groggy from painkiller, but she opened her eyes when Erin whispered her name. "We're here, honey. The doctors are going to take good care of you, and we'll be there when you wake up."

Cory took Kayla's hand in his. "Remember we love you, okay?"

Kayla gave a little nod before her eyelids closed again.

"I wish Skipp were here to give her a priesthood blessing," Erin said, wiping her cheeks.

Cory had been excommunicated some months after their divorce. Not because he was gay, but because he'd had a partner and was hoping one day to be in a committed same-gender relationship. "I may not be able to give her a blessing," he said somberly, "but I can pray for her."

Erin gripped Kayla's limp right hand as Cory made an impassioned plea for God's blessings to be upon their daughter. She felt the unmistakable presence of the Spirit as he spoke. Overwhelmed by sweet comfort, she understood why. Love was present.

Erin brought Kayla home after a week in the hospital and three surgeries with a rod in her leg and a pair of crutches. Cory, worried about Kayla negotiating the stairs, had set up a corner in the great room for her with a bed, her stuffed animals, and her CD collection. He'd scrapped the trip he'd planned to take with the kids, offering instead to take Hannah and Mark on local jaunts and to entertain Kayla, who was suffering both from pain and frustration.

Erin was grateful for his help. It gave her time to work on the design of a large living room redo, a frustrating job because the client couldn't say what she wanted, only that it be unique and impressive.

A stream of visitors came the first weeks Kayla was home. Girls from her Beehive class. Megan, who slunk in and out as if the accident had been her fault. Coaches and friends from the figure skating club, who encouraged Kayla, saying she'd be back on the ice in no time. Erin didn't point out that Dr. Mancuso had said the loss of flexibility in her ankle—the break was just above it—might make competitive skating difficult, if not impossible.

Relatives came, too. Cory's mother, Linda, helped out with Hannah and drove Mark to his swimming and piano lessons. Joanna and Jake, whom Erin thought of as a Buddha with suspenders, stopped by in the evenings after closing their antiques store, often with carryout for supper. Andrew brought Lottie once, but mostly she stayed in contact by phone.

The Jays, Cory, and his parents were all there when Ben came over one Saturday with a stack of feel-good videos for Kayla. Erin happily introduced him to the group, but she could tell he was uncomfortable being the object of scrutiny. He stayed only long enough to be polite. At the door, he gave Erin a quick kiss and promised to call soon.

But he didn't. After a week passed, Erin asked Caitlin if she knew what was going on. "I'm sorry, Sis," Caitlin murmured. "Alex says Ben doesn't 'do sick.' He sees enough of it in his work."

Erin told herself she didn't care, but she was in a funk when her friend Lucky Brown dropped by with her daughter, Shakeela. Kayla and Shakeela hadn't spent much time together since the days when Erin, Cory, and the kids had gone roller-skating with the Browns, but Lucky and Erin had remained close.

Lucky listened while Erin let loose with her frustration over Ben. Then she made a rude sound. "If Ben scares so easily, he's no great loss."

"But we had fun together," Erin said. "I miss having fun."

JUNEAU

E-mail, August 6, 1996
Deenie and Erin,

Trace and Cath are married! We all drove up to Utah and Idaho for the festivities. The ceremony was in the Logan temple, since it's closest to Cath's home in Mink Creek. Cath was radiant and Trace wept when the officiator told them to look in the mirrors and see themselves reflected on and on into infinity. He said he finally understood eternal family. That was especially poignant, since the room was full of Cath's family, but not a single person from his had come for the wedding. I doubt if he invited any of them. Of course, they wouldn't have been at the temple, anyway, since they're not members.

The reception that evening was at the pretty Mink Creek

church, and everyone in town was invited. There was food and dancing, and Trace played his guitar while he and Cath sang a duet of that Pete Seeger song, "There Is Love."

I really thought Misty and Gideon would show up. I'd about given up hope when the illustrious Whitford Morgan arrived. I looked for Misty and Gideon to be with him—Misty has intimated in what little communication we've had that she and Whitford are an item. When it was clear they weren't with him, I asked Whitford if he knew where they were. He said she'd asked some time ago if she and Gideon could spend this weekend at his cabin near the Tetons. He hadn't realized it was the same weekend as the wedding.

He apologized for having been part of Misty's disappearance. Then Greg said he hoped Whitford would bring her and Gideon down to California sometime soon to get to know the family. From the look Whitford gave him, it's clear he doesn't think of Misty in a romantic way. Her notion of their being an item is nothing but fantasy.

Greg decided to enlighten him about the situation with Misty and Gideon. Whitford, to his credit, offered to do what he could to help us get Giddy back. He said he loved Giddy but felt that he was unhappy. Now he understood why. We all agreed to move carefully for fear Misty might disappear with him again.

When we gathered to send Trace and Cath on their way, we found that Beto and Ira (they drove up there with us) had decorated Trace's car with miles of tissue paper roses, a custom at Mexican weddings in our area. Cath loved it. Trace grumbled about starting their honeymoon in a car that looked like a float in the Rose Parade.

Love,
Juneau

P.S. The next day, we dropped Nicole off in Provo to start her last year at Brigham Young University. Poor Beto! He had a hard time saying good-bye. They've been "on" since she got home from her mission.

Chapter 5

WILLADENE

Deenie wiped the sweat from her forehead. Even with the air conditioning running full blast, it was too hot a day to be ironing. But it was important that the uniform Evvy would be wearing to St. Anne's look perfect.

St. Anne's was a private school that offered free tuition to the children of Academy staff, and visa versa. Deenie had been ambivalent about having Evvy attend a school that would separate her from her everyday neighbors, but Marsha had assured her that St. Anne's offered some of the best education to be had in the entire county. Since Roger had agreed they would pull Evvy out the minute she picked up any elitist ideas, Deenie was content with the arrangement for the moment.

While she ironed, Deenie listened to Evvy humming as she tried to read all the big words in a disclosure statement that had come from St. Anne's. "What does this mean, Mama?" she asked pointing to the final paragraph. Deenie set down the iron and joined Evvy to look over the words that troubled her.

"They're asking us to agree to have religion based on Christian principles taught in the classroom."

"Christian means that you believe in Jesus, doesn't it?" Evvy asked.

Deenie sat down next to her at the kitchen table. "Yes."

"Then that's okay. Mormons believe in Jesus."

"Yes, honey," Deenie said. "Mormons are Christians, but not all Christians believe the same things we do. If you ever have any questions about what your teachers say you'll be sure to ask us, won't you?"

Evvy nodded. "I wish Christiana was going to St. Anne's," Evvy said referring to her first new friend in their Florida ward.

"I do too." Deenie knew Evvy might be the only Mormon child enrolled in the private girls' school. That would be different from anything she'd experienced.

When she finished Evvy's uniform, she ironed Roger's shirts and the tan linen skirt and white silk shirt she'd chosen as her uniform when she hosted tours of the public rooms at Gobb Hill. Then she sat down to update the COBs. *Dear COBS,* she began, her fingers flying on the keyboard.

> Roger loves his job, Lizzy loves England, and from his phone calls it sounds like Paul may be falling in love with Dani. (Did I tell you he's decided he wants a career in the Church Educational System?) Evvy has a new friend at St. Anne's named Mandy Love-Bassett, and I've found one in my new visiting teaching companion, Sister Ethel Bernice Hobbs, known to all as Miss B.
>
> Miss B is a real Southern gentlewoman, seventy-five years old and with a drawl so thick she says her last name in two syllables—How-obbs. She's determined that I get to know the real South and takes me on field trips after we go visiting teaching. She is teaching me to like local specialties, starting with boiled peanuts!
>
> I wish Delia and I got along as well as Miss B and I do. No matter how careful I am, I'm on the wrong foot whenever we meet. Last week she caught me as I was finishing a run around the soggy track with Bear (we're getting in shape to join Search and Rescue here) and asked me ever so politely not to use the track when students were arriving or leaving the Academy campus. Since the track is right by the main drive, it would be inappropriate for them to see the assistant director's wife in such dishabille. She actually did say that word! I had to look it up when I got home.

Deenie smiled as she sent the e-mail, hoping that she'd given her friends a taste of life in Florida. And a chuckle or two.

ERIN

August was a roller-coaster for Kayla, and Erin rode it with her. Early in the month, Dr. Mancuso took out Kayla's stitches. Kayla was delighted until he said it looked like she might have a slight infection and wrote a prescription for antibiotics.

A week later, a reporter from a local newspaper wrote an article on Kayla: "Young Figure Skater's Dream Broken in Crash." As Erin had hoped, Kayla brightened in the attention she received after it ran. But she was disappointed that no one turned in the boys who'd caused the accident. "It's not fair for them to get off scot-free," she groused.

When Kayla asked Erin if she could visit girls' camp one day, Erin thought, *Why not? It might cheer her up.* As it turned out, spending time with the girls and leaders made both of them feel better. Until Kayla ended up back in the hospital on IV antibiotics for a bone infection. She came home three days later with the IV line in place, so she could get antibiotics through it for the next six weeks. She would still be getting them when school started after Labor Day.

Sitting at Kayla's bedside in the hospital, Erin discovered that The Griff—The Great What If—had a partner, The Griffly, short for The Great If Only. The Griffly stirred up thoughts like, If Only I'd noticed the redness was back. If Only I hadn't taken Kayla to girls' camp. If Only I'd asked Hannah why she and Rascal had been anxiously hovering around Kayla.

Erin felt even guiltier when Colleen Harrington, her friend and business partner, brought her children, Ricky and EJ, to visit. "I'm sorry I haven't been holding up my end of the Big Barn business," she apologized.

"Don't worry," Colleen said, a smile on her fresh face. "Naieem has a nose for finding the good stuff. Wait 'til you see what she's brought out to the barn."

"Don't worry, be happy!" Ricky echoed. His perpetual enthusiasm, typical for kids with Down Syndrome, was a little too loud for a hospital. And at nine, he didn't realize how strong he was—when he gave Erin a bear hug, she thought her ribs would crack.

In contrast, EJ, who was sporting black lipstick and fingernails, was gloom personified. She said only a few words to Kayla before slouching in a corner chair.

"What's with EJ?" Erin asked when she and Colleen took a turn down the hall.

Colleen's expression drooped. "She says she's a nobody—she isn't cute, or popular, or smart, or talented."

"That's not true."

"Try telling that to a seventeen-year-old who doesn't believe it. Most of the kids at her school and at church are high achievers. They write off kids who are average but good like EJ. So those kids write themselves off." Colleen shook her head. "I think that's why she's going for a semi-Goth look. It gives her some identity."

"Bless her heart." Erin hugged her friend, whispering a prayer for both their girls. She knew that Kayla, who'd gotten so much of her identity from skating, would feel lost if her injury ended her competitive career.

JUNEAU

September arrived, and Giddy was still in Idaho. Whitford Morgan had warned that it would take time to make the necessary legal preparations for his return. Juneau was grateful she had the writing class to occupy her time and thoughts. Shan Beldon had signed up for it, and because her house was on the way to the college, Juneau picked her up each Thursday night.

Juneau enjoyed Shan's company but found it curious that Shan sometimes came to class wearing those big dark glasses. She mentioned this odd habit to Greg, but he was so distracted with the contracts he and Arnie were working on that he shrugged it off, saying maybe the light hurt her eyes. She wished she could talk to Clyde about it. But they didn't have private talks anymore.

Then one Thursday night Clyde stopped Juneau and Shan as they were leaving the classroom. "Your discussion of thematic material reminded me of what Mrs. Jarvis used to say, Juneau. Would you two like to go with me to the cafe and talk about it?"

Juneau started to say no, but Shan said, "I'd love to. I've never taken a writing class before, and I've got a lot to learn. Can we stay a while, Juneau?"

When they were settled in a booth, Clyde asked Juneau about her family. She had so much wanted to talk to him about Giddy that it all poured out. "I'd hoped having Whitford on our side would speed things up, but it's taking so *long*," she wailed.

Clyde patted her shoulder. "You know that old saying, 'The mills of the gods grind slow but exceeding fine.' Things will work out. You have to rely on your good Mormon optimism and patience."

Juneau snorted. "Hah. I'm not sure I ever had those qualities."

"You've always given that impression."

"You're the optimistic one," Juneau said.

"What do *you* think, Shan?" Clyde asked.

Instead of answering, Shan glanced at her watch and said, "I'm sorry, but I need to go home. Now."

Shan's sudden change of demeanor was odd, but Juneau gathered up her things and bade Clyde a hasty good-bye. When they pulled up in front of Shan's house twenty minutes later, Juneau saw Dex, Shan's husband, standing on the front porch, obviously watching for them.

She waved to him as Shan scurried up the walk, and he waved back. A contractor of some kind, he'd been friendly when she'd met him at church, but Shan's rush to get home perplexed her. It didn't feel right.

She hoped to talk it over with Greg when she got home, but the house was dark. A message from Greg on the answering machine said he and Arnie were working late on a project.

Juneau was working at her computer the next morning when the phone rang. She answered it absently, but when she heard Whitford Morgan's voice, a premonition turned her cold.

"Misty's gone," Whitford said.

"What? Where? Why?"

"I don't know. She must have overheard me talking to Trace's lawyer or maybe read some of my e-mails about Gideon. Her apartment is cleaned out. She's gone, and Gideon is gone with her."

ERIN

E-mail, September 21, 1996
Juneau and Deenie,

Juneau, I couldn't believe it when you called to say Misty's taken off with Gideon. Again! It's got to be awful, wanting to do something for Gideon but not knowing what. I feel that way about Kayla. And Colleen's EJ and my protégé, Melina.

Melina's the girl I took under my wing when I first taught Beehives, the one whose mother is a hoarder and never leaves the house. A week ago her dad, Gerald, said he couldn't take living in a trash house any more and left! Just like that.

Althea was so shocked, she had a panic attack. Melina thought it was a heart attack, so she called 911. The EMTs wanted to transport Althea, but when they realized she wasn't going anywhere unless they drugged her into oblivion, they stabilized her and turned the situation over to Human Services. If Melina hadn't been eighteen, Child Protective Services would have gotten into the act.

So it's a real mess. I feel like I should be doing more for Melina, but with the Big Barn Sale next month, taking care of my own kids is all I can do.

Speaking of the Sale, it's not even close to being ready, even with the help of Naieem, Caitlin, The Jays, and Colleen's husband, Steve. We're still working out logistics with vendors and the county (we cause a traffic jam along Colleen's road), and there's a lot of pricing and bookkeeping to be done. The effort doesn't seem worth the income any more.

No word from Ben. Probably a good thing, because I'm exhausted. Believe it or not, I'm in bed at nine these days.

Erin

WILLADENE

A rainy fall day in October found Deenie struggling. She missed the change of seasons she'd grown up with—the crisp mountain air and the brilliant colors of the leaves in Sardine Canyon as they painted the mountains in vivid autumn shades. More than that, she missed her mother's support and Aunt Stella's tough-love advice and Grandma Streeter's gentle wisdom. She needed all three.

It helped to have something to do. Roger had requested that she compile a list of things she thought needed attention at the Academy. "It would help me to have your take on things," he'd said.

She'd gone about making her assessment and recording it with the same full-throttle enthusiasm she always had when writing lists. She was looking forward to presenting it that afternoon at the fall luncheon of the Faculty and Board Wives' Association, the group that spearheaded keeping the Academy up to date.

Deenie knew she'd made a mistake when she showed up at the "work" meeting in her favorite cropped pants and a plaid shirt. They were freshly ironed and still crisp in the damp weather, but the others in the group were dressed in what the folks in Wellsville would have called Sunday best or uptown casual.

Nevertheless, when Delia, the current president, asked if there was any new business, Deenie, looking forward to making her contribution, stood up and launched into her list. She started with the deplorable state of the track field and ended with the insufficient study space in the library. When she finished her report and sat down, Delia put her in her place so fast and so slick Deenie didn't know what had hit her.

"Mrs. Rasmussen," Delia said with pointed patience, "the Association is well aware of those problems, and we're addressing them in order of priority. Of course, all projects hinge on our ability to finance them. Unless you have discovered a way to pay for the improvements you've suggested, we should get on with the business of the day."

Deenie wanted to slide down and hide in the cushions of her chair. She still felt like hiding when she got home.

Instead she sat on her fancy, down-filled couch, looking out the small-paned glass windows of her living room at the rain that came every afternoon and the leaves of endless green. What would Sally Greenwood think of her attempt to be part of her new community?

"Think of moving to Gainesville as an adventure," Sally had said. "You have a rare opportunity to test yourself and all you've learned in a brand-new setting. And for the first time in your life, you'll be without that family safety net you've always counted on. Wow! What a trip!"

The idea of being without a safety net hadn't comforted Deenie. But Aunt Stella had another take on Sally's advice. "She's not suggesting you live without a safety net, dearie. She's saying you'll have a chance to custom-build one of your very own." After a pause she added, "Remember that you'll be the new kid on the block and the other kids are going to need time to get to know you."

Delia's had four months to get to know me, Deenie thought, *and she still doesn't like me.* The worst thing was that Deenie couldn't seem to get away from her. Except at church, Delia was part and parcel of every activity at the Academy and at St. Anne's—even the ones Deenie was in charge of herself. Organizing St. Anne's costumes for the Thanksgiving pageant. Having Thanksgiving Dinner at Gobb Hill for all the resident students who couldn't go home for the holidays. Hosting the yearly planning meeting for the Faculty and Board Wives' Association coming up in April to be held at Gobb Hill.

I've got to find a way to make friends with that woman before then, Deenie thought. But she didn't know how.

It seemed as if Deenie could hear her mother saying, "Pray for Delia, dear. Pray for her until you genuinely care for her welfare. Pray for her until you love her." She knew it was excellent advice, but right then, she didn't think she could do it.

ERIN

E-mail, November 29, 1996
Dear COBs,

Happy (belated) Thanksgiving! Kayla's finally on the mend, and I'm feeling hopeful for the first time in months.

It looked pretty grim in October. The infection in Kayla's leg flared up yet again, and X-rays showed the break hadn't even begun healing. So Dr. Mancuso took out the rod, cast her leg, and put her on a six-week IV course of a "last-chance" antibiotic.

His calling it "last chance" scared me, but the antibiotic worked! Kayla's free of infection, the cast is off, and she's started on the last round of oral antibiotics. Now all I have to do is fatten her up!

Other good news. Deenie, you were right when you said

something positive might come out of Gerald's leaving. Health Services assigned Althea a caseworker and sent a doctor to the house (!) to evaluate her and prescribe meds. When she's stabilized, she'll get counseling and behavioral therapy. Melina's getting help, too.

It's hard to believe that something that seems terrible can look entirely different as time passes, although the problem of the house remains. If there's a lesson in this, it's that even traumatic events are only a part of the story and that we don't know what they mean until we get past them.

I hope Kayla will be able to say that about her accident one day.

Erin

P.S. Ben called. No apologies, no explanations, just an invitation to a Vikings game with Alex and Caitlin. His breezy attitude bugged me, but I can't expect him to act like we're serious when we're not. So I said yes. It'll be good to have an evening out again.

WILLADENE
E-mail, December 1, 1996
Dear COBs,

Our Christmas tree is up and decorated, a garland drapes the mantel under Gabby's pioneer painting, and our cards are ready to mail. We are finally feeling settled enough to have holiday guests.

Because the guest suites at Gobb Hill won't be needed during the holiday and nothing's scheduled for the public rooms, the board has given us permission to use the whole house to entertain our family for Christmas. Though Lizzy will be in Germany with Miss Addie—and is she ever loving her adventure!—Carl, Paul, Aunt Stella, and my parents will be here. Remember Roger's sister, Bert, and her husband, Hal? They'll stop here, too, with their children, Timothy, Ami, and Atsu, on their way to Ghana to visit the girls' grandparents. (Jenny, Keith, and the girls will be going to California to spend the Christmas with Wilford and NeVae at their winter condo since Bert and Hal will be gone.)

They'll all arrive in time to see Evvy and her new friend, Mandy, perform in the Christmas pageant at St. Anne's. (What a blessing that little girl has been for Evvy.)

It will fill my Christmas cup with joy to have them all here. I have missed them so.

This year Pat will be sending the traditional chocolate torte to all y'all as usual. So watch for the yellow boxes. I'll be getting one myself, and I can't wait for that taste of home.

Christmas blessings on all y'all and your families.

Love,
Deenie

Chapter 6

1997

WILLADENE

On New Year's Day, 1997, Deenie's mother, Margaret, her Aunt Stella, Miss B, and Deenie herself gathered in the apartment kitchen at Gobb Hill. Deenie's father, John, husband Roger, and sons Paul and Carl had been banished to the library, where they were noisily watching a football game. Evvy was playing in the garden with two of the Academy students who had stayed at the school over the break, so the women had the place all to themselves. Miss B was demonstrating to the others how to prepare the traditional Southern good-luck meal of black-eyed peas with ham hocks (to be served with a variety of hot sauces ranging from ouch to unbearable), collard greens, and corn bread.

Deenie sniffed the steam rising from the pot of black-eyed peas appreciatively. "Should we start the collard greens?" she asked Miss B.

"Not until the corn bread's in the oven," Miss B said.

"I can take care of that," Aunt Stella said, rising from her chair at the table.

"And I'd be right grateful, Stella." Miss B wiped the perspiration from her forehead with the corner of her apron and sat down in the chair Aunt Stella had vacated.

"Who's the redhead watching out for Evvy?" Margaret asked, looking down at the gardens below.

"That's Leo Flynn," Deenie answered. "He's one of the four resident students whose parents are stationed overseas. He sees his family only during summer break. In the meantime, he's made Gobb Hill a second home. He's become Evvy's hero and protector on campus and one of her three best friends."

"Are her other best friends the girls you talk about in your letters?" Margaret inquired. "Christiana and Mandy?"

Deenie nodded.

"Are any of them Mormons?" Aunt Stella asked.

"Only Christiana."

"Has being a Mormon caused any problems for Evvy?" Aunt Stella said.

"No, and I'm glad for that." Deenie replied. "Roger and I have met a few adults who were sure we had horns and tails. Everybody loves Evvy."

"Do Mandy and her family know you're members of the Church?" asked Margaret.

"It's no secret," Deenie said, gesturing to all the Mormon markers visible in the apartment. There were temple miniatures on the mantel, glossy big books on the Restoration and the life of Joseph Smith on the coffee table, and open scriptures and a family home evening manual on the dictionary stand next to Roger's favorite chair.

"But those things might not register with a nine-year-old girl. Have her parents ever visited?" Margaret said.

"No. I have no idea how Gwen and Glen might feel about our faith. The thing is, I don't want to make an issue of it, but I don't want it to come out in some manner that would hurt Evvy. Maybe I should bring up the subject the next time Gwen and I volunteer together at St. Anne's."

"Good idea." Aunt Stella checked the cornbread. "This is almost done. Time to set the table, I think."

Deenie got to her feet. "Thanks for the advice. After we have our good-luck meal, maybe you can help me plan the menu for the Faculty and Board Wives' Luncheon in April. Marsha says it's never too soon to submit a menu to the Academy kitchen staff."

JUNEAU

E-mail, January 5, 1997
Dear Deenie and Erin,

Misty called us Christmas Eve! She wouldn't tell us where she and Giddy are, nor would she let us speak to him, but she says they're fine, she has a good job, and Gideon likes his school. And if we give up the idea of gaining custody, perhaps they'll come for a visit. I'll believe it when I see it.

On a cheerier note, we had Christmas at Trace and Cath's apartment in Studio City. They have a room all ready for

Gideon when he comes to live with them. They don't waste time on negative thinking and always say *when* rather than *if*.

Ira brought a delightful girl named Shoshana to Christmas dinner. She's an assistant producer of the pickle commercial he does that's been such a success. She says Ira could quit school and be a full-time pickle, if he wanted to. He has higher ambitions, but it's a great way to pay for his Ph.D.

Nicole was here from BYU with tales of dating both Reece and Ryan Crafton. Beto spent Christmas Day with his own family, but he and Nicole went on a couple of dates while she was here. I don't ask.

Greg is happy about the way Smoketree Systems is going. Now that we have the money to do things, he has no time to do them. Isn't that the pits?!

And now, ladies, I have a proposal: Greg and I were going to line up a condo timeshare week in England, but he says he's too busy. I have an idea for a book, and I'd like to spend a week in Sedona, Arizona, to make some notes. I could trade a timeshare week for a condo there. Would you like to join me?

> Much love, and Happy New Year,
> Juneau

ERIN

Erin celebrated New Year's Eve with Ben at a big party in a downtown hotel, complete with a five-course meal, dancing, and a disco ball descending to mark the arrival of 1997. Caitlin and Alex weren't with them—they'd gone their separate ways. "No reason," Caitlin had said. "It was time to move on."

"Another catch-and-release," Erin had murmured

Erin was in a festive mood as she and Ben enjoyed the sumptuous meal. She felt beautiful in her black dress with sequin trim, and she knew she and Ben, who wore a European-style jacket and purple dress shirt, made a good-looking couple.

While waiting for the dessert course, Ben said, "Shall we dance?"

"I haven't danced for a long time."

"No problem. If the music is fast, stand facing me and do what I do. If it's slow, put your arms around me and sway."

Erin laughed as he led her to the dance floor. Exhilarated by the atmosphere, she had fun dancing to jitterbug and disco tunes, but then the band turned to slow songs. Hesitantly she stepped into Ben's arms. After a few minutes he said, "Relax. Sway."

She couldn't, not feeling the way she did. She kept her eyes closed so he couldn't read what was in them and thought, *Oh, boy. I'm in trouble.*

Caitlin said the same thing when the family got together on New Year's Day. "Have you thought about where your relationship is headed? And how far you're willing to let it go?"

"No," Erin said. She didn't want to. It would complicate the wonderful feeling of being in love.

Thoughts of Ben intruded into everything Erin did that month, but they only went out twice. She was too busy staying ahead of the train marked "work" and taking care of her family. She wasn't doing a very good job of either.

She felt things were looking up when Kayla was given a clean bill of health shortly after her birthday and a referral for rehab. Although Dr. Mancuso warned Kayla that it wouldn't be easy—her muscles were atrophied and her ankle virtually immobile—both Kayla and Erin were ecstatic.

The first session at the rehab center brought them down to earth. It was hard for Erin to watch her daughter go through therapy that seemed more like torture. And harder yet to see the look in Kayla's eyes as she understood what was ahead of her.

While Kayla was struggling, Mark was roaring full speed ahead. He practiced even more than usual, as if that would protect his dream. Erin didn't have the heart to tell him there weren't any guarantees.

It did get him ready for his home recital in February, at which he would play the entire Book III of the Suzuki repertoire by heart. He invited all the family, his whole Scout troop, the Harringtons, and Melina.

Erin was more nervous than Mark the night of the recital, but the joy he felt when playing was evident. When he took his bow after playing "The Wild Rider," he grinned and said, "I like playing that so much, I'm going to play it again!" Erin and Cory exchanged a glance that said, *That's our kid.*

At the end of the recital, Mark and Melina played a ragtime duet. As always, their age difference (eleven and eighteen) didn't matter when they sat at the keyboard. After they took their bows, Melina announced that she'd gotten an early acceptance letter from Augsburg College, where she planned to study music therapy. "I was inspired when I saw how much music has helped Ricky," she said, acknowledging Colleen's son with a wave.

"I *love* music!" Ricky cried. "Can I sing? Mark, play 'Here Comes the Ox Cart'!"

Later, as the guests were enjoying dessert, Cory motioned to Erin. "Let's go into the great room. I want to talk to you."

She expected him to say something about Mark's delightful performance. Instead, he asked, "What's going on with this Ben character?"

Erin bristled. "This *Ben character?* Nothing that concerns you."

"Kayla and Mark have been talking about you two. It concerns them, so it concerns me."

"Hold it. I don't ask about your private life, and I think that may be more disturbing to the kids than my going out."

Cory's eyes flashed. "I agreed not to have anyone over when the kids are with me, and I don't."

"I don't bring Ben home, either."

Then he asked the same question Caitlin had asked. "Where is this relationship going?"

"I don't know," she snapped.

But she did know. She and Ben had driven headlong into an immovable roadblock.

JUNEAU

In February, Clyde sold a story to a mystery magazine. The class cheered the night he told them about it. Afterward Shan suggested that she and Juneau treat him at the cafe. He accepted with a grin.

"You're doing well, too, Shan," Clyde said as they ate his choice of treat, a large order of french fries. "You'll be selling soon. Don't you think so, Juneau?"

"I know so," Juneau said. Shan wrote happy-ending stories that reminded Juneau of the romances she and Erin and Willadene used to read. Deenie had said she liked reading them because she knew they would come out right. Maybe that was why Shan wrote them.

Shan waved a hand dismissively. "We're talking about *your* success tonight, Clyde. I guess your family is mighty pleased, aren't they?"

Clyde put down a ketchup-laden fry and sat back in his chair. "My wife died several years ago. But my daughter in Tucson and my grandchildren are pleased that Grandpa sold a story." He glanced at Juneau and then picked up the abandoned french fry, holding it as if it were a glass of champagne. "Hey, aren't we here for a celebration? Let's eat a toast to my story!"

Juneau and Shan each picked up a fry. All three touched their strips of potato soggily together and then ate them.

"May it be the first of many," Juneau said.

The next week Shan didn't attend class, but Clyde brought a new story about a man dealing with loss. It was eloquent and moving. After class, he approached Juneau's desk. "I'd like to talk with you," he said. "Can we go over to the cafe?"

She suspected his story came from personal experience and that Clyde needed a listening ear. "All right," she said.

When they walked outside, they saw crowds of people on campus. "Must have been an event at the auditorium," Juneau commented. They could see before they crossed the street that the cafe was filled to overflowing.

Clyde stopped. "Well, scrub that. Let's go somewhere else."

"I'd rather talk here," Juneau said.

"How about sitting in my car?" Clyde stopped beside a blue sedan and unlocked the door. "I can tell you don't want to go anywhere with me."

"You're right," she said. "I'm sorry, Clyde."

Without warning, he put his arms around her in a brief, light hug. "Oh, Juney," he said, "you're so implacably, unrelentingly *good*."

He let go and opened the door. Feeling a little disconcerted, she started to get into the car. But as she did, she looked up and saw Greg's partner, Arnie Gilbert, and his wife two cars away. They were looking directly at her.

"Hello, Juneau," Arnie called.

Juneau was curled on the sofa feeling a mixture of guilt and defensiveness when Greg arrived home. He stood in front of her, looking down. "Is there anything you want to tell me?"

"Apparently Arnie scurried back to the office with tales to tell," she said, keeping her tone light.

"He said some guy was hugging you in the parking lot and then you got into his car. Is it true, Juneau?"

"Mostly."

"How about you tell me what part is 'most' and what part is 'ly.'"

"Clyde's a student in my writing class. He was troubled and needed to talk."

"In a dark car in a dark parking lot?"

Juneau stood to face him eye to eye. "I didn't get into the car after Arnie saw us. I came right home. Clyde and I have been friends for a long time, in Mrs. Jarvis's class and in mine, now that I'm the teacher."

"That gives him the right to hug my wife? How long has this been going on?"

"Nothing's been 'going on.' We're friends. I enjoy talking with him. He's like me, always quoting stuff." When Greg didn't respond, she added, "I tell him what's on my mind. He gives me good advice."

Greg's face darkened. "You used to ask *me* for advice."

"I still do, Greg," Juneau protested, "but you're either on your computer or too tied up with the business to talk."

"So now it's my fault."

"I didn't mean it that way."

"If Arnie hadn't seen you, what would you have done?"

"We would have *talked.* In a public place. That's all."

Greg sat down. He seemed weary and sad, and Juneau was ashamed to be the cause. She took his hand. "I'm sorry, Greg. I should have told you about Clyde a long time ago. Keeping secrets has always been my thing, I guess."

"*Guilty* secrets, you used to call them."

She nodded, her eyes stinging.

He paused and then said, "Juney, I understand wanting to talk about work with colleagues, both men and women. But it's something you have to be very careful about. It can be misinterpreted by the other person, not to mention observers."

As he left the room, Juneau had the feeling that something indefinable had been lost, or at least altered, by the revealing of her secret relationship with Clyde.

ERIN

E-mail, February 16, 1997

Dear Juneau,

Deenie asked for an update about Melina when we talked today, so I thought I'd give it to you, too.

I'd hoped that with Health Services in the picture the Franks' situation would be better by now, but Althea's problems are tough to deal with. It turns out she's not actually agoraphobic, because she doesn't fear leaving the house. She fears that if she does, someone will take all her stuff! (That's what Gerald and the elders quorum did years ago while she was at work.) The official diagnosis is obsessive-compulsive disorder and anxiety.

At least enough junk has been removed from the house to prevent it being condemned. Althea's caseworker got people from public health to organize a cleanup day when she could be there to help Althea survive another raid on her things.

I call Althea every few days, and we talk about the weather and local news—everything but what's really going on with her. Melina says that her mom looks forward to my calls, so I'll keep up with them.

Your Erin

JUNEAU

Shan didn't come to class the last week in February, but she did come in March, once again wearing those large dark glasses. As they drove to the campus, Juneau told how Arnie had seen her and Clyde and reported it to Greg.

"I hope we can still talk with Clyde," Shan said. "I'd miss our discussions. Renaissance men are always fascinating."

Renaissance men, Juneau thought. Men of broad interests and wide knowledge of a vast number of subjects. That was Clyde, all right.

"Of course we can talk with him," Juneau said. "But I won't keep it a secret. I've always been good at secrets."

"Me, too," Shan muttered.

Juneau was sure by now that the dark glasses hid one of Shan's secrets, but this wasn't the time to ask about it. Instead, she told Shan about Clyde's story. "I think it was about the loss of his wife," she said. "It's the best thing he's ever done."

"Sorry I missed it," Shan said.

Juneau turned into the parking lot. "He wants to talk about it."

"I can stay for a little while tonight," Shan said.

But although the three of them—Juneau, Shan, and Clyde—went across the street to the cafe after class, Clyde didn't bring up the subject of his story. Instead, he asked about Shan's dark glasses.

"Eye problems," Shan said.

He turned his gaze to Juneau. "And all is well with you?"

She knew he was asking about Greg and his reaction to their being seen together. "All is well," she said. Under her breath she added, "Mostly."

Juneau made a point of telling Greg about meetings with Clyde or anyone else after that. Greg made an effort to come home earlier and to turn away from his computer whenever she spoke to him. And the next week, he suggested that they resume their Wednesday evening square dancing, something that had fallen by the wayside the last couple of months.

But despite the revitalization of her relationship with Greg, there was still the void left by Gideon. If only he were home.

And then one balmy March day he was.

When the knock came at her door on a Monday afternoon, Juneau got up from her computer, ready to tell whatever salesman was there that no, she didn't need a new roof or her chimney cleaned. She wasn't prepared to see Gideon standing there, with Misty beside him, holding his hand.

Wordlessly Gideon sprang forward and wrapped his arms around Juneau's waist. With a cry she bent over him, enfolding him to her, kissing the top of his head with its newly buzz-cut hair. He seemed much taller than he'd been the last time she'd seen him and more filled out.

"Oh, Giddy, Giddy," Juneau whispered, "I'm so *happy* you're home." She raised her eyes to Misty, who stood there watching impassively.

"Time to kill the fatted calf, Mom," Misty said. "The prodigal has returned."

E-mail, March 7, 1997
Deenie and Erin,

I'm sure I was babbling incoherently when I called to say Gideon was home. I can still hardly believe it. Maybe writing the details will help me wrap my mind around it.

I thought my heart would burst with joy when I saw Misty and Gideon standing on the doorstep. I didn't want to let him go, but after many hugs and kisses, Gideon wanted to assure himself he was really home. He ran around the house touching things, nuzzling Numbtail, scurrying out to the pomegranate tree to look at the "graves" there.

He was happy about the marker we put where we buried the T-shirt he sent us, but finding his bedroom as it was when he left seemed to touch him the most. He climbed onto his bed with Numbtail in his arms, saying he needed a little snooze. Before he went to sleep, he asked if I remembered when I'd saved Numbtail from the nasty boys. It seemed to me he was asking why I hadn't saved *him* when Misty snatched him away. I made a resolve never, ever to be so wimpy again.

Greg burned up the road getting home after I called with the news. He and I shared some tears as we watched Gideon sleep. But the minute we joined Misty in the living room, Greg lit into her, asking her if she had any idea of the harm she'd caused Gideon and Trace and us. She countered by saying we'd done harm to her by trashing the good thing she'd had going with Whitford Morgan when we told him the truth about Gideon.

She said she could have been a great asset to him in his ambition to be governor. I could picture what she had in mind: Whitford with his handsome chiseled features in a photo with her, slender and beautiful, each with an arm around Gideon, a typical kid with freckles and big, toothy grin. She said Gideon could have been the governor's son someday.

Fantasy. All fantasy.

After Greg and Misty calmed down, we had a surprisingly good conversation. Misty said she brought Gideon back because he needs a family. She said I should teach him all the old songs that I used to sing to her and Nicole. Can you believe it was the slim thread of remembered lullabies that made her decide to bring him back?

She also said one very sensible thing when we told her that Gideon might be going to live with Trace and Cath. She said, "Why don't you ask Gideon what *he* wants? He needs to have some control over his life."

The next morning she was gone. Gideon said she came into his room while it was still dark and told him good-bye. She didn't say anything to Greg and me. So the strange Misty saga continues. But the good thing is, Gideon is home!

Love,
Juneau

Chapter 7

WILLADENE

That spring the months passed quickly. Whenever Deenie attended Church meetings or participated in a Church activity, she thought, *Here's a place where I know what to say and how to act. Here's where I'm okay.*

When Roger was called as the new high priests group leader, Deenie jumped into the activities with an enthusiastic splash. Since Devon Kenady, Cleo's husband, was also a high priest, it was natural for Deenie and Cleo to spend more and more time together. Their blossoming friendship helped Deenie start to put down small tentative roots in the Florida soil.

And then there was Miss B.

"She's Aunt Stella, Grandma Streeter, and Leila Jeffrey rolled into one," she told Roger after spending an entire day visiting teaching with Miss B. She instinctively knew that Miss B was someone she could turn to no matter what.

The three days a week when she didn't have to be available to host tours of Gobb Hill, Deenie was busy working to qualify herself and Bear for Search and Rescue in Florida and volunteering at St. Anne's. She saw Mandy's mother, Gwen, frequently during that time, often sharing lunch in the teachers' lounge. But the opportunity to discuss religion never seemed to arise, and as the day for the big Association function on Gobb Hill came closer, Deenie put aside her concerns and concentrated on making the perfect impression on the wives of the board and faculty.

ERIN

In April, Ben invited Erin to dinner at Campiello, a white-tablecloth Italian restaurant in Uptown, for her birthday. The Jays, who were going to watch the kids for the evening, arrived as Erin finished dressing and walked downstairs. "Don't you look lovely," Joanna said.

"Thanks, Mom." Erin rubbed her hands together—they were cold, a sure sign she was nervous.

Joanna warmed them in hers. "You've not told him, have you?"

Erin shook her head. "I can't believe I let things go so far. I knew better."

"The heart and the head aren't always in agreement, dear," Joanna said, giving her a hug.

Erin had a speech ready, explaining all the reasons she and Ben had to stop seeing each other, but what could she say when he arrived at her door with a smile that dazzled her?

All the way through the meal, Erin felt herself grow warmer under his gaze. By the time they were enjoying their dessert of chocolate truffle cake, she felt as if she were drowning. And that scared her.

Ben seemed to see it in her eyes. "The Mormon Mother has reappeared, hasn't she?" he said. "The one who didn't want to fall in love."

"Yes." The truth fell from her mouth. "But I did anyway."

"Is that so bad?"

"No—if there's a future possible."

"And there isn't?"

"Not unless you want to convert and marry me and be a father to my children."

He made a sound that might have been a laugh. "I guess we both knew it would come to this."

"I'm so sorry."

"Not your fault only." He placed a box on the table. "Happy birthday."

E-mail, April 19, 1997
Dear COBs,

Ben took me out on my birthday. We acknowledged we'd fallen in love, he gave me a simple diamond pendant (diamond is the April birthstone)—and we broke up.

After I bawled my eyeballs out, I made a promise to myself: I'm done with men, period. Whatever relationships have to offer, the pain isn't worth it.

Then, wouldn't you know it, the bishop called me to the ward activities committee. He said he hoped I would come up with some exciting new things for the singles to do!

Erin

WILLADENE

On the day of the Faculty and Board Wives' Spring Luncheon and Planning Meeting, which was always held in April, Deenie fussed for an hour over what to wear. She finally settled on her favorite new Sunday outfit. The white mid-calf linen skirt and lemon-yellow silk top made her feel classy and in charge. And her new uptown shoes made her taller. *I wonder if looming over Delia might give me the social stature I lack,* Deenie thought.

To her great relief, everything was ready when the ladies arrived, and the luncheon, served with the gracious efficiency that the Academy kitchen staff was famous for, was as tasty as Marsha had promised it would be. Still, even after almost a year at the Academy, Deenie still felt like the new kid on the block. She watched with painful empathy as other new members tried to find their way through the conversation dominated by the long-timers.

As dessert was served, Marsha shocked Deenie by launching into the story of how Deenie had earned the nickname Dead-Eye. Roger had told it with relish one evening when Marsha had joined them for dinner. Thinking it would remain among those present, Deenie hadn't asked Marsha not to pass it on. Looking at the faces of the women—some intrigued, others scandalized—she fervently wished she had.

Hiding her chagrin at being the center of unwanted attention, Deenie smiled and said, "I'm always a little worried about how folks will respond to that story. And to my having a red pickup and a monster dog."

One of the other newbies laughed out loud. "Why, Deenie! Half of Alachua County have big dogs, own guns, and drive pickups."

"Yes, but they are usually driven by men, never by staff of the Academy." Delia patted her lips daintily with her napkin.

In the silence that followed, Delia stood, usurping Deenie's place as hostess, and invited the ladies to adjourn to the reception room for their meeting. With Delia in charge, the official business was handled in short order, and the ladies dispersed. No one lingered to visit the way Deenie had hoped they would.

She watched them leave, thinking, *What a disaster.* Then Marsha, who was following Delia down the front steps, looked back to give her a wink and a thumbs-up.

A week later Deenie sat on the front porch with Bear waiting for Evvy's school bus to arrive. Evvy was so excited about her school's Stranger Danger project—a month-long personal safety unit—that she wanted an instant audience to whom she could report on each day's presentation.

While Deenie waited, she picked up a notepad and started a rough draft of a letter to Juneau and Erin, trying to sort out her feelings about Delia Tucker and the Wives' Association as she wrote.

April 20, 1997
Dear Juneau and Erin,

If where we are determines part of who we are, does a new where require a new who? It feels like it.

The old who (me) and the new where (here) don't fit together. Some days I feel I'm losing myself in trying. I wonder who that other person is—the one who's picking and choosing what she says and developing a drawl. Is she really me or someone I am pretending to be? I don't know. What I do know is that I'm hopping my way through a gauntlet of cultural preferences and expectations with one foot on the ground and the other in my mouth. If I ever needed Gabby's advice and insight, I need it now.

Other news: Lizzy is in Ireland, and Paul is in love.

Deenie put down her pen at the sound of the school bus braking to a stop. A solemn Evvy trudged up the front walk, dropped her bag on the porch, and wriggled between her mother and Bear. Deenie put her arm around Evvy's shoulders. "How was school today?"

"Okay."

"Are you excited about taking Bear to school tomorrow for your Stranger Danger talk?"

Evvy shrugged. She'd been thrilled to get permission to bring Bear as a visual aid for her report on what to do if you got lost. Now all that lovely enjoyment was gone. Concerned, Deenie gently questioned her daughter. "Did anyone give a report on Stranger Danger today?"

"Mandy."

"Did she do a good job?"

"Teacher thought so." Evvy picked up her school bag and began rummaging through it. "Mandy's church had a Stranger Danger day last summer. She got some pamphlets from her pastor to share with the class."

She handed Deenie a small brochure with "The Strangers at the Door" emblazoned across the top. Underneath was a picture of two young men in suits. "It's about the missionaries, Mom," she said in a tiny voice and began to cry.

Deenie couldn't believe what she was reading as she scanned the text of the pamphlet. It vilified fine young Mormon missionaries, like Carl and Paul had been. And all of Evvy's classmates had gotten one exactly like it.

When they showed it to Roger at suppertime, he was as upset as Deenie. They both tried to comfort Evvy, but she was inconsolable.

"How should we handle this situation?" Deenie asked Roger after Evvy was in bed.

"Pray hard. And do whatever Evvy wants us to do."

At breakfast the next morning, Evvy offered her own solution. "I think I'll wait until everyone really likes me and knows I'm not dangerous. Then I'll tell them I'm a Mormon."

Evvy's wisdom and courage amazed Deenie. When she sat down to finish the letter she'd started the day before, she had a whole new story to add.

JUNEAU

The question of where Gideon was to live couldn't be avoided forever. On the day Trace and Cath came over to talk about it, Juneau, remembering her vow not to be so wimpy anymore, glanced at Greg, and said, "Misty left a sensible thought. She said we should let Gideon choose where he'll live."

Trace and Cath sat silently for what seemed a long time, and then Trace said, "You know where he'll choose."

Cath took his hand. "Maybe Juneau's right, Trace. Giddy *needs* to feel he has some control over his life. He's been yanked around enough."

Trace seemed to struggle with the idea. But finally he nodded and said, "All right. We'll ask him. We'll abide by what he says."

Gideon looked surprised when they called him in and posed the question. "I want to be home," he said simply.

Juneau gripped Greg's hand with relief, but she couldn't rejoice, seeing the expression on Trace's face when he told Giddy how much he and Cath loved him and how they hoped he would visit often.

After that, things went fast. Trace dropped the custody suit he'd been preparing, and Greg and Juneau took the necessary legal steps to ensure their guardianship was strong and binding. So it was done.

WILLADENE

E-mail, May 19, 1997
Dear Erin and Juneau,

We took Mandy's parents, Glen and Gwen Love-Bassett, to dinner, told them we are LDS, and explained how the pamphlet Mandy brought to school had upset Evvy. I was sick at my stomach, not knowing what to expect, but I didn't have to worry. Gwen was appalled and apologized profusely. She thought Mandy had taken a booklet on safety rules for biking!

Glen said how much they liked Evvy and what a good influence she was on Mandy. And they both agreed to let Evvy tell Mandy when she thought the time was right.

I wish I'd been there when Evvy told Mandy she was a Mormon. Apparently Mandy's response was, "No, you're not. You're not wearing a long skirt and a long-sleeved blouse. Mormons wear them all the time. My pastor says so." When Evvy insisted she was a Mormon, Mandy asked her if her daddy had more than one wife. When Evvy said no, Mandy claimed Evvy couldn't be a Mormon, "'Cause Mormons have lots of wives. My pastor says so."

It took Gwen saying that Evvy was a Mormon before Mandy would believe it. What a strange world we live in.

Our Elizabeth returned to Wellsville with Addie on May 15. She's already registered for summer school at Utah State University. She insists she's going to live with my parents. She doesn't want to play gooseberry to Paul and Dani. I think she's miffed that Dani fell in love while she was overseas. They'd always planned to date and marry twin brothers so they could go through the whole process together.

We'll be spending the summer here. Roger has to oversee the renovation of the junior dorms. We'll suffer out the summer wearing as little as morally possible and drinking tons of ice-cold minted lemonade. Thinking about it makes me long for our trip to Sedona in September. In the meantime, Bear and I are officially on the roster of the local search and rescue unit and have made two easy searches with the team.

Deenie

ERIN

E-mail, May 22, 1997
Dear COBs,

Melina graduated last night! The kids and I sat with her dad, who hasn't entirely disappeared from the scene. We clapped like crazy when she walked across the stage.

She got a great financial aid package from Augsburg. With a scholarship, grants, student loans, and working part time, she'll be able to manage her tuition obligation and other school expenses. I'm so thrilled she's going to be able to pursue her dream of being a music therapist.

And so sad when I see how little progress Kayla has made toward reclaiming her own dream of figure skating. She's stronger, thanks to swimming and weightlifting, but her right ankle is terribly stiff. During the two sessions she's had with her coach, she looked as awkward and unsteady on the ice as a beginner. It's partly fear, I think.

Your Erin

P.S. I'm not coming up with any good ideas for our singles group, probably because I'm not interested in it. I went out with Ben because I thought it was safe. I don't want to meet someone I could really get serious about.

In mid-June, a month before the anniversary of Kayla's accident, Erin got a call from Don Munroe, the reporter who'd written the article on it. He wanted to do a follow-up. "It'd be a human interest story with a photo of her skating. You know, showing her triumph over adversity."

Erin wasn't sure it was a good idea—Kayla's progress since getting back on the ice had been excruciatingly slow, hampered by her lack of conditioning and the stiffness caused by the break being so close to the ankle. But remembering how her daughter had perked up after the first article appeared, she told Kayla about Don's request. Kayla said, "Tell him to come."

Erin sat in on the interview. She could see how much Kayla was enjoying the reporter's attention. Until he asked what it was like dealing with six months of infection and pain followed by two months of rehab and how she felt about the boys who ran into her.

When he asked what it was like seeing other skaters go on while she was still struggling, Erin said, "I think we're finished here."

But Don had one more question. "May I snap a photo of you taking a turn around the rink?"

Kayla blinked rapidly. "I can't do any big moves yet. My range of motion stinks."

"No problem. Just strike a pose."

E-mail, June 21, 1997
Dear COBs,

Say a prayer for my Kayla, please. She's had a big setback—she was at the rink so a reporter from our local newspaper could get a photo of her to go with an article he's writing. She was skating the perimeter (she's still unsteady and fearful of reinjuring her leg) when a bunch of kids passed her going really fast. The next thing I know, she's hanging onto the boards, shaking. I think the motion of other skaters passing her brought back the moment the bikers ran into her.

And then that wretched article ran in the paper: "Will Brave Teen Ever Compete Again?" It downplayed all of Kayla's progress and made a big deal about the boys who got away with doing something that caused so much suffering.

Kayla's terribly upset and says she'll never go back on the ice again. I got her in to see a counselor, which I should have done a long time ago. Vickie Bouchard is a former member of the University of Minnesota's gymnastics team, has a degree in psychology, and is a certified personal coach. Kayla liked her right off. Luckily, Cory's got the kids on his insurance. It will cover the first several visits completely.

I hope she perks up when Cory takes the kids to Wisconsin Dells (a family fun/water park destination) next week.

Your Erin

JUNEAU

E-mail, June 22, 1997
Dear COBs,

Erin, I'm so sorry about Kayla's problems. I hope Vicki can help her.

Deenie, it seems Nicole has decided between the Crafton twins, and the winner is—drum roll!—Reece! Her letters the last few months have been filled with mentions of him. She's even told Beto about him. The other day, Beto asked me if I thought Reece was the kind of good Mormon boy every good Mormon girl is looking for. He looked so forlorn, I had to hug him.

With all that's going on in our families, I don't have to look far for possible plots!

Juneau

Every year Juneau anticipated the appearance of luscious red and yellow Rainier cherries in the produce section of Ralph's Supermarket. "These are great, Mom," Gideon said when she brought some home after a shopping trip. "Let's take some over to Serenity and her mom. It could be a surprise."

Serenity came to the door in answer to their knock. "Hi," she said guardedly.

Juneau held up the bag of cherries. "We brought something for you."

Serenity reached out to take it. "Thanks," she said.

"Is your mom here?" Juneau asked.

"She's sick."

"Oh, I'm sorry," Juneau said. "Is there something we can do?"

"Mama said I shouldn't let anybody in."

Juneau had a strong sense that something was wrong. "Serenity, honey," she said, "I need to talk with your mother. Please let us come in."

Serenity gazed steadily back at her. Juneau could tell she had a major conflict going on inside. Should she disobey her mother's orders or reach out for help?

Slowly she opened the door. "Mama's in her bedroom."

Serenity's suitcase was out again, with a map and a box of Band-Aids inside, along with a flashlight and a small packet of cheese and crackers. And a sweater Juneau knew belonged to Shan. Was the child planning to take her mother with her this time?

"Serenity," Juneau said, "maybe you and Gideon could watch a video while I talk with your mom."

After setting the kids up with a movie, Juneau approached Shan's closed door. "Shan," she called softly, "may I come in?"

There was a brief hesitation, and then Shan said, "Oh. Juneau. Could you come back another day?"

"No," Juneau said. "I need to see you now."

Another hesitation and then, "Just a minute."

Eventually the door opened to reveal Shan standing in the darkened room wearing a long-sleeved dressing gown—and dark glasses.

"I'm not feeling so well," she said. "What did you want to see me about?"

"I brought you cherries," Juneau said. "And a listening ear. Which do you want first?"

Shan peered down the hallway. "Is Serenity okay?"

"She and Giddy are watching a video," Juneau said. "Let's turn on the lights, Shan, and have a talk."

Shan hesitated and then walked to a bedside table where she switched on a lamp. Motioning for Juneau to sit on the bed, she took off her dark glasses and slid the dressing gown from her arms. "Is this what you wanted to see, Juneau?"

Juneau didn't say anything to Greg about what she'd seen until after Giddy had gone to bed and they were sitting on the sofa with the TV on low, tuned to a sitcom they weren't really watching.

"Shan has a horrible scar," she said. "It covers most of her left arm from elbow to wrist. It's red, and the skin is puckered. She says it's a birth-mark."

Greg pinched his lower lip as he stared at the TV screen. "That accounts for the long sleeves. What about the dark glasses?"

"She says she has an 'eye thing.' She said she was holed up in a dark bedroom today with cramps. She gets them bad."

Greg turned to look at her. "What do you think, Juney?"

"I think something is not right there."

"So do I," Greg said.

Chapter 8

ERIN

E-mail, August 18, 1997
Dear Friends,

You won't believe this, but Caitlin's most recent guy dumped her! He told her he didn't want to spend time and emotional energy on a lightweight relationship, and when she figured out what she wanted, she should let him know!

When Caitlin told Kayla and me, she protested that she knew exactly what she wanted in a man. I pointed out that she'd morphed his challenge from *what you want* to *what you want in a man*. Then Kayla brought us both up short when she asked, "Isn't it as important to know what men want from women?"

What *do* men want from women? I have to admit, I don't know. That's sick, considering how long I was married to Cory and the year I went out with Ben. You two have been married a lot longer than I was. Do you have an answer to that question?

Erin

P.S. Hannah starts Montessori preschool this fall. How time flies.

JUNEAU

Juneau was so happy to have Gideon home again that she almost cancelled the timeshare reservation she'd made in Sedona, Arizona, for her and Erin and Deenie. But Greg and the Guys Club, reinstituted by Gideon, wouldn't let her.

"We'll get along just fine," they assured her.

So Juneau went with a light heart concerning Gideon and a sense of purpose for the vacation. She hoped to get the information and the feeling she needed for her new young adult novel about a girl, part Hopi and part Caucasian, and her search for a missing brother.

"I mainly want to let the place sink into my consciousness," Juneau explained as she, Erin, and Deenie sat watching evening light play over the red rock cliffs from the patio of the luxurious three-bedroom condo. "I'd like to start out tomorrow with the trolley tour of Sedona and then explore a ghost town I've heard of. And there's a Hopi lecture I want to go to in the evening." She paused. "If that's okay with you."

"Fine by me," Deenie said, and Erin agreed.

They had supper at the Mexican restaurant recommended by the concierge. As they ate, Deenie regaled them with stories of her adventures in Florida, her words flavored with softened and lengthened vowels and periodic y'alls.

"Do you realize you don't sound like a Utah girl anymore?" Erin asked with a laugh.

"I hate hearing that."

"Why?" Juneau asked. "It's charming."

"Because I still feel like Willadene from Wellsville."

The next day was all Juneau had hoped for. She paused often to scribble notes in the little pad she'd brought for that purpose. She scribbled almost nonstop during the lecture that evening by Ray Red Hawk.

Juneau had had to prod the others into attending with her—they'd protested they'd done enough for one day—but before long they were rejuvenated by the energy surrounding the lecturer. Ray Red Hawk exuded enthusiasm as he spoke of the First People, which was what the Hopi called their ancestors. "They understood the connection between man and earth," he said. "They understood the nature of themselves."

"Ancient Hopi secret," Erin whispered to Deenie. "I hope he lets us in on it."

Juneau hushed Erin. She didn't want to miss any of what Ray Red Hawk was saying about words being sacred, and silence, too. Then he spoke of something that focused Juneau's attention on her own life.

"I have a personal belief," he said, "that each decision we make in life puts together a package that will inevitably be opened at some time in the future. Some decisions we make without conscious awareness, and some we make by choosing *not* to choose in a given situation, thus not thinking about consequences.

"But," he went on, "decisions can also be made as the result of look-ing ahead to what we want our lives to be. This gives us something to live into. Even little things begin to put together packages to be opened in the future."

Like me singing to Misty and Nicole, Juneau thought. *How could I have known that those remembered lullabies would one day convince Misty to bring Gideon home?*

She shared her insight with the women after they got back to their condo, adding, "That was a real surprise package."

"Surprise package," Deenie mused. "I like that. We can't tell what things we set in motion when we make a choice. Like me finally agreeing Roger should go back to school, which eventually moved us to Florida. Who'da thunk it?"

"Like me marrying Cory," Erin said. "I thought I was putting together the perfect future, and it turned out to be a melodrama."

"At the time, it looked like the perfect future," Juneau said.

Erin nodded solemnly. "I hate that even when we're doing the best we can, we can still end up in a train wreck."

"The thing that gets me is," Juneau said wonderingly, "how the little things can end up counting the most. Like singing my girls to sleep."

"Then everything we do matters," Erin said. "Thinking about that could drive a person crazy."

Deenie nodded. "But Miss B would say, 'Say your prayers and do the best you can.'"

"Don't we always do that?" Erin asked.

"Sometimes more than other times," Juneau said.

"I wonder what kind of packages we're putting together right now," Deenie mused.

"I don't know about you," Erin said, "but after all the food we've been eating, I've wrapped up a package of jeans that no longer fit!"

Deenie chuckled, but Juneau didn't join in. She was wondering about the package she'd put together with Clyde. What surprises were still in that?

The next day Juneau filled her notebook on their tour of Old Oraibi and Second Mesa. She would use all of those places in her story of a girl searching not only for her brother but also for her own identity. There would be obstacles as the girl began to uncover secrets of the past. Juneau hoped she would be able to put it all together so that it said something. About life. About inward directions. About packages to be opened in the future.

There was one more place Juneau wanted to visit. On their last day in Sedona she said, "I was thinking that today we should climb up to the cliff dwellings that the guide pointed out on our trolley tour. How about it?"

"I don't know," Erin said. "I'm not much of a climber. A day by the pool is more my speed."

"Come on," Juneau urged. "Think of the history. Think of the ghosts. Think of my displeasure if you fink out."

It took them almost the whole morning to spot the dwellings in the cliff-lined canyon and then climb up the steep trail strewn with boulders.

The climb was worth it, at least in Juneau's opinion. Signs had been put up recounting the evidence of how people had lived here long ago. The caves went far enough back into the cliffs that they must have been quite snug and relatively invulnerable because the only access was at the front. Standing at one of the crumbling walls, Erin looked out over the valley before them.

"Hey, guys," she called. "Have you noticed that you can look only ahead here? No need to watch your back. You can focus on what's coming at you."

Juneau thought about that. "Unless it's coming from within. That's where a lot of my 'enemies' live."

"Ah, yes," Deenie said, "the seventh direction." She perched on a rock at the edge of the cave. "Sit. Let's talk."

They talked for a long time about the Hopi and Ray Red Hawk and packages they were putting together by the decisions they were making. Then they sat in silence for a moment before starting back down the steep hill.

They were halfway to the bottom when Erin cried out as she lost her footing. Horrified, Juneau saw her tumble over rocks and brush, coming to rest several yards down the canyon. She lay without moving, blood trickling from her forehead.

Juneau and Deenie scrambled after her. Deenie immediately checked Erin's vital signs. Juneau knelt at her head, pressing two fingers against the forehead wound, one of the few things she remembered from the First-Aid course they'd had in Relief Society. "It's my fault," she said. "I shouldn't have . . .

"Save it, Juneau," Deenie said tersely. "Here's my cell phone. Find a place where you can get a signal and call 911."

As she ran down the hill, Juneau flashed on another fall at another time and another place and the terrible guilt she'd felt over it. But she hurriedly pushed it back down into the dark place where it had lain hidden for all these years.

ERIN
E-mail, September 22, 1997
Dear COBs,

Well, ladies, that was some vacation! I loved being with you, and we had some fantastic experiences before "The Fall," but I have to say I'm glad I'm home.

The kids swarmed over me the minute they saw me, wanting to know for themselves that I was okay. Hannah especially needed hugs and reassurance. She snuggled up next to me, sucking her thumb, while I talked. I'd hoped she was getting past that.

Before The Jays left, Mom asked me what I learned from my vacation. It sounds like the kind of question you'd ask a kid after some misadventure: *Now, what did you learn from that?* But she didn't mean it that way. Whenever you two and I have vacationed together, I've always come back with some insight that I've shared with her.

My answer was directly related to the accident: *Listen to the inner voice.* I had the feeling I shouldn't make the climb to the ruins, but I let myself be talked into going.

What's been bothering me since coming home is, how are we supposed to tell which of the fleeting feelings and random thoughts we have every day are worth paying attention to? If "Don't make the climb" had been in neon red, believe me, I never would have gone.

Your Erin

P.S. Still headachy, but ribs doing much better!

JUNEAU

E-mail, September 24, 1997
Dear Erin,

I wish I could transfer your headaches to me. It's my fault that you fell, because I insisted you climb up that mountain. I'm so sorry I coaxed you into ignoring your inner voice. I'm sorry. I'm sorry.

Contrite Juneau

WILLADENE

E-mail, September 25, 1997
Dear Erin and Juneau,

My inner voice is telling me you both need serious chocolate. Look for those bright yellow packages from Crafton Catering to arrive soon. Instead of sending them for the holidays, I asked Pat to ship them now—same-day delivery!

I could use some of that chocolate myself. Even though we're planning our first big holiday open house here in Gainesville, the kids have opted to spend Christmas in Wellsville to be with NeVae. She and Wilford usually spend the winter in California, but she's been doing poorly and wanted to be home with family for the holidays.

I think Paul's decision has as much to do with Dani and his new studies toward being a seminary teacher as being with his grandparents. So we'll miss the boys this year, but at least we'll finally get to see Elizabeth when she comes at New Year's.

Re: Ray Red Hawk and Sedona—I'm practicing really listening to what people have to say. Then I take my time answering, honoring what we learned about the sacredness of words. Roger and Evvy have responded as though I were suffering from a synapse shortage.

Evvy can manage about a ten-second wait before saying, "What!" When I answer that I'm thinking, she gets a look on her face like I've grown another head. Roger says to save it for the evening. He doesn't have enough time during the day for my new thoughtfulness. So I'm going to try it out on Gwen. If it works, I might even try it on Delia.

Miss B and I are exploring the more rural areas of the county so I can see the Real South. Bear's going with us. I wonder what her reaction would be if I suggested bringing my Smith and Wesson. (I got my concealed carry permit.) Dead-Eye Deenie in a picture hat and a hoop skirt. Can you imagine that?

Deenie

ERIN

E-mail, October 13, 1997
Dear Juneau and Deenie,

Deenie, thanks for the fabulous chocolate! It definitely made me feel better. Hope it did the same for you, Juneau. Take my advice and clean out that guilt closet of yours. I don't know what's moldering in there, but my fall doesn't need to be added.

Here's a news flash: My sister met a landscape architect named Sam Powers a couple of weeks back, and she's talked of nothing and no one else since. He's medium height and medium weight with medium brown hair and medium hazel eyes. But when he smiles at her, he looks like Prince Charming to me!

Regina's girls were getting older now, ready to train as knights and maids-in-waiting to the queen. But Daphne, the oldest girl, was holding out for love.

"There is a prince waiting for me," she told Regina. "I'll recognize him when I see him."

"What does he look like?" asked Regina. "How will I recognize him among all the knights in the king's court?"

Daphne frowned. "I don't know. In my dreams he's always wearing armor and a helmet!"

Your Erin

Early in November, Lottie called Erin to say she would host Thanksgiving that year. "I want to have everyone sitting around my table. You, the kids, and your mother and Jake." She paused. "And The Grandparents McGee."

"You can't mean to have my mother in the same room with Andrew's parents!" Erin said. "That's asking for trouble."

"Joanna's already said she'd come," Lottie said with satisfaction.

Despite her concerns, Erin didn't dwell on Thanksgiving. There was a more important family event occupying her thoughts. Mark would soon turn twelve, which meant he would be ordained a deacon. It was one of those times that reminded Erin of how much had been lost since her divorce. Cory should be the one ordaining him, not Skipp.

She knew Cory no longer went to church, but she hoped he would at least join the family and the Harringtons in the bishop's office to witness this milestone in his son's life. He didn't, and in the end, she was glad of it. It would have made Mark uncomfortable, which was the last thing she wanted.

Mark's eyes glowed with pride as he shook hands after the ordination. Ricky, who couldn't contain his excitement, pounded Mark on the back and said he couldn't wait to be ordained so he could pass the sacrament, too. His eagerness touched Erin. She knew that wouldn't happen soon—Steve and Colleen would wait until they were sure he understood what it meant to hold the priesthood.

As the Harringtons took their leave, Colleen hugged Erin and said, "Call me tomorrow. We need to talk."

All afternoon and into the evening, Erin kept coming up with possible reasons for the requested call, each more dire than the one before. Finally, she pressed in the Harringtons' number. "I know you said to call tomorrow," she said without preamble, "but I won't be able to sleep unless I know what's up. So, what's up?"

"Nothing bad," Colleen said. "At least I don't think so." She paused.

"I know your heart isn't in the Sale anymore, Erin, even though you do as much as you can. Naieem would be thrilled if you'd be willing to let her buy you out. She's already looked into getting a small business loan."

Erin was speechless. She'd concluded she needed to sell, but getting an offer so soon caught her off balance. She and Colleen had created the Big Barn Sale, and with years of hard work they'd turned it into a Twin Cities institution. She couldn't imagine not being part of it, but she also knew Colleen needed an on-the-spot partner.

"We'll still be friends, even if we aren't business partners," Colleen said into the silence.

Sighing, Erin said, "Let's set up a meeting with Naieem."

"So far so good," Erin said to her mother. They were standing in Lottie's kitchen, putting finishing touches on individual plates of cranberry Jell-O salad in preparation for Thanksgiving dinner. All the guests had arrived and greeted each other politely. *A miracle in itself,* Erin thought. Now Sean McGee and Lottie were talking to Caitlin's boyfriend, Sam, while Andrew, Jake, and the kids were downstairs playing billiards.

"Look at that." Caitlin pointed to where their grandmother, dressed in her signature black with pearls, was shifting name cards at the long dining table. "Can you believe it? She's changing the seating arrangements."

"No doubt I'll end up below the salt," Erin said, using an expression from historical romance novels she'd read when she was younger.

"Do you want me to put the place cards back where they were?"

"No. It's not worth the fuss."

When they took their places at the table, Erin saw that Margaret had arranged the cards so that she and Sean were seated near Andrew at the head of the table with Mark and Kayla next to them. Then came Caitlin and Sam. At Lottie's end of the table were The Jays, Erin, and Hannah, who perched on a booster seat.

Andrew greeted the assemblage and gave a traditional Catholic blessing on the food. Then he carved the turkey, sending small platters of white and dark meat around the table. Other dishes were started, and everyone focused on enjoying the meal until Andrew stood again, goblet in hand.

"It's our very great pleasure to have you all here today," he said. "The older I get, the more I realize the importance of family. I propose the toast from the movie *Moonstruck*: 'A la familia.'"

Several minutes later, Sean stood. He spoke of the meaning of Thanksgiving and of his gratitude for his wife, Margaret. He said how lucky Andrew was to have Lottie and thanked Lottie for the loving way she'd raised Caitlin. "To Margaret. To Lottie."

Everyone raised their glasses, whether sparkling cider or wine, and drank.

Then Sean went on to compliment Caitlin for having recently completed special training on environmental design. "I'm green now," Caitlin said, laughing.

Erin held her breath, wondering what Sean would say about her. But he spoke next of Mark and Kayla, saying he and Margaret could see parts of themselves in the two, especially in their early accomplishments. He drew a smile from Hannah when he said she could always make him laugh.

Erin's ears flamed as she raised her goblet. She couldn't believe Sean would ignore her so cruelly. She was angry that no one called him on it and angry at herself for still hoping and wanting, after all these years, to be acknowledged as a McGee.

The meal continued, but Erin was too upset to eat. Jake put his arm around her. "Let it go," he said softly. Lottie added, "Trust Andrew. I don't think he'll let it pass."

She was right. A little later, Andrew rose. "I propose a toast to Joanna. She also raised a daughter of mine to be a lovely young woman. She did it in the most difficult of circumstances, which I regret being partly responsible for. And to my daughter, Erin," he continued. "I couldn't be prouder of what she's accomplished in her life, especially of the way she and Cory are parenting Kayla, Mark, and Hannah."

As everyone raised goblets to Joanna and Erin, Hannah crowed, "To me!"

"To Hannah," Andrew said, "whose delight in life delights all of us."

Sam stood, clearing his throat. "Uh, this seems like a good time to make an announcement."

Caitlin looked up at Sam with glowing anticipation.

Sam's grin was a mile wide. "I've asked Caitlin to marry me, and she said yes."

WILLADENE

The evening of the open house, Gobb Hill twinkled with fairy lights from the eaves to the boxwood hedges that outlined the front gardens. They reflected off the leaves of the fresh magnolia wreath Deenie had hung on the front door, catching the colors of the pomegranates, figs, and apples that nestled there.

"Perfect!" Deenie sighed. She closed her eyes and said a quick prayer for the evening to come. It was so important. She'd finally gotten the courage to gather all the tenuous threads of her life in Gainesville together and hoped to see the beginning of that safety net she was missing.

Saying a fervent amen and then reminding herself not to chew off her lipstick, she smoothed her hands over the skirt of her cherry red sheath, took a deep calming breath of the crisp air, and went back inside. She stepped into a medley of holiday aromas—mulled cider, bacon-wrapped scallops, and crab-stuffed mushrooms. Candles glowed, and Gobb Hill crystal and silver gleamed in the firelight.

She was enjoying the final moment of peace before the guests arrived when Roger came down the stairs. "Deenie, everything looks spectacular. Including you."

"Thank you, kind sir," Deenie straightened his Christmas tie. "I hope this doesn't turn out to be a disaster. We're mixing an odd bunch here tonight—Church members, Academy staff, new friends, parents of non-residential students, *the board* . . ."

"The whole point of this gala is to share the Christmas spirit with all the people who are important to us," Roger reminded her. "Everything is going to be fine. You worry way too much. Relax and enjoy yourself."

"Happy Christmas," Evvy caroled in her most grown-up voice.

Deenie looked to the top of the staircase where her daughter posed dramatically. In that second she had a vision of who Evvy would be when she grew up. Then the doorbell rang, and guests began arriving. First on the scene were Mandy and her parents with their pastor in tow. Deenie and Gwen had decided the open house would be a great time to introduce Pastor Wilmot to some real Mormons, and the Love-Bassetts, with a great deal of effort, had persuaded him to accompany them.

As if it had been planned, Bishop Shurl Nunn and his wife arrived directly afterward. Deenie gathered her courage and dived into the introductions. She hid a grin when Bishop Nunn said, "Mighty fine to meet you," and gave the pastor's hand a hearty shake. "Don't you love this time of year when we celebrate the birth of our Savior?"

"Certainly do," Pastor Wilmot said, looking slightly flustered, but he returned the handshake with equal enthusiasm.

As the evening wore on, Deenie noticed that people from the various areas of her life congregated together, Church folk with Church folk, school with school. Then Miss B arrived with Cleo Kenady, her husband, Devon, and Christiana, and the chemistry of the evening changed. Along with Marsha, they moved from group to group like social blenders running on high. Deenie smiled widely when she realized that her *made* family, as Juneau would call them, were doing exactly what her Wellsville family would do—helping to make the evening a success.

After the last guests left and Evvy had gone to bed, Deenie and Roger raided the first-floor kitchen for leftovers of all the food they hadn't had time to taste. Back in their apartment, Roger lit the fireplace while Deenie laid out the spread of goodies and opened a bottle of sparkling cider.

"This will go down as one of the best evenings of my life." Roger reached for a slice of sweet potato cheesecake. "Everything was great. The house, the food, you. Even Delia said so."

"I'm glad she approved." Deenie was warmed at the thought of the many wonderful things had happened, such as Ferris entertaining everyone with his recitation of the The Night Before Christmas and Delia getting teary when the girls sang "Silent Night." But the highlight of the evening was when Pastor Wilmot offered to bless the house before he left, and everyone came together to listen to his prayer.

Deenie raised her glass to Roger. "This was one of the best nights of my life, too."

Chapter 9

1998

JUNEAU

As Juneau mused on the positive events of 1997, she put Gideon's return at the top of the list. Somewhere down in the middle she put the week in Sedona with Erin and Deenie. She'd enjoyed it tremendously and had got what she needed to move forward with her book. But she was still haunted by her thoughtless insistence on climbing to the cliff dwellings and Erin's frightening fall. It had shaken awake memories of another fall she'd caused, many years before, something she'd filed away in a place called Don't Look.

But she wasn't going to think about that now. She turned her thoughts to how grateful she was that Erin wasn't blaming her. In fact, Erin had e-mailed last fall urging Juneau to clean out her guilt closet and close the door. It was good advice—it could have come straight from Gabby's mouth.

What Juneau did was hang the guilt on Catalina, the protagonist of the book she'd been researching when they were in Sedona and was now writing. She made Catalina guilt-ridden because she felt it was her fault her brother had run away, and that drove her to follow his path deep into Hopi country. During the twists and turns of Catalina's search for her brother, Juneau forced Catalina to face the truth about herself and learn Ray Red Hawk's lesson—that when there was a decision to make, she needed to think ahead to the possible consequences.

As she wrote the girl's story, Juneau felt as if she were learning the same lessons as Catalina. After finishing one very satisfying chapter, Juneau e-mailed Erin.

> Just wanted you to know I'm tackling that guilt closet you referred to. Only I'm going to clean it out before I close the door!

Despite the optimistic tone of her e-mail, the very thought of tackling that closet was daunting to Juneau. It was full to bursting with packages from the past, all the way back to her childhood when she'd promised to write to Starette, the girl in the trailer park in Washington. But she never had. What was the point? She'd never see her again. Didn't *want* to see her again. Then there was Misty. And Gideon. And Clyde.

And Greg. Perhaps Greg was the package to start with. But what could she do that would let him know she wanted their relationship to improve? Or that would please him? Actually, that was an easy question to answer. She shut down her computer and went shopping for a slinky new nightgown.

ERIN

E-mail, January 1, 1998
Dear Friends,

I was marking all the birthdays and anniversaries in my new 1998 calendar, and I realized I turn forty this coming April! I don't know why that seems like such a big deal, but it does.

Kayla has a significant birthday, too. She turns fifteen in a few days, which means she can get her learner's permit. I'm glad she has something to balance the bad news her coach gave her before Christmas—her ankle isn't flexible enough to do some of the moves necessary to requalify for competitive skating. I think Kayla already knew, but hearing him say it hit hard. Her counselor, Vicki, is helping her get through it.

Caitlin and Sam have chosen August 12 as the date for their wedding, and they've reserved the rotunda of one of the Carlson Towers in Minnetonka for the ceremony as well as a block of hotel rooms at a Ramada Inn for out-of-town guests. Caitlin's so lucky to have found Sam. Their romance has been effortless and uncomplicated—why couldn't I have had one like that?

Remember the question, What do men want from women? I discovered it's not a good one to ask single Mormon men—they think it's a signal I'm interested in them!

I went to a singles dance before Christmas. I felt I had to since I did part of the planning. As Deenie would say, Aargh! The

men were either interested in twenty-something blondes or
. . . Well, let's say they're single for a reason.

Of course, that's true about me, too.

Love,
Erin

P.S. I've sold my interest in the Big Barn Sale. I'm relieved but
sad—it was part of my life for twenty years. Still will be, to some
extent. I'll help familiarize Naieem with her new responsibilities, and I'll lend a hand on actual sale days. That's where the
fun is!

WILLADENE

A cold winter mist lapped at the foot of Gobb Hill as Deenie dressed
for her morning run with Bear. She needed the time alone to think about
the difference she'd immediately noticed in Elizabeth as she stepped off
the plane the last week in December.

It was the first time Deenie had seen her daughter since she had
returned to the States in May. Outwardly, she seemed her cheerful, ebullient self but with a new maturity and self-assurance. However, Deenie
sensed a deep change, something she couldn't quite put her finger on.

Evvy noticed it, too. "I think Elizabeth's sad," she'd said. "She looks
like she's lost something important, and she can't find it anywhere."

That described it as well as anything Deenie had come up with, but it
didn't explain it, and Deenie was worried sick. *How am I going to get her to
tell me what's troubling her?* she wondered as she ran. She'd spoken to her
mother about it, and Margaret had said she thought it had something to
do with all the letters Liz was getting from Brad Donaldson. That news
had set Deenie's teeth on edge. What was he doing corresponding with
Elizabeth? He was Sunny's sweetheart!

There were now only two days left before Liz was to go back to Utah,
and Deenie had to find a way to get her to confide what was bothering her.

With her thoughts spinning in circles, Deenie ran until even Bear had
had enough. The phone was ringing when she dragged herself through the
back door of the apartment. Paul was on the other end of the line.

"Mom, Dani and I have something to tell you," Paul said.

"Hold on. Let me get everyone on other phones so they can hear, too." When Deenie hollered, "Family phone call," Roger and Evvy scrambled for extensions. Elizabeth listened with Deenie, who'd turned on the speakerphone.

Deenie said, "Everybody's here," and Paul and Dani shouted together, "We're engaged!"

"That's great news," Elizabeth said, but her enthusiasm was muted.

"Now you'll really be my sister," Evvy crowed. "Can I be a brides-maid?"

"I wouldn't have it any other way," Dani said.

Roger interrupted as Evvy began again. "Let a father get a word in here. We couldn't be happier, Dani. You've been a member of this family for years, and now it will be official."

"When's the big day?" Deenie asked.

"We'll be sealed in the Logan temple on the twenty-third of July," Paul said, "so Dani can have her hoedown reception the next evening on the farm."

"But that's Pioneer Day," Deenie protested, referring to the Utah holiday.

"We know," Paul said. "Won't it be great? Everyone will be in town for the holiday anyway. They won't even have to change their plans."

"That's not much time to plan a wedding, girlfriend," Elizabeth said. "Besides, I thought we were going to get married on the same day."

"If you've got the guy, we'll have a double ceremony."

"You know that's not possible," Elizabeth said.

"Sorry I asked," Dani said regretfully. "I should have known better."

Hearing the exchange, Deenie's fears about Brad and Elizabeth were confirmed. And Elizabeth was unwilling to tell her about it.

"Sister Rasmussen, are you there?"

Dani's voice over the speakerphone brought Deenie back to the conversation. "Sorry, dear. I'm listening."

"I was saying we have all the reception plans made. I'm going to wear a simple summer suit. Pat's already signed up to do the cake and desserts, and everyone else has offered to furnish the usual potluck pioneer dinner."

"You mean everyone else already knows?" Deenie asked with a sinking feeling. Surely all the plans for her son's wedding hadn't been made with-out her.

"Well, we wanted to have everything in order before we called so you wouldn't worry," Paul said.

"Mom and Dad are moving back to New Jersey in August to take care of my grandma, Sister Rasmussen," Dani added. "We wanted to get married before they left and do it without adding more stress for them."

"Then what can I say but congratulations and welcome to the family, Dani dear," Deenie said.

God bless them, Deenie prayed silently, as she began her nightly tour of Gobb Hill, checking doors and locking windows. *God bless Elizabeth, too.* She was thrilled that Paul would be her first child to be married, but she feared that Elizabeth might be the first child on both sides of the family to consider marrying outside the Church. If so, would she, Deenie, be able to face it with as much equanimity as Juneau seemed to show?

JUNEAU
E-mail, January 22, 1998
Dear Deenie and Erin,

Erin, months ago you asked us to ask our husbands what men want.

After nearly thirty years of marriage, I've discovered that Greg, age fifty-two, wants much the same things as Gideon, age almost ten! Greg wants to be cherished, appreciated. He wants to be significant in my eyes. Remember years ago when I told you about Gideon's saying our dog, Philip Atwater, thought he, Gideon, was Somebody? Greg wants me to think he's Somebody.

I'm working on it. We still speak two different languages, but we're trying to put together a pleasing package for the future.

I was thinking the other day that I miss Regina and Reginald. I wondered what packages they've put together since we last saw them.

"Reginald," Regina said pensively, gazing across the table at Burger King, the only place they could afford to eat out now that the twins, triplets, and quadruplets were all headed for college and missions.

"We've been through so much together. Have I changed? Do you still see me the same as in the old days?"

Reginald's face was tender as he said, "Oh, Regina darling, yes, you've changed. What I see is so much more than the old days." His eyes explored her face, coming to rest on her full red lips, enhanced these days by Revlon's brightest shade.

Regina smiled flirtatiously. "And what more do you see, my love?"

"Oh," Reginald said, "about forty pounds, I'd guess."

As he picked himself up off the floor, he said, "Let me change that, my lovely, to say that you're a sight for sore eyes!"

Love,

Juneau

ERIN

Erin sat in bed flipping through the March issues of upscale housing magazines looking for trends and room treatments she thought might intrigue clients. She heard a noise and looked up to see Kayla standing in the doorway.

"May I come in?" Kayla asked.

Erin moved the magazines to her nightstand and patted the space beside her. "Sure."

Kayla climbed in and leaned her head on Erin's shoulder. "Did you know the McCandless Competition was today?"

"It was? I wish you'd told me. We could have gone."

"No. I would have hated watching other girls skate their programs." Kayla's voice broke. "I loved skating. I don't know what to do with myself now."

"I'm so sorry." Erin hugged Kayla and kissed the top of her head. Her hair, which in her skating days had been long enough to pull back, was now a short mop of curls.

"I'm not a part of anything anymore, Mom. I feel like a nothing. I don't belong anywhere."

Erin remembered Colleen saying that was how EJ felt. "You aren't a nothing, Kayla Johnson. And you belong to a family who loves you."

"I *know* that, but I don't *feel* it." Kayla sighed. "Maybe if I had a fairy godmother to zap me with her wand . . ."

Erin could feel Kayla's yearning for something to make her feel significant, to use Juneau's word. To feel welcomed by and a part of her community of women.

The word *welcome* turned on the light bulbs. The next day Erin called Lucky Brown, who'd done the Baby Welcome for Hannah. She explained Kayla's situation and said, "Do you think you could pull off a Woman Welcome, something to give young women faith in themselves and a sense of belonging?"

"Dang, girl!" Lucky said. "I should have thought of that myself. Shakeela needs some womanlove and direction, too. That girl is too sassy for her own good."

With Lucky's agreement, Erin planned to schedule the Woman Welcome right away. But then Andrew called to say Lottie was in the hospital.

WILLADENE

Lark Donovan, Dani's mother and Deenie's close friend, called early on a March morning, bubbling over with contagious excitement. They talked over the wedding plans, which to Deenie's keen disappointment already sounded etched in stone. Then Lark dropped another surprise in Deenie's lap. Because she and her husband were moving to New Jersey and wanted to sell their house as quickly as possible, they were going to clear out most of their furniture to make it look bigger.

"We've offered Paul and Dani their choice of items. Is it all right with you if we pack away some of your things to make space for them?"

"That's fine," Deenie managed before the shock of yet another change took over and left her speechless.

That afternoon she vented her feeling of life moving rapidly out of her control in an e-mail to Juneau and Erin.

I've asked Elizabeth to see that all my things are packed away safely, but I still worry. Not only about my things but also about how I'll feel when I walk into my house and see someone else's things in their place. It's good we'll be coming right back to

Florida after the reception. I can't fathom two Mrs. Rasmussens in the gray house at the same time.

Regina stood on the veranda of the mansion house looking down at her luggage in dismay. Virginia, the bride of her eldest son, Denzel, stood in the doorway with her arms staunchly crossed and her feet spread wide.

"Why, Mama Regina, I thought you understood. We can't have two Mrs. Snodgrasses in the big house at the same time. Papa Reginald understands. He's already packed up Daphne; the triplets Hazel, Philbert, and Wally; the quads Daisy, Maizie, Margie, and George; and the dogs Cleopatra, Wolf, and Hound; the birds Tweet, Cheep, and Twitter; Bubbles the fish; and Venom the snake and moved into the potting shed beyond the back gate."

At least I have the battle with Delia to keep me distracted from what is going on in Wellsville. For the present we are trying to out-polite each other while we jockey to see whose choice of project is going to be funded by the board first, hers or mine. Aargh!

Roger, Evvy, and I leave for Wellsville and wedding preparations on June 8. Since Bear's going with us, we're taking two vehicles. Considering our previous experience with Bear's motion sickness traveling cross-country, I'm not looking forward to it. Meanwhile, if you don't hear from me, no news is good news.

Love,
Deenie

ERIN
E-mail, April 7, 1998
Dear Friends,

Lottie's had another bout with pneumonia. She's back home after several days in University Hospital, weaker but in good spirits. I think a cheerful heart is her special gift. When Caitlin told Lottie that she and Sam were thinking of moving the wedding up to May, Lottie said August was fine—she wasn't planning on dying yet!

Caitlin and Sam did scrap their plans for an extravaganza—

Caitlin's heart wasn't in it anymore. They've opted for an intimate wedding in Andrew and Lottie's living room. Caitlin's mother, Brenda, is arriving the week before the wedding to act as field marshal so Caitlin can spend as much private time with Lottie as possible.

That's such a big-hearted thing for Brenda to do. I can't reconcile the woman I know with the young mother who left her daughter to be raised by someone else. I wonder why she did it.

Erin

An hour before guests were to arrive for the Woman Welcome, Caitlin called to ask Erin to put the ramp in place. "I'm bringing Lottie."

"Is that a good idea?" Lottie had been weak since her recent bout with pneumonia. Erin knew that overexertion could cause a setback. "Melina's mom is going to be here via speakerphone. Lottie could do the same."

"She wants to come."

Lucky and Shakeela arrived after Erin and Mark had wrestled the wheelchair ramp into place. Lucky enveloped Erin in a sea of kente cloth. Her eyes sparkled, and her grin was wide. "Girl, you're too skinny!"

"I don't know about that. Shakeela, give me a hug."

Shakeela complied, and then Erin held her at arm's length. "Wow! You're a stunner."

Lucky snorted. "Any dude start coming around, I'll show him who the stunner is."

Over the next few minutes, the house filled. Caitlin, Lottie, and their housekeeper, Theresa, arrived first. Then Joanna, Linda, and Melina, followed by Colleen and EJ, who now had five piercings up the scroll of her left ear.

Lucky took her place before the living room fireplace, around which Erin had arranged a circle of chairs, and the ceremony began. Lucky talked about what it meant to be a woman, bearer of such gifts as the ability to bear and nurture children, comfort those in need, pass on enduring values, and protect those unable to stand up for themselves. Striding into the circle, she looked at the girls and delivered her conclusion with the fervor of a Southern preacher, "Your title of Woman comes not by degree or decree but from the beating of your heart."

Erin felt goose bumps rise as she realized that Lucky had defined what it meant to be a COB and wished Juneau, Deenie, and Gabby—and Grams—were there, too.

The gift-giving part of the ceremony was magical. Erin saw Shakeela seem to grow more beautiful as she stood in the middle of the circle and received her gifts.

Kayla's eyes glowed as Theresa gave her the gift of courage and kissed her cheek. But when Theresa said in rapid-fire Spanish, "*Vivir con miedo, es como vivir a medias!*" Kayla frowned. "What does that mean?"

"A life lived in fear is a life half-lived."

"Is it a Spanish proverb?"

Theresa's black eyes gleamed. "No. I heard it in a movie, *Strictly Ballroom*. You should watch it, *querida*."

When it was Melina's turn to receive, Althea's voice came over the speakerphone clear and strong. "I haven't been the mother you needed or deserved, Melina. I'm worried that my problems have made you feel different, like you have something to hide. So I give you the gift of knowing that you're a wonderful young woman, no matter what our circumstances are."

Erin looked at Kayla, EJ, and Melina and murmured, "Amen to that." Later, she sat at her computer and wrote:

I wish you could have been at the Woman Welcome tonight. It did everything I'd hoped for Kayla. She looks happier than she has in a long time. She even seems taller!

She wants to get a sterling silver bracelet engraved with "A life lived in fear is a life half-lived," which Lottie's housekeeper says is from a movie that's worth watching.

I think EJ felt better afterward, too. I hope so. Colleen says she's still floundering. She'll graduate this spring but doesn't have any plans for additional education or training. She seems happy to squeak by grade-wise, work as a cashier, and watch movies or listen to music with her friends. Girls, who, according to Colleen, have as little direction as she.

Chapter 10

JUNEAU

One May day Juneau and Gideon stopped at an Albertson's supermarket in a different part of town on the way home from his guitar lesson. They were contemplating what kind of cereal to buy when Juneau looked up to see Clyde coming down the aisle, pushing a shopping cart in which a cucumber rode in solitary splendor. He'd been to class only once since the night he'd brought his moving story about loss. The night Arnie had seen them together. She'd wondered what had happened to him but hadn't called to find out.

At first she didn't recognize him. She'd never seen him in anything but the crisp khaki pants and neat shirts he wore to class. The man before her was dressed in ratty blue jeans worthy of a teenager and a green T-shirt that had seen better days. He was thin, and his brown hair showed more gray than she remembered. There was an aura of loneliness about him that called up a memory of the man who'd wanted to talk with her at the truck stop south of Provo all those years ago and then changed her flat tire for her.

Seeing Clyde in this new light made her wonder if in the time they'd been friends she'd ever really taken stock of him. Added him up as a person. She was looking right at him when he glanced her way. His gray-green eyes lit up. "Juneau," he said, smiling. "How nice to see you. If I'd known *you'd* be here, I would've changed out of my gardening clothes."

"It's good to see you, too, Clyde. And you don't need to dress up for *me*." Juneau put an arm around Gideon, who regarded the newcomer with interest. "This is Gideon," she said. "We're doing a bit of shopping."

Clyde put out a hand to Gideon. "Glad to meet you," he said. "I was hoping I'd run into somebody who could give me some advice. How about it?"

"Who, me?" Gideon looked uncertain as he briefly clasped hands with Clyde.

"You." Clyde pointed at the rows of cereal boxes. "I'm tired of corn-flakes and am looking for something really killer. What would you rec-ommend?"

Gideon considered Clyde as if determining if he was being put on. Then he said, "Well, it depends on whether you like a lot of sugar or not."

"Not," Clyde said.

Gideon nodded. "Okay, this." He pointed and then moved his finger along the row. "This is good, too. Has strawberries in it but isn't icky sweet. And this."

Clyde picked all three boxes from the shelves. "I appreciate your opinion. When my grandson visits, he helps me shop. But he hasn't been here for a while."

Juneau absorbed that bit of information. She remembered only once that he'd ever mentioned his daughter and grandchildren. Why had she never asked about his family? Was it because she'd felt their relationship would be less intimate if she didn't know anything more about him than what he presented in class?

"Clyde," she said, "we miss you on Thursday nights. We all wish you'd come back."

His slight smile told her he'd noticed the plural pronoun. "I didn't think you wanted me to," he said. "After. . . ." His eyes went to Gideon.

"After what?" Gideon asked.

"After he wrote a very good story," Juneau finished. She looked up at Clyde. "It *was* good, you know. Have you done anything with it?"

Clyde shook his head. "There's not much of a market for personal stuff like that."

So it *was* personal. "Maybe not," she admitted. "But it was a depar-ture from the journalistic articles you've done. Why not try more stories? You're good at mysteries, like the one you sold. There's always a market for them."

"Maybe I will come back," Clyde said. "I've been out of town for a while, but I can probably make it tomorrow night." He paused. "How's your friend Shan?"

His eyes said more than his words, letting her know he saw more in

Shan's life than she ever talked about. Just as Juneau did. "Maybe she'll come, too, tomorrow night," Juneau said. "I'll give her a call."

They parted then, and Clyde headed toward the checkout with his three boxes of cereal and the lone cucumber.

Gideon watched him go. "I like him. He didn't ask how old I am or what grade I'm in at school."

"He's a nice man," Juneau affirmed.

Clyde *was* a nice man. A decent man. If their relationship had been in any way inappropriate, it had been as much her fault as his.

"Gideon," she said, "pick out the cereal you want and put it in the cart. I'll be right back."

She hurried after Clyde, calling his name. He turned, gazing at her as she reached him. "*I* would be very happy if you'd come back," she said.

He acknowledged the change of pronoun with a smile. "I'm glad to hear that. D'you think we can talk tomorrow tonight?"

"After class," she said. "In the classroom."

That evening, when Gideon was parked in the family room doing his homework, Juneau told Greg that she'd be meeting with Clyde the next night.

"Oh?" Greg busied himself stashing tableware in the dishwasher and then straightened up. "Did he call or something?"

Juneau rinsed a plate and handed it to him. "Gideon and I saw him at Albertson's. He was so nice to Giddy that I think he has a fan."

Greg glanced at her before taking the plate and depositing it in the machine. "Is he back in your life, Juney?"

"He's a friend, Greg. And an excellent writer. I want to help him, if I can."

"As a friend."

Juneau nodded and then added, "Also as a teacher. Like you helped Polly Norton." Juneau named a student she knew Greg had mentored. "You managed that without it turning into something else, didn't you?"

Greg stopped, dish towel in hand. "Yes."

"And I bet you didn't talk only about business," Juneau said.

"No." Juneau saw the slightest of grins tug at the corners of his mouth. "We talked sports, too."

He talked sports with Polly? Like she talked poetry with Clyde. Mutual interests.

"So what do you think?" Juneau asked.

Greg regarded her solemnly. "You'd go ahead even if I did object, wouldn't you?"

Juneau was about to say yes. But Greg deserved better than that. "Probably not. Your feelings are more important to me than Clyde's writing."

"Thank you," Greg said. "For the record, I don't object."

WILLADENE
E-mail, June 23, 1998
Dear Sisters in COBhood,

What do you do when coming home isn't coming home? Nothing is the way I expected to be. My whole house has been Dani-ized! Everything's been streamlined inside and out, and there's not a pastel in sight.

A brightly colored piece of Lark's illustration artwork hangs over the fireplace. The basket of crocheted afghans now holds chenille throws in purple, orange, and green to accent the painting. Even Bear's and Rauf's favorite spot by the fireplace has been preempted by a giant copper-glazed vase. It's a gift from Roger's sister-in-law Jenny from her collection of pottery she did at the university. I never thought she would part with any of them. Now there's one in my family room.

To be fair, I should tell you Dani created homey touches, too— a favorite afghan made by Grandma NeVae over the back of my recliner, fresh flowers on the dining room table, and chocolates on the pillows in our bedroom. She even took the time to plant forget-me-nots on faithful old Rauf's grave. She and Mom decorated Evvy's room with Sunny treasures, which pleased Evvy to no end.

It's hard to see so many changes. When I told Roger how I felt, he reminded me that while it may be our house, it's no longer our home.

I still believed I'd feel at home in the community. There would be tasks that needed doing—a meal to plan, a dress to hem. Not so. Roger's sisters-in-law, Jenny and Charlotte, have teamed up with Lark and Pat, and they have everything under control.

The final straw? My nose misses Florida, even if the rest of me doesn't! I've had to sleep with a wet cloth over it to compensate for the lack of moisture in the air. Roger is vastly amused.

Thank heaven Mom has asked me to help at the Cache Valley Senior Advocacy Center and Reading Room and the folks at the Pioneer House Rest Home have invited Bear back for a visit.

Deenie

JUNEAU

Clyde didn't come to Juneau's class on the night he said he'd try to make it. Shan had called to say she wouldn't be coming, either. Juneau was disappointed on both counts, but she didn't dwell on it long. She was deep into the plot about Catalina, the girl searching for her missing brother. She spent hours each day working on it while Gideon was in school so she'd be free to spend time with him after he came home.

Juneau could always tell when Gideon, now ten, was remembering what she called his hostage year. Those days, he stayed close by her side. The rest of the time, he seemed fairly well adjusted and happy. He was very much involved with Cub Scouts and mentioned once that his old nemesis, Tanner Melton, was in the same troop. They'd become friends. "He's not so bad," Gideon explained, "now that I got him to dump that stink eye stuff."

Juneau remembered that when he was younger, Gideon had been upset because Tanner Melton had told him he'd put a stink eye on him. "How did you get him to dump it?" she asked.

"Oh," Gideon said lightly, "he was talking about it one day, and I said, 'That's babyish, Tanner. Grow up.' He hasn't said anything about it since."

Juneau chuckled to herself. Gideon was learning how to deal with his world.

Misty called faithfully every week to talk with Gideon, barely exchanging a sentence with Juneau before asking to speak with him. Juneau asked once where she was, but Misty merely replied, "Not too far away, distance-wise." So what did that mean? That ties-that-bind-wise and family-connection-wise she was worlds away?

On the plus side were the short, hurried e-mails from Nicole, who was attending the University of Colorado School of Medicine in Denver. "Can you believe it?" she'd written recently. "I'm on my way to becoming an actual for-real *doctor!* I feel as if I'm living a dream. Except I know it's not a dream because I never get time to sleep!"

Juneau noticed she seldom mentioned Beto. But then, she didn't mention Reece Crafton, either.

One Thursday night Clyde came back to the class. He brought a story, a light, funny tale about a man who feeds his sharp-tongued, abusive wife something called Green-O and turns her into a tree.

"It's saleable," Juneau declared after she finished reading it to the delighted class. "Let's talk about a couple of weak spots, and you can bring it back next time."

Clyde came up to her desk afterward. He seemed elated. "Do you really think it has a chance? My story, I mean."

Juneau nodded. "I'd wager a big order of fries on it, some night when Shan is here, too."

He nodded, apparently understanding what she was saying. "You're on. Mind if I sit down?"

"I wish you would," she said. "We have things to discuss."

He sat at the desk directly in front of her. "I hope we can still be friends, Juneau. I thought your husband might come and punch my lights out after his friend saw us together."

Juneau smiled. "He thought about it."

Clyde nodded slowly. "I would have deserved it. I guess I was going for more than I should have."

"Maybe I was leading you on," she said soberly.

"Maybe, maybe not." He gave a self-deprecating shrug. "I'm a guy, Juneau. Guys tend to test the boundaries."

"And I didn't set strong enough ones." Juneau paused. "I have now."

Clyde nodded and then stretched his arms out as if relaxing. "Tell me about Gideon. Great kid. He seems okay now that he's back home."

She found herself telling him at length about Gideon and the guilt she felt about allowing him to have been snatched away.

"'Bless the beasts and the children,'" Clyde quoted, "'for in this world they have no voice.'"

"I should have been his voice," Juneau said.

"It's past. Leave it there. It will all work out."

"I hope so," Juneau said. "He likes you, Clyde. He said you made him feel like a person."

Clyde chuckled. "I was a boy once myself. I know how it is."

When they finally left the classroom, Clyde walked her to her car, waving cheerfully as he headed for his own. They parted as easy friends, and Juneau felt that at the age of fifty-one she had taken a baby step toward true COBhood that Gabby would have been proud of.

WILLADENE

Deenie quickly learned that her task as the future mother-in-law of Danielle Donovan included keeping her head down, her ears open, and her mouth shut. No one needed her to be Deenie-in-Charge. And no one wanted her to.

Her input wasn't wanted when it came to family issues either, especially not by Jenny. When Deenie expressed her worry about NeVae's failing health and doubts about her decision to live out the rest of her life on the farm, Jenny said, "It's not your concern. Those of us who are here will take care of NeVae."

All the listening skills Deenie had been practicing since Sedona flew right out the window. "Just because I don't live here anymore doesn't mean I'm not part of the family."

"No. But you're not in charge, either."

"I never wanted to be in charge," Deenie protested.

"Well, it always ended up that way, because it was easier for us to yield than to argue," Jenny said.

Deenie was astounded. Years ago, when her sister-in-law Bert had spearheaded getting the family to help finish renovations on the gray house, Deenie had been impressed by how she got others to do things without causing resentment. She'd tried to follow Bert's example, but obviously, it hadn't worked as well for her.

Later, she sat on the stairway landing in her parents' home with her head in Margaret's lap, as they'd done many years before. "What's wrong with me?" she asked. "I don't fit in Gainesville, but I don't fit in Wellsville anymore, either."

"There's nothing wrong with you. But you've changed, and so have all of us. We need to be patient and kind as we learn to adjust to those changes."

Deenie felt her mother's soft caress. Here, at least, she felt at home. "I'll try, Mom. I'll really try."

She did try to be more open to all the changes in her family and community, but it was hard. She missed the close involvement she'd once had with her friends. But she had a chance to experience it again when Lark Donovan came to visit her one day, brimming with delight. "Shawn and I are going to receive our endowments. Then we can be at the wedding and be sealed at the same time. Would you be my escort?"

The invitation to be present for Lark at that special occasion, as she had for Lark's baptism, put Deenie's heart at ease. *This is what it's all about,* she thought. *It's why we're here. To be a family, despite our differences.* "I'd be honored," she said.

For the rest of the Wellsville visit, Deenie kept that thought foremost in her mind. She focused on it during the temple ceremony and through the reception on the farm she'd had little to do with. She kept it close to her heart as she shared a tender private farewell with Dani and Paul after the reception and later when she stood with the others, tossing rose petals and calling good-bye as they left for their honeymoon. No matter what changed—and she acknowledged that change would come no matter how hard she tried to hold it at bay—being a family was what mattered.

Chapter 11

JUNEAU

E-mail, July 5, 1998

Deenie and Erin,

We have breaking news! Trace and Cath are having a baby! They told Gideon first, and he couldn't wait to announce it at our Fourth of July backyard picnic. He hollered, "I'm going to be a brother!" as soon as we were all assembled. You've never seen anyone as pleased as Trace, Cath, and Giddy. And me and Greg and Nicole and Beto and Ira and Shoshana and Marisol—well, you get the picture.

As we chowed down our hot dogs, each person present offered a gift to the coming baby, somewhat like that Baby Welcome your friend Lucky Brown did when your Hannah was born, Erin. Ira inducted him/her into the Royal Order of Picklehood, and Shoshana offered lifelong free entry into any movies that are made from screenplays she writes. There was a lot of hooting about that, because she hasn't sold a screenplay yet, but she said, "It will happen!"

Beto (he and Marisol were invited; he and Nicole seem to be "on" again for the summer) offered free health care for the baby but said he/she will have to come to the little Mexican village where he'll be practicing in order to get it! Nicole said she'd be the "aunt at the picnic" to celebrate his/her first Fourth of July next year, and Giddy said his gift was to be the best big brother in the total entire world. Marisol, Greg, and I, being old and wise in years (ha!), offered sincere gifts of love and family.

So, Greg and I will be grandparents again. Not by blood but by choice.

When it started to get dark, Greg invited us all to climb up on the roof to watch the fireworks displays all over the valley, including the Rose Bowl. Marisol and I remained down below on the lanai, and she asked if I thought we'd ever have mutual grandchildren. I wouldn't hazard a guess. Marisol said that Beto had told her he can't go on much longer the way they are. He said he's planned to marry Nicole ever since they were four years old and can't get interested in anybody else.

So I guess he hasn't given up hope. I don't know what will happen. *Que sera, sera.*

Love,
Juneau

The day after Juneau wrote the e-mail, Nicole came home from an afternoon with Beto at the beach. Looking sunburned and somber, she pulled a chair close to Juneau's computer desk and said, "Can we talk?"

"Of course." Juneau closed her file and turned to her daughter.

Nicole stared out of the window. "Beto wants us to get married next summer, after he graduates from med school and I finish my second year."

"And?" Juneau's calm voice belied the jumble of emotions she was feeling.

"I love him, Mom, but I can't ignore our religious differences." Nicole gulped down a sob. "Beto says our kids would have to be raised Catholic. He says it's the sensible thing, anyway, since we'd be in Mexico where it's the dominant religion. I reminded him that there's always a pair of *camisas blancas*—'white shirts,' as they call the missionaries—in the little town where the clinic is and a small LDS chapel about eight miles away. But he wouldn't even consider changing his mind."

"Sounds like you two are at a standoff."

"More like caught between the proverbial boulder and hard place," Nicole said with a watery smile. "I went on a mission because I love the Church. I want to be married in the temple and have an eternal family. I want to teach my children the things that mean so much to me. But I love Beto, too."

Juneau could feel Nicole's pain as all the years of Beto and Nicole being like one entity flashed through her mind. "What answer did you give him?"

"The only one possible. That I couldn't marry him. He looked out at the ocean for a while and then said, 'Okay.' Oh, Mom!" Nicole cried, her shoulders heaving. "I love him so much."

Juneau held her weeping daughter, shedding tears of her own. She wasn't sure whether they were of sorrow or relief. Or both.

Two days later, Beto came over to say good-bye. "I called Dr. Vasquez in Mexico," he explained as the family stood in the living room. "He's happy to have me work with him until school starts in September. And I'll be happy to be there with *Abuelo* Hernandez and others of my mother's family."

The air was heavy with what Beto had not said as he gave Juneau a brief hug and shook hands with Greg and Gideon. He turned to Nicole, and Juneau ceased breathing as she saw the longing and pain in the look they exchanged. Then he was gone.

ERIN

E-mail, July 29, 1998
Dear Friends,

Did you hear the news? We're getting a temple, one of the small ones, on the St. Paul side of the Twin Cities. The groundbreaking will be in September and the open house next December.

I haven't gone to the Chicago temple much since Cory and I were divorced. I always leave a session feeling uplifted but also sad and confused, wondering why I had such a feeling of rightness on the day we were married, considering what was to come. That leaves me distrustful of my feelings, spiritual or otherwise.

I just now stopped to read what I'd written, and it made me mad. Not at Cory but at myself for dragging those feelings, plus distrust and regret, into every new day for the last four years! How stupid is that? Cory has gone on with his life—why haven't I? Time to put together a new package!

Your Erin

P.S. Preparations are in full swing for Caitlin's wedding, and Lottie is holding up well.

WILLADENE

Gobb Hill looked the same to Deenie on the hot day in August when they returned to Florida as it had the day they left it. But change was waiting to bite Deenie in the ankle the minute she opened the mail. The first envelope on the pile was from Addie Spencer, who wrote:

> I didn't realize you were leaving so quickly after the wedding. I thought we'd have time to talk over my latest project, but I missed the opportunity, so here it is. Since Elizabeth and I returned from our adventures, I've been writing travel articles on the places we stayed. Elizabeth has been a great help. She has quite a bent for journalism.
>
> To my delight they have sold well, and I have been asked to do a series on April in Paris for the young and young at heart. I couldn't manage the "young" part without Elizabeth. How do you feel about another trip abroad for your daughter? It would be on the same conditions as before, expenses and salary. I'd like to book our accommodations before the end of the year. Looking forward to hearing from you.
>
> Addie

The next letter in the pile was from Elizabeth. She wrote:

> I expect you've heard from Addie by now, Mom. I'd really like to take that trip. Since I managed to test out of so many classes while I traveled with her, it won't put me behind in school. In fact, I'm thinking of changing my major from French to journalism. I know I could get credit for my work with Addie. If you and Daddy approve, I'll finish up early at Utah State, spend Christmas through April with you, and leave for Paris from there.

As Deenie read the letters, she didn't experience any of the dread she had felt the first time Elizabeth traveled overseas. She could only feel relief that the trip would put some distance between her daughter and Brad.

That small respite from her concern over Elizabeth would give her the time she needed to concentrate on keeping in closer touch with Carl. With his ROTC commitments, she had barely seen him during the summer and knew she was missing out on knowing the man he was becoming.

It seemed to Deenie that fall that school started again before she'd had time to unpack from their trip. Leo Flynn and his cadre started showing up for morning runs with her and Bear. Roger jumped back into work at the Academy with his usual enthusiasm, and Evvy started ironing her own uniforms for St. Anne's—she wanted them to look just so. Deenie knew her little girl was growing up quickly.

And then there was Delia. No matter how hard Deenie tried to follow her mother's advice, they were still at loggerheads. This time over repairing the track and field versus expanding the music program at the Academy. Deenie knew they were both worthy projects, but she couldn't get on board with Delia about the music when every time the boys worked out they squished in the damp of the low-lying field.

By the middle of September Deenie was already longing for Christmas vacation and a break from it all.

ERIN

Erin smoothed the back of Caitlin's raw silk going-away suit, trying hard not to get weepy again. Her sister's wedding, which had been awash in love, had stirred up all Erin's ambivalent feelings about men and marriage and brought up longings she preferred not to acknowledge.

"You were a beautiful bride, sis," she said. "Everything was perfect."

"It was, wasn't it?" A glowing Caitlin sat on her bed to put on her high heels. "Hannah was the cutest flower girl ever. Give her a kiss from me on her birthday, okay? And tell Mark everyone loved the romantic songs he played during the reception. I know that's not his favorite kind of music."

"He'd rather play Beethoven." Erin couldn't hold back the laughter bubbling up. "Caitlin, did you see our grandmother's face when she saw Brenda walking you up the aisle with Andrew and Lottie? I swear she looked exactly like a guppy!"

Caitlin chuckled. "Poor Grandmother. She was rather overwhelmed by Sam's family, too. But Lottie held up well, didn't she?"

"She looked happier than I've seen her in a long time." Erin saw a secret smile light up Caitlin's eyes. "What?"

Caitlin pulled Erin down beside her. "Concern for Lottie wasn't the only reason Sam and I decided on a small wedding. We're going to use the money saved to try for a baby through in vitro fertilization."

Erin squealed in delight and gave Caitlin a fierce hug. She knew that an infection years ago had scarred Caitlin's fallopian tubes. This was the only way she could conceive.

"Don't get too excited, Erin. It's a complicated process, and I may not get pregnant the first time. Or the second."

Erin felt a warm flood of emotion. "But you will."

In the days after the wedding, Erin felt at a loss. She'd always known where she was headed and what needed to be done. That's why she'd been particularly concerned about Kayla and EJ not having a sense of direction. But now she felt directionless herself.

She began questioning everything. Was she a nice person? A kind, lovable, loving person? Was she making a difference in the lives of others? Giving her children what they needed, despite being a working mother? Doing the right thing by staying single? Or would her children tell her someday that they'd always wished for a stepfather to anchor their home?

These questions pulled her away from her work. She would suddenly realize she'd been sitting at her desk, pen in hand, thoughts far away from the project in front of her. They intruded into her thoughts while fixing dinner and reading bedtime stories to Hannah, who'd just turned four. They kept her awake at night.

She was in the throes of this self-examination while weeding a flower bed one sunny August afternoon when Kayla joined her.

"Mom, how old were you when you got your patriarchal blessing?" Kayla asked.

"Uh . . . I've never gotten it."

"Mom! Why not?"

Erin sat back on her haunches. "At first, I put it off because I wanted to be prepared. Then I met your dad, and . . . Why do you ask?"

"I think I'd like to get mine." Kayla yanked out a clump of quack grass and tossed it onto the growing pile. Then she looked at Erin. "Why don't you get yours at the same time?"

The fear of not being ready—not being worthy—to receive her blessing ran up Erin's spine. It was followed by the sure knowledge that her blessing would give her the direction she'd been seeking. She just had to take the step forward.

"I could do that," she said.

"Cool." Kayla gave Erin a hug and headed for the sandbox. "Hey, Hannah Banana! Want someone to play with?"

E-mail, August 23, 1998
Dear COBs,

Today Kayla and I got our patriarchal blessings. I was so nervous driving over to the patriarch's house that I left wet handprints on the steering wheel. Kayla was more excited than nervous, but her blessing left her perplexed because of what the patriarch said about making the most of her talents. She's been of the mind that she had only one real talent—skating. Now she's wondering what else she might be good at. She says it must be something she's never tried doing before.

What can I say about my blessing? I only remember one part, but I remember it in perfect detail. It stuck with Kayla, too. On the way home, she kept babbling, "Mom, he said you're going to go to the temple with someone that's worthy. That means you're going to get married again! And that part about spirits in heaven calling you their mother? It must mean you're going to have more babies!"

Me, having babies? At my age? That's hard to imagine, especially since the prospective father of said babies hasn't presented himself! I can't brush it off, though. I don't think I've had a spiritual experience like that since I received my temple endowment.

Your Erin

JUNEAU
E-mail, September 1, 1998
Deenie and Erin,

We never stop being "mama," do we? Nicole is almost twenty-five years old and a second-year med student, yet she's still my little girl. My *hurting* little girl. I want to kiss it and make it better or put a Band-Aid on the owie. But she needs more than a Band-Aid.

Beto came home from Mexico last week, but he's not living with his mother next door any more. He rented an apartment close to USC because he says he needs to be near the med school now that he'll soon be starting his third year. Marisol and I both think he wants to remove himself from his old life.

Nicole has returned to Denver for her next year of study, and we two mothers have said good-bye to the dream of mutual grandchildren. Which, I might add, is made even more poignant because Marisol seems intrigued by our concept of eternal families. Ever since Manny divorced her, she's felt she isn't a good Catholic—they don't believe in divorce, you know. So she's been attending church with me at least twice a month. She says she enjoys our meetings, especially Relief Society.

Greg and I are enjoying our weekly square dance class. Last week as we do-si-doed I was analyzing why it's so much fun. I like it on several levels. I like my swingy-skirted, gingham square dance dress with all the ruffly petticoats. I like totally forgetting all our problems for a couple of hours, lost in the music and intricate routines. Best of all I like the feel of Greg's hand in mine, on my back, reaching out to me, guiding me, leading me, just being there. There's something symbolic about that, and when I figure out what it is, I'll let you know.

Love,
Juneau

ERIN
E-mail, October 14, 1998
Dear Friends,

Juneau, you asked me a while back if my blessing had got me thinking differently about men, marriage, and babies. It might have, if I weren't dealing with a gangly, touchy, stinky twelve-year-old.

Joking aside, I'm worried about Mark. Going through puberty would be tough enough without his worrying about his sexuality. He won't talk to me about his fears, but Jake told me he skirts around the subject when they're together. He does what he can to reassure Mark, answering the questions Mark won't ask directly.

Cory knows that Mark's troubled, but he's not in a position to help. Mark refused to go the last two times the kids were to spend the weekend with Cory. All he would say is, "I don't want to." Juneau, remember when I asked you if you thought knowing the truth about Letitia made things better or worse? I have to think Mark would be better off now if Cory had held his tongue until Mark was mature enough to handle knowing the truth.

If Mark is pulling away from Cory, Cory is distancing himself from us, too. He has a life that we have no part in. Maybe it's because he knows I don't want him to have anyone over when the kids are at his place. And that his father can't bear even the thought of him having a partner.

Hannah has a four-year-old's unreserved love for her daddy. I hope nothing ever changes that. She's so cute. She loves Montessori preschool and is still wild for animal movies. Rascal is always by her side when she watches them—I think his personal favorite is *Air Bud!* A while ago I took all the kids to a movie about a parrot. Big mistake. All she's talked about since is getting a parrot!

Erin

JUNEAU

E-mail, December 1, 1998
Dear Friends,

I guess you can include Misty in the list of those who are doing what they have to do. She's searching for *something*, but I don't think even she knows what it is. The last time I talked to her, I invited her for Christmas dinner. I doubt she'll come.

We'll be having Christmas dinner at our house with the extended family, including Nicole. It'll be festive and fun—Ira and Trace will see to that—but I'll still feel Misty's absence. And Beto's.

Love,
Juneau

ERIN

On Christmas Eve Day, Erin got a call from Linda saying that Harold

Johnson, now ninety-seven, wasn't up to coming even for a short visit that night.

"We'll take Christmas Eve to him, then," Erin said. She put together a plate of goodies, knowing full well Harold would give most of them away, took his presents (Tabernacle Choir CDs) from under the tree, and in late afternoon hustled the kids into the car.

They met Linda at the retirement home and followed her to Harold's room. Propped up in bed, the old fellow was glad to see them and accepted his gifts graciously, but his eyes were dull, and Erin had the feeling he was tired of life.

On the way home, she was thinking about how important family was when she had a flash of inspiration. She changed directions, explaining to the kids, "We're detouring to Melina's house to sing carols for her and Althea."

"If Melina isn't there, Althea won't even open the door," Mark said.

"So we'll sing on the steps. We won't freeze."

"Not if we sing really loud," Hannah said.

No one answered when Erin rang the doorbell, but after they began to sing "We Three Kings," Melina peeked out the window and, recognizing them, gave them a wave. Then Erin heard the sound of multiple locks being undone. Melina had told her the caseworker had helped Althea install locks on all doors and windows, in the hope that if the contents of the house were protected, Althea might be able to go on short outings to the neighborhood grocery store and library.

Melina joined them on the steps with a happy smile. Then, to Erin's amazement, a woman stepped into the doorway. She was shorter and wider than Melina, and her dark hair showed signs of gray, but the similarity between them was striking when she smiled. Althea.

"Thank you." Althea reached out a tentative hand to touch Erin's.

Erin clasped Althea's hand in hers and held it while she and the kids sang "Silent Night." The special closeness ended with the song, but Erin's feeling that she'd witnessed a miracle lingered the rest of Christmas Eve.

Chapter 12

1999

JUNEAU

E-mail, January 1, 1999
Dear Deenie and Erin,

Happy New Year to you all! We had a nice holiday, thanks to
Gideon's enthusiasm. He loves everything Christmas, so he kept
us stoked. Trace and Cath (she's as big as a house, baby due in
five weeks) were here, and so were Ira and Shoshana. In their
honor, we had not only red Christmas candles on our table but
a menorah with candles of every color. We even had a phone
call from Misty! To coin a phrase, a lovely time was had by all.
Except Nicole. She tried to pretend otherwise, but without
Beto she's deeply depressed.

Love,
Juneau

ERIN

As her sixteenth birthday approached, Kayla started lobbying for a
car of her own. Erin had her doubts about whether that was a good idea,
but Cory was all for it.

"I'd rather have her driving a smaller car than your SUV," he argued.
"It's too much for a sixteen-year-old to handle. Why don't I look for
something reliable—it'll be a present from me and my folks. Then I'll take
her out on practice drives so she can get used to it before she takes her
test."

Erin had to agree when the argument was presented in that light. But
it irritated her how Cory often stepped in with a grand gesture when the
kids wanted something she couldn't or wouldn't provide. Like telling
Mark he would pay for an expensive weeklong piano camp in Duluth that
August.

Not that that will change Mark's feelings any, Erin thought. From the time Cory had told the kids his reason for the divorce, Mark had walled himself off from his father. Erin still got chills when she remembered Mark's words: "I don't think I like you anymore."

She couldn't fault Cory's choice of car when he called to tell her what he'd purchased for Kayla. An older Ford Escort, it definitely wasn't the type of car a teenager would show off in. And she loved seeing the gleam in her daughter's eyes when Kayla burst into the great room after taking her driving test, crying, "Mom! I passed!" She cavorted around the room, the slight hitch in her gait barely noticeable.

"How's the mother of the new driver holding up?" Caitlin asked when she and Sam came to visit a few days later.

"Still breathing." Erin was only partly joking. She'd often found herself holding her breath when Kayla was driving on her own.

Kayla tugged at Caitlin's sleeve. "Let me take you for a ride."

"If you hang this over your rearview mirror." Caitlin handed Kayla a box. She laughed at her niece's perplexed expression when Kayla held up a medal on a chain. "It's a Saint Christopher medal. He's the patron saint of travelers. And first-time drivers." Caitlin looked at Erin. "If it's okay with you."

"Absolutely. We can use all the help we can get." Erin pointed to a similar medal on the chain Caitlin was wearing. "That's not Saint Christopher, I'm guessing."

"Nope. Saint Anne, patron saint of women who want to get pregnant. Sam and I need all the help we can get, too. Including your prayers."

Two weeks later, Bishop Daley called to ask that Erin visit him in his office to talk about a new calling. She was surprised at the regret she felt. She'd come to enjoy meeting with other members of the activity committee. The singles firesides and parties, too, once she stopped thinking of them as matchmaking events.

She played with guessing what position he might have in mind for her, but she was floored when Bishop Daley asked her to serve as second counselor in the Relief Society presidency. She'd always felt that the women who held positions in the presidency of the women's organization were far more spiritual than she. What could he be thinking?

She remembered what another bishop had said when she asked why he'd called her to be the Spiritual Living leader. "You try harder than anyone I know." But Bishop Daley gave her a different reason for this call. "The women of the ward need your compassion."

Two weeks later, she e-mailed the COBS:

> I love this new assignment. Working with Valerie (president, tall, blonde) and Gail (first counselor, round, long gray braid) is a blessing in itself, and being responsible for Enrichment activities is giving me a chance to know the sisters of my ward in a whole new way.
>
> For years, I've thought I was different from other Mormon women because of my family background and marriage to a gay man. What an odd sort of pride! The kind of issues some sisters are dealing with humble me.
>
> My special assignment is to be Althea's visiting teacher. Our visits will be over the phone—only her caseworker and the fire department liaison are allowed inside her house. Or with me standing on the front step and her in her doorway. But that's a start.
>
> Love,
> Erin

WILLADENE

After family prayer and a blessing on breakfast, Roger took his place at the head of the kitchen table. Deenie could see the pleasure in his face as he smiled at his daughters.

"I feel like an eastern potentate with all this feminine beauty around me," he said.

"What's a potentate?" Evvy asked. Elizabeth and Roger dived into the chance for a family word game.

"A leader," Roger said. "What's a potentato?"

"Mashed with garlic," Elizabeth quipped.

The rest of breakfast was accompanied by lots of laughter, and later, when Deenie set off to face the one-on-one meeting Delia had requested, she was filled with good humor. Until Roger reminded her as she passed his office that *compromise* wasn't a dirty word.

Am I really so hard to deal with? Deenie wondered as she headed for the room set aside for meetings of the Faculty and Board Wives' Association. She thought about Jenny's comment last summer in Wellsville that it was easier to yield to Deenie than to argue with her. *What she really meant was it's easier to yield to me than deal with me. Not a pretty picture. Except if I'm right*—and this time I'm right. *Who in the world would ever choose a music program over track for a boy's school, anyway!* she thought as she entered the room.

Delia greeted her politely and invited her to sit in one of the two chairs she'd positioned face to face. She took the other. "I asked for this meeting because our being on opposite sides of this issue has created a real problem."

Before Deenie could protest, she continued, "If you hadn't campaigned with the board to put sports first, we could have completed the expansion of the music department. *And* already started on the track and field."

"If they'd started on the track first, the team would have a decent place for spring training," Deenie countered.

"Sports have never been a major part of what attracts students to the Academy," Delia said.

"With the facilities here, no wonder."

"But music has," Delia said as if coaching someone slightly daft. "There are three extremely talented students planning to register next year—depending on the completion of the music department expansion. A lot of money and influence would come with them. Money and influence the school needs to promote other programs as well."

Deenie sat back in surprise. "Why didn't you say so?"

"Why didn't you read the literature I sent you on the music program?" Delia asked.

Because they were from you, Deenie thought.

She was distressed by that recognition, and on the way home, she wondered if she'd dismissed things Jenny had said in the past the way she'd dismissed what Delia had been trying to tell her.

"Don't take it so hard, Mom," Elizabeth said when Deenie arrived home still reeling. "You're the one who's always saying not to sweat the small stuff, and if it doesn't affect your eternal salvation, it's all small stuff."

"Being stiff-necked with pride in my own wisdom might."

"Hey, you know better, you do better."

Deenie put her arm around Elizabeth. "You sound like Aunt Stella."

"Where do you think I learned that bit of advice?" Elizabeth asked as she rested her head on Deenie's shoulder.

"Have I told you how glad I am that you're here?" Deenie said and gave her daughter a hug.

"Yes, I'm glad to be here, too. In fact, I think I'll plan a special family dinner for Valentine's Day. I'll do the shopping and the cooking and everything. What do you think?"

"I think that would be wonderful."

JUNEAU

Trace and Cath and Gideon hoped their baby would arrive on Gideon's birthday, February 1.

It didn't. Adrienne, Cath's mother, had been poised to fly down from Idaho to help once things started happening. But then she called with the news that Cath's father had to have emergency heart bypass surgery. He did well enough with it, but Adrienne had to give up her plans in order to care for him. Juneau, to her great joy, was asked to act as standby grandma.

Days went by, and still the baby didn't come, much to everyone's frustration. But Juneau had cause to be grateful she was still home when Serenity called on February 5. In a scared little voice Serenity said, "Mama is sick, and I don't know where my dad is. He was going away in his car when I got home from school."

Juneau dropped Gideon off at Tanner Melton's house and hurried over to Shan's. Serenity, waiting at the door, pointed toward the family room. Shan was on the floor, huddled in a fetal position.

Juneau quickly knelt beside her, brushing her hair back from her forehead. "Shan! What happened?"

Shan groaned. "I'm all right. Just . . . just terrible cramps."

"Cramps, my foot," Juneau snorted. "Your face is bruised."

"I stumbled and hit my cheek on the coffee table."

Yeah, right. She'd been beaten, and Juneau was positive her husband, Dex, had done it. "I'm calling 911," she said.

"You don't need to do that, Juneau. I'm all right." Shan staggered to her feet. Serenity came over to hug her and help her to the sofa, murmuring encouragement, as if she'd done it many times before.

Juneau wasn't buying it. She picked up the telephone by the sofa, but Shan snatched it out of her hand, hissing, "Juneau, if you tell anybody, I'll never speak to you again." Turning to Serenity, she said, "Go to your room, kiddo, and do your homework."

Serenity knelt and wrapped her arms around Shan's waist. "No, Mama, I want to stay here."

Juneau knew how to get the girl out of the room. "Serenity," she said, "would you go to the phone in your mother's bedroom and call Gideon for me, please? Tell him it will be a while before I pick him up at Tanner's." She scribbled Tanner's number on a scrap of paper from her purse and turned Serenity toward the hallway.

With a lingering look back at her mother, Serenity went.

"Okay, pal," Juneau said, sitting in a chair near Shan. "Tell me what happened. The truth."

After some hesitation Shan said, "Dex came home from work early because he was stewing about an argument we had last night. And . . . well, I made him mad again."

"So mad he beat you to a pulp?"

"It's not that bad." Shan said weakly.

"It *is* that bad. It's battery. It's abuse. *It's dangerous.* For you *and* Serenity. You've got to get away from here."

Shan snapped upright. "Absolutely not. I love Dex. He loves me and Serenity."

"Well, you can't go on like this. If you won't allow me to contact the police, I'm at least going to call Bishop Palmer."

"No! Why can't you understand? *It's my fault.* I'm so muddle-headed that I say things all wrong, and he has to smack some sense into me. He'll be really sorry when he comes home again. He'll bring me flowers and apologize and make it up to me. Really."

Juneau felt her stomach knot with anger. "Is that what he was doing, smacking sense into you?"

"Sometimes I need it. I'm so dumb. But it's going to be better now."

"You are *not* dumb. And it won't be better. He'll do it again. He's an abuser—that's not going to change."

"Yes, it will," Shan insisted. She turned her head to avoid Juneau's gaze. "It was only today . . ."

Juneau turned Shan's face toward her. "Shan, what kind of a friend would I be if I didn't help you now?"

"What kind of friend would you be if you ruin it for me and Serenity?" Shan shot back. "We like Pasadena. We don't want to move again. If you tell, Dex will have us out of here before you can blink. Juneau, please. Don't mess things up for us."

Juneau wondered if Shan realized how much she had just revealed about her life with Dex. "Does he hurt Serenity, too?" she asked slowly.

Shan looked at her as if she'd said something unthinkable. "No! Never! Dex is a wonderful dad."

"Really? Seeing what he does to you has affected her, even if he doesn't hit her. Why do you think she runs away?"

"She doesn't really run away. She goes only as far as the gate." Shan took a deep, shaky breath. "If you really want to do something for me, Juneau, you could get some ice for my face."

When Juneau returned with a plastic bag of ice wrapped in a dish-cloth, Serenity was standing at her mother's side.

"I talked to Gideon," she reported. "He says you don't need to hurry. He's having fun at Tanner's."

"Thank you." Juneau was handing Shan the bag of ice wrapped in a dishcloth when the phone rang.

"I'll get it," Serenity said. "Maybe it's Gideon calling to say I can come over to Tanner's." She eagerly answered the phone. Then she handed the receiver to Juneau with a sigh. "It's Gideon's dad."

"Cath's baby must be coming." Juneau cried, taking the handset.

"Cath is on her way to the hospital," Greg said. "Trace wants you to meet him there."

"I'm on my way."

Juneau picked up her purse, and then stood paralyzed. She was anxious to be on her way but worried about leaving Shan and Serenity alone.

"Go. We'll be all right," Shan said. When Juneau still hesitated, she added, "I'm sure."

But as Juneau moved to leave, Shan clutched her arm. "Please, please, please," she pleaded, "don't tell *anybody*."

E-mail, February 11, 1999
Dear Friends,

I've been through the grandma gauntlet! I found it's one thing to have a baby; it's a whole other ball game to sit and wait for someone you love to get it done.

Rhiannan Cassatt arrived safely, and no baby in history was ever more welcome! Trace cried, and Cath cried, and I cried—and Rhiannan howled! You recognize the name, of course. They named her after my lovely niece who died in the Lockerbie plane crash back in 1988. Trace's first love and Cath's good friend.

I'll be staying at Trace and Cath's place for a few more days doing grandma duty. Trace got two weeks' paternity leave from Smoketree Systems (after all, he's the boss's son-by-choice) so he can help Cath. This morning, as I was showing him how to bathe Rhiannan, he stood back and gazed at her in awe. Then he said, "I love her so much. It's like God reached into my heart and tore out a chunk and said, 'Here's part of you in a new form.'"

I cried, of course.

Love,
Juneau

After she sent off the letter, Juneau sat back to think about how special this time in Trace and Cath's home had been. She'd grown closer to Trace and Cath and been enchanted by little Rhiannan. It had been such a lovely time, she couldn't help but contrast the feeling in their home with that in the Beldon home.

Thinking about the difference heightened Juneau's concern about Shan and her abusive husband. But when she called, Shan said, "Everything is fine, as I said it would be. Dex has been a darling since he came home."

Still, Juneau wondered.

WILLADENE

On Valentine's Day Deenie was rewarded for her efforts to call and write Carl more often. A long letter came filled with his deeply thought-out reasons for being part of the military: his love for his country and his desire to protect the cradle of the Church. *It feels like an extension of serving the Lord,* he wrote. *I'll wear my uniform with the same pride and dignity I wore my white shirt and tie on my mission.*

Deenie was brought to tears by his words. She couldn't wait to see him graduate from college in June and receive his commission in the Air Force.

"What are you doing still home?" Elizabeth asked as Deenie started reading Carl's letter for the second time. "I'm in charge here today. Don't you have an appointment for a massage or a haircut or something this morning? And aren't you spending the afternoon at St. Anne's?"

"Yes," Deenie looked up at her daughter's flustered face and wondered what on earth was going on.

"You can't come home until Evvy's out of school and then no peeking in the kitchen and the dining room until I say so. This is my surprise, so don't ruin it!"

"Okay," Deenie said. "But is it all right if I shower and get dressed before I leave?"

"Of course."

Elizabeth could barely contain her excitement, and Deenie headed for her bedroom, wondering what her daughter was up to.

Deenie spent an hour volunteering in the library. She met Evvy after classes were over, and on the way home, the two of them speculated on what Elizabeth had planned for them. They opened the door to a sparkling clean apartment filled with delicious aromas. There was a sign on the mantel that read, *Please dress for dinner.*

"Whoa, what's gotten into Elizabeth?" Evvy asked.

Deenie shook her head and retired to her bedroom to nap out the wait until dinner.

That evening the menu included beef Wellington and cherries jubilee. But the flaming dessert wasn't the biggest surprise. That honor went to Elizabeth's guest. As the family assembled, Brad Donaldson arrived dressed in a suit and carrying chocolates and roses. *He looks like a man who's come courting,* Deenie thought.

She was ill at ease with the situation, but Roger and Evvy kept up a lively conversation with Brad and Elizabeth, who looked at Brad with glowing eyes. Brad told them about the new job he'd accepted with a firm headquartered in Atlanta. He was excited that it would require both his training in international corporate law and his police experience. Then he described his recent visit to his parents in their new retirement home in Orlando.

By the time Brad shook her hand in farewell and kissed Elizabeth on the cheek late that night, Deenie was aching for a private talk with her daughter. She managed to wait until the cleanup was done, Evvy had gone to bed, and she, Roger, and Elizabeth were sitting together around the kitchen table.

"So tell us about it," Deenie said, not trying to hide her worry.

Elizabeth went straight to the heart of the matter. "Mom. Dad. You know Brad's been my ideal since he dated Aunt Sunny. When he kept the promise he made and sent me flowers for graduation, we started keeping in touch. I've learned a lot about him since then, and he's still my idea of a perfect sweetheart." She paused, smiling sofly. "I think he's beginning to feel the same about me."

"Falling in love is wonderful, baby," Roger said gently. "But loving Brad doesn't solve the problem of your age difference or the fact that he isn't a member of the Church."

"I know, Daddy."

"How are you planning to handle that?" Deenie asked.

"We're not making plans, not really. Brad has that new job in Atlanta, and I'm off to Paris in April. So don't worry."

Not yet. Elizabeth didn't say those words, but Deenie heard them as clearly in her mind as if she had.

After Elizabeth kissed them both good night, Roger said, "Most of the time I think she's way too wise for her years, but tonight I feel like she's my little girl."

"Is there anything we need to do?" Deenie asked.

"It's already done," Roger said. "We raised her to have faith in herself and trust in the Lord. We'll pray for her and love her as we always have, but the final decision on where her relationship with Brad will go isn't ours to make."

Chapter 13

ERIN

E-mail, April 21, 1999
Dear COBs,

I've been heartsick ever since I heard the news about Columbine. How can something like that happen?

After Hannah went to bed tonight, Mark and Kayla and I watched a special on the tragedy. They couldn't understand how those boys could have done what they did, even if they were harassed. So we had a talk about how individuals get from point A to point Z by taking one step at a time and making one choice at a time.

Kayla said, "What if you don't know when you make a choice where it's going to lead? Are you still responsible?" I said we may not know what consequences a choice or act will have, but it's our job to think ahead and choose wisely. Then she said, "You're talking about me again, aren't you? You want me to say it was partly my fault that my leg got broken!"

Kayla still refuses to accept responsibility for her choices that day, which leaves her feeling like a victim, full of bitterness and anger. Thinking this might be a teaching moment (aargh!), I said, "Isn't it? You chose to put on the rollerblades when you'd promised your coaches you wouldn't. You chose to skate down to Lake Harriet and go on the bike path. In fact, every choice you made that day contributed to your being on a collision course with those boys."

Kayla went ballistic, wanting to know why I didn't take her side. Then she ran upstairs without saying goodnight. Mark said, "Nice try, Mom," and followed her.

On the positive side, I've been getting closer to EJ lately. Much to Colleen's distress, she moved into an apartment with her friends after she graduated last spring and got a job at a biker/tattoo shop owned by the father of Sahrita, one of her roommates. I've taken to stopping by the shop when I drive out to the Dwyer development in Maple Grove, and we've had some nice chats.

The other day while we were talking, a bruiser with a ponytail and tattoos covering his arms came out from the back workspace. EJ introduced him as Sahrita's dad! He looked scary, but it turns out he's quite a nice fellow. He's a child of the 70s, but he runs a drug-free shop, according to a sign behind the counter. His sister, who lives in LA, calls herself Flower!

I don't know if my visits help any, but at least EJ knows that someone's thinking about her.

Time to go to bed. I wish I had someone to snuggle up to for comfort. Guess I'll call Rascal.

Your Erin

WILLADENE
E-mail, April 24, 1999
Dear Erin and Juneau,

The day Elizabeth left for Paris, Evvy came home late from school. She'd stayed after hours at Mandy's invitation to listen to her practice a solo with the school choir. Evvy was riveted. She's determined to learn how to read music and sing this summer so she can audition for choir in the fall. And if she has anything to do with it, I'll be volunteering in the music department rather than the library.

Do you suppose there's some quirky cosmic payback going on here for how I opposed Delia's plans for the music department at the Academy? By the way, we are skirting each other civilly now, but I still haven't gotten to the point where I want to pray for her.

The whole thing has made me think about the ripple effect of choices we make and how sometimes what we get isn't what we thought we chose. If I hadn't invited Brad Donaldson into my home all those years ago, he wouldn't be courting Elizabeth now. But if I hadn't, he'd never have met Sunny, and she would have missed out on all the richness of emotion and experience he brought to the final years of her life.

Ever since Columbine I've wondered what the outcome would have been if anyone had paid better attention to those boys and acted on the clues they dropped. It's the same question I ask myself about you, Juneau, with Shan and Dex. What are the possible outcomes if you don't intervene, given what you know? How will you feel the day you get a phone call that Shan's in the hospital or you have to ask yourself, "Why didn't I do something sooner?" Think about it.

> Love,
> Deenie

JUNEAU

E-mail, April 25, 1999
Dear Deenie,

I've endlessly asked myself the same things. But if I tell, and Dex whisks Shan and Serenity out of Pasadena to who knows where, how can I help them?

> Worried,
> Juneau

ERIN

E-mail, May 11, 1999
Dear COBs,

On Mother's Day, I noticed that the pendant Caitlin was wearing wasn't the one of St. Anne. (Deenie, isn't Evvy's school named for St. Anne?) My heart fell—I thought that meant she and Sam were already giving up on in vitro. But the new pendant is of Elizabeth, *patron saint of expectant mothers!* She and Sam are having a baby in November.

We're all excited, Lottie most of all. She's delighted us by rallying. She's determined to hold her new grandchild.

This month, The Jays are celebrating their tenth wedding anniversary with a Caribbean cruise. They're so cute together. Mom says she's gotta love a man who brings her the newspaper and orange juice in bed every morning and laughs at her jokes. Jake teases that the best thing about marrying Mom was that she came with a ready-made family. (He's never been close to his son, who grew up on the East Coast with his mother.) Mom got a keeper in Jake.

Love,
Erin

WILLADENE

Deenie would always remember the summer of 1999 as the year she started contributing to the community of Gainesville, all because of Bear. The day the family returned home after attending Carl's graduation from Utah State University and seeing him receive his commission in the Air Force, she and Bear were called out to join a search for two small children lost on Payne's Prairie.

Since Bear was cross-trained to search over water as well as land, he was first on the list to look for the missing tots in the 21,000-acre preserve of grass and wetlands. The search ended with a happy reunion and Bear's picture on the front page of the paper, along with an article that described his career as a rescue and therapy dog.

Invitations started arriving for Deenie and Bear to share their story at various summer programs and retirement centers. The responses there were overwhelmingly positive. It was what Deenie had been looking for— a way to feel that she mattered in the community outside of the Academy. Stacking books on library shelves at St. Anne's hadn't done it for her.

The new students who were attending summer session gravitated more and more to Gobb Hill in their spare time. At first, they came because of Bear, but after the novelty of being with a celebrity dog wore off, they still kept coming. It was clear to Deenie that many of them saw Gobb Hill as a second home, and she began to see it through their eyes.

When the gun safety teacher had an accident that took him out of the picture and Deenie assumed his responsibilities, she began to have a mystique of her own for the students.

"Big dog, big truck, qualified to teach gun safety, concealed-carry permit. You're every young boy's dream crush," Roger teased.

Deenie was pleased to see Evvy becoming part of a community of her own. She had Leo Flynn and his cadre of friends as big brother surrogates and backups, Mandy to teach her music, and Christiana to accompany her on the guitar. And Miss B had become to Evvy what Aunt Stell had been to Deenie.

"Roger, I think I'm beginning to see some knots in our new safety net," Deenie said.

"That's good," he said. "You never know when you might need it."

They needed that safety net sooner than they thought. The week before fall session was to begin, Ferris Tucker suffered a major heart attack. Roger had to become Ferris on campus, and Deenie had to become Delia, who refused to leave Ferris's side. Roger, who'd trained his whole life to take on such a job, handled it better than Deenie did. She'd always assumed that if she had the chance she could do Delia's job as well as Delia. But she soon learned that she had neither Delia's connections nor her finesse, both of which were necessary to get anybody to do anything.

JUNEAU

E-mail, June 29, 1999
Dear Friends:

Marisol came over today to read me an interesting letter from Beto, who's in Mexico working with Dr. Vasquez the way he did last summer.

He wrote that the Mormon missionaries in the little town have been helping to build an addition to the clinic whenever they have time. Church members (there are more in the town than Beto had realized) often stop by to see what they're doing.

One day Beto heard some of the kids singing "I Am a Child of God," which he remembered from when he used to attend Primary with Nicole. He really surprised them by joining in the singing, and ever since then the kids have called him "*Hermano* (Brother) Sanchez."

He ended the letter by suggesting his mother show it to me. He didn't mention Nicole at all. When I sent him a note saying how pleased I was that he remembered that Primary song, I didn't mention Nicole, either.

Love from Juneau

P.S. Marisol told me she's been offered a position as a French instructor at Pasadena City College. She's been teaching at a high school since Manny skipped out, and she's thrilled with this new opportunity.

ERIN

Skipp and Linda were out of town on the Fourth of July, so the next Saturday they hosted a barbecue for the family. When Erin and the kids arrived, Cory and Skipp were setting up a badminton net and Linda was putting snacks on a table on the patio.

"Daadeee!" Hannah cried. She hugged Cory's waist and then shouted, "Jay-keeee!" and zoomed toward Joanna and Jake. Cory pounded in the last stake and tossed Kayla a badminton paddle. "Wanna play?"

Erin watched as Kayla and Cory took on Mark and Skipp. The elder Johnsons' home was neutral territory that seemed to give Cory and her children freedom to enjoy one other. She was grateful for her in-laws. Technically they were her *former* in-laws, but she never thought of them that way. They'd been unwavering in their love and support not only for their grandchildren but for her, too.

Sounds of conversation, children playing, and friendly competition filled the air as the afternoon faded into early evening. They'd eaten their supper of bratwurst and potato salad and were ready for ice cream cake when Erin noticed Hannah wasn't in the backyard.

"Anybody know where Hannah is?" she asked.

"Try looking inside," Cory said. "Mom got her a new animal video."

But Hannah wasn't in front of the family room TV. Erin went into the kitchen where Linda was dishing up the cake. "Have you seen Hannah?"

"No." Linda frowned. "I thought she was in the backyard."

Erin felt a frisson of alarm. She and Linda split up and made a sweep of the house, meeting at the front door. It was partially open. "Oh, no." Erin dashed outside and looked up and down the street. No Hannah.

"I'll go this way," Linda said, pointing left. Erin ran the other direction, saying a prayer.

She was nearing the corner when a tall man wearing a baseball cap rounded it. One hand held Hannah's, the other held the leash of a strange-looking dog with curly hair.

"Hannah!" Erin cried.

"Are you missing someone?" the man asked pleasantly.

Erin pulled Hannah into a hug. "Where did you find her?"

"In my parents' backyard. Apparently my dog needed company, and Hannah decided to provide it."

"Curly Dude was barking. He wanted to come play with us," Hannah said, patting the dog's head. "You were all busy. I didn't think you would care."

"A rule is a rule," Erin's fear made her voice stern. "You don't go outside alone. Period." Holding Hannah close, she looked up at the man. "I'm sorry she bothered you."

"No bother. Curly Dude loves kids."

Linda hurried up to them. "You found her. Thank goodness."

"She was visiting this gentleman's dog," Erin said. "Uh . . ."

"Vince Gerlach. My folks, Russ and Anne, recently moved in around the corner."

"I met them the other day," Linda said. She pointed at his message T-shirt. "You must be the son who's a veterinarian."

Erin read the words aloud: "The more I'm around people, the more I like dogs."

"It's not really true." A smile crinkled the corners of his hazel eyes. "I like dogs and people. And yes, I'm a vet. I have a clinic and animal hospital in Golden Valley."

Linda held out her hand. "My name's Linda Johnson, and this is my daughter-in-law, Erin."

Erin made a sound, and Linda corrected herself. "Former daughter-in-law, I should say."

"Pleased to meet you," Vince said. He shook Linda's hand and then Erin's. "This is Curly Dude, my goldendoodle."

Hannah giggled, and Erin said, "You're making that up."

"I'm not. Scout's honor. His mother was a standard poodle, his father a golden lab. Therefore . . ."

"Goldendoodle," Erin finished. She could see it now. Curly had a face and coloring that looked much like Rascal's, but his soft curls and a regal stance reminded Erin of a poodle in her neighborhood. Except Curly had a poodle puppy cut—no pompom tail for him.

"D'you want to meet my daddy and my other grandparents?" Hannah asked, looking up at Vince. "You can bring Curly Dude, too."

Vince glanced at Linda, who said, "We were just going to have dessert. Please join us."

Erin was surprised that Linda, who'd never had an animal in her house, would second Hannah's invitation to both man and dog. Taking Hannah by the hand, she followed Linda, Vince, and the dog back to the Johnson house.

They were about to go up the front steps when Vince stopped. He pointed at a decorative piece of concrete to the right of the steps. "That's an interesting piece of yard art."

"It's a sunstone," Linda said. "A reproduction of a stone used in building the Mormon temple in Illinois."

Erin cocked her head, curious as to what his response might be.

"I thought that's what it was," he said. "I saw some like it when I was in Nauvoo about . . . say, ten years ago."

"What took you there?" Erin asked.

"I drove down after I joined the Mormon church. I wanted to see Nauvoo and Carthage."

"Well!" Linda beamed at him. "Welcome to our home, Brother Gerlach. We're Mormons, too."

JUNEAU

As time went by, Juneau began to wonder if Shan might have been right when she'd said everything would be fine after Dex beat her so badly in February. Shan said it had awakened him to what he was doing and he'd promised never to lay a hand on her again. She seemed happy, and she'd started attending the writing class regularly, so perhaps the bad times were over. Perhaps Dex had changed.

When Juneau told Greg about her concerns and the promise Shan had extracted from her, he said, "That's hard to believe. When I've been around him at church, he's seemed like a nice guy. And he's offered good advice when we've had problems with our building. He's in the construction business, you know."

"He may seem nice, but I know what I saw," Juneau said.

Greg thought about it and then said, "Could we invite them to dinner or something? I think it's a good idea to get better acquainted with him."

"I'll see if they'll come," Juneau said.

She called the next day to extend an invitation. "We'd love to," Shan said. "I've been wanting you to get to know Dex. When do you want us to come?"

"Five-ish on Saturday. Bring Serenity. Gideon would be thrilled to tell her about his baby sister and let her get acquainted with Numbtail."

"Terrific." Shan hesitated. "Juneau," she said and then paused again. "Juneau, you won't say anything about . . . about what happened, will you?"

"No," Juneau said. "Not if you don't want me to."

The dinner was a great success. Juneau had chosen a menu she felt confident about—salmon with mango salsa and scalloped potatoes (from a Betty Crocker box, but with some parsley garnish and a little paprika sprinkled on top, who could tell?). For dessert she made Great-Grandma Letitia's Danish pudding, hoping they liked rhubarb, which they did.

When they finished, Dex said, "That was a tasty meal, Juneau. I hope you'll give Shan the recipe for the rhubarb pudding. It was your great-grandmother's, you say?"

After Gideon and Serenity and Numbtail went off to look at the "graveyard" under the pomegranate tree, Greg asked Juneau to tell the story of Great-Grandma Letitia and her empty grave, which she did, wondering all the while if she should censor the ending where Letitia whacked her miserly husband with a shovel. She decided to tell the whole thing.

"Served him right," Dex said when she finished. "That Orville didn't have a clue, did he!"

Juneau wanted to yell out that old Orville wasn't the only one who didn't have a clue. But she'd promised Shan she wouldn't bring up the subject. And besides, Dex had been behaving himself admirably. He'd given Serenity a big kiss before she went off with Gideon, and he was loving and sensitive to Shan.

The evening ended up with Greg telling Dex and Shan about the house additions he and Juneau hoped to do someday. Dex was enthusiastic and asked Greg to explain what they wanted. "This is a great add-on house," he said. "It wouldn't take much to expand your dining area just by pushing out that wall. Why don't you show me what else you're planning?"

So while Juneau and Shan cleared the table, Greg took him for a tour. When they came back, Dex said, "Juneau, you're going to have the most fabulous second-story workroom in town. There'll be a great view whichever direction you look."

"Dex says he can give us good advice all the way," Greg said. "He says we should get started soon."

"I'd like to," Juneau said.

When Shan and her family left, Juneau watched Dex open the car doors, depositing his "womenfolk" safely inside. She looked at Shan's happy face, but she still had a bad feeling.

Gideon hadn't come outside to say good-bye. Back in the house, Juneau and Greg found him huddled on the family room sofa.

Greg hurried over to sit down beside him. "What's the matter, buddy?"

Gideon raised a worried face. "You're not going to change everything, are you?"

Juneau knelt down beside him. "Change what, Giddy?"

"Everything." Gideon made a gesture with his arm that seemed to include his whole world. "The house," he said. "I don't want it changed.

I heard Serenity's dad talking about tearing out walls and building a stairway and a lot of stuff. *I don't want anything changed.*"

Juneau and Greg each put an arm around Gideon. "Okay," Juneau
said. "We don't have to change anything. I like our house the way it is."

"So do I." Relief washed over Gideon's face, and Juneau realize that
he'd been more deeply affected by having been snatched away than she
liked to admit. To divert his thoughts, she asked if he had enjoyed entertaining Serenity.

"Yeah," Gideon said. "She's great. She liked our graveyard. She says
she'd like to bury something there."

"And what would it be?" Juneau asked.

Gideon shrugged. "I don't know. She said she'll bring it when she has
to run away from home for good."

Chapter 14

ERIN

E-mail, August 19, 1999
Dear Friends,

My little Hannah turned five today. She'll start kindergarten in Lake Harriet Community School in September. I can hardly believe that this fall all of my kids will be in school!

She got what she wanted for her birthday, an animal-themed party and two special guests—Vince Gerlach and his dog, Curly Dude. Vince is the man I told you about who brought Hannah back when she was lost. You should have seen how Hannah took over when he arrived at our house. The way she led him by the hand and introduced him to Lottie and Andrew made me realize that Hannah thinks of him the way she thinks of Rascal: "He's mine!"

She also got her wish for pets. Mark gave her two goldfish in a bowl. Cory's gift was two hamsters in a fancy three-story cage. Vince gave her a turtle. He told Hannah she could call him any time if she had a question about it or any of the other critters. I have a question for him: "Why didn't you ask me if I wanted a turtle?"

Hannah is much taller than Kayla was at her age. She often has the same knowing look she had when I saw her before she was born. I think she has an innate ability to pick up on what people and animals—especially dogs—need. A special empathy, I guess you could call it. I see it in how she interacts with Kayla. She sometimes sits next to her big sister, the way she sits next to Rascal, not saying anything, just being there. Once in a while, I see her patting Kayla's arm as if to say, "It's all okay."

Kayla's been very inward since the accident, and I've had to accept that she's a different girl than she was before, one who's still trying to find her way. She's decided to take some of her classes at the University of Minnesota this fall, through a program that lets juniors and seniors enroll there with tuition paid by the state. The classes she takes will count twice—for high school and college credit.

I didn't think it was a good idea, because it will separate her further from kids in her class. I felt a little better when she said she would keep going to seminary and also enroll in an institute class. The building's near the U of M campus.

Love,
Erin

P.S. Vince entertained us with stories of taking Curly Dude to the children's ward at North Memorial. So now Hannah plays nurse with Rascal as therapy dog. She gets Mark and Kayla to pretend they're sick, and then she and Rascal make them "feel all better."

JUNEAU

E-mail, September 5, 1999
Dear COBs,

Guess what! Greg and I have joined the twentieth century, now that it's almost over. We bought—TA DA—cell phones!

Usually Greg is right onto anything electronic that comes out, but he's been working so hard he hasn't had time to check out which one he wanted. He's teaching a graduate seminar at Cal State again as well as working overtime at Smoketree Systems—which, by the way, now has six employees. They're becoming regular tycoons! But our fun square dance nights have been a casualty of his work. Greg says we'll get back to them soon.

Gideon and I spent some time in August at my parents' little house in the big woods in Oregon. I enjoyed the visit, although it's scary how feeble Dad seems to be. Mom is doing all right. Still spends most of the day working on their next novel, with Dad dictating dialogue from his easy chair.

I've got a fun project. Our stake was doing Broadway shows every other year for a while—remember, I was Eulalie Mackechnie Shinn in *Music Man!* Well, Dr. Tim Hart is on the

activities committee again, after taking a couple years off following the death of his wife, and he revived an idea we had
back in the late 80s that I should write a script for a musical
revue. It'll mainly be just some connective material for something we'll call *Millennial Madness,* since a new millennium is
almost here. We'll use existing music, except for a couple of
songs that Dr. Tim is writing. He wanted to be a composer
when he was young but didn't think he was good enough, so he
went into medicine.

The only other news is that Beto will be coming back from
Mexico soon to start his internship. He and I exchanged letters
all summer after I sent him that note in June. He seems grateful
that Greg and I haven't cut him out of our family now that he
and Nicole are no longer together. How could I ever cut him
out? He'll always be like a son to us, no matter what.

I don't know whether to hope he'll arrive before Nicole returns
to Denver in a couple of days to resume her studies. She's moped
around all summer long, looking like a bad case of London fog.
Even a visit from Reece Crafton didn't cheer her up.

Love,
Juneau

Juneau sent off the e-mail and then went to the family room where
Greg was reading the *Los Angeles Times* and Nicole and Gideon were staring at the TV. She was about to join Nicole on the couch when there was
a knock at the door. She opened it and gasped. "Beto! You're back."

"I just got in. Is Nicole . . . ?"

Juneau motioned toward the family room, and Beto marched past her
like an army going to battle.

"Nicole," he said, "I hope you didn't take a ring from that Mormon
guy, because if you did, you're going to have to give it back. You're *my*
woman. You've always been my woman. I love you."

Taking her hand, he pulled her to her feet and gave her a kiss worthy
of the one Rhett Butler gave Scarlett in *Gone with the Wind.* Then he
said, "Nicole Caldwell, will you marry me?"

Juneau couldn't take her eyes off the scene as Nicole's face turned from
red to white to glowing pink. Then she said, "Of course! Who else in this

whole entire world would I marry, Beto Sanchez?" Wrapping her arms around his neck, she gave him a kiss to equal the one he'd given her.

"Uh," Greg said, "should I be covering Gideon's eyes?"

"No way, Dad," Gideon said.

That made everybody laugh, and the emotion in the room turned festive. It wasn't until later that Juneau allowed herself to feel her misgivings.

She wasn't the only one feeling them. The next night Nicole joined her and Greg on the patio after she'd finished packing for her return to Denver. "Do you think I'm making a mistake?" she asked, taking a chair opposite them.

"You mean marrying Beto, I presume," Greg said.

Nicole nodded. "He caught me by surprise last night, and I just followed my heart. But nothing has changed. We're still in opposite camps when it comes to religion."

Juneau looked to Greg. He made a slight motion indicating she should speak first. "Beto has been like a member of our family ever since he was a baby," she began. "We love him dearly."

"But?"

"You know all the buts, sweetheart," Greg said.

Nicole's eyes glistened in the patio lights. "Yes. I've gone over them a thousand times in my prayers. My head acknowledges I'll be giving up the blessings of a temple marriage. But my heart insists that marrying Beto is the right thing to do." She paused. "I wouldn't feel that way if it weren't, would I? I have to believe Beto will soften about our kids being brought up in the Catholic faith."

"And if he doesn't?" Juneau asked. "I can't bear the thought of you and Beto wounding each other—even growing to hate each other—over what church you'll bring up your children in."

Nicole put up a hand in protest. "We love each other too much to do that."

"How many young couples have gone down that path and lived to regret it?" Greg asked. "No matter how much we like to believe love conquers all, it ain't necessarily so, as the song says."

"Are you telling me not to marry Beto?"

"It's your choice," Greg said. "But you're young. You could find some-one else."

Nicole shook her head fiercely. "Never. It's Beto or nobody." She gave them a rueful smile. "Maybe I should go back to my one-time ambition to be a nun. Like Audrey Hepburn in *The Nun's Story*."

They shared a brief chuckle, but Juneau's heart wasn't in it. Wishing this could be a moment of unadulterated joy, Juneau asked, "Have you set a date?"

"We want to get married in June. Cross your fingers that Beto will be able to get a residency in Denver so we can be together while I finish med school."

ERIN

E-mail, November 6, 1999
Dear COBs,

I'm an auntie! Lindsay Marie Powers arrived early this morning, with all the requisite fingers and toes and duck down for hair. Caitlin and Sam are thrilled. No, the better word is *transformed*.

Caitlin wants Lottie to spend as much time with Lindsay as pos-sible, so she and Sam and the baby will be staying in Caitlin's old room at Andrew and Lottie's for a while. It will be a full house, because Caitlin's mother, Brenda, is arriving tomorrow, and she'll be sleeping on the entertainment room hide-a-bed. How's that for family togetherness?

Erin

Lottie was propped up in her bed when Theresa led Erin and her kids into the master suite where the family was gathered. The baby rested in a Moses basket beside her, wrapped in the soft yellow blanket Miss B had sent and wearing a matching headband.

Lottie's smile was beatific. "Come see your cousin, kids."

Mark, Kayla, and Hannah carefully climbed on the bed, taking turns stroking Lindsay's head and touching her little hands.

Erin hugged Brenda. "What a miracle she is."

Brenda nodded. "I never thought I would see the day."

"God is merciful," said Margaret, who was sitting straight-backed in a chintz lady's chair.

"Give modern medicine some credit, too," Sam said dryly.

"Is the baptism dress ready?" Margaret asked.

Lottie pointed to a box, which Andrew handed to his mother. With great care Margaret removed a long, creamy dress trimmed in lace. "This dress is almost ninety years old. It was made from my mother's wedding gown. I was baptized in it. Andrew and Caitlin, too."

Hannah giggled. "Grandpa! You got baptized in a dress!"

"I was too little to mind," Andrew said. "Now if I'd been a Mormon and eight years old when I got baptized . . ." His words drew delighted laughter from Erin's children.

"You know, kids, I wouldn't be married or have this little treasure if it hadn't been for your mother," Caitlin said. "Her love for you made me want to have children of my own."

"Isn't it strange how things turn out?" Brenda looked at Margaret as she spoke. "Everything you did to separate Andrew from Erin—and from me—has actually worked toward bringing us together today."

Margaret gave Brenda a withering look. Leaning on Sean's arm, she rose. "I think it's time for us to go."

Erin felt the energy of the room shift, as if a storm front had just blown in. She had a sick feeling that reminded her of how she used to feel right before Grams started shrieking at her mother.

"Don't go yet, Mother." Andrew turned to Brenda. "What did you mean about Mother driving us apart?"

"Now's not the time," Margaret said. "Lottie needs her rest."

"I'm fine." Curiosity brightened Lottie's sallow skin. "I'd like to hear this. But the kids don't need to."

"I couldn't agree more," Erin said.

When Erin returned from taking the kids down to the family room, Caitlin said, "Mom? I've always wondered what was so awful that it was easier for you to leave me than to stay. What happened back then?"

"Ask her." Brenda gestured toward Margaret.

Andrew frowned. "Yes, Mother. Explain."

"You don't really want to get into this." Margaret tipped up her chin.

"You don't want Caitlin to know her mother almost killed them both driving drunk."

Caitlin gasped. Brenda turned on Margaret with fiery eyes. "And you don't want Caitlin to know you told me it would be best for her if I got out of her life and stayed out. And that you paid me to go!"

Andrew's "What?" overlapped Caitlin's "You didn't!"

Erin had heard enough. "This doesn't concern me. I'm taking the kids home."

"But it does," said Brenda. "Margaret and Sean bought your mother off, too."

"Everyone agreed to it," Margaret snapped. "Including Joanna's parents. And you agreed to go, Brenda. Don't forget that!"

"I didn't know what else to do."

Erin saw Brenda look at Caitlin in a silent plea for understanding. "I didn't know how to be a wife or a mother, Caitlin. Andrew was never home, and Margaret and my mother pointed out everything I was doing wrong. So I developed a nice little ritual. A bottle for you, a bottle for me, and a long naptime for both of us." She shook her head. "I hate to admit it, but I was often asleep when your father left in the morning and asleep when he got back."

"I let you down." Andrew's regret was clear. "I should have spent more time with you and Caitlin."

"It wouldn't have changed anything," Margaret insisted. "We paid for Brenda's treatment at Hazelton, Caitlin. But less than a week after she got home, she was driving drunk with you in the car. She's lucky you weren't killed in the accident. And yes—I did tell her it would be best for you if she left."

"How could you do that!" Andrew's anger was genuine, but it infuriated Erin. It was far too little, far too late.

"She was a danger to your child!" Margaret's voice was sharp. "Who knows what might have happened if I hadn't intervened?"

The loud voices woke Lindsay, and she let out a wail that silenced them all. Caitlin picked her up, holding her protectively. Erin was proud of her sister when Caitlin said in a tone that allowed no compromise, "Lindsay's baptism is this Sunday. I can't imagine it without you—especially you, Grandmother—but unless all of you can do what it takes to let go of the past and forgive each other, I don't want you to come. I mean it."

JUNEAU
E-mail, November 25, 1999
Dear Friends,

You won't believe this, but Marisol was baptized last week. By Greg! She's been coming to church with me for some time, attending the Gospel Essentials class. She and Greg and I have had many long conversations, sitting in either our backyard or hers. We always ended up talking about the doctrine of eternal families, which she's quite taken by. But it wasn't until she read the Book of Mormon (in Spanish) and took Moroni's challenge to pray about it that she really got a testimony. There's something so splendid about the testimonies of new converts!

Beto, who attended the service, was most impressed by the fact that Greg had the authority to do the baptizing. Afterward, he hugged his mother and wished her well. I could only wish he would take the same step.

Marisol was relieved that Beto was so supportive. She'd been worried about telling him—and also her father in Mexico—that she'd left the religion of her ancestors. Her father's response was written in the words of a Spanish proverb: "Dios te escuchara no importa la ropa que te cubre." Translation: "God listens no matter what cloak you wear."

I'm so very happy that Marisol is my sister in the gospel. The next thing to look forward to is Nicole being home over Christmas. I'm sure we'll be making wedding plans.

Love,
Juneau

WILLADENE
E-mail, December 1, 1999
Dear Erin and Juneau,

I am sad, sad, sad. NeVae's now bedridden and on oxygen. She has made a special request that the whole family come for Christmas, and everyone has arranged to be there. Us, too. It sounds as though she wants a chance to give us all her blessing and say good-bye while we're together. Roger says he's been expecting it. Paul confirmed those feelings by telling us of his own prompting not to let a day go by without telling his grand-mother how much he loves her.

As if that weren't enough, Mom called to say Aunt Stella fell at home and is in the hospital, and Leila Jeffrey died in her sleep.

Do you remember my telling you about the smiley face quilt Leila gave to Sunny one Christmas when she was so sick? And how Sunny used that same quilt to wrap around Rauf so he wouldn't be cold when we buried him? I've been thinking a lot about them both and how they had such hearts for helping in the right way at the right time. Certainly a quality to strive for.

But, as Miss B says, there's always reason to be joyful. Evvy and Mandy will close the Christmas concert at St. Anne's singing "Bring a Torch, Jeanette Isabella" with Christiana Kenady as guest guitarist. I love to hear those cute girls. It will be the only Christmas event we'll attend here before heading to Wellsville. We're looking forward to being with our families over Christmas and especially spending time with NeVae.

Pat will be sending something new from the bakery this year. I'll get a taste when I arrive in Wellsville. Best blessings of the sea-son to you all.

> Love,
> Deenie

ERIN

E-mail, December 30, 1999
Dear COBs,

I can't end this year without sharing with you what I've learned the last two months. Miracles happen. Love can soften even the hardest heart.

First, all of the McGees were present for Lindsay's baptism. I didn't think it would happen after the brouhaha I told you about, but you can't write off Margaret McGee.

The threat of being barred from Lindsay's baptism hit her hard.

She got us all (including Mom and me) to meet with her spiritual advisor, Sister Rita. After a wrenching afternoon, Margaret humbled herself and asked for forgiveness, and we all acknowledged our part in the family drama, however small. If only you could have been flies on the wall!

Second, the kids and The Jays and I spent Christmas Eve with the whole McGee clan at Sean and Margaret's antiques-filled garden home, which is part of a continuing-care retirement community in St. Paul. (They're very independent and don't want Andrew and Caitlin to have to worry about them.) Anyway, because of Lindsay, there's a wonderful new relationship between us. She finished what Kayla started when she smiled her way into Andrew's heart.

After Christmas, I went through the St. Paul temple twice during the open house. First, I went with the kids, Skipp and Linda, and The Jays. The next time, I took the McGees— Andrew, Lottie, The Grandparents McGee, Caitlin, and Sam. Brenda, too. She hadn't planned on staying for Christmas, but when Lottie asked her to, she switched her flight to January 3rd.

Lottie was most affected by the experience. She didn't want to leave the celestial room and said afterward that her heart was comforted by being there.

All the best in the coming year and may the spirit of the Lord be with us all in both our joys and our sorrows.

Your Erin

Chapter 15

2000

JUNEAU

E-mail, January 1, 2000

Well, dear friends, we've passed into the year 2000 smoothly. The world didn't end at the stroke of midnight as some predicted it would. Now that the global computer meltdown has been avoided, Greg can stop wearing his T-shirt that says "I'm Y2K OK, R U Y2K OK 2?"

We loved having Nicole home from Denver for the holidays. Of course she spent all her time with Beto planning their June wedding. They've chosen a Mexican fiesta theme. They'll set up the ballpark just south of our church parking lot with a grid of sparkly little lights overhead and a portable dance floor. And they'll hire a mariachi band.

She is so happy. But oh, how I wish . . . No. I'm not going there.

I'd hoped for a full house over Christmas, but my folks couldn't come from Oregon as planned because Dad didn't feel up to it. And Misty didn't show. We managed to fill the house for dinner, though! I invited Shan and Dex and Serenity because they don't have family close by. Dex was on his best behavior.

I also invited the man named Clyde from my class. I thought he looked a bit forlorn on the last class night, so I asked if he was going anywhere for Christmas dinner. He said his daughter and family, who live in Tucson, were spending the holidays with her husband's parents. You should have seen his face light up when I asked him to join us.

It was the right thing to do. He got along famously with everyone, including Greg. He parried jokes with Ira like a pro, and he joined with Trace and Gideon for a mighty fine trio rendition of an old Homer and Jethro song with guitar accompaniment. He and Gideon had a long talk together about animal rescue after Giddy told him how I'd saved Numbtail from the nasty boys. Seems Clyde is very active in animal support groups.

So here's hoping the next thousand years bring peace and prosperity. We should be so lucky!

I almost forgot—I finished the manuscript for *Millennial Madness*, the production I wrote for our stake young people and adults, too, to present this summer. It will go onstage in July.

Love,
Juneau

P.S. Nicole will be flying home in March so she and Marisol and I can shop for her wedding dress together. We sent an e-mail to Misty inviting her to join us, but she said she couldn't make it. As usual, she offered no explanation.

WILLADENE

For Deenie, the turn of the year was beset by grief. It was difficult for her and Evvy, but especially for Roger, to leave Wellsville knowing how ill NeVae was. But NeVae had given her blessing, saying, "Go home, son. We've said our good-byes."

They'd been back in Gainesville only long enough to start unpacking when the main doorbell rang. Deenie guessed it was Miss B, who couldn't manage the outside stairs to the apartment entrance. Hurrying in stocking feet to let Miss B in, Deenie failed to notice the stair steps had been waxed and buffed while they were gone. Halfway down the staircase her feet slipped out from under her and she landed headfirst at the bottom.

Woozy and in pain, her first thoughts were of Roger. Not wanting to leave him and Evvy after their emotionally trying trip, she tried to convince him not to call 911. But Roger didn't listen. *At least, Miss B's here for Evvy*, Deenie thought as she closed her eyes and let the EMTs load her into the ambulance.

She was diagnosed with a mild concussion and a cracked tooth, and after staying the night in the hospital, she was released with a prescription for pain medication and a reminder to visit her dentist as soon as she could. Her face was reminder enough. It throbbed and her head spun as

Roger eased her into the car. Even so, she noticed how worn Roger looked. Not just worn but grief stricken.

There could only be one reason. "Roger?" she inquired, laying a tentative hand on his arm.

"Keith called last night," he said gruffly. "Mom passed away Tuesday morning, shortly after our flight took off. I should have stayed." He paused, swallowing hard. "There wasn't anything here that needed doing that Ferris couldn't have done. He's back at work part-time now and is getting better every day. I should have stayed."

Deenie was silent, knowing no words could comfort him. *At least I can help get ready for the trip back,* she thought, but when they got home, Roger banished her to the bedroom. She didn't even have Bear's comforting presence to cheer her. He was still at Marsha Warrington's, where he'd spent the holidays while they were in Wellsville. At the news of NeVae's death, Marsha had offered to keep him for as long as the Rasmussens needed.

They took the only return flight with three available seats, a red-eye on Friday night with a layover in Atlanta. Roger's regret over leaving Wellsville mere hours before his mother's death hung over them the whole trip. "Everyone else stayed," Roger kept saying. "I was the only one not there when Mom died."

Deenie held Roger's hand, the only comfort she could offer. Her own distress over NeVae's death coupled with the physical pain in her face had drained every ounce of her energy. She was grateful that Evvy, who'd been comforted by Miss B and was sure that her grandma was having a super time with Aunt Sunny, was at peace.

They arrived at the gray house in Wellsville with barely enough time for them to change clothes and for Deenie to reapply foundation over her darkening bruises. Then they crossed the street to the church, where the family had gathered in the Relief Society room for the viewing.

Despite the touch up, Deenie's bruised and swollen face garnered almost as much attention as the remains in the mauve casket. She told the story of what happened over and over again until Jenny whispered, "Why don't we open the room next door so you can have a receiving line of your very own?"

The unexpected cruelty of the comment made Deenie want to run and hide, if only just long enough to catch her breath and reset her smile. Then Carl was at her side, tall and handsome in his Air Force uniform, putting his arm around her shoulder. "Looks like you could use a little backup, Mom," he said and stayed by her side during the remainder of the viewing.

The funeral, which was filled with love and laughter as well as loss, lifted Deenie's spirits. And for the first time Roger wept freely. Deenie said a silent prayer of gratitude on his behalf, seeing his tension and guilt dissipate as the shared emotions brought release.

The next morning Roger and his brothers sat with their father, discussing the farm. The women in the family met under the direction of Bert, Roger's only sister. She was the executor of NeVae's personal effects, which were beautifully displayed on the dining room table.

Deenie noticed how Jenny went straight to the sea-foam green Roseville vase NeVae had kept on a pedestal by the window. Deenie had often heard Jenny say how its pastel colors and graceful lines satisfied something in her that nothing else did. As Bert pulled out NeVae's handwritten will, Deenie prayed silently, *Please let Jenny get the vase.*

Bert began reading the bequests. Evvy delightedly received a treasured antique dress clip made of sky blue enamel grapes with sculpted vines and leaves of fourteen-karat gold. When she was younger, Evvy had worked hard to earn the privilege of holding it on visits to the farm. For Elizabeth, there was a cross-stitch sampler of the characteristics of a virtuous woman, worked by NeVae's mother. Charlotte, Gordon's wife and the genealogy guru in the family, had already accepted stewardship over all NeVae's personal papers and photographs. Now she was happy to get NeVae's well-worn and cherished wooden lap desk.

Jenny and Deenie were the last to have their bequests read. Only two items remained on the dining room table, the Roseville urn and the family Keeping Book, a hardbound treasure from NeVae's side of the family containing four generations' worth of housekeeping advice, medical notes, and favorite recipes.

Deenie held her breath, but the look on Bert's face told her that Jenny hadn't been left the vase.

"Mom's will leaves the vase and pedestal to Deenie and the book to Jenny," Bert began. At Jenny's sharp intake of a breath, Bert held up her hand. "Hold on. Mom told me at Christmas she realized she'd made a mistake. She knew that you, Jenny, would cherish the vase and Deenie would love the book. She was planning to change her will the day she died."

"But it's not in the will now, is it?" Jenny's voice was brusque.

"No," Bert answered. "But Mom told me she meant you to have the vase. She knew how much you love it." She picked up the vase and held it out to Jenny. "Mom even told Keith to clear stuff out from under the living room window so you'd have a place to put the stand."

"You're not making this up?" Jenny asked.

"Keith will tell you."

Jenny took the urn in her arms, cradling it as though it were a precious child. And Deenie accepted the Keeping Book with the same care.

Later that evening, after the family dinner, Deenie found Jenny standing on the front porch. "You still seem upset about the vase mix-up," she said.

Jenny shook her head in disbelief. "Don't you get it yet, Deenie? It's not about the urn. The only thing I ever really wanted from NeVae was to be as important to her as you were."

"But you were," Deenie insisted.

"I never felt it. She never had time for me or my girls. You and your constant dramas were always more important. For heaven's sake, Deenie, you even had to be center of attention at NeVae's funeral!"

"It wasn't like that," Deenie protested, afraid there might be a grain of truth in what Jenny was saying. It wasn't the first or even the second time Jenny's resentment of her had come up. "Jenny, I'm sorry for whatever you think I did."

"You're only sorry I see through your Miss Perfect act." Jenny stalked off, leaving Deenie wondering how she could have hurt someone so badly and not known about it.

But I did know she resented me, Deenie confessed to herself. *I just never bothered to ask why.*

ERIN

E-mail, January 11, 2000
Dear Deenie and Juneau,

Deenie, you and your family have been in my thoughts since I heard about NeVae's passing. Even when our loved ones have lived a rich life, as NeVae did, we still mourn. I think as a family we're already mourning Lottie. Repeated bouts of pneumonia have taken a devastating toll. Every time the phone rings, I expect bad news.

Lottie's situation got me thinking about the twists and turns in my personal history that brought her into my life. My decision to join the Church opened a whole new set of possible futures. I can't imagine who or where I would be if I hadn't taken that step.

Certainly, I wouldn't have met you two and Gabby. I was trying to explain our relationship to a client the other day, and no matter what I said, it fell short of expressing how I feel. You've been my safe haven, my confessors, my teachers, and the mirror in which I see myself more clearly. And my playmates during "recess," which is what Jake calls our vacations!

We've been doing this dance for twenty years, ladies—just five years to go before our Pact is fulfilled.

Blessings,
Erin

JUNEAU

E-mail, January 13, 2000
Dear Deenie,

I hope this card conveys my sincere sympathies. NeVae and I became good friends while she and Wilford were here in California. She was quite a lady. Please give Roger a loving hug from me and Greg.

I don't know what to say about Jenny. I have a friend who says when someone acts in a way you can't figure out, you should try to understand where she is coming from, and if that doesn't help, then you might try apologizing, even though you don't know what for.

And Erin, I can't bear to think of Lottie's imminent passing. Getting older wouldn't be so bad if we didn't have to lose all these dear people.

Lots of love,
Juneau

WILLADENE
E-mail, January 15, 2000
Dear COBs,

Thank you for your loving cards and sympathy. I miss NeVae a lot. But I like thinking of her and my sister, Sunny, together. Roger's feeling better. He gets a lot of comfort from the weekly phone calls he puts in to his dad, brothers, and sister. The Rasmussens are closer now than they have ever been. And administrative problems at the Academy keep him busy.

I tried to apologize to Jenny as you all suggested. She said she might be willing to listen when I figured out what I should be apologizing for. Aunt Stella said to remember that Jenny owns fifty percent of the problem. I'm grateful our spat hasn't come between Roger and his brother.

Missing you both,
Deenie

P.S. I've begun reading NeVae's Keeping Book. It's funny, touching, and eye-opening. I can see how the four generations of women who wrote in it evolved from young wives and mothers into COBs in their own right. Sometimes I read a section out loud to Evvy, who has a genuine taste for family history.

Deenie put off making the recommended appointment with her dentist out of sheer cussedness. She just didn't want to go. But when she awoke on the morning of Evvy's twelfth birthday party with a fever of 102 and a painful abscess from the tooth she'd broken the day before NeVae died, she called for an emergency appointment.

She felt terrible having to cancel all the festivities. "Next year, Mom," Evvy said as she helped her mother into the car for the trip to the clinic.

The dentist wasn't as understanding. "Why didn't you call immediately so I could get you on antibiotics? You know how risky it is to do dental work without it for someone with a heart murmur like yours. Now we have to worry about that as well as this nasty abscess. The cracked tooth will have to wait."

Three days later Deenie was still running a fever, her face still hurt, and her stomach refused to hold anything more than clear liquids and crackers. With Roger's help, Evvy did the best she could to keep the house on an even keel, but Deenie could feel the disorder creeping in on her. Miss B tried to put things into perspective when she came to visit. "Nobody's counting those bugs on your kitchen floor, and they won't keep you from getting into heaven, so just settle down."

Deenie hadn't known she had enough bugs on the kitchen floor to warrant counting. "How humiliating," she murmured.

"Take a deep breath, dearie. You've lived in the South long enough to know everybody has bugs."

"Not Delia," Deenie said. "Bugs wouldn't dare live in her house."

"From what you've told me, she's not likely to stop in for a friendly visit, is she?"

But Delia did. Ten minutes later she arrived, carrying a savory-smelling pot of chicken soup. "Ferris insisted," she said when Miss B led her into Deenie's bedroom. "He says my chicken soup can cure anything. After all, it got him through recovering from his heart attack."

Deenie murmured her thanks and then winced as Miss B put a bag of ice on her colorful cheek.

"That must hurt something awful," Delia commiserated. "I hope you're able to eat. Marsha's bringing butter biscuits to go with the soup and doing a cold molded salad, so you're set for dinner. What else can I do to help?"

In a panic that Delia would discover the bugs that needed sweeping up in the kitchen, Deenie assured her everything was taken care of. She was relieved when Delia left with cheery best wishes and the reassurance that either she or Ferris would be checking in daily.

"I don't understand that woman one bit," she said to Miss B when the door closed behind Delia.

"There's no mystery," Miss B said. "Delia's doing what we all do. She's being the heroine in her own life."

"Delia, a heroine?"

Miss B studied her thoughtfully. "Why, sugar, did you think you were going to be the heroine in Delia's life? Deenie to the rescue of us all?"

Deenie ducked her head as she recognized herself in Miss B's words.

"Let's have none of that," Miss B said kindly. "You just need to realize being born and raised in the Church doesn't make you better than the rest of us. God loves us all the same, in the Church or out. We're all common dirt. And without the mighty grace of a good God, we stay dirt."

At that, Deenie burst into tears. She felt terrible. Her face hurt, and her worst flaw had just been handed to her on a platter. With a sympathetic "Tut-tut," Miss B wiped Deenie's cheeks. "Don't take it so hard, now. We all have warts, and we love one another anyway."

She kissed Deenie's forehead and said, "Get some rest." Then she left, shutting the bedroom door behind her.

But Deenie couldn't rest. She spent a restless night in self-examination. By morning, she'd come to the weary conclusion that along with absorbing gospel teachings as she'd grown up, she'd somehow absorbed the notion that being born under the covenant and having a wonderful Mormon heritage set her apart from—and above—others. The realization shamed her.

ERIN

E-mail, February 22, 2000
Dear Juneau,

Lottie's still with us—I don't know how she hangs on. I'm writing for another reason.

My friend Colleen's daughter, EJ, has moved to California with Sahrita, her housemate and the daughter of the tattoo artist she worked for. She wanted to see what life was like in some other place, and since Sahrita was headed in that direction . . .

The girls are living in Culver City with Sahrita's aunt, Flower Telford. EJ's twenty, but Colleen still worries about her being so far away. Would you mind calling EJ so she knows there's someone she can turn to if necessary?

So far, she's doing fine. She's thrilled to be in the Golden State, except for missing her brother, Ricky. Now that he's a "real Boy Scout," his goal is to fill his sash with badges, the way he and Mark did when they were Cub Scouts. He e-mails EJ with updates on the badge he's working on. Colleen and Steve are rightly proud of his accomplishments.

I wish I could say Mark and Ricky are friends. They've worked together on Cub Scout and Boy Scout badges for years, starting when Colleen's husband, Steve, stepped in to help Mark after the divorce. But friendship means sharing more than activities, doesn't it? Mark's started having friends over on weekends, but he never invites Ricky.

Sorry I got sidetracked. Let me know if you're willing to call EJ.

Your Erin

JUNEAU

E-mail, March 1, 2000
Dear Erin,

I spoke with EJ on the phone. She said Flower Telford is really good to her and Sahrita, she has a part-time job restacking books at the big downtown library but is looking for something that pays better, and she loves the ocean.

I think she was happy enough to hear from me. I invited her and Sahrita to come to my house for dinner next Sunday. She said they couldn't make it, but maybe they could come some other time. So she left the door open.

Love,
Juneau

Nicole flew home the following weekend to shop for her wedding dress, and looking at her, Juneau understood in a new way the meaning of the term "all atwitter." The dedicated medical student was nowhere to be seen. In her place was a young woman deliriously excited about her coming wedding to a boy she'd loved all her life.

She giggled; she blushed; she glowed. She tried on dresses until she found the perfect one—pure white with lacy bodice, slightly puffed sleeves, nipped-in waist with a hint of bustle in back from which a small train flowed.

When she turned to face Juneau and Marisol, she looked so much the embodiment of a happy bride that Juneau cried. Marisol, too. "I wish I'd brought a camera," Marisol said, snuffling. "This moment should be preserved for posterity. For your eternal family."

Nicole laughed happily. Turning back to her reflection in the mirror, she turned this way and that, looking at herself. Then she stood still, gazing straight ahead.

She stood that way for a long time. Finally she said, "I'll have to think about the dress," and abruptly headed back to the dressing room. When she came out in her street clothing, Juneau was shocked to see that the happiness had drained from her like air from a balloon.

"What happened?" Marisol whispered as she and Juneau followed Nicole from the store.

Juneau shook her head. "I don't know." She tried to engage Nicole in conversation on the way home, but Nicole veered away from any mention of weddings. Instead she commented on Gideon's being twelve now and a deacon and mentioned how anxious she was to see little Rhiannan, who had recently turned one year old.

When they were alone in their house, Juneau took Nicole by the shoulders and asked, "What happened at the store?"

Nicole's façade crumbled. "I can't do it, Mom," she cried. "I can't marry Beto."

Juneau enfolded her daughter in her arms, letting her sob her heart out. Then she eased her to the sofa, handed her a tissue and said, "Want to tell me about it?"

Nicole wiped her eyes, now red and swollen. "I guess I just woke up from my dream world, thanks to what Marisol said. "

Juneau drew a blank. "What—?"

"About posterity and eternal families. I was looking in the mirror at the time, and all I saw was myself. No Beto. No family. I was alone."

"I'm not following."

Nicole shuddered. "Think of the mirrors in the sealing rooms of the temple, Mom. Remember how when Trace and Cath were married, Trace said he understood about eternal family when they looked at themselves reflected on and on and on as far as they could see? And now Rhiannan is part of that picture."

Juneau nodded.

"If I marry Beto, it won't be like that. I wanted so much to believe we could get around the religion question, but it's too big, seen from an eternal perspective. Our getting married would be only until death do us part, with no going on as a forever family. Like me looking into the mirror and seeing just myself, with nothing beyond. I would be standing alone in eternity."

Nicole again collapsed into sobs, and Juneau held her, not knowing what to say. What *could* she say?

Later she e-mailed the COBs a terse note:

> The wedding's off. Nicole told a brokenhearted and pleading Beto today. Then she left on the earliest flight she could get to Denver.

ERIN

E-mail, March 19, 2000
Dear Friends,

> Lottie passed away yesterday afternoon. It's been very hard on my father. Thank goodness he has Caitlin and Lindsay. And Brenda, for a few days yet. She was going to leave the first week of January, but when Lottie's situation turned critical, she delayed her flight again. She and Lottie had become fast friends. The fact that they'd both been married to Andrew, mothered Caitlin, and dealt with Margaret gave them a unique understanding of each other's experience.

> Margaret and Sean wish it had been them crossing over, not Lottie. Oddly, they're comforted that Lottie rests near their plots in a historic St. Paul cemetery. Andrew, too, when the time comes.

> Your Erin

A cloud hung over the McGees the following weeks. Erin and Caitlin took turns visiting their father, who hadn't yet gone back to work. He often wandered around the house as if looking for something, according to Theresa, and he had begun spending more time with his parents at their home in the continuing-care retirement community. They'd recently moved into one of the newer garden homes on the campus, the tighter construction of which would save on heating and cooling costs.

"They're in their late eighties and infirm," he told Erin. "They could go at any time, too."

"We should get Grandpa Andy a dog," Hannah said. "He needs one."

Erin smiled, absently patting Rascal's head. When he yelped, she looked in his ear and discovered a nasty abscess. "Looks like we need to take Rascal to the vet," she told Hannah.

"To Vince?" Hannah asked hopefully.

"No. Our regular vet takes good care of Rascal."

But Hannah insisted, so Erin drove to the Gerlach Animal Clinic and Hospital in Golden Valley. Vince was surprised and pleased when he saw Rascal was his next patient. It didn't take long for him to treat Rascal. When he was finished, he explained to Hannah everything he'd done, and then listened patiently while she described how she lined up her dollies and pretended she and Rascal were visiting them in the hospital.

"Why don't you enroll Rascal in a therapy dog class?" he asked Erin. "He's got the perfect temperament. He's curious, calm, and does well in unfamiliar surroundings. And he knows basic commands."

Hannah jumped up and down. "Yes, Mama, let's do it!"

"I can recommend a program if you decide to sign up," Vince said.

Erin found it hard to resist their enthusiasm. "I'll think about it," she said.

Other things took precedence, however, such as the upcoming Relief Society anniversary party, which Erin, Gail, and Valerie were beginning to plan. After spending so much time on the phone with Althea and getting to know other sisters in her ward better, Erin had a thirst to know all of them. "What about a night focusing on the sisters themselves?" she asked. "Interesting things about their pasts? Their talents we may not know about?" And the plan was put into motion.

Also high on Erin's list was her concern about Kayla. The more social fourteen-year-old Mark became that spring, the more Erin worried about Kayla. She was seventeen and had never gone on a date.

"She's busy," Joanna said. "She has an unbelievable schedule."

That was true. Kayla divided her time between Edina High School, the university, and the gift shop where she worked part-time. When she was home, she was either studying or watching TV—or studying while watching TV, something Erin couldn't understand.

When Kayla spent yet another Friday night at home, Erin perched on the arm of the great-room couch and ruffled Kayla's curls. "It's got to be boring, sitting at home on a Friday night."

"I don't mind it."

"Wouldn't you rather be out with friends? Or on a date?"

Kayla gave her a long look. "If you're trying to ask me something, the answer is no."

She thinks I think she's attracted to women! Erin thought with shock. "That wasn't what I meant. I'm just concerned that you don't have a social life."

"I don't have a social life because I'm not interested in 'hanging out.' I don't date because I've never been asked."

"I can't believe that. You're so cute and—"

"You're so *cuuute,*" Kayla mimicked. "Boys must be hanging on you." She paused. "*Not.* But I don't care. I don't believe in love."

Erin put her arm around Kayla's shoulders. "Don't give up on love because your father and I didn't make it."

"That's not why. I'm following your example. You don't need a man in your life."

Again Erin was shocked to know what was going on in her daughter's mind. "I've done without a man, true. But it doesn't mean I wouldn't like to have one."

"Could've fooled me. You haven't dated since the dermatologist."

"I go to singles events at church, but the choices aren't so good for women my age."

"That's just an excuse. Aunt Caitlin found Sam."

"Lucky her." Erin regarded Kayla with cocked head. "How about you? Isn't there anyone you're interested in?"

Kayla hesitated. "Maybe."

"Does he know you're interested in him?"

"I'm not any good at flirting."

"Why not ask him out? That's perfectly acceptable these days."

"Really? I haven't seen you asking anyone out."

Erin gave an exasperated huff. "How come you always bring things back to me?"

"To bug you?" Kayla said with a crooked grin. "Listen, Mom. If you're so eager to get me to ask someone out, you go first." Her grin widened. "You could ask Hannah's pet vet, Vince Gerlach."

E-mail, April 2, 2000
Dear Friends,

Our Relief Society anniversary party was tonight. Gail and Valerie and I found out something not generally known about each sister. We set up a sort of round robin in which every sister present was acknowledged for a particular talent or gift or service. What an amazing group of women we have! We closed with Valerie giving a talk about using our talents to bless others, which is what Relief Society is all about.

Kayla and I have a dating challenge going. Much to Caitlin's amusement, I've asked out the vet I told you about. He's not my type, but he's kind to kids and animals. That's something.

Erin

Chapter 16

JUNEAU

The night before Ira and Shoshana's wedding, Juneau and Greg invited all the guests who flew in from New York and Connecticut to a catered backyard party after the rehearsal at the country club in Alhambra where the wedding would take place.

It was the kind of meeting-of-the-clan event that Juneau had always wished for as a girl. Her parents, the Peripatetic Paulsens, had never taken her and Flint to Idaho where the relatives were. Now that she had her own diverse *made* family, Juneau was determined to enjoy it to the fullest. She even invited Misty, when Misty called to talk to Gideon.

"I don't know where you are," Juneau said, "but if you're close enough to come, please do."

"Why would I *want* to come?" Misty asked.

"To wish Ira well," Juneau said, "since you were once married to him."

"Past history," Misty said. "Tell him *mazel tov* for me. Now may I speak with Gideon?"

Maybe it was just as well, Juneau decided.

Ira had asked Uncle Schlomo to be the master of ceremonies for the evening, so there was a lot of joking and kidding and easy family banter. It was very late before the festive party finally broke up. Both Ira's parents and Shoshana's hugged Juneau and Greg and thanked them tearfully for being so good to their children. Juneau and Greg, equally emotional, assured them that it was a pleasure and honor.

E-mail, April 31, 2000
Dear Deenie and Erin,

Ira and Shoshana were married today at 5:00 P.M., and I've added a number of new words to my vocabulary: 1. *Klezmer*— A pickup band with various instruments, this time a violin, hammered dulcimer, saxophone, clarinet, and tambourine.

2. *Ketubah*—A beautifully illuminated marriage contract.
3. *Chuppah*—The canopy under which the bride and groom stand during the ceremony. (This one was held up by Trace and Cath and Shoshana's brother and his wife.)

The ceremony was beautiful, and the feeling of tradition so strong I could almost hear Tevye from *Fiddler on the Roof* saying, "Because of our traditions, everyone knows who he is and what God expects him to do."

Marisol and I completely lost it when Shoshana came down the aisle, escorted by both parents. What is it that makes us weep at weddings? Maybe the sheer beauty of it all, the joy and hope in the faces of the young couple, the solemnness of those age-old rituals. Or maybe for Marisol and me it was thinking about Nicole and Beto—neither of whom attended—and how their differences of religion had finally separated them.

Thankfully, Marisol doesn't resent our family for the pain her son is feeling. She's just as sad as I am about the end of the relationship. We have to keep assuring ourselves that it's better for them to split now than later.

Well, to go on, the rabbi was a delightful thirty-something woman who started off by saying that the first time Ira and Shoshana had come to her synagogue, a little boy said in a loud whisper, "Mama, there's that pickle guy from TV." She quoted some advice from the Talmud and was just about to get into the vows when Gideon touched my arm and said, "My other mom's here."

I thought he must be mistaken, but there was Misty, sitting in the back row, dressed all in black. Her hair was dyed black again, the way she used to do it when she was a teenager. I want to think she's trying to find her true self, what with all her wanderings and personal changes. But the image that came to my mind was of the evil fairy going to Sleeping Beauty's baby party. Why else would Misty decide to come when she said she wouldn't?

When the ceremony was over, somebody brought two chairs on which they put the bride and groom. Lifting them up, they paraded them around the room while everyone called out

"Mazel tov" and danced the *hora*. Gideon and I went to find Misty, who stood watching from the sidelines, an odd expression on her face. After she hugged Gideon and he ran off to join the dancers, she turned to me. "You think I came to make trouble, don't you?" She saved me from answering by saying, "You're right. I did." She said she'd had mischief in mind but had been so touched by the centuries-old traditions and the beauty of the ceremony that she'd decided just to wish the newlyweds well and go on her way. Which she did.

Will I ever understand my daughter? Will I ever find out where she's living?

Puzzled,
Juneau

WILLADENE

Spring that year was all about new beginnings. Having been humbled by Miss B, Deenie was consciously letting go of her previously unrecognized belief that her background made her better than others. It wasn't easy, but when she succeeded, Deenie found herself also able to let go of her need to live up to that belief. It was a wonderful relief. Her change in attitude was rewarded by a subtle shift in her relationship with Delia. They weren't friends, but between Deenie's new insight and Delia's chicken soup they were no longer enemies.

In March Paul and Dani announced they were expecting. Deenie celebrated by getting out her knitting and setting up a quilting frame in the attic and inviting Miss B to help her make a baby blanket.

"You're happier, Deenie, dear," Miss B said as they worked. "It shows on your face. I like it."

May brought a quick trip to Wellsville for Elizabeth's graduation. Brad was there, too, and seeing how he gazed at Elizabeth, Deenie knew he was a man on a mission. But he left abruptly before the evening was over with the terse comment, "She said no."

"Can you tell me about it?" Deenie asked when she found Elizabeth crying in her room.

"Do I really have to explain what happened?" Elizabeth asked through her tears.

"No, dear," Deenie said. She lay down next to her daughter and pulled Elizabeth's head to her shoulder and let her cry.

It was a strange, emotional visit for Deenie. Her concern for Elizabeth was offset by her joy in feeling Dani and Paul's baby kick. Misery and miracle, side by side.

JUNEAU

E-mail, June 1, 2000

Dear Deenie and Erin,

I just received the jacket for my new book, *Package of Silence*. It's the one I started in Sedona, about the girl searching for her brother on the Hopi reservation. I like the jacket, which has a suitably mysterious desert scene.

With no deadlines, I'm happily immersed in rehearsals for *Millennial Madness.* We have about seventy-five teenagers in the cast, plus a number of adults, including Marisol. My old friend Dr. Tim Hart wrote a delightful number for the production involving a fussbudget dad reeling off all the things that were apt to go wrong in a world adjusting to Y2K. To counterpoint that, the laid-back mom breaks into the old Doris Day song, "Que Sera, Sera." Dr. Tim plays the dad, and I talked Marisol into taking the mom part. I wish you could see her and Dr. Tim together—they make a great comic team.

On the way home from our *Millennial Madness* rehearsal last night I told Marisol that I think Dr. Tim, who's been a widower for several years now, likes her. She giggled and blushed like a teenager!

By the way, I've been investigating "mysterious places" to set my next book, and I've settled on Williamsburg, Virginia, after reading a book titled *The Ghosts of Williamsburg* that a friend gave me. I can trade a timeshare week for a condo there. Greg says I shouldn't count on his being available, so would the two of you like to join me? Probably September of 2001?

Love,
Juneau

P.S. Do you think I'm becoming more like my parents? I mean, I'm traveling to the sites of my novels just the way they did. I've heard that eventually, sometime during her life, a woman becomes her mother.

ERIN

E-mail, June 19, 2000
Dear COBs,

Juneau, book that vacation! I'll make it work.

About women becoming their mothers, I'm more like Caitlin than I'm like my mom, which makes me wonder if both Caitlin and I will end up becoming our grandmother, Margaret McGee. The reformed version, I hope. I'm discovering she has a rather sly sense of humor. The kids and I have had dinner with The Grandparents McGee every other week or so—they're great storytellers and love showing the kids family memorabilia.

Remember the dating challenge Kayla and I had? I went to a concert with Vince the Vet, so she asked a boy she likes to a stake dance next month.

Vince and I had a pleasant afternoon when I took him to a concert at the Lake Harriet band shell, but we don't have a whole lot in common. He's five years younger than I am, has a house in Golden Valley near the animal clinic and hospital he's co-owner of, plus a cabin up north where he spends as much time as possible during the summer.

He reciprocated by taking me fishing on Lake Minnetonka. I don't like to fish—and I don't like watching someone else fish! When he didn't even take me to lunch at Lord Fletcher's, a restaurant with a boat dock on the lake, I was ready to write off the day as a total disaster.

Then on the way back to his slip we cruised right by Angie Dunmeyer's lakeshore home. I've known her for ages—she was my buddy in my first job as a hairdresser at Stefani's. Odd to think that before our "troubles," Cory (and Steve) gave her the discussions that led to her baptism. Anyway, she was working in her yard, so I had him tie up at their dock. Angie and her husband, Norm, insisted we stay for supper.

Angie got Vince talking about his past. I found out he got

interested in the Church when he helped some LDS Scouts get their merit badge for veterinary medicine, and he's been Scoutmaster in his ward. He's been married once. His wife was killed in a car wreck. They had no children. When Angie asked if he'd ever consider remarrying, he smiled and said, "Depends on if I can find a woman George approves of."

George, it turns out, is a yellow-nape Amazon parrot that sings "How Much Is That Doggy in the Window?" and is very noisy when he wants food or attention. My prediction is that Vince will remain single—what woman would agree to be vetted by a parrot?

Erin

JUNEAU

E-mail, June 27, 2000
Dear COBs,

Last Saturday was when Nicole's wedding would have taken place had she not called it off. She phoned that day to cry a little, but she still feels she did the right thing. Shades of Elizabeth and Brad!

We were all kind of morose about it, but then we had a surprise that put it out of our minds—Misty showed up at our house and she brought Colleen's daughter EJ with her.

Misty told us she's been volunteering after work (something to do with computer programming) at a place called Covenant House, which does outreach to young women. Covenant House had a booth at a fair near where EJ is living. By total coincidence, EJ stopped by when Misty happened to be staffing the booth! They started talking, and when EJ mentioned that her mother and a friend named Erin put on a Big Barn Sale every year, Misty made the connection. Apparently Misty has taken EJ under her wing.

When I invited them to dinner the next night, EJ said yes for both of them, and Misty acquiesced. Actually, I think she was happy to have an excuse to come home. Turns out she's been working right here in Los Angeles most of the time since she brought Gideon back, except for a few months she spent in a commune up near Big Sur (said she decided it wasn't for her).

EJ didn't have a lot to say to Greg and me when they came to dinner, but she talked for a long time with Gideon while Numbtail napped in her lap. Gideon says they just talked about "stuff." He's a good listener and quite wise for his age. He says she misses her brother, Ricky. While they talked, I asked Misty if EJ needed help. She said, "No. She has to figure out what she wants out of life. Like all of us. But if you want to help, just take her in, like you do everybody else who comes along. She needs somebody to love her just as she is."

The compliment almost floored me. Who knew Misty felt that way? It profoundly affected me. Remember back in our younger days when we wondered what God expected of us? Perhaps that's my mission, and Greg's, to take in the lost and the lonely and provide a safe harbor. *Who'da* thunk it?

Love,
Juneau

Chapter 17

ERIN

"You left something out when you did that Woman Welcome for Kayla," Erin said to Lucky Brown. It was a bright July day, and they were enjoying a pizza supreme on the patio of a chain restaurant.

"Lay it on me," Lucky said.

"When you listed the things women do, you didn't say we would spend our adult lives worrying about people we love." Erin was thinking of Elizabeth, EJ, and Nicole as well as her own children.

"How dumb of me." Lucky spoke around a mouthful of pizza. "That Shakeela keeps my worry beads busy. She's doing fine, studying to be a dental assistant, but I can always see things she should be doing different. She tells me my idea of what her life should be like isn't her idea."

"But you keep trying to help her, don't you?"

Lucky sat back. "Tell Mama what's bothering you."

"Kayla. She's never gotten back her sparkle. And she hasn't given any thought to what she'll do after she graduates next spring."

Erin paused. Lucky waited.

"And Mom. She's afraid of getting Alzheimer's, like Grams did. She's constantly on the Internet, looking for what she can do to protect herself." Erin smiled grimly. "She bought a tandem bike so she and Jake can get more exercise. She's had all her mercury fillings replaced, and she makes sure she eats fifteen pounds of vegetables a week."

Lucky chortled. "Guess fifteen pounds of pizza don't count."

"She's driving herself crazy doing all sorts of activities meant to keep her brain cells working. She takes classes she's not even interested in, just to be learning something new."

"That woman is going to die of exhaustion," Lucky said.

"There's got to be something I can do for them, but I don't know what."

"You can't make life perfect for them, girl. It's not your job."

"I know. But what if there's something I'm supposed to do? I don't want to wake up one day and realize I've missed the boat."

"Oh, babycakes. That's going to happen no matter how hard you try."

On the way home, Erin stopped in Hopkins to visit The Jays. She was talking to her mother when she noticed Jake and a thin man with a ponytail sitting on the deck overlooking the flower garden Grams had loved. "Who's that?"

"Oh, that's Tomas Kitt, our renter," Joanna said.

"You never told me you'd rented Grams's apartment."

"I didn't?" Joanna frowned. "I thought I had. I can't keep anything straight these days."

"I have days like that myself," Erin said reassuringly. "Now, tell me about this renter."

"We saw him looking at postings for apartments at Lakewinds Natural Foods. Jake started talking to him, and the rest is history." Joanna smiled in Tomas's direction. "He's an odd duck, but I think you'll like him."

"What does he do?"

"He's a *tai chi* master. He owns Swooping Crane Studio. Come on, I'll introduce you."

The men stood when Joanna and Erin walked onto the deck. Jake said, "We were just discussing the meaning of life. Want to join us?"

"Unfortunately, I don't have time for that." Erin smiled and held out her hand. "I'm Joanna's daughter. Erin Johnson."

"Tomas Kitt."

Erin had the confusing impression of softness and steel when she shook his hand, and his smile held a sweetness that made her feel like crying. She was enormously relieved that when he spoke, he sounded completely ordinary.

"I've signed up for a class at Tomas's studio," Joanna said. "I'm thinking of asking Kayla to come with me. It might do her good."

"My daughter broke her leg several years ago, and it took a long time to heal," Erin said to Tomas. "Her ankle still gives her trouble."

"Tai chi will be good for her," Tomas said.

Kayla didn't say much about the class she and Joanna were taking, but Erin often noticed her practicing the graceful movements of full circle tai chi on the back lawn, Hannah imitating her from behind. Mark sometimes joined them, laughing as he parodied the routine. Erin expected Kayla to react with anger, but she shrugged it off. The more Mark teased her, the stronger her focus became.

As the anniversary of the accident drew near, Erin realized Kayla had gone several weeks without trotting out her perennial complaint about the boys on the bikes. When Erin hinted at the subject, Kayla waved her hand dismissively. "Anger is a waste of chi."

"What's that?" Mark asked.

"Life energy," Kayla said.

Mark grunted. "That tai chi is making you weird."

"But weird in a good way," Erin said.

Later, Kayla said, "I don't know how to explain it, Mom, but doing tai chi makes me feel alive again. I think I shut down when my leg was such a mess. It was easier to deal with the pain and frustration that way. Now I feel like I live in my own body, the way I used to feel when I skated."

"Then you keep it up, dear." Erin gave her daughter a hug. "Don't worry about what Mark or anyone else thinks."

Tomas Kitt's class seemed to have a positive effect on Joanna, too. When Erin mentioned it to Jake, he said, "That class was the best money I've spent in a long time."

Joanna and Kayla were having so much fun that Joanna proposed they take a beginning pottery class through community ed. "Sign me up, too," Erin said. "I don't want to miss out on the fun."

So Erin was there to see the light go on in Kayla's eyes as she rolled clay to hand-build a vase. "It's like playing in mud when I was little," she said, giggling. Erin watched with amazement at how easily Kayla created a small vessel out of the coiled clay, one with a beauty of shape that belied it was a first attempt.

The teacher was also impressed. "You have a nice touch," she told Kayla.

Two weeks into the class, Kayla was already talking about taking pottery classes that fall. It was the first time she'd been that excited in years. Four years, to be exact.

JUNEAU

E-mail, July 30, 2000
Dear Friends,

Our *Millennial Madness* show went off even better than expected. And I'm wondering if I've started a romance by pairing up Dr. Tim and Marisol. Just call me *Yente*.

My whole "family" helped with the show. Misty and EJ came to help with the dancers, Clyde acted as prompter. Shan sewed costumes, Ira and Shoshana had good advice on production, Serenity and Gideon were among the more than seventy-five kids in the show and now they're totally stagestruck . . .

It was a blast!

Love,
Juneau

WILLADENE

When Roger and Deenie returned to Gainesville they discovered that Evvy had picked up playing the banjo while staying with Miss B, and Ferris Tucker had announced his retirement as head administrator effective immediately due to another cardiac episode.

When Deenie told her mother over the phone that Ferris had retired, Margaret said, "So Roger's head administrator now."

"No, Mom. He's only filling in while the board interviews other candidates for the job."

"We thought it would be a sure thing when Mr. Tucker retired," Margaret said.

"So did we. But Ferris is still on the board, and he's pulling for Roger."

Deenie tried to sound upbeat, but she was furious that the board had put Roger in such an awkward position. He was faced with making important decisions that might be overturned any day. The stress was beginning to show. He responded to Deenie's efforts at lightening the situation with a grim smile. *Even if he does get the job, how is he going to have a decent working relationship with the men who put him in this untenable situation?* she wondered.

The tension on Gobb Hill was almost unbearable by the time Ferris Tucker arrived Friday morning with the news that Roger had been appointed head administrator of the Academy. Instead of the great sigh of relief Deenie had expected, Roger nodded his head and said, "Guess I better get to the office."

Before Ferris left, he handed Roger a box of stationery with the school crest, Roger's name underneath, and the word *Headmaster* below that.

Deenie saw relief followed by satisfaction cross her husband's face as he opened the box. "You must have been pretty sure I'd get the job," he said.

"Of course." Ferris flashed one of his hearty smiles. "I trained you, didn't I?" Then he took a five-inch-thick spiral binder out of his briefcase and handed it to Deenie. "Delia asked me to give this to you. She said you'd be needing it." It was labeled Faculty and Board Wives' Association. Deenie took the book with a weak thank-you, and Ferris and Roger left for the day. The weight of the oversized binder was nothing compared to the weight Deenie felt on her shoulders. She'd always been a little snide about the way Delia handled things. Now for all intents and purpose Deenie was going to have to be Delia on campus. *Aargh!*

E-mail, September 1, 2000
My Dear Friends,

The board has decided to close Gobb Hill to the public (Yippee! No more tours to lead) and make it the official chief adminis-trator's home. I think it's their way of keeping us here. They like the convenience of Roger being on campus 24/7.

Too convenient for me! More than once, I've been caught drinking juice on the veranda in my jammies by someone look-ing for Roger. Now I Dress, with a capital D, first thing in the morning, even if all I do is end up referring visitors to Marsha, who always has an answer for everything.

Roger sets the alarm at five every morning so he can get an early start on the day. If I want him to eat anything at all, I have to be up with him and have something made that he can gobble on his way out the door.

I miss having him here for scripture study and family prayer with Evvy. But I've insisted that no matter what's on the docket at work, Monday nights still belong to the family.

Last Monday we had a joint family home evening with the Love-Bassetts and the Kenadys. Christiana and Evvy played a very simple banjo and guitar duet with Devon, Christiana's dad, accompanying them on the harmonica. The short lesson was punctuated with all three girls raving about their new choir teacher at St. Anne's. (Christiana is now there, too.) According to them, Miss Winsome is the epitome of what every St. Anne's girl wants to grow up to be. Not only is she beautiful and smart and can sing but she's also spiritual and starts each choir practice with a thought on what it means to be a friend to Christ.

If Miss Winsome has become Evvy's idol at St. Anne's, Leo Flynn has become her hero on campus. He calls her by her full name, Evangeline Rose, and she calls him Mr. Flynn, the way the teachers do. I bet he doesn't preen for the teachers the way he does when Evvy uses that name.

I find myself in the peculiar situation of trying to fill Delia's shoes on campus. I wish I could ask her for advice. Miss B says the best thing I could do to get to be friends with Delia is ask her to help me. What do you think about that?

In the meantime, I'm having a just-because luncheon for all my new friends in Gainesville this afternoon. I'm serving pumpkin soup in a pumpkin and Grandma Streeter's cornmeal rolls.

Love,
Deenie

P.S. I invited Delia to join us. She said yes. Roger asked me if I really want to be friends or if I want to be friends because I need her help and advice. I think the answer is yes to both. I'm tired of the conflict, and I need her advice.

As Deenie set the table in the apartment dining room for the luncheon, she began thinking of all the luncheons she had hosted in Wellsville for family and friends. She imagined how those dear folks would look here and now, sitting at this table.

Mom would sit at the head of the table. Deenie put down a place card for Marsha Warrington. *I'd put Pat here, to her left.* There she set the card for Cleo Kenady. *I'd put Lark by me so she could see the fall flowers from the front window.* Down went the place card for Gwen Love-Bassett. For Aunt Stella, Miss B.

"I've found someone wonderful for almost every empty slot in my heart," Deenie said out loud as she gave a final loving pat to the center-piece of autumn leaves and dried bittersweet berries. "But if I had to replace me, who would it be?" Who, of all the women she knew in Gainesville, would be the most likely to have Band-Aids and antibiotic cream in her purse? Who was the one most likely to show up with the heal-anything chicken soup?

"Delia!" Deenie sat down with a thump as she answered her own question.

Miss B was so right. I did charge chin-first into Academy society, expecting priority placement in a slot already happily and competently filled by someone else.

In the days following the luncheon, which was a wonderful success, Deenie enjoyed a greater sense of belonging in Gainesville and on cam-pus. She and Delia had moved beyond just being civil with each other to reaching out tentatively toward friendship, and Deenie felt her safety net was finally taking shape. Oddly, she didn't feel as safe as she'd thought she would when she achieved that goal. She was pondering that strange dichotomy when she was unexpectedly, suddenly overcome with a feel-ing of sorrow so immense her knees buckled.

The Griff? she wondered as she collapsed on a kitchen stool. No, this feeling was completely different. It was sorrow without the fear and hope-lessness of the Griff. A prompting, then? Deenie remembered the con-versation she'd had with Aunt Stella after NeVae's funeral. Deenie'd asked why Stella got so many promptings and she so few. "Maybe because I'm listening," Stella had said.

"I'm listening now," Deenie said. The answer came quick and clear. It was about Dani and the little girl she carried. Sarah Beth Rasmussen was delivered stillborn, four weeks early and twenty-four hours after Dani noticed she'd quit kicking. Twenty-four hours after Deenie had been brought to her knees in sorrow.

She hadn't been the only one. Paul had known the minute the small heart had stopped beating. Stella, too. There was nothing any of them could have done. And unlike the aftermath of Sunny's birth when everyone felt guilty, there was no question of blame in Sarah Beth's passing. The doctor said so, and the post mortem confirmed his findings.

"Some babies die before they're born for no discernible reason." The words, repeated over the phone by a devastated Paul, cut Deenie to the core. She knew there were no guarantees. But she depended on knowing the reason things were the way they were. The greater plan. The big picture. How could perfect little Sarah Beth being born without breath fit into that?

Deenie asked Miss B the question after she, Roger, and Evvy had returned from a quick trip to Wellsville for the burial.

"Don't know," Miss B said. "Don't need to. God's God, and I'm his child. I trust in that." Miss B took Deenie's face in her hands. "Don't you trust that God is taking care of you and me and Sarah Beth and every other one of his children, here or in heaven?"

Deenie couldn't answer. She couldn't think beyond the hurt in her heart. "They are so stricken, Paul and Dani, by sorrow. You should have seen them at the grave. How are they ever going to recover from this?"

"They're not," Miss B said. She led Deenie to a seat in her tiny kitchen and offered her a glass of cold water. "Not completely. Even after the grief mellows, the loneliness for that child will always be there. But even that pain's bearable with the good Lord's grace and mercy."

"The dirt and grace thing again?" Deenie asked, remembering Miss B's comment that everyone was common dirt except for the grace of God.

Miss B nodded, her white curls bobbing up and down. Deenie found her pragmatic approach to faith unexpectedly comforting.

ERIN

E-mail, October 10, 2000

Dear COBs,

Deenie, my heart is with Paul and Dani. And you, too. I know how you were anticipating the coming of this child.

Here's the next installment in the Vince serial. He invited me to go to Duluth to see the colors. What he didn't say was that we were flying—in the Cessna 182 he owns with his dad! I don't know why, but the thought of going up in it threw me for a loop. He tried to make me feel better by saying he's been flying since he was thirteen and that "statistically speaking," I'd be safer in the air than I would on the road! It didn't help.

He was very gracious when he realized I wasn't kidding about not getting in his plane. We spent the day driving around, looking at all the places I'd called home. We started at the little house in Nordeast where Mom, Grams, and I lived and then went to the apartment I had Uptown when I first met Cory. Over lunch at Figilio's, I told Vince my next apartment was over the garage at Angie and Norm's. Vince really likes the Dunmeyers, so he had me call to see if they were home. We spent the afternoon on Lake Minnetonka in the 1953 Chris Craft cabin cruiser Norm rebuilt. I don't remember ever being so relaxed.

When Vince dropped me off, Hannah captured him for an hour, telling him what we'd learned in our obedience training classes. (I'm amazed at all the things I didn't know about dogs—and people!) Then Mark talked to him for the longest time about his airplane. Mark's always been interested in doing the aviation merit badge, and Vince said he'd be glad to teach him airplane mechanics and take him up. I'm as nervous about Mark flying with him as I was about me! And I'm not sure how I feel about how easily Vince has made a place for himself in our lives.

Your Erin

P.S. Kayla's applying to the University of Minnesota with the idea of majoring in fine arts. She's been fired up by the encouragement she's gotten from the artists at Northern Clay Studio where she's been taking classes. She says she's finally found the talent spoken of in her patriarchal blessing! Then she asked, "Have you found the man in yours?" Who knows.

JUNEAU

E-mail, November 27, 2000

Dear COBS,

Remember back when I was in a tizzy because so many guests were invited for Thanksgiving Dinner? Well, I had an overflow crowd this year and hardly batted an eyelash. I wouldn't say I've turned into "a hostess with the mostest," but I actually look forward to having our house full of friends and family. Good thing, because Greg's asked me if I'll throw a holiday party for Smoketree System employees!

Sometimes I wonder if I'm making any personal progress in my old age, so it's gratifying to see that some things have changed.

I haven't told you this before (talking takes away the impetus to write), but I'm deep into a new book called *Backstage Ghost,* half of which I wrote during the production of *Millennial Madness.* It's about kids in a high school drama group who have to placate a ghost named Orson who died on the school stage when a backdrop of Mount McKinley fell on him. It's fun, doesn't take a great deal of thought, and I'm confident the publisher I'm working with will like it.

I wonder why I'm "haunted" by these ghosts—Orson and the ghosts of Williamsburg, who will end up in my next book.

Juneau

ERIN

In November, Mark finally told Erin he'd decided on an Eagle project—a Christmas program to present at Great-Grandpa Harold's retirement home, the assembly room at The Grandparents McGee's retirement community, and at the ward Christmas party. For the next month, the Johnson house was full of music and laughter as the crew Mark had gathered practiced their numbers.

Erin felt quietly proud as she, Linda, and Skipp sat by Harold watching the premiere show in early December. It started with a quartet of students from his school singing popular holiday songs while interacting with the audience. Next they passed out percussion instruments and led a sing-along. Then it was Hannah's turn. She delighted the oldsters by reciting *The Night Before Christmas*. The program ended with Mark and Melina playing Mark's arrangement of Christmas carols and then an appearance by Santa Claus—Jake in full costume and beard—followed by refreshments.

What Erin liked best about the program was that Mark had enrolled a whole troupe of helpers instead of making himself the star. This performance was more about serving others than impressing others. She saw in his eyes how the seniors' appreciation touched his heart in a way that accolades hadn't.

The surprise of the evening was when a woman showed up unannounced with a therapy dog dressed up as an elf. Hannah followed them around the whole time they were there, and in the days afterward she went back to lining up her dollies in a pretend hospital ward, putting a tie or cap on Rascal, and taking him to visit them.

After making her rounds one day, Hannah approached Erin. "Mom, we need to take Rascal to therapy dog class."

Erin barely looked up from her work. "I don't have the time for that. Sorry," she said.

"But Mom, the old people need him!"

When Hannah said that, the thought *Althea needs him* popped into Erin's mind. She didn't know where it came from, but she'd been trying to be more open to intuition and inspiration, so she signed up for the eight-week first-level course beginning in February. Then she bought Hannah what she wanted for Christmas: doggy dress-up items that Rascal could wear when she took him to visit her sick dollies.

ERIN

E-mail, December 30, 2000
Dear Friends,

I'm in trouble. Vince kissed me under the mistletoe. I mean, really kissed me! Oh, he is one good kisser. All of a sudden, things look a whole lot different. He's the same person he was before, still Vince the Vet who sometimes wears sports caps in the house and thinks a great vacation is spending a week at his cabin Up North, fishing. But that doesn't seem to matter anymore.

I don't understand what's happened, but he's all I think about day and night. Every cell of my body aches to be with him. It can't be love, can it? Maybe it's pheromones or the drive to perpetuate the species (except I'm too old, aren't I?). Oh, help! What am I going to do with myself?

Your Erin

ERIN

> E-mail, January 10, 2001
> Dear COBs,
>
> What a year this has been so far. First Caitlin's announcement
> that she's pregnant again—and the ultrasound picked up two
> heartbeats! She's due in July. Then the news that Cory's grand-
> father, Harold, had passed away in his sleep two months shy of
> one hundred.
>
> When Cory and I cleared out Harold's room at the retirement
> home, we found a bundle of Cory's mission letters. Cory doesn't
> have anything to do with the Church these days, so I was sur-
> prised to see tears in his eyes when he saw what they were. I
> thought he might talk—really talk—to me, but he didn't, and
> we seem farther apart than ever.
>
> A week later, Skipp called to say he's taking the whole family
> to Salt Lake for the 2002 Olympics! I thought he was joking,
> but his father's death got him thinking about the relative
> importance of things, and he decided to use on a family vaca-
> tion some of the money he's been salting away.
>
> He's already booked rooms for the last week, and he's working
> on getting tickets to one of the figure-skating events. I don't
> think it will really sink in until next year when the kids and I
> start packing our bags.
>
> Your Erin

WILLADENE

> E-mail, January 20, 2001
> Dear Erin,
>
> With all the losses our families have experienced, having some-
> thing to look forward to sounds good. The 2002 Olympics in Salt
> Lake City, huh? You're putting ideas in my head. We wouldn't

even have to rent a place to stay. That is, if I can pry Roger away from the Academy and Evvy away from her banjo and Mr. Flynn. She'll be thir*teen* soon and is taking it very seriously.

Love,
Deenie

P.S. I'm taking up the harmonica.

JUNEAU

Gideon turned thirteen at the beginning of February. Juneau was still trying to wrap her mind around having a teenager in the house again when she experienced her first hot flash. Since she was fifty-four, it wasn't unexpected. Still, it made her a little anxious. "I don't know how hot flashes and teenage hormones are going to mix," she wrote to Deenie and Erin.

Greg grinned when she told him. "You mean no more PMS?"

Juneau gave him an arch smile. "You wish. Maybe I'll just have it all the time now!"

"My cue to exit," he said, grabbing the lunch she'd prepared for him and heading off to work.

Despite hot flashes and hormones, life ran smoothly until one Saturday afternoon when Juneau answered the phone to hear Gideon's voice, hoarse with urgency. "Mom! You gotta come over here."

"Here" was Serenity's house. Gideon had been invited over to watch a video.

"Giddy, what's happened?" Juneau cried. "Are you all right?"

"Yes, but Brother Beldon hit Serenity. Her arm is hurt. Hurry."

Juneau's heart thumped. "I'm coming. Call 911 when I hang up."

"Sister Beldon already did," Gideon said.

Juneau tried to call Greg on her cell phone as she dashed to her car. No answer. She drove to the Beldon home as fast as she dared, asking herself, *What would Deenie do?*

The paramedics and police were already there when Juneau arrived. She ran to the door, but a burly cop blocked her way when she tried to enter.

"Sorry, ma'am," he said politely. "You can't go in."

"But my boy's in there," Juneau protested. "Gideon. He called me." She felt her face flush. The presence of so many uniforms unnerved her.

"It's my mom!" she heard Gideon cry from inside the house.

The policeman stepped aside, and Gideon came and flung his arms around her. "I saw the whole thing, and I told the policemen all about it," he whispered.

As she hugged him to her, Juneau saw Shan on the sofa, one hand holding a tissue to her bleeding nose and the other arm around Serenity, who sobbed softly as a paramedic examined her arm. Dex stood to one side flanked by two police officers. "Juneau!" he called. "It was an accident. You know I'd never hurt Shan and Serenity. Tell them, please!"

Juneau's fury made her words icy. "What I know is what I've seen. The bruises. The dark glasses. The *burn on her arm*." She put special emphasis on the last item.

"If you have information about this situation, we'll need to take your statement," the policeman nearest her said.

"I'll give it gladly," she said. Looking at Dex, she added, "I'm calling Bishop Palmer. I should have called him a long time ago."

Dex's face crumpled. "Juneau, don't do that. I didn't mean to hit Serenity. Shan and I were just having a little argument and . . ." When Juneau began pressing in Bishop Palmer's number, he started toward Shan but was blocked by one of the officers. "Sweetheart, tell her not to do this. Tell her it was an accident."

Juneau paused before hitting the last number, looking at Shan, who gazed steadily back at her. "Call him," Shan said.

The paramedic who'd been examining Serenity stood up. "Her arm is broken. We're taking her to the hospital."

Bishop Palmer met them all at the emergency room entrance. After Serenity was lifted onto a gurney and taken inside with Shan, he asked what had happened.

"Gideon saw it all," Juneau said.

The bishop turned to Gideon, who said, "Me and Serenity were watching a video when we heard some thumps and went to see what was happening. Brother Beldon shoved Sister Beldon against the wall, and Serenity yelled at him to stop. She ran up behind him and grabbed his arm. He went like this." Gideon made a backward sweeping motion with his right arm. "He hit Serenity in the face and knocked her over a coffee table and hurt her arm."

Bishop Palmer's expression was grave as he turned to Juneau. "Is this a regular thing with him, do you know?"

"He's hit Shan before," she confessed. "She pleaded with me not to tell anybody. But I should have told you, shouldn't I?"

Bishop Palmer nodded. "Yes, but it's too late for regrets now. The police will be holding Dex. Can you take Shan and Serenity home until we can get them admitted to Haven House? I'll ask them to alert you immediately if he gets out on bail."

"I'll be glad to," Juneau said. "For as long as necessary." She felt limp. This was such scary stuff. She'd read too many articles, heard too many stories, to believe Dex's problem would just clear up. But as Bishop Parker said, it was too late for regrets.

Serenity fell asleep the minute Shan and Juneau tucked her into one of the twin beds in Juneau's apple-tree guest room. Gideon asked if he could sit watch in case she stirred. "Remember how you stayed by my bed after I came home from having my head sewed up?" he said to Juneau. "It was nice to have you there."

She hugged him. "You may sit here as long as you wish."

The bruises on Shan's face had darkened by the time Juneau got her to sit down in the family room. The rest of her skin was pale, and her nose still leaked a slight trickle of blood. "I'll be all right," she said when Juneau handed her a tissue.

"I'm not so sure," Juneau said.

"Really," Shan insisted. "This was a wake-up call. I should have listened to you a long time ago, my friend."

"Yes. You should have."

Shan ducked her head. "I loved him. I still love him. But I have to put him out of my life—and Serenity's."

"Can you do it?" Juneau asked.

"I don't know," Shan answered honestly. "I'll need your backup. Your strength." She paused. "I wish I could be like you, Juneau. You're strong, you know what you want, you stand up for what you know is right, you know where you're going. You're . . ." Shan searched for a word.

"A COB," Juneau said. "A Crusty Old Broad." Briefly she told Shan about how she and Deenie and Erin had met Gabby and adopted as their goal becoming like her, a self-described Crusty Old Broad, a triumphant survivor of all life had thrown at her.

"What does it take to join the club?" Shan asked.

"You made a start when you called 911," Juneau said. "Now you need to follow through on what you've decided about Dex."

E-mail, February 12, 2001
Dear Deenie and Erin,

Dex Beldon has been locked up where he belongs. He must love Serenity very much, because he made a plea bargain (pleading to assault and battery and other charges) so she wouldn't be asked to testify about what happened. He's also facing a Church disciplinary council.

Shan has signed on to become a Crusty Old Broad. Before she married Dex she was a paralegal, so she's convinced she can support herself and Serenity. The ironic thing is that she met Dex when the lawyer she worked for was his defense attorney in a previous case with his first wife. She knew what he was when she married him. She says she was positive she could change him. Aaargh!

Shan is looking to me for strength. As Gabby was to me, I am now to Shan. Can you believe it?

                         Love,
                         Juneau

P.S. Deenie, thanks for the advice you gave when you called. Shan says she'll make sure she knows when Dex is up for parole, just like you do with Rod Tulley.

ERIN
E-mail, February 15, 2001
Dear Juneau,

I've been thinking about you not believing that someone would think you are strong. I love you dearly, but it's time you dropped that "What, me?" shtick when someone says you're a strong woman. It seems that either you're being disingenuous or there's something inside that keeps you from seeing it yourself. What could that be?

You can pin my ears back if you think I'm out of line, but isn't part of COBhood being willing to risk anger to say something that might make a difference?

Your Erin

WILLADENE

Every February when Evvy had a birthday, Deenie found herself brooding over those terrible months of depression after her youngest child's birth. She wondered what surprises were yet to be opened from that package. Roger reminded her to stick with *what is*, not *what if*. Miss B quoted scripture: "Love thy neighbor as thyself," stressing the word *thyself*. And Luvy, the Relief Society president, said to listen to Miss B.

Deenie was worrying the subject like a dog with a bone when a special delivery letter arrived from Elizabeth addressed to Mrs. Willadene Rasmussen. Because Elizabeth was prone to phone calls and quick e-mails, the fat envelope Deenie signed for filled her with dread.

She put off the reading of it until she had taken care of Bear, showered, and dressed for the day. Then she sat down on the porch and opened the letter.

Dear Mother,

When Dani and Paul lost their baby girl last fall, I stopped what I was doing and took stock. I asked myself where I was going and what I wanted out of my life. Adventure? Family? Love? Fame? With the help of Grandma Margaret, Great Aunt Stella, who moved in with us last week, and a dozen other dear people, I have come to some serious conclusions.

I want it all. But first I want what you and Grandma Margaret and Dani have. I want a man who stays and a relationship based on temple covenants.

I thought of how Dad stayed after Evvy was born and you were in the hospital. I was afraid he might leave, too, but he promised me he never would. He said loving you wasn't just about the good times, it was about the bad times, too, and it was about forever.

Then you came home, and it was hard and messy and ugly and wonderful, but you and Dad both stayed in the ring. I could see how much you loved each other—with a love that was far more than romance. It was about serving and abiding and wanting what's best for each other and sharing the gospel together and so many other things I can't list them.

But I want them, and I am starting my plan to acquire them by putting in my mission papers and receiving my endowment. And no matter what happens after that, I am holding out for forever. I almost chose a different path with Brad, but when it came right down to it I couldn't say yes. It hurt something awful.

So Mother, dear, and Daddy, too, you say I've been a blessing, and I know I've been a brat. The truth of who I am lies somewhere in between, anchored in the faith and love you've shown me.

I love you and Daddy loads.

Elizabeth

Deenie felt a split second of sorrow for that awful time after Evvy was born, but the letter was about how they'd grown since then. Seeing herself as Elizabeth now saw her was the blessing Deenie had needed. She put the letter in her pocket, walked down the hill to the administration building, and stepped into the hall leading to Roger's new office suite. She caught him as he hurried out, carrying a pile of folders.

Deenie fell into step next to him, nodding at the folders. "More applications for assistant administrator?"

"Yes. I think Marsha's the one for the job, but you know the board," Roger said.

When they turned the corner down a smaller hall, Deenie moved closer to Roger. "Have I ever thanked you for sticking with me during that terrible time after Evvy was born?"

Roger looked at her curiously. "Yes, you have. But I never mind hearing it again."

"Thank you for staying when a lesser man would have hightailed it for the hills." Deenie tucked Elizabeth's letter in the breast pocket of his suit jacket. "Read it when you have a private moment," she said, giving it a pat. Then she kissed him soundly on the lips to the appreciative hoot of a group of students emerging from Marsha's office.

"Way to go, Mrs. R," Leo Flynn hollered. Much to Deenie's delight, a faint hint of blush colored Roger's cheeks. But when he threaded his way through the boys, she saw he was smiling.

Deenie smiled to herself as she walked down the corridor. It was turning out to be a very good day after all. Maybe she'd have that heart-to-heart to completely clear the air with Delia she'd been promising herself.

The talk had to be postponed. That afternoon Ferris suffered another heart attack and was rushed to the hospital.

ERIN

Erin carefully picked her way across the icy theater parking lot, grateful for Vince's steadying arm around her waist. "I'm glad you suggested we see *Finding Forrester*. It's so uplifting."

"Maybe we could have a movie night with your kids when it comes out on DVD," Vince said.

"I think they'd like that."

As he helped her into the car, Erin mused at how easily Vince had slipped into their lives. Through the back door, so to speak, which Hannah had held wide open. He'd been to dinner several times and once to family home evening, which gave Erin a chance to see him interact with Mark and Kayla. They liked him well enough, but Erin sensed that Kayla worried about being disloyal to Cory.

Vince started up the car and then cleared his throat. "My mom's beginning to think you're avoiding her and Dad, and I don't know what to tell her. Could I pick you up after church tomorrow and take you over there for dessert?"

Erin hesitated. She'd been reluctant to meet his parents, afraid that they might not like her, or worse, they might like her too much. But now her reasons seemed rather pitiful. "Yes, I'd be glad to meet them."

She liked Russ and Anne immediately. Russ had the girth and gimpy knees of the former college football player he was. A retired airline pilot, he loved outdoor activities, War II history, and anything to do with airplanes. Vince's mother, Anne, was a foot shorter than Russ and trim. She kept her house very orderly, with a separate room for her scrapbooking and sewing projects. In her free time she volunteered at a Crisis Center. A *Lutheran version of Molly Mormon,* Erin thought.

Dinner was enjoyable, and Erin had begun to think the afternoon was going well when Vince's sisters Suzanne, Margo, and Karen showed up with their husbands and children. They filled the house with such noise and activity she couldn't keep names and family units straight. The single impression she left with was how much Vince loved his nieces and nephews. And how crazy they were about him.

When she e-mailed the COBs about her encounter with the Gerlachs, she ended with:

> On the way home, Vince said he regretted not having children and still hoped to have some one day. Hah! He knows I'm forty-three, so he must not be thinking of having them with me!

JUNEAU

The week after the incident with Dex Beldon, Juneau told Clyde all about it after class. Shan hadn't come that night, and Clyde asked if she was okay.

Juneau motioned for him to sit on the chair next to her teacher's desk in the classroom after the other students left. Because Clyde had become a good friend to Shan as well as to her, she told him everything. "Since Dex hurt Serenity, Shan knows what a serious problem he has," she said.

Clyde nodded thoughtfully. "Do you think she'll gut up now and dump the guy?"

Juneau smiled at his phrasing. "If I have anything to do with it, she will."

"She's lucky to have a friend like you," Clyde said. "You're a fine example of a strong woman."

"Hah! That's twice in one week that someone's told me I'm strong. I guess I should apply Mrs. Jarvis's writing rule—if it's said three times, you know it's important and should pay attention."

Clyde nodded. "What about the little girl? How has all this affected her?"

Juneau told him about Serenity's fake runaways. "It's been devastating. Gideon has been great about helping her, though. What he's been through has made him sensitive to others' pain. He sat with her through the first night after her arm was broken. The next day he and she sat talking for a long time, with Numbtail stretched across both their laps like a bridge."

"Numbtail?" Clyde looked puzzled.

"Cat," Juneau reminded him. "Gideon told you how we rescued him from some nasty boys."

"Ah, yes." He steepled his fingers under his chin. "Numbtail, Gideon, and Serenity have a lot in common." He was silent, seemingly deep in thought. Then he said, "Juneau, I have a suggestion that might be helpful."

"And that is . . . ?"

"Let's call it a therapy group. I'll be going there Saturday, and I'm inviting you all to join me." He smiled. "I think you'll enjoy it."

E-mail, March 1, 2001
Dear Deenie and Erin,

Here's the follow-up you requested when I phoned you about Dex Beldon's meltdown.

We're all going to a therapy group Clyde suggested. We call it the Barker Clinic, and its practitioners all have big ears and cold noses! Dogs, if you haven't guessed. Abandoned dogs. Mistreated dogs. *Rescued* dogs. They all have scars themselves, as we do. Yet they face life with enthusiasm and joy, when they are given a chance.

Molly, the earth angel who owns the dog rescue kennel, always needs people to pay attention to the animals. We spent most of the afternoon there walking dogs, playing Frisbee with them, petting and talking to them, or just sitting quietly in the shade with a warm, happy presence, or maybe two or three, at our sides. Serenity and Gideon can hardly wait to go again.

I think the Barker Clinic will go a long way in helping to heal what ails us.

Love,
Juneau

ERIN

E-mail, March 19, 2001
Dear COBs,

Juneau, Vince loves your Barker Clinic! He's seen the healing power of dogs when he takes Curly Dude to visit children in the hospital.

My sister never ceases to amaze me. She just put earnest money down on a house. Without asking Sam first!

It's one of the small Victorians built for railroad workers in the historic Milwaukee Avenue District east of the Mississippi. She renovated it for the owner a couple of years ago and told him to call her if he ever wanted to sell.

I can't believe she would do that. Sam's easygoing, but it must bother him when Caitlin charges ahead without consulting him. There's a line that says, "This is too much." I hope she never finds out where it's drawn.

The thing is, I'm an awful lot like Caitlin. I've been making decisions on my own for seven years, and I like being in charge. If Vince the Vet and I ever get serious, will I be able to share decision-making with him? I wonder.

I've finally met his parents and sisters and their families. It was clear they were sizing me up as in-law material. From the looks on their faces, I passed.

Your Erin

P.S. Deenie, how is Ferris doing? And Delia?

Chapter 19

WILLADENE

Deenie did her best to rub the tension from Roger's forehead after a particularly difficult day. "I had no idea how much Ferris was smoothing my way with the board," he said wearily. "With him completely out of the picture since the bypass surgery, the board is stalling on every request I put in front of them. They're even balking at hiring Marsha to fill my old job, though she is clearly the most qualified person we've interviewed."

"Isn't there anything more you can do?" Deenie asked. She was as eager for a resolution as Roger was. He was burning the candle at both ends, and she and Evvy were spending long evenings home alone.

"Keep interviewing more candidates until the board figures out on their own that no one else has Marsha's qualifications," he said.

Deenie wished with all her heart that she had the kind of pull with the directors Delia had, or that Delia would step in and ease the way for Marsha. But that was out of the question. Delia hadn't left Ferris's side since he'd returned home from the hospital. That afternoon, Deenie decided it was time to return the chicken soup favor and ask Delia for advice.

Delia burst out laughing when she saw Deenie standing on the doorstep with a soup pot in her arms. "We really are two peas in a pod, aren't we?" she said and invited Deenie in.

Deenie offered Delia the soup along with an apology for being so contrary when they'd first met. Delia accepted the soup and the apology, and the two women sat down at Delia's elegant kitchen table and talked over the past.

"I guess I thought what I needed to do here was what I'd done at home," Deenie said sheepishly. "Make lists. Take charge."

Delia smiled. "There's nothing wrong with that approach. I'm partial to it myself. But in this case. . . ."

"Someone else was already doing it?" Deenie said.

"I could have been nicer about it all," Delia acknowledged. "But I was already worried about Ferris's health, and I wasn't going to put up with anything that added the least stress to his life."

Deenie understood. She was already feeling protective of Roger as he struggled under the weight of his new responsibilities. She'd confront anyone who made life more difficult for him.

The afternoon wound down as the conversation turned to more mundane topics. Then Delia walked Deenie to the front door, saying, "Please tell Roger to come and visit when he can. Ferris needs the distraction."

"As soon as all this hiring fiasco clears up, I know Roger would love to spend time with him," Deenie said.

Delia paused with a thoughtful look on her face. "Let me make a few phone calls and see what I can do. Thank you again for the soup," she paused and gave Deenie a kind smile, "and the apology."

Deenie left the Tucker mansion feeling as though she had taken a big step toward COBhood—owning up to and cleaning up after your own mistakes. *I'll add that to the Keeping Book,* she thought.

That evening dinner was interrupted by a ringing phone. It was Elizabeth announcing she had received her mission call to the Romania Bucharest Mission.

"That's so far away," Deenie gasped. Then immediately changed tack. "What do you need us to do and when's the farewell?"

"Remember me in your prayers—and I'm not having one."

"What? Why?" Deenie sputtered into the speakerphone.

"I want to keep my focus on my calling and not be distracted by what would end up being a big family reunion."

"I can understand that," Roger said.

The conversation turned to the myriad tasks that needed to be completed to prepare for a foreign mission. All of which, it seemed to Deenie, were going to be handled by someone other than her.

"Don't worry, Mom," Elizabeth said. "I'm a grownup. I've got it covered. But I will need you to write me tons of letters filled with love and inspirational thoughts."

Later that evening she wrote the news to the COBs, adding:

After Roger and Evvy turned in for the night. I watched an old episode of Star Trek while I was eating and blubbering. There was a scene where a new, completely computerized Enterprise was going on its shakedown mission. Because Captain Kirk supposedly wasn't needed, he was snidely referred to as Captain Dunsel (a part on a ship that has no use).

That's exactly how I was feeling. Obsolete in my own family. Elizabeth has grown into adulthood without us. Addie and even Brad Donaldson have had as great an effect on her amazing maturity as we have. It's an odd feeling to realize you gave birth to this remarkable human and raised her and loved her but in the end she is who she chooses to be.

Dunsel me,
Deenie

Two days later the board finally hired Marsha as assistant headmaster and Richard Harker, an eager young man with a degree in public administration, to fill her previous position. Deenie, grateful to Delia and Ferris for their help and encouragement, spent the afternoon in the kitchen at Gobb Hill making a heart-healthy version of Pat's hazelnut chocolate torte as a thank-you.

ERIN
E-mail, May 17, 2001
Dear Juneau and Deenie,

Rascal, Hannah, and I have passed the first level of therapy dog training with flying colors. We're taking the second level now, where we learn how to handle situations that might come up when we visit nursing homes or hospitals.

Rascal's already working his magic. I took him with me when I gave Althea the April visiting teaching message. She usually stands in the doorway, but Rascal enticed her out on the front steps, and we talked while she petted him. I've taken him over once since then at her request. Her caseworker drove up while we were there. She watched Althea with Rascal and said, "I think you need a dog!"

There was a hook, though. The caseworker said the house would need to be deemed safe for a dog. Like the house is "safe" for Althea now but not for an animal? Althea said she'd do what it takes to have a dog of her own. We'll see.

Your Erin

P.S. When Vince came over for a movie night, he introduced us and The Jays to a classic named *Harvey*, starring Jimmy Stewart and an invisible rabbit. It's our new favorite.

WILLADENE

"You are one handsome man," Deenie said as she did one final brush across the shoulders of Roger's new dark blue suit. He was dressed to officiate at the first graduation of his administration. Deenie thought he looked exactly like a headmaster of a prestigious private school should, even down to the gray hair that was beginning to show at his temples. "See you at the ceremony," she said and gave him a kiss.

Roger smiled, picked up the folder containing his speech, and walked out the door with exaggerated dignity, which left Deenie laughing. Later, as proud Deenie watched Roger hand diplomas and awards to the graduates, she thought of all the years of study and work and choices that had brought them here. And she felt at peace with the decision that had brought them to Gainsville.

Later in the day, after the reception for the graduating students, Deenie sat on the balcony of the apartment overlooking the gardens. She thought about packages. Putting them together and opening them. How when she'd put Deenie in Charge to rest, she'd discovered Deenie the Careless hiding in the wings. She hoped she was putting together different packages after learning from Miss B what constituted openhearted, no-holds-barred, Christian kindness.

She had a deep need to share her feelings but not with friends in Florida. With Juneau and Erin, her almost sisters who knew the *before* Deenie and would value the changes she had made. In the quiet of the evening she wrote:

With all the changes in our lives for the better, it feels like fate has conspired to make me grateful for the move to Florida. I'd

gotten so stuck in a rut in Wellsville, especially in the way I saw
the world and the people in it. I've come to the conclusion that
there is something new to learn every day, if you're willing to
look for the lessons and accept that teachers come in all sizes,
colors, and levels of education.

Missing you and chomping at the bit for our visit to Williamsburg,

Deenie

P.S. In an effort to live my life with greater faith and less I'm-
in-control-of the-world, I'm trying to give up my lists!

JUNEAU

E-mail, June 23, 2001
Hi, Deenie and Erin,

Greg, Gideon, and I flew to Denver for Nicole's graduation
from medical school. She's now officially Dr. Caldwell! She's
staying in Colorado for the summer to start an early internship
at a hospital in Pueblo. She tried to make us think she's happy.
Maybe she is. She's dedicating herself to her work, which she
loves. She's not dating. Says she doesn't have time.

Love,
Juneau

Juneau was pleased that Greg enjoyed walking the dogs at the Barker
Clinic fully as much as Gideon and Serenity and Shan did. She didn't ask
what problems he might be working through. Greg was a lot like his
parents—kind, loyal, loving, but very private. He saw his parents, who
lived quietly in Arizona and had no desire to travel, even less often than
she saw hers. They loved one another, Juneau was sure, but there was
definitely lack of communication between them.

Juneau had thought for some time that she and Greg had the same
problem. They'd been married now for more than thirty years, they'd
raised a family and a half, they'd had successes and failures, they'd
rejoiced together and cried together. That should have built a strong
bond between them, but somehow, their words often fell flat. Unheard or

not understood. Different languages. Me Juneau, I speak woman. You Greg. . . .

One day she heard a talk show guest say that one of the best ways to convey your love to your mate was to give him/her your undivided attention. Because she was going off to Williamsburg with Deenie and Erin in September, Juneau figured she owed Greg some time. One evening she said, "Greg, I want to talk."

He gave her a quizzical look. "What about?"

"About you," she said. "You work so hard, and between the two of us, we've made enough money to do just about anything we want. Is there something you'd really, really, really like to do? Take a cruise and dance under the stars on the fantail of the ship? Go hiking in the Tetons? Maybe white-water rafting?"

"Did that with the boys when I was Scoutmaster."

"Did you like it?"

"Loved it."

"Would you like to do the same thing with *me?*"

"I didn't think you cared for that kind of thing."

"I might. If you leave your computers behind, I'll leave my writing behind. We can go wherever you want, do whatever you like. How about it?"

He looked at her warily. "Did you have a Relief Society lesson on pleasing the man in your life?"

"It's my own idea," she said with a grin. "I figured you were due for some pleasing."

"There *is* something I'd like to do." He turned so he was looking full at her. "I'd like to go to the Winter Olympics in Salt Lake City next February. A whole week of events, especially the downhill skiing."

"What?" Juneau squawked.

He grabbed her hands, enthusiasm lighting his face. "Juney, I wasn't going to mention this, but one of the guys we're doing a major project for owns a vacation house outside Park City. The people who booked it for the Olympics just cancelled, and he's looking for someone to take it over. It's ours, if we want it."

The thought of the crowds and the noise and sitting in the cold watching downhill skiing gave Juneau a headache, but the light in Greg's face was something she hadn't seen for a long time.

"Call him," she said. "Tell him we'll take it."

He jumped to his feet, and for the second time in recent memory, she saw him leap into the air and click his heels together.

ERIN

E-mail, June 28, 2001
Dear COBs,

Caitlin had twin ginger-haired girls yesterday, Grace and Hope. All three are doing fine. The twins will be coming home to the Victorian, which Sam loves as much as Caitlin does.

We've had two graduations this month: Kayla from high school, and Rascal, Hannah, and I from level two of therapy dog training!

Kayla's headed for the University of Minnesota this fall. She's already filled many of her basic requirements with the classes she's taken there the last two years, so she can focus on her art classes. Rascal, Hannah, and I are doing an internship. Our first official outing in the company of a trainer was to the retirement home where Harold lived. The residents' appreciation made me feel like I was the one being served.

Here's good news: Althea's caseworker has begun bringing a little "pocket dog," a chihuahua/toy fox terrier mix, when she visits. With the dog in hand, Althea has been able to go farther afield than ever before. Maybe one day she'll be able to do it without her caseworker. Wouldn't that be something!

Erin

P.S. Deenie, no way would I give up my lists! I couldn't manage without them.

That summer, Erin and Vince often took their dogs for walks around Lake Harriet. For some reason, they felt freer to explore relationship issues when they were in the company of Rascal and Curly Dude. They talked about how they would handle finances, division of household chores, parenting. Hypothetically, of course.

Erin found Vince's approach aggravatingly simple. Do what best serves the needs of those involved. Show love.

"Give me something more specific," she said as they walked along the north side of the lake one day. "Like, how would you create a relationship with Kayla and Mark?"

"The same way I would if I got a new dog," Vince said without even a hint of a grin. "Establish who's pack leader. Set clear boundaries. Create a safe environment. Make sure they have what they need. Give them tasks to do and acknowledge when they've completed them."

Erin stopped short. "You'd treat my kids the way you'd treat a dog?"

"Well, yeah." He gave her a wry smile. "Except the issue of pack leader would be tricky. You and Cory are co-leaders. Having me in the picture would confuse things."

"Maybe not so much. Their feelings for Cory are . . . complicated."

He lifted one eyebrow questioningly.

She'd been waiting for the right time to tell him about Cory. This was it. She kept her eyes on Curly and Rascal as she explained that she'd stayed with Cory—and had Hannah with him—after she knew the truth. "I suppose you think less of me."

He lifted her chin and looked into her eyes. "No. I think you're a complicated and intriguing woman. A good woman. You and Cory have done an amazing job of raising your children."

Erin's step was much lighter as they came around the south side of the lake. She chattered away, telling Vince about the little elf door in the base of a tree they were nearing. "People leave gifts and letters for the elf. He answers them when he's in residence. He goes away for the winter, you know."

"Really. Have you ever left a letter?"

"Hannah has. She wanted to know what elves like to eat. She got the cutest letter back—our elf prefers nuts, cheese, and beer." Erin knelt at the base of the tree. "Here it is."

He joined her in examining the cunningly fitted door. "Does anyone know who the elfmeister is?"

"Nope. Knowing would take the fun out of it, don't you think?"

She reached for Vince's hand as they continued the last part of their circuit. It was strong and warm, and his sturdy presence made her feel protected. Against reason, she loved him. Years earlier, she'd broken up with Ben the dermatologist because she knew relationships didn't stand still. Was she willing to go where this relationship was headed?

When they'd completed their circuit, Vince leaned against his pickup, idly stroking Curly Dude's head. "How about I come to your ward tomorrow?"

"If you do, everyone will think we're serious."

"Aren't we?"

The expression in his eyes made her catch her breath. "Would you take 'I think so' for an answer?"

"Coming from you, that's as good as a yes."

E-mail, July 1, 2001
Dear COBs,

This morning, Vince left for a week at his cabin in the North Woods. I'm already missing him. I don't know what draws us together, unless it's a simple case of opposites attract. Whatever it is, he's found his way into my heart.

Your Erin

WILLADENE
E-mail, July 11, 2001
Dear COBs,

Equation for the day: Deenie in Charge + No Lists + Midsummer Faculty and Board Wives' Association Planning Meeting = Disaster. Said disaster averted by the kind rescue of Deenie-Deer-in-the-Headlights by Delia-Does-It-Better.

"There are lists, and then there are lists," Delia says. "Unless you're a Mentat from *Dune*, bring a planner." Who knew she read sci-fi? What a gal.

Egg on my face but still standing,
Deenie

In the months after Gobb Hill was closed to public tours, Rasmussen family life trickled its way out of the apartment and down the stairs into the rest of the house. Unloading the groceries in the main floor kitchen was so much easier for Deenie than lugging them up to the apartment. Evvy decided she needed more room and moved into one of the guest suites. Roger and Deenie did the same. The third guest room became Deenie's office. And before Deenie knew it, the apartment was emptied of all their personal things and set aside for guest use.

Deenie kept the main rooms of the house company-ready at all times, so she noticed immediately when Roger started leaving piles of paperwork on end tables, on the dining room table, or on the bottom step of the staircase. It was obvious that he was distracted.

He came home from his school office the week before the new year was to start carrying a bag of mail from parents asking questions about the Academy.

"Shouldn't Mr. Harker or Marsha be helping you with those?" Deenie asked as Roger, who sat at the kitchen table, opened the twentieth letter.

"They could, but I need a handle on how parents are feeling," he said.

Deenie began to wonder if the Deenie-in-Control-of-Everything syndrome she was working so hard to get rid of was contagious. Now that Roger had the reins of the Academy in his hands, he seemed reluctant to relinquish any control, even to Marsha, no matter how competent she was.

"Here's something different," Roger said, holding up an envelope. "It's from Brad Donaldson to both of us. It was delivered to my office by mistake."

Deenie opened the envelope, wondering what Brad could have to say to them since Elizabeth had turned him down. She dumped out the contents. On top was a photograph of Brad standing in front of the Perth Australia Temple. The accompanying note read:

> When I was in Perth in May, I attended the open house in honor of Sunny and Elizabeth and the family who have been so kind to me. I was touched and amazed at the beauty of the temple. I have a deeper understanding of why Elizabeth made

the choices she did. I would like to write and tell her so if you think it would be all right.

"I think Elizabeth would be pleased to hear from him," Roger said. "As long as he doesn't distract her from her work," Deenie added.

E-mail, September 1, 2001
Dear COBS,

Elizabeth has jumped into her mission experience with her usual enthusiasm and already feels connected to the people there. She's sent us a list of things to collect for the children in her area. Our ward is pitching in. Would you like to help, too?

She closed her letter by sharing a beautiful testimony of the work. Then she added a P.S. that she'd received a card from Brad wishing her well on her mission. It made her cry. That made me cry.

I don't dare make a comment on choices or consequences around here. I guess I've overdone it. Evvy swears she'll run out of the house screaming if she hears either word one more time. Maybe it's time to start practicing silence again.

Bear and I have had a busy summer with search and rescue. (Anything over two calls a season is busy, and we've had three.) We are both suffering from knee problems, and the vet has suggested we consider being on the reserve list instead of active. He's put Bear on meds for pain and for his joints. My doctor has done the same for me, but we are stilling running. Bear won't stand for anything less.

I'm already packing for Williamsburg. See you soon!

Love,
Deenie

Chapter 20

Deenie laughed at the expressions on Erin's and Juneau's faces as she unloaded the Southern treats she'd brought to Williamsburg in her carry-on. Butter biscuits and homemade mango chutney from Miss B. Black-eyed peas. A special collection of Southern spices. Boiled peanuts and an assortment of barbeque sauces from the Cluck You Chicken Stand.

"That's its name, honestly," Deenie said.

Sitting at the table in their condo, the COBs nibbled on the rich biscuits while catching up on family news. Then they talked about what they wanted to see in the area.

"Colonial Williamsburg, of course," Juneau said. "I absolutely want to go on a ghost tour. That's why I came."

"I want to see the mansions on the James River and the furniture-making demonstrations," Erin said.

"I don't know what I want to see, but . . ." Deenie pulled out a roll of receipt paper and gave it a flip with her wrist. It streamed over the table showing a numbered, handwritten list. "Roger was on the phone with Ferris last night, making a list of every historical site they thought we should visit."

"How many weeks do we have at this condo?" Erin asked, laughing.

"Don't worry," Deenie said, feeling deep pleasure at being in the company of her friends. "The top thing on my list is to see you."

They spent Monday morning in Colonial Williamsburg, where Erin volunteered to try the hand lathe at the furniture-making demonstration and Deenie set off a security alarm in the textile exhibit by leaning too close to an antique quilted undergarment while trying to count the stitches per inch. That evening they attended a ghost tour, during which Juneau took notes at a furious pace by lamplight.

Tuesday they planned to visit Jamestown after breakfast, for which they drove to a restaurant famous for Southern cooking. After drooling over the menu, they ordered biscuits with red-eye gravy, real Virginia ham, and cheesy grits. Deenie asked for hot sauce to spike her tomato juice.

They were enjoying their meal when they heard a waitress say, "Did you hear that a plane hit one of the Twin Towers in New York?" Not long after, a shout of disbelief came from the kitchen area. A man burst through the doors, hollering, "Another plane's hit the other tower. They're both burning!"

The waitress who was refilling their water glasses cried out, "My brother works at the World Trade Center." Her hands shook as she set the pitcher on the table and pulled out her cell phone. "All circuits are busy," she said. She dropped into the empty seat next to Deenie, who put a comforting hand on her arm.

A manager came into the dining area and set up a portable TV. Customers and employees alike were riveted by the images on the screen. Deenie was still trying to absorb what she was seeing about the Twin Towers when news of a third plane hitting the Pentagon flashed on the screen, followed by footage of the south tower collapsing.

Is this war? Deenie thought, terrified. Her mind flew to Carl, her son in uniform. He could be in harm's way right now. Her heart sank. Holding fast to Erin's and Juneau's hands as the images repeated, she whispered a fervent prayer, "Lord, keep my Carl safe."

They hurried back to their condo, hoping to reach their families, but jammed phone circuits made calls and e-mails impossible. They paced, watched the endlessly looping TV coverage, sat with arms around each other for comfort, and talked about all the things they wished they'd said but hadn't.

"I hate it that we're here and our families are thousands of miles away," Juneau said.

"Me, too." Erin pulled them closer. "But if we have to be stranded, there's no one else I'd rather be stranded with."

"Amen," Deenie said, but she didn't want to be stranded, no matter with whom. She wanted to be doing something.

By Wednesday morning, Deenie couldn't stomach any more TV coverage or inactivity. "I've either got to get away from this or move toward it. I don't have Bear with me, but there are things I can do, and I feel I should be there, doing them."

She dialed the number of the first fire station listed in Williamsburg and identified herself and her training. "They're looking for teams," she said when she hung up. "They need me and Bear."

She dialed Roger's number, hoping against hope that the call would go through. To her amazement, it did. After reassuring Roger they were fine, Deenie explained the situation and requested that he arrange to get Bear and her equipment up to Williamsburg where she would connect with a team from that area.

She could hear the intake of breath. "Honey, I know where your heart is and how you feel about finding the lost, but we're lost here without you. You've got a daughter frantic for her mother, a husband wanting his wife, and all the boys for whom you are the stand-in mother asking when you are coming home."

Deenie hung up the phone and said, "Roger wants me to go home. I guess there are other places where I have something to offer that's needed."

Erin looked at her as if she were dopey. "Well, duh!"

Ten minutes, half a box of tissues, and numerous calls to several airlines later, they realized that none of them was going home that day. Needing distraction, they decided a quiet trip up the James River would help them calm down.

Being on the smooth, glassy water bordered by tall rushes with bright sun overhead and the sound of birdcalls in the air was exactly what Deenie needed. They all found it comforting that in the midst of cataclysmic change, nature offered sanctuary and healing.

During a lull in the tour guide's commentary, Erin said, "Deenie, remember way back when we sat in your orchard and I asked how you can know if you love someone and if marrying that person is the right thing?"

"Of course," Deenie said. "You were wondering if you should marry Cory."

"And now you're wondering if you should marry Vince!" Juneau clapped her hands.

"Since yesterday, I've been thinking how much I would regret it if I didn't tell Vince I love him," Erin said. "If I do that, he'll ask The Question. I know he will."

"And?" Deenie asked.

Erin gave a helpless grin. "I'll say yes."

The excitement of Erin calling Vince that night brightened their spirits, but it wasn't enough to quiet their anxiety. As the hours went by, it became clear that they all wanted to go home, *needed* to go home. The nearest of their homes was Gainesville. They called the rental car company to change the drop-off point, packed their bags, and drove through the night.

ERIN

Three days after the COBs arrived in Gainesville, both Erin and Juneau were able to get flights home. When Erin arrived in the Twin Cities, her children swarmed over her. They sat with knees, shoulders, and hands touching, telling how it was the day the videos played over and over on TV and the heart of the nation changed.

"Where would we live if you didn't come home?" Hannah asked.

"Don't worry about that, Hannah Banana. I'm here. I'll—"

Mark interrupted. "Don't say you'll always be here. It's a promise you can't keep."

Hannah made a small sound and started sucking her thumb. Erin pulled the girl onto her lap. "I'm here now, and I'll do everything I can to make sure I'm always here." But Hannah wasn't reassured. When it was time for bed, she insisted Erin lie down beside her until she fell asleep.

Back downstairs, Erin asked Kayla and Mark to join her in the living room. Two months shy of sixteen, Mark was growing into his father's good looks. It was especially noticeable since he'd begun wearing contacts. But now his handsome face was sullen.

"Mark, you were right about my not being able to promise I'll always be here. But Hannah's only seven. She doesn't need to hear that life is uncertain. Or unsafe."

"But it is!"

Erin prayed to find the right words. "None of us knows what's going to happen the next hour or the next minute, son. We can either let uncertainty paralyze us or trust God and move forward."

"You can say that after what's happened?" Mark demanded.

"Oh, grow up," Kayla said. "If you want a guarantee, buy a vacuum."

Mark whirled on her. "You of all people should be angry. You didn't deserve to get blindsided by those idiots on bikes."

"*C'est la vie.*" Kayla's voice was even. "You have to deal with what comes, whether you deserve it or not. Because that's all there is."

"I guess you do have to be philosophical about it," Mark retorted, "since you can't skate anymore."

Kayla gasped, and Erin cried, "Mark Johnson! Are you completely without empathy or did you mean to hurt your sister?"

All the anger drained out of Mark's stance. His eyes glittered with sadness and confusion.

"Apologize, now," Erin insisted. "And you better mean it."

Mark touched Kayla's shoulder. "Sorry, sis. I didn't mean what I said. I wish the accident had never happened."

Kayla gave a slight nod, but she refused to look at him.

"Kayla, please. You're my sister, and I love you." His voice cracked. "The thing is, everyone loves you, no matter what. I wish they felt that way about me."

Kayla wiped her eyes with the back of her hand. "I do, you silly goof!" The two held each other, murmuring things Erin couldn't quite hear. But she'd heard enough to know that underneath his arrogant façade, her son was just a little kid, hungry to be accepted and loved.

It was almost midnight when Erin called Vince, as she'd promised she would. "I'm back and I'm fine, but I need to see you. Can you come over?"

"I'll be there before you hang up the phone."

She waited for him on the front step, glad for the deep quiet of night. On the airplane, she'd imagined a heartfelt reunion with her kids, but the reality had been exhausting. Flesh-and-blood children had sticky issues. Life tossed up unexpected obstacles. You had to keep taking the next step, doing the best you could, making changes when they were called for, and when necessary, forgiving and accepting. Love demanded every-thing one had, but was there any other real choice?

When Vince pulled up, Erin tore across the lawn and into his arms. She kissed him as she'd always wanted to, giving in to the yearning and need that had built up over the summer.

When they came up for breath Vince smiled broadly. "When do we get married?"

"Slow down, buckaroo. I thought another question was supposed to come before that one."

He grinned. "You must mean the Will You Marry Me question. Do I really have to ask it?"

"Absolutely," Erin said. "When Hannah wants to know how you pro-posed, I want to be able to tell her you got down on one knee."

"What about when a child of our own asks that question?"

The words tumbled from her mouth of their own accord. "That, too."

Joy lit up his face. "Then I'd better do it right."

JUNEAU

E-mail, September 20, 2001
Dear Deenie and Erin,

Congratulations on your engagement, Erin! I'm thrilled for you and your Vince and so glad to hear that something good has come of this disaster.

My family all gathered here on Monday night to give thanks for my safe return. I cried the whole time! It's heartbreakingly reas-suring to be back home in my familiar world, now when every-thing is so crazy. I watch the rescue operations at Ground Zero on TV, and I weep for all those people who were killed and for their families who must face the loss. It's like a disaster movie, but we're not sitting safely in a theater, knowing we can leave the disaster once we exit. We're living it, if only on the fringes. But even the fringes don't seem safe any more.

Erin, Misty brought EJ for my welcome home. We had a few minutes to talk together about what it's like being far from home and dealing with terrible things. I think she was missing her family, and being with us gave her a sense of belonging.

I get the feeling that she left Minnesota looking for something. (Shades of Misty! Maybe that's what they have in common.) She hasn't found it yet, though she *has* found a better job. She's working in an office now, thanks to Misty having taught her how to use Microsoft Office Suite. She said she's also taking some classes at a community college.

As always, she spent time talking to Gideon and Serenity. (Serenity stays here after school until her mother gets home from work.) Gideon urged EJ to join us at the Barker Clinic sometime, and she said she'd love to. So our family now has three new members: Shan, Serenity, and EJ.

Deenie, I'm so glad I got to see what your life in Florida is like. As long as I had to be stranded somewhere, I'm happy it was with your loving family. And helping to comfort the boys did wonders to keep me calm until I could get a flight home.

With tremendous gratitude for all the good things in our lives,
                                        Juneau

WILLADENE

E-mail, September 22, 2001
Dear Juneau and Erin,

Congratulations, Erin! I thought that might happen after our conversation on the river.

Both of you will be receiving an official thank-you from the board for the way you helped comfort the boys who gathered at Gobb Hill after 9/11. But I wanted to send a special thank-you from Roger and me. You were terrific. The kids needed you, and so did I. I smile every time I think of your instant affinity with Delia, Erin, and yours with Miss B, Juneau. Just look at all the good work a bunch of Crusty Old Broads can do when they put their minds to it.

We're still fielding calls from worried parents who want assurance about the school's safety. What can we say? There are no measures we can take that will guarantee that, but we're doing what we can.

I've been going nonstop with responsibilities at home, at the

Academy, and at St. Anne's. Every day Evvy asks if I will be at her school—my being there makes her feel better. After I've spent a session on the phone with worried parents, I hie myself to Roger's office and spend some time with him. That makes *me* feel better.

This morning, I'm packing a lunch to take down the hill and share with him after I finish helping field phone calls from parents. The board has also been rumbling about remodeling the executive suites. Marsha says we should strike while the iron's hot, so Roger and I will look over some applicable catalogs while we eat.

Love to all y'all,
Deenie

Deenie finished her session in the office chatting over administration business with Marsha. They were continually interrupted by Richard Harker, the new executive assistant, who found one reason after another to poke his head in the room. When he was finally called away Deenie asked, "How is Mr. Executive Assistant Harker these days?"

"Way too interested in everybody's private lives," Marsha said.

"But he's good at his job?"

"Can't fault him on that. More's the pity," Marsha said.

"You don't like him, do you?"

"I don't like the way he does things. He could get ahead fine using the skills he has, but it appears he's planning to climb the ladder one body at a time."

Marsha's last comment was on Deenie's mind as she grabbed her purse and picnic basket and headed for Roger's office.

"How many phone calls did we get today?" Roger asked as Deenie spread out lunch on his desk.

"Not as many as usual. And more were about making the kids *feel* safe than about what added security measures are being taken. One mother had a huge list of things she thought would help her son feel looked after, from flannel sheets when the weather gets chilly to clam chowder and corn bread on Thursday nights."

Roger nodded. "You never know what will comfort a child."

"What made you feel safe when you were little?" Deenie asked as she leaned against Roger's desk.

Roger put his arm around her waist. "Let me think . . . A light on in the window when it was cold and dark out and we were coming in from milking. Waking up to the sound of Mom in the kitchen and Dad praying out loud in his big voice. I thought the chain of command was my mom to my dad to God, and as long as Dad was talking to God, we were okay."

They sat in silence for a time. Then Deenie said, "Miss B and I have been talking a lot about what it means to be safe. She says spiritual safety is the only safety there really is—everything else is illusion."

"And?"

"And nothing. She says no matter how much we've learned or how much others share, each of us has to find our individual pathway to spiritual peace alone."

Chapter 21

ERIN

E-mail, September 30, 2001

Dear COBs,

Vince and I are proceeding as if there will be a wedding some-time before the first of the year, but who knows? We'll schedule a sealing room in the temple after we've received the letter from the First Presidency saying that my request for a cancellation of sealing has been approved. Vince is sure it will come within weeks, not the months I think is more likely. He's a man of unquenchable optimism and faith.

Writing the letter outlining the circumstances of my divorce from Cory was a very interesting exercise. Quite freeing, actually. From the distance of seven years, I can honestly say that whatever my faults, I was totally committed to us as a couple. But that wasn't enough, because we were married under false pretexts.

Cory had to write a letter, too. When I asked him to, he seemed oddly relieved. As if he doesn't have to feel guilty about us if I've moved on.

Now it's a waiting game. While the countdown's been running, life's going on: school conferences, the Gerlach family gathering on Boulder Lake in October, and Mark's sixteenth birthday in late November.

Cory and Skipp are already scouting for a reliable car for Mark—they set a precedent when they bought one for Kayla when she turned sixteen. I haven't the faintest idea how we'll manage having four vehicles (counting Vince's pickup truck) and a two-car garage. Just one of the logistics Vince, the kids, and I have to work out. Guess we'll be buying headbolt heaters!

Your Erin

JUNEAU

Greg had told Juneau in August that his business partner Arnie and his wife, Nelda, had bought a new home, but she didn't see it until a golden October Saturday when they were invited there for lunch. It was out near Diamond Bar, about twenty-five miles east of Pasadena. Gideon wasn't interested in going, so they left him with Tanner Melton's family and enjoyed the car trip by themselves. Greg seemed pensive as they drove along past the summer-browned mountains.

"I've been thinking a lot since 9/11," he said. "Something like that makes you realize how fragile our lives are. Who knows what will happen tomorrow?"

He seemed to be leading up to something. "And?" Juneau prompted.

"And I think that whatever it is we want to do, we should do it now," Greg said.

"Like?"

"Oh, like taking that trip to England to see the land of Shakespeare and Milton."

"I'd love that," Juneau said. "We have timeshare weeks in the bank. But, Greg, it's too scary right now, after the Twin Towers attack."

He nodded and didn't say anything more, but Juneau had the impression he had something in mind.

Juneau admired Arnie and Nelda's home when Greg turned into their driveway. Like most of the other houses in the development, it had two stories in earth tones, with pillared entryway, arched windows, and a triple garage. A black Mercedes sat in the curved driveway.

"Pretty impressive, isn't it?" Greg said.

She nodded. "Very handsome."

It was beautiful inside, too, with spacious, sun-filled rooms and a vaulted ceiling in the great room, which sported a graceful stairway curving up to a balcony. Juneau had yearned for that kind of space when the girls were young. She could imagine the fun they and their friends would have had putting on a play of their own making on that sort of balcony. But those times were past.

Greg was enthusiastic during Arnie's guided tour. Juneau could tell how much he liked the place, especially when he excitedly pointed out the view from Nelda's upstairs quilting room. The windows looked down into a canyon with the mountains in the background.

"Wouldn't you like to have a room like this rather than that dinky garage space?" he asked when they were alone on the patio.

The tone of his voice aroused a suspicion. "What are you getting at, Greg?"

He grinned broadly. "Juney, a house just like this went on the market this week, two blocks away. I'd really like to think about buying it."

She almost gasped. "But it's too big," she protested. "We don't need this much space any more."

"We could use it," Greg said. "We'd each have our own office. I could have a hobby room in the garage."

"That would be nice," Juneau said, but her thoughts were of her cozy house, small, yes, but holding so much. She'd longed for it while she and Deenie and Erin had been stranded in Williamsburg. For the family pictures on the wall, the penciled marks on the kitchen doorframe showing growth height and dates for Misty, Nicole, and Giddy. For the pomegranate tree in the backyard, with its little memorial cemetery underneath.

"Let's go see it after lunch," Greg said. "The house, I mean. It's open today."

He seemed so excited about it that she couldn't say no. Besides, wasn't it the kind of house she'd dreamed of during those cramped Airstream trailer days of her youth?

JUNEAU

E-mail, October 14, 2001
Dear Friends,

Greg offered me a brand-new, just-built house! A magnificent palace, twice the size of our present home. Oh, the space! Oh, the newness! Oh, the trash compactor and walk-in closets!

Would you believe I said no? Partly because of 9/11 and wanting to feel safe in familiar territory, I think. Also because I don't want to leave my friends and the ward I love, to say nothing of my neighbor and almost-sister Marisol. And I'm too danged practical and don't want to spend money on space we don't need now. More has never been my mantra.

I told Greg how much it meant that he'd offer me a palace. We talked about it at length on the way home. If his enthusiasm had lasted, perhaps I would have gone for it. But there was grid-lock traffic on the way home (probably an accident some-where), and Greg commented that Arnie was frequently late in the mornings due to freeway congestion. He said it would be hard to get used to an hour-long commute when he is just ten minutes from his office now.

When I told him I'd rather he'd spend the time with me, he smiled. And before we got home, we'd mutually agreed that we'd forego the palace.

One more item: Dr. Tim told Marisol he thinks they would make a good pair. She told him she likes him a lot but is very content with her teaching career and doesn't want to compli-cate her life. What's the matter with her and me? We're offered good things and turn them down!

I'm secretly relieved because I don't know what I'd do without my dear friend next door.

Lovence,
Juneau

P.S. *Lovence* is a term Shoshana uses all the time. I take it to mean something like enhanced love.

ERIN

The last day of the Big Barn Sale in October, Erin came home exhausted after helping out from dawn to dusk. The smell of pizza and the sound of game-playing greeted her as she walked into the kitchen where the kids were playing 10,000 with The Jays.

"I saved some pizza for you," Joanna said.

"Thanks, but I'm too tired to eat. I'll just have some herbal tea." Erin gave everyone a hug or a hair-ruffle and then put water on to boil. She began flipping idly through the mail stacked on the kitchen counter.

Halfway through the pile was the letter she'd been waiting for. Her hands trembled as she read it, hardly daring to believe her eyes. The way was clear for her and Vince to marry in the temple.

"Hey, Mom," she cried. "It's time for you to start making my dress. Vince and I are getting married!"

After the hubbub died down, Jake said, "Guess it's time for you all to figure out how you're going to fit Vince into the family. And the house."

Erin glanced around the great room. She'd decorated it to her tastes. It was perfect as it was. However was Vince going to fit in?

The next day an ebullient Vince joined the family for Sunday dinner. Kayla and Hannah matched his mood, and even Mark reluctantly joined in the celebration. After dinner was over and the kitchen cleaned up, Vince and Erin sat at the kitchen table to make a list of what needed to be done.

When the list was finished, Erin leaned back and said, "You know, we've never talked about what you're going to bring from your place."

He looked around the great room. "Maybe just a suitcase. Looks like you and the kids use every inch of the house."

It stung that he thought there wasn't space for him. "Bring whatever you want—we'll make room."

They decided his favorite chair and ottoman would go in the great room, the desk and bookcases that had been his grandfather's in her upstairs office, and his woodworking bench and equipment in the basement rec room. *One more thing handled,* Erin thought.

Then Vince said, "What about Curly Dude? And George, my parrot? His cage will need to be in the great room, where there's a lot of company."

Erin covered a gasp with a cough. She'd forgotten about George.

"Don't worry," Vince added. "I'm not asking you to take over his care and feeding."

"I'll help," piped up Hannah, who'd wanted a parrot for years. She beamed at both of them as if they were getting married just for her.

The weekend before Thanksgiving, Kayla and Hannah enthusiastically helped Erin clear shelf and closet space for Vince. Mark was less enthusiastic. Erin had to ask him twice to help her move a new dresser for Vince up the stairs—she wanted it in place before Vince came over for supper. Mark grumbled during the process, and as they positioned the dresser, he made a snide remark about needing some soundproofing between her bedroom and his.

Erin felt her cheeks flame. "I'm going to say this only once, so pay attention. Vince and I will be living here as man and wife. And what goes on behind our bedroom door is our business. Do you understand me?"

He started to speak, but her upraised finger stopped him. "One more thing. You will treat Vince with the respect he deserves. Maybe he'd rather watch football than listen to classical music, but he's a fine man, worthy of your respect."

"Okay," Mark said after a long silence. "As long as you don't try to make us all one big happy family."

WILLADENE
E-mail, November 15, 2001
My Dear Friends,

We are still dealing with the fallout of 9/11. Nightmares and fights among the students. Unexpected visits from families just to check up on things. In the middle of this, we received a letter from Carl telling us that he did so well at squadron officer school, he's been invited to be an instructor. I never know whether I should cheer or be worried when I hear he's moving up the military ladder. I say congratulations and pray harder on his behalf and for the whole world than I ever have before.

Happily, he also said he'll be able to join us for the closing ceremonies at the Olympics. The whole family is now on board. We'll see all y'all there!

May you have a Thanksgiving filled with gratitude and a Christmas filled with peace.

> Love,
> Deenie

ERIN
E-mail, November 29, 2001
Dear COBs,

Everything's going light speed here!

Vince made honeymoon reservations for us at the La Mansion del Rio Hotel in San Antonio. Our room has a view of the famous Riverwalk, which will be lit up for the holidays. Very romantic.

Mom has the dress I'll be wearing at the reception, which will be at our house, ready for the final fitting. She's doing a fabulous job. It's three-quarter length, of cream-colored heavy crepe and lace with a crossover front that flatters my figure. I love it.

Brenda and Caitlin hosted a shower for me the weekend after Thanksgiving. (Did I tell you Brenda's back in town? Seems there's something going on between her and Andrew!) The gifts all ran to silk and lace, so I definitely won't need to stop at lingerie boutiques when I go shopping for honeymoon clothes. I'd be quite happy if it weren't for Mark being a stinker.

Erin

The night of her shopping trip, Erin was laying the new purchases on her bed to see if she still liked them when Hannah came into her room. "Hey, you," Erin said. "It's late. Why aren't you in bed?"

"I couldn't sleep." Hannah touched a soft cashmere sweater. "Oh, look at all your pretty things."

Erin gave Hannah a chance to look at each item, and then she set them all aside. "Time for bed. Want to climb in with me for a bit?"

Hannah nodded. She snuggled close, and Erin could hear she was sucking her thumb. After a second, she pulled it out of her mouth with a slurpy sound. "My Primary teacher says temple marriage glues people together. How come you and Daddy came unglued?"

"Unglued. That's a good way to put it." Erin paused. "Hannah, getting married in the temple isn't like gluing two pieces of wood together. It's more like setting two plants in the ground close enough to each other that they can grow together as the years pass. If they grow together so much that you can't tell where one begins and the other ends, then the Holy Spirit blesses them to be . . ."

"Forever Plants!" Hannah chortled.

"But if those plants—that husband and wife—let something or someone get between them, or if one starts growing in a different direction, they don't intertwine."

Hannah sighed. "Is that what happened to you and Daddy?"

"Unfortunately."

"Mark says when you and Vince go to the temple, us kids won't be part of your Forever Family. Whose family do I belong to?"

Erin mentally shook Mark for causing Hannah yet more concerns. "Don't worry about what Mark says, honey. Your daddy and I love you. Your grandparents love you, all six of them. Vince loves you. You're part of a very big family, I'd say."

Erin smoothed back her daughter's ash-blonde hair. "Some things seem complicated now, Hannah Banana, but Heavenly Father knows how to sort them out. We have to trust that he will take care of them. And us."

She spoke to herself as much as to Hannah. As the wedding approached, whenever The Griff tried to poke doubt and fear awake, she whispered, "Love Vince, trust God, have faith." She repeated those words the morning of the wedding two weeks before Christmas when she awoke with eagerness and anxiety tingling along every nerve. She repeated them silently as she and the kids got ready to go to the temple. And later as Colleen helped her into her temple dress.

But when Erin knelt across the altar from Vince and looked into his eyes, the words transformed from a mantra against fear into a promise for their future.

ERIN

E-mail, January 3, 2002
Dear COBs,

A New Year, a new life as Mrs. Vince Gerlach. I am so happy, it's ridiculous. The physical side of marriage isn't everything, but honestly, I had no idea of the amazing bond it can create between two people.

It's so strange to have a man—plus parrot and dog—in the house. Vince takes up a lot of space and not just physically. His presence has shifted all our relationships, the way a mobile would be thrown out of balance by a new, heavy element. We're barely beginning the adjustment phase, trying to find a new way to balance. Right now, Vince and the kids (even Mark) are making every effort to accommodate one another.

Looking back, I wonder if I would have had the courage to marry Vince if it hadn't been for 9/11. That tragedy changed a lot of other people, too, prompting them to do things they might otherwise not have done.

Kayla's had a little miracle facilitated by our local elf (try Googling "Lake Harriet elf door"). He sent her a letter containing a note someone had left behind his door after 9/11. It was an apology to her from one of the boys who'd caused the accident six years ago!

EJ's come home for a visit. Instead of feeling helpless and cynical in the aftermath of 9/11, she seems determined to make something of herself. It's a big change from the girl who went wherever the wind blew.

Here's the biggie—Brenda is once more Mrs. Andrew McGee! After Lottie's death, Caitlin and I speculated on what it would be like if Dad and Brenda got back together. It didn't look like that was going to happen. Then Andrew flew to Hawaii in

October and Brenda flew here for Thanksgiving. She stayed for my wedding—she said. She and Andrew were married by a justice of the peace a week later!

With all this excitement, the trip to Salt Lake for the Olympics has been the farthest thing from my mind. But now I'm getting excited about it, especially about you meeting Vince and us all getting together with Gabby's family. I'm so glad Cecelia and Junior suggested that!

See you all soon!

Your Erin

P.S. Vince is teaching George to sing "Pretty Woman" when he sees me! Mark is trying to teach him the first intervals of Beethoven's Fifth—da ta ta DAH, da ta ta DAH!

WILLADENE

Deenie returned home after a long afternoon at the Academy to find the side porch of Gobb Hill overrun with teenagers.

"Hey, Mom," Evvy said cheerfully. "Miss Winsome asked the three of us girls to design banners to decorate the auditorium for the spring concert. The theme is 'Our Friends in Christ Are . . . ' We're supposed to fill in the blank with the ideas she's given us in class. Leo and the gang wanted to help, and I promise we'll clean up when we're done."

Deenie looked at the posters spread out over the newspaper-covered porch. "Looks like you're doing a good job."

"Thanks. I wanted to get everything finished and up before we leave for the Olympics," Evvy said.

Christiana waved to Deenie. "Sister Rasmussen, come look at my banner."

Deenie noticed that everyone but Mandy looked puzzled at Christiana's use of the word *sister.* "It's a Mormon thing," she explained as she joined Christiana.

"Mom says to remind you that the new choir robes will arrive next week," Christiana said. "She and Mandy's mom are counting on you to help with the hemming when you get back from Utah."

"Thanks for the reminder," Deenie said with a grin. "Now I have something to look forward to the minute I get home."

She heard Christiana and Evvy giggle as she headed for the kitchen. Thumbing through the mail on the counter she found a delightful letter from Elizabeth reporting the first baptism in a family she was teaching. Deenie relished the words that revealed how much her daughter loved serving the Lord in the mission field.

The next letter from Paul and Dani was filled with equally good news. Paul had been offered a job as a seminary teacher in a small town south of Provo. He was thrilled to finally get the job he'd worked so hard for. Just like Roger. Deenie remembered how excited Roger had been when he received the offer from the Academy.

Now he seemed more burdened than happy with his job. No one expected him to have all the skills and connections Ferris had developed over years of running the Academy, but Roger expected it of himself. He was determined to justify Ferris's faith in him before another school year passed by. He was working twelve-hour days to make certain that every contingency that could arise while they were at the Olympics was handled before the family left for Salt Lake City. Deenie wondered if he would be able to relax enough to enjoy the trip.

JUNEAU
    E-mail, February 1, 2002
    Dear Gals,

    It's Gideon's fourteenth birthday, so of course we're having a family party tonight. But I just had to write and say how happy I am that we'll all be at the Olympics and at Jonas's ninetieth birthday gathering in Provo afterward. Bless Cecelia and Junior. Gabby would be proud of them for making her dear friend part of their family.

    FYI, I've chosen the title *The Speaking House* for my book set in Williamsburg. It starts on 9/11. I have only the first chapter done so far. I'm curious to see where it leads!

                        Love,
                        Juneau

The house Greg had rented in Park City was a rustic delight and cozily warm, which made Juneau happy because the outside temperature was 12 degrees above zero Fahrenheit. "Perfect for winter games," Greg exulted. "Brrr," Juneau shivered.

Gideon immediately picked a room whose window looked out on the snowy mountains. Juneau, captivated by the twinkling lights, chose a bedroom for her and Greg with windows overlooking the valley below. After they unpacked, she made supper from the groceries they'd stopped to pick up on the way, after which she crawled into the electric-blanketed bed, leaving Greg and Gideon to watch TV coverage of the Olympic events of the day. She fell asleep listening to them laughing and cheering.

The next morning they had tickets for the ski-jumping competition. Juneau had never followed the sport—it seemed ridiculous to purposely launch oneself into the air with two sticks tied to one's feet. She did, however, remember clips of Eddy the Eagle, the hapless ski-jumper from England who had come in last in the 1988 Olympic Games but whose name had nonetheless become a household word.

As they approached the ski-jump venue, they got caught up in the crowd and the excitement. Juneau had never been to an event where the air fairly vibrated with anticipation as it did that morning. Soon she was cheering and gasping with everyone else at the sheer audacity of what the contestants were doing. Greg and Gideon had their favorites, having studied up on who was competing. But Juneau cheered for them all, especially the jumper who, according to Gideon, had sustained a serious injury just a year before but had overcome it.

By the end of the week she'd become something of a Winter Games junkie, but even so, her fervor was mild compared to Greg's and Gideon's. She'd never seen Greg quite like this, except maybe when they'd first met and she had reluctantly gone with him to a couple of sports events.

On the night before the closing ceremonies, Juneau and Greg sat together in front of the fire after Gideon had gone to bed. "This has been amazing, Greg," she said. "Thank you for bringing us."

"I'm glad you're having fun, Juney."

She couldn't help noticing how happy he looked. Younger, even. As if he'd been rejuvenated by simply being there. "I'd forgotten how much you enjoy sports," she said. "Makes me wonder why we haven't gone to more than one or two Dodgers or Lakers games since we got married."

He rubbed his chin. "I guess because I knew you wouldn't enjoy it. And then I fell into the computer pit."

"We should've gone more," she murmured.

He nodded thoughtfully. "It was my choice, Juney. I could have gone if I'd really wanted to, but I preferred doing something with you."

It had never occurred to Juneau that for her, he'd given up something he enjoyed. It made her wonder if he would even have suggested coming to the Olympics if she hadn't asked him back in June to tell her something he really, really wanted to do. That had been her attempt to listen to him and then try to speak his language. She was glad she had. He was a different person here. More *alive*.

She told him as much, adding, "I'm sorry you didn't do things you enjoy doing because of me or work. I think you missed it more than you realized."

He was silent for so long she thought he hadn't heard her. Then he said, "Sometimes we leave behind parts of ourselves that we didn't need to."

It wasn't the kind of thing Greg normally said. And it was exactly the sort of sharing she'd always longed for. Touched, she kissed his cheek softly. Who said he didn't speak *her* language?

The day after the closing ceremonies of the Olympics, Greg, Juneau, and Gideon drove down to Provo, where they had been invited to join the Farnsworths to celebrate Jonas's ninetieth birthday. Erin, her new husband, Vince, and children Mark, Kayla, and Hannah would be there, as would Deenie and Roger.

Memories washed over Juneau as Greg stopped the car in the driveway of Gabby's pioneer house embellished with gingerbread.

"Nice place," Greg commented.

"Yes." Juneau stared at it. "Except for the snow, it doesn't look all that different from when I first saw it back in 1980." She didn't know why she'd thought it should, except she had changed so much she figured nothing could be the same.

It wasn't the same, actually. Gabby wasn't there.

But Gabby's clan was. Before they could ring the doorbell, Kenny flung open the door and pulled Juneau and the men inside to smiles and happy greetings. Erin, who looked more beautiful and happier than Juneau had ever seen her, proudly introduced Vince to them. They were joined by the Rasmussens, Junior and Cecelia, and Jonas for a hug-in and a sorting-out of families. Then the adults began talking like old friends while the young people scattered in groups through the house.

Juneau hovered to one side watching Gideon, who was face-to-face with Evvy Rasmussen. *Poor boy,* she thought, seeing his ears turn bright red as he gazed down at Deenie's daughter who had more cutes than any one girl needed. Evvy seemed equally disconcerted by the meeting.

Coming to the rescue, Juneau introduced herself to Evvy and started them talking about what they'd liked best at the closing ceremonies of the Olympics. When Evvy spoke enthusiastically about the Native American dancers, Juneau turned away. They didn't need her any more.

"Nice save," Deenie said, joining her. "Come on, let's get Junior and Cecelia to introduce us to all the new little Farnsworths."

"It's amazing," Erin said to Gabby's son after he'd done the honors. "Three generations of Farnsworths are gathered here: Gabby's children, grandkids, and great-grandkids."

Cecelia nodded. "Junior and I see something of Gabby in each of them, her eyes in one little face and her smile on another. We do every-thing we can to ensure they carry her values inside their souls. We want her legacy to go on."

Bryan, whom the women had first met in 1980, joined the group as they sniffled nostalgically into tissues. "I was thinking about the profound effect your grandmother had on my life," Juneau said.

"Mine, too," he said. "But you know, you and your friends affected my life just as much." He paused. "Remember that day in 1980 when I came here demanding that Grandma let me take Grandpa's old Cadillac? When she wouldn't, I called her a crazy old broad."

"I remember," Deenie said. "You were a mouthy brat, weren't you!"

"No kidding," he said with a rueful grin. "Grandma told me later that you three changed my terminology to '*crusty* old broad,' which she thought fit her to a T. And that you decided you wanted to learn to deal with life the way she did. Up to then, I'd never seen my grandmother as somebody with discipline and character—and attitude. That was when I started listening to her."

Impulsively, Juneau hugged him. "Bryan, if we contributed in any way to what you are today, I'm so danged proud I could cry!" She found it endearing that he was a little teary himself.

He cleared his throat. "Well, I think I'll join your husbands. They're off with Kenny, having a great time in the computer room talking about the latest and greatest."

"The Guys Club lives!" Juneau laughed as they watched him go.

The COBs moved on to have a special chat with Jonas, whose birthday they'd come to celebrate. At ninety, he looked his age. His formerly ramrod posture was now stooped. His mane of white hair had thinned dramatically, and his face was a celebration of wrinkles. Still, his eyes were bright, and he was as sharp as ever.

"I'm glad you three could be here." He pressed Deenie's hand between his gnarly ones and then Erin's and Juneau's. "I've been lucky to count the Farnsworths as my family. I think of you as family, too."

He peppered them with questions. It wasn't until all three had given him a full report that Juneau had the chance to ask him how he was. "And tell me the truth," she added.

He held her hand a little tighter and a wistful expression crossed his face. "Remember Gabby's favorite line from Tennyson's *Ulysses*, 'Tho' much is taken, much abides'?"

"Yes," Juneau said. "It's meant so much to me over the years."

"There's more to it, but I don't remember. Do you?"

She nodded and her eyes stung as she recited:

> *And tho'*
> *We are not now that strength which in old days*
> *Moved earth and heaven; that which we are, we are.*

"That's how I am," he said.

"Oh, Jonas," she said, "what if Deenie and Erin and I hadn't come here all those years ago? What if we'd never known you and Gabby?"

He gazed steadily back at her. "And what if we'd never known the three of you?"

That theme seemed to be on everyone's mind, Juneau thought, when, after celebrating Jonas's birthday with toasts and cake, Cecelia and her daughter Sophie drew the three friends into a quiet corner. "It's hard to think where we might all be right now if you hadn't come into Gabby's life," Cecelia said. "Every time we're together as family, I'm grateful you pushed Gabby to the realization that allowed for healing."

Sophie nodded in fervent agreement, adding, "It could have gone another way, especially with Kenny. Thank you all from the bottom of my heart."

It was almost too much to assimilate. Overcome with emotion, the COBs put on their coats and went out onto the porch. Deenie blew out a cloud of frosty breath. "*Who'da* thunk it? When I came to Education Week in 1980, I wasn't hoping to influence anyone for good. I was just trying to find myself."

"You were not," Erin said. "You were trying to find some new yogurt recipes."

They laughed together, remembering.

"Don't you feel like all this was meant to be, right from the beginning?" Juneau asked. "Makes it seem as if there's some grand cosmic plan."

"If there is," Erin said, "I wish I had a clue as to what's on the next page. That way, I could do—"

"—what it takes to be a good Mormon woman," Deenie finished. "Like when we first met, remember?"

"Touché," Erin said, smiling. "I'd like to think I've changed a little since then. Or at least learned something about myself and others. We can't celebrate completing The Pact in 2005 and declare ourselves COBs unless we've learned something from twenty-five years of striving for it."

"It would be pretty sad if we haven't learned a thing or two since 1980," Juneau said wryly.

"You got that right," Deenie said. "We should get some benefit from what we've gone through."

"Something that can go in our *COBs Little Book of Wisdom*," Erin said.

Juneau giggled. "Or our *COBs Book of* Little *Wisdom*."

Linked by love and memories, they stood in the crisp night air, gazing at the outline of jutting mountains against the wintry sky.

ERIN

E-mail, March 2, 2002
Dear COBs,

We're still trying to come down from the high of our Utah trip. I tell you, watching that little Sarah Hughes skate her long program raised the hair on my arms. Kayla was thrilled to see her win the gold but sad, too. She said compared to the final skaters, she was never that good. I reminded her that she'd had her own success at the semifinals at regionals in 1995. That brought a smile to her face. She said, "I did, didn't I?" I felt her finally let go of her lost dream, and it was all right.

Now it's back to what's become the "new normal" for our house. The noise of the two dogs playing together, the parrot asking, "Where's Vince," phone calls for the vet at odd hours from distraught pet owners, Mark playing Bach preludes and fugues (his attempt to put some order back into his life), and the scouts who invade the place at Vince's invitation—he's the new assistant scoutmaster in our ward. They've turned the rec room into a clubhouse.

Sometimes all this activity and noise—especially when Vince and the kids are playing games—is too much to take. Then I escape to my office or bedroom for some alone time. But I wouldn't have it any other way.

Your Erin

JUNEAU

E-mail, March 10, 2002
Dear Deenie and Erin,

What fun it was to see you and meet your families at Gabby's old house. And the Farnsworths. Isn't it interesting how our lives intertwined with theirs to the benefit of all of us! Despite your "whack upside the head" a while back, Erin, I still find it hard to believe I've had a positive impact on someone's life.

Gideon was very quiet on our trip home. We knew he was thinking about your cute Evvy, Deenie. Every now and then he'd venture out of silence to tell us Evvy said this or Evvy said that. He was mighty impressed about your being Dead-Eye Deenie; Evvy told him all about it.

The first message waiting for me when I got home was from my mom. She asked me to fly up to Oregon to be with her and Dad next week. That bodes ill; normally she would never ask me to come. I hope I can bring them some comfort and cheer or whatever else they need. In the hope that they'll come live with us sometime soon, we're finally adding on to our house.

When I saw how excited Greg was about the remodel, I asked him if it would suffice for the palace near Arnie he'd had his eye on. He said, "More than, and we don't even have to move!"

Gideon, who has been against changing anything more than necessary, has decided it's okay to build on for his grandparents. We've got all the permits and have lined up a good contractor to get started. (*Not* Dex Beldon, who is still in jail.)

> Love to you dear ones,
> Juneau

WILLADENE

E-mail, March 12, 2002
Dear COBs,

It's hard to believe that after so much planning and anticipation, our Olympics were over so soon. There should be extra hours in the days with big events so they stretch out longer. I'm with Vince, Erin. I wish we lived close enough to get together for birthdays and national holidays. Or just because.

What a visit we had in Provo. It's amazing to me how much has come from the original stay in Provo with Gabby. It occurred to me that finding Gabby was an answer to our prayers, but we were an answer to hers as well. Her influence in our lives set us on the path to becoming the women we are, and our intervention in her life was the key to restoring her family. Pretty amazing, huh?

By the way, didn't you think Carl looked too handsome for words in his uniform at the closing ceremonies? I felt safer with him by my side in that huge crowd. Ripples from 9/11, no doubt.

Roger says Carl talked to him about the future as if there may be another wedding in the offing, but we haven't even heard a girl's name in his conversation so far. I wonder what's up!

It would have been grand to have had a few days free when we got home to relive and relish all the memories from Salt Lake City, but Roger's already putting out fires at the Academy and I'm scheduled to join Cleo and Gwen at St. Anne's tomorrow, hemming the new choir robes for the spring concert. I'm going to stop in the auditorium first to see the "Our Friends in Christ" banners Evvy and her friends made for the program.

I hope when you read this you can hear my voice as if I'm talking right to you. Talking face to face with you in Utah was so much better than e-mails. I'm proposing more phone calls. How about it?

Love,
Deenie

"Say, what did you think of the banners in the auditorium?" Cleo asked as she, Deenie and Gwen set up the school's sewing machine outside the costume closet in the choir room. It was the perfect place to work, well lit and cool.

"I thought they were terrific," Gwen said. "The premade letters and borders the kids used made them look professionally done. Not that Miss Winsome would tolerate anything less."

"And don't we know it," Deenie said. "My favorite was the banner Leo Flynn made. *Our Friends in Christ Are Reasonable*. Not exactly a quotation from Miss Winsome but clear and to the point."

"It's almost time for choir practice to start," Gwen said. "I think if we spend the hour pinning hems, we won't disturb the class."

"Good," Deenie said. "I'd like to get a peek at how The Winsome One mesmerizes the girls."

"They won't even notice us," Gwen said.

When the bell rang for class, clusters of chattering thirteen- and fourteen-year-old girls spilled into the room. But the chatter ceased abruptly when the door from the choir director's office opened and Miss Winsome stepped out carrying a large vase of long-stemmed pink roses. She was delicate and fair, her straight blonde hair held back from her face with a pearlized headband. She wore a linen skirt and silk sweater in lavender accented with a strand of pearls around her throat. Her gray shoes had a strap across the ankle.

She nodded absently to Deenie and her friends in the back of the room, placed the roses on the piano, and said, "Good morning, class," in a melodious voice.

"Good morning, Miss Winsome," the class responded in equally refined tones.

Miss Winsome ran her fingers over a rose and smiled at the girls. They responded with a universal sigh.

"Good grief," Deenie whispered behind her hand to Gwen. She, Gwen, and Cleo leaned forward to hear what Miss Winsome would say next.

"This weekend Pastor Bagger and I—" the girls sighed again—"had a special opportunity to attend a lecture by one of our great Southern Christian leaders on the topic of knowing our friends in Christ. I was so impressed I wanted to share some of that information with you." She made two headings on the blackboard, Christians and non-Christians. "Now, what churches do people who believe in Christ belong to?"

The girls in the room fired off the Catholic Church and the names of every Protestant church Deenie had ever heard of—and then some. When Miss Winsome asked for the names of non-Christian religions, the list went as quickly. Hindu, Muslim, Jewish, Buddhist . . .

"Now this next group is the hardest to identify," Miss Winsome said as she wrote the word *Cults* on the board.

"People who belong to these groups will often say they believe in Christ to put you at ease, but then they will try to convince you a little at a time that what they believe is better than what you believe. They're very tricky, and you have to be careful not to trust them. One of those groups is called the Mormons."

Deenie gasped and started forward, but Cleo held her back as Christiana jumped to her feet, waving her arm at the teacher. "Yes?" Miss Winsome said.

Christiana smiled widely. "Ya'll might not know it, Miss Winsome, but I'm a Mormon. And the name of our church is The Church of *Jesus Christ* of Latter-day Saints."

"Well, now. Isn't that interesting?" Deenie could tell by her reaction that Miss Winsome hadn't expected any such response from her class.

Then Evvy stood up without waiting to be called on. "I'm a member of The Church of Jesus Christ of Latter-day Saints, too," she said.

Deenie was so proud of Christiana and Evvy. And of Mandy, too, who stood and declared, "Mormons do believe in Christ. I'm not a Mormon, but I could be, if I wanted to."

Miss Winsome raised her eyebrows. "Your parents might have something to say about that."

At that, Gwen stepped forward and said, "As a matter of fact, I do have something to say about that, Miss Winsome. If my Mandy were to choose to join the Mormon church when she's old enough to understand it, Glen and I would support her choice."

Miss Winsome's porcelain expression turned even paler. "Well. Well." She stumbled over how to respond. "It looks like we'll have plenty to talk about then, doesn't it?"

"We certainly will," Deenie promised.

Miss Winsome scurried to the piano at the side of the room. "Now, class," she said and struck a chord. "Warm-ups."

The three women returned to their corner and finished out the hour of choir practice quietly turning up hems. Deenie was surprised at the absence of anger in her heart. Other feelings, positive feelings, were filling her up. It felt as if heaven was highlighting what loving friends she had made in Florida. Evvy, too.

Deenie sought out Evvy's face in the choir, feeling her heart swell at the unexpected strength her daughter had shown.

Chapter 23

ERIN
    E-mail, May 12, 2002
    Dear COBs,

Happy Mother's Day. I wish.

In Minnesota, an otherwise progressive and sensible state, the fishing opener falls on Mother's Day weekend! In an effort to resolve this conflict, the Department of Natural Resources once did an ad campaign calling it "Take-a-Mom-Fishing Weekend."

I used to find it amusing. When Vince told me (before we got serious) that he, his father, and brothers-in-law always go up to Mille Lacs for the opener, I said something like, "Give your sisters and mother my condolences." I never thought he'd keep up the tradition after we got married.

Well, he did! I tried to entice him to stay home, but he said it was a tradition in his family and we'd celebrate Mother's Day after he got back. So the kids and I spent the afternoon with Mom and Jake. It was nice, but I couldn't shake my resentment. I didn't do a good job of hiding it, either. Mom told me to let it go, that it wasn't that important in the grand scheme of things. Later, when Tomas (the tai chi master) joined us, he rested his hand on my shoulder and whispered, "Breathe!"

I gave myself a talking-to all the way home, and I'd done a pretty good job of convincing myself that one day out of 365 wasn't that big a deal. Until I found a big bouquet from Cory on the front step with a card acknowledging me as the mother of his children. I sat on the steps and had a good, long cry.

You can guess how it went when Vince came home. The honeymoon's definitely over. Which is why I'm in my office at two in the morning while he's sleeping the sleep of the clueless.

    Your Erin

JUNEAU

E-mail, May 13, 2002
Dear Erin,

Why don't the moms of Minnesota declare Father's Day as "Go Shopping" Day? Oh dang, that won't work for us, will it, since it's on a Sunday. Oh well.

Juneau

WILLADENE

On May fifteenth, Deenie celebrated her fiftieth birthday by accepting a call to teach the nine-year-olds in Primary. She was delighted with the chance to connect with younger members of the ward.

Later that day a delivery person arrived with a vase of exotic flowers from Roger. They were beautiful, but Deeni knew that if Roger had ordered them himself, they would have been daisies and daffodils. Marsha must have done it. It was another worrisome reminder of how busy and complicated Roger's life had become, running the school and doing battle with the board.

Evvy gave Deenie a handmade card containing a coupon for a mother-daughter activity of her choice. Deenie was pleased. Since Evvy had roared into teenage social life, they hadn't spent much time together, just the two of them.

Then the pièce de résistance arrived in the mail from Paul and Dani. It came in a small, bright aqua box with a card that said, "Happy birthday, Grandma." Inside was a homemade desk calendar with September 12 stamped with a baby cradle and a little note that said, "See you then."

Deeenie let out a whoop of delight that brought Bear to her on the run. "Paul and Dani are having another baby," she crowed and gave the big dog a hug around the neck. "They're so brave. I'm so happy! Come on, dog. Let's go tell Grandpa. That's got to make him feel better."

ERIN

Vince stood in the doorway of the master bathroom a week after Mother's day, watching Erin work mousse through her hair. "I'm sorry I disappointed you. I don't fish on any other Sunday, but this is an important family tradition." When she didn't respond, he added, "My mom and sisters are okay with us guys going fishing on Mother's Day—and you did say it was fine. Or is *fine* a code word women have for something men don't understand?"

"You should have known I wanted you with me on that day." Erin started on her makeup. She was meeting with a potential client, and she wanted to look her best.

"So you'll make me pay for not doing things your way." He sighed heavily. "When I got married, all I wanted to do was to be with you. But you . . . you have a whole list of expectations. I don't know who you want me to be, Cory or Prince Charming."

Her head jerked toward him. "I don't want you to be like Cory! And I've never believed in Prince Charming."

"Will you let me make it up to you? I've got to open the cabin over Memorial Day weekend. I usually go up on Thursday and come back on Monday. If you can get someone to take Hannah for that long, we could have some time alone."

He looked so forlorn that Erin was taken aback. What in the world was she doing, holding onto resentment and making this dear man miserable? The sudden fear that she could ruin this second chance at love made her shudder. She put down her mascara and hugged him tight. "I'd love to," she said.

E-mail, May 21, 2002
Dear COBs,

Congrats, Deenie, on the coming baby. You're a grandma-to-be, and Juneau is a grandma. If I'm following in your footsteps, I should be anticipating grandmotherhood. Instead, Vince and I are thinking of having a baby!

We both know it's risky at my age, so we went to see Dr. Lamont, my gynecologist. She said there've been so many advances in gynecology that "forty is the new thirty-five" when it comes to childbearing. She laughed when I said, "But I'm forty-four!" and added that I wouldn't be the oldest prospective mother she sees! That doesn't mean I'll actually get pregnant, so don't start crocheting a baby blanket yet.

Melina has graduated from Augsburg College with a degree in music therapy, which is a great achievement. She'll do an internship at Methodist Hospital before taking the licensing exam.

Althea wasn't at the ceremony. She still can't be away from home for long stretches. But her caseworker brought her and the pocket dog to a nearby Chili's where we met for dinner afterward.

It's interesting to see that in the middle of her mess, literal and figurative, Althea has created a life that works for her. I'm thinking that qualifies her to be a COB. We're all trying to make something meaningful out of what we're handed in life, aren't we?

Love,
Erin

P.S. I'm going with Vince to open his cabin over Memorial Day weekend. I have no idea what I'm in for.

Very early the morning Erin and Vince were to leave for his cabin, Joanna came over. She and Jake were going to hold down the fort during the long weekend, getting Hannah off to school on Thursday and Friday and being there if Mark or Kayla, now sixteen and nineteen, needed them for any reason.

All the way north, Vince told stories of summers spent at his parents' cabin on Boulder Lake, which they'd purchased when he was little. "It gets pretty noisy now when all my sisters and their families are there. I bought my cabin so I could escape when I needed some peace and quiet."

After lunch at a café in downtown Duluth, they took the narrow road north to Boulder Lake and then a rutted dirt road through the thick forest of pine, birch, and maple. It ended at the lake where a small cabin and some outbuildings stood. The cabin was weathered a silver gray, the porch sagged, and moss grew on the shingles of the roof.

"It's great, isn't it?" Vince unlocked the front door and waved Erin in with a flourish. Her first impression was of dust, mouse tracks, and sun-bleached curtains. "Wow," she said. The main room had an old sofa and a recliner, a small bookshelf, and a rectangular table with four rickety chairs. In one corner was what passed for a kitchen. There were two bedrooms—one with a double bed, the other with two bunk beds—a bathroom, and a washer on the closed-in back porch.

"I'll get the water turned on for you first," Vince said. "Then I've got to start working on the dock. It always needs repair in the spring." He gave her a big smile and a quick kiss. "It's so great to have you here."

When they'd unloaded the truck, Erin made a mental list of what jobs needed to be done. First was to wash the linens, which after a long, wet winter were slightly damp and smelled of mold. She was carrying them through the main room when a motion at the back of the sofa caught her eye. A little mouse with soft fur and large pink ears was peeking over the back of the sofa.

She stifled a shriek. Where there was one little mouse, there were other little mice. And a mother mouse.

She ran down to the dock calling Vince's name. "Do you have a mousetrap?" she asked. "I think there are mice living under the couch."

"I don't know. We'll probably have to buy one."

"Give me the keys. I'm driving to Duluth for the trap and some other things I want to get."

At the nearest Target, Erin grabbed a cart and went up and down the aisles tossing things into it. The more she put in, the more she thought of. Cleaning supplies and rubber gloves, new kitchen and bathroom textiles, new bedding for the bedroom, rugs and curtains for every room. Mousetraps and D-Con.

When she got back, Vince looked at the bags in the back of the pickup. "I didn't think it was that bad."

"Women see things men don't," she said. "Will you give me a hand?"

They worked nonstop the rest of the afternoon and into the evening. They swept and dusted and scrubbed. Then together they hung the curtains, dressed the bed with the freshly laundered linens and the new bedding, and placed scatter rugs on each side. In the main room, Erin put a cheery oilcloth on the table, tied matching cushions to the chairs, tossed a throw over the sofa, and put a rag rug in front of it. As a final touch, she put a jar full of pretty flowering weeds on the bookshelf.

"Now it looks like home," she said, deeply satisfied by the result. "Do you like it?"

He nodded slowly. "Only it's not mine anymore. It's yours."

Erin felt like crying. "I was trying to make it ours."

JUNEAU

E-mail, June 20, 2002

Dear Deenie,

While cleaning out my closets today (blame it on our house renovations), I thought about Elizabeth's request for clothing for the Saints in Romania. So I'm putting all the things I think they could use in a suitcase I don't need any more and shipping it off to you. I'll have so much closet space when the work on the house is done, I won't know what to do with it—a walk-in upstairs in the master suite and another big one in my writing room.

Our good news is that Nicole has finished her internship with high praise for her work. That helps a lot in her efforts to build a life without Beto. She has been offered an obstetrical residency in Pueblo, south of Denver, which she is very pleased to get. As for Beto, he just finished his second year of residency here in LA, and he'll be heading for Mexico soon to live out the dream he and Nicole had of running Dr. Vasquez's clinic when he retires. She sent him a card wishing him well. I'm praying that all goes well for both of them.

Lovence,

Juneau

WILLADENE

"So there'll be no summer vacation this year?" Deenie asked, trying to get a grip on Roger's startling news.

"That doesn't mean you and Evvy can't go to Wellsville," Roger said. "But with Marsha on family leave to take care of her mother and Harker taking his vacation at the same time, there's no way I can be gone. Besides, I already used one week of vacation for the Olympics. I'm saving the rest for the holidays. Don't worry about me. Go. Enjoy the summer."

"Not without you," she said.

Roger argued until Deenie finally compromised. "We'll take a week. I did promise Dani I'd help her paint the nursery in their new apartment in Springville, and I want to attend some temple sessions with Mom and Dad. But after that we're coming home."

The days before Deenie left for Wellsville were filled with tension. Roger kept insisting he'd be all right if they stayed in Utah longer. "I'm perfectly capable of taking care of myself," he said almost resentfully. Deenie wondered if she'd hit a sore spot. Had someone been questioning his abilities? Had he been doubting himself?

She wanted to ask but couldn't figure out how to without causing more tension between them. She might have been careless with Delia's feelings and even Jenny's, but she wasn't going to be careless with Roger's.

Deenie spent a week in Wellsville with Evvy as she'd planned, but worry about Roger kept her from fully enjoying it. The one really bright spot was the happy news that Carl was in love with Chan-Sook Wagner, the daughter of an LDS officer at Maxwell Air Force Base and his Korean wife.

Deenie and Evvy arrived home to even more good news. Brad Donaldson had sent a letter containing a photo of himself dressed in white standing in front of the baptismal font in an LDS church. He had written:

> I was so touched by what I saw at the Perth Australia Temple open house that I invited the missionaries to give me the discussions. I investigated because of Elizabeth, but I was baptized for myself.

While Deenie was pleased that Brad had found the Church on his own behalf, she worried about what that would mean for Elizabeth, who still had six months left to serve on her mission.

"Why does the thought of Elizabeth ending up with Brad still worry you? Especially now?" Roger asked when Deenie voiced her concern.

"He's so much older than she is," Deenie said. "Ten years is a generation apart these days. They'll see life so differently."

"I thought the greater distance had to do with differing faiths. Now that he is a member of the Church, that no longer exists. So tell me. What's *really* troubling you?"

Deenie thought seriously about it before the answer finally dawned on her. "What bothers me is that he once belonged to Sunny. It doesn't seem right that he should be in love with Sunny's niece."

"Maybe not," Roger said. "But it looks like it's an objection you're going to have to get over."

All the good news seemed to have had a positive effect on Roger, which was a great relief to Deenie. He seemed to have gotten over whatever had been troubling him. He'd never told her what it was, and she was afraid that asking him now would bring it all back up again. Besides, if it had been something she needed to know, he would have told her. Wouldn't he?

ERIN

Despite Erin's willingness to try for a child with Vince, she hadn't really believed she would get pregnant. Until the morning her stomach did flip-flops at the smell of bacon. A visit to Dr. Lamont confirmed what she already knew. She was going to have a baby!

Vince and Hannah were ecstatic at the news, Kayla was amused, and Mark was embarrassed. The Jays and Andrew and Brenda were happy but concerned about her health. Erin's own concerns went beyond the pregnancy. Delivering a healthy baby was just the beginning. She would be forty-five when it was born. Fifty when it started kindergarten. Sixty-two when it graduated from high school.

"I'm too old for this," she muttered as she and Vince climbed into bed after saying their prayers. "How am I ever going to make it through until this kid's able to take care of himself?"

"You won't be raising him by yourself, you know." Vince snuggled up behind her and put his arm around her waist. "I'm here. There are three sets of grandparents gearing up to spoil this kid. Our sisters will be marvelous aunts. And think of all the cousins he'll have to play with."

"That's nice," she murmured. "I didn't have cousins to play with. Neither did my kids until Caitlin's brood came along. I always felt they'd missed out on something special."

"With this one, we'll have a whole tribe helping us out."

She told Cory about the baby when he called the next evening to talk about the two weeks when he had their children during the summer.

"Congratulations. Actually, Kayla told me when she called to say she was passing on coming to my place this year. Mark, too. Do you know anything about that?"

"Uh, they mentioned it. I told them they needed to talk to you."

"Come on, Erin."

Erin leaned her head against the hand not holding the receiver. "They've got their own plans. Kayla's taking as many ceramics classes as she can, and Mark's getting ready for piano camp in Aug—"

"I get that they're busy, but I was looking forward to spending time with them. I've got some activities lined up. Mom and Dad are looking forward to having them stay a few nights there as well."

"I'm sorry. But Kayla's nineteen and Mark's nearly seventeen. Kids that age don't put spending time with their parents at the top of their list. They don't spend that much time with me, and we live in the same house."

"I don't think that's the whole story." When she didn't say anything, he asked, "What about Hannah?"

"She's already got her bags packed." She paused. "I'll get Mark and Kayla to make time for a few of the activities you've planned."

"I appreciate that," Cory said. "You take care of yourself and that baby."

I will, Erin thought. *By going to bed right now.* It was only eight-thirty, but Hannah was already in bed, so she kissed Vince goodnight and crawled under the covers. As she closed her eyes, she crossed her fingers that Vince wouldn't get an emergency call from his clinic in the middle of the night—they always woke her up with her heart pounding. She didn't need that.

JUNEAU

E-mail, July 17, 2002

Dear Erin,

Well, dang, girl! How about being mom again! For the most part I say, "Better you than I." I get my baby fixes from grand-kids these days, and there's going to be another one—Trace and

Cath are expecting. Rhiannan is three and a half now (so cute I could just gobble her up), so it's time for a brother. Or sister. Or one of each (Trace says there are twins in his family).

Anyway, congratulations to you and Vince!

EJ and Misty came up last Saturday to go with us to the Barker Clinic. When we got home, I ordered in pizza, invited Marisol and Dr. Tim over, and we played games all evening—dominos, Uno, Monopoly. EJ is one of the family now. Once she got past being shy, she's quite delightful.

Did I mention that Beto has gone to Mexico for good now that he's finished his internship and residencies? He came over before he left to say what a big part of his life our family has been. He didn't ask about Nicole, just said he would stay in touch. I love that boy! Why does life have to be so hard?

Love,
Juneau

ERIN

E-mail, August 17, 2002
Dear Friends,

Mark baptized Hannah today. I'm attaching two photos I took at the family dinner afterward. One is a group photo—the unfamiliar faces belong to Vince's people. The other is of Hannah with her McGee great-grandparents. If you look closely, you can see the sterling silver butterfly pendant they gave her as a baptism gift. Bless Margaret. I can imagine her fretting over what would be an appropriate replacement for the cross pendant she would have preferred giving Hannah.

Life is full of Who'das. The Grandparents McGee have been more than gracious to the kids and me, and they've even made peace with Brenda about being part of the family. I do love seeing Dad and Brenda back together after all these years and all her marriages! I think Lottie would approve.

Erin

P.S. Juneau, I love that you and Misty are part of EJ's support system. Blessings on you both from Colleen and me.

WILLADENE

E-mail, September 1, 2002
Dear COBs,

Wahoo! Paul just called from Logan, borderline hysterical, to tell us Dani has delivered a healthy baby boy. Three weeks early. In the living room of my folks' house. Into the waiting hands of Aunt Stell. They have named him Daniel Paul, Dee for short.

Aunt Stell being there so she could help bring our Dee safely into the world seemed meant to be. Any lingering sadness over the birth of Sunny in that house has been replaced with abundant joy over the safe arrival of our little man. We will be flying to see him as soon as arrangements can be made.

The excitement over Dee has been tempered by our concern over Elizabeth, who will be coming home early due to a lingering illness—a virus, the doctors there think. She's spent time in the hospital there but is still weak, so she'll stay in the mission home until she's fit to travel.

Brad must have found out about her condition as soon as we did. He called us from Australia to say that with our permission he'd like to be here when our girl gets home.

In case you're wondering about all the clothing we collected to take with us to Romania, it is still going but now as part of a drive sponsored by St. Anne's. I told Gwen about Elizabeth's request for clothing and school supplies, and before I knew it, voilà! The Romanian Project came into existence. St. Anne's is also planning a gala to raise funds for the shipping. Isn't that splendid?

Toggling between joy over our new baby boy and distraction over our dear daughter.

Deenie

Chapter 24

ERIN

Once she got over morning sickness, and the oppressive summer heat and humidity had given way to sparkling fall days, Erin felt energized. She was a whirlwind of activity, keeping the house clean and laundry done. Meeting with the Relief Society presidency. Visiting Althea and other sisters. Working her network for contacts that might result in new clients.

"Slow down," Joanna told her one afternoon. "You don't have to do all this—the kids can help out with the house. And it's not necessary for you to work."

"Yes, it is. I stopped getting child support for Kayla last year, and I need to make up the shortfall." Erin read Joanna's expression and said, "I don't expect Vince to help with the kids' expenses. His house hasn't sold yet, so he's still making payments on it."

"You haven't even talked to him about it, have you?" Joanna said. "You still think you have to do it on your own, don't you? I wouldn't be surprised if you have a rainy-day fund you haven't told Vince about."

Erin flushed. "It came in handy when Cory and I got divorced."

"Erin, Erin," Joanna chided. "You're still trying to protect yourself against the future."

Erin knew her mother was right. So many things were happening over which she had no control. This baby growing inside her. Vince's presence changing her quiet home into a hub of Scout activities—boys were over every weekend to work on badges in the basement rec room. Kayla and Mark making plans that had nothing to do with her.

When the family went up to Boulder Lake for the October Gerlach reunion held over the long weekend of the teacher convention, both contacted people they wanted to see in Duluth. Kayla made plans to meet with the Pulanskys, a husband-wife team of potters she hoped to apprentice with in the coming summer. Mark was having lunch with a music professor he'd met at piano camp that summer after using one of the university practice rooms.

After dropping Mark at the university fine arts building and meeting the Pulanskys, whom she liked very much, Erin went on to the library to check for business e-mails. She replied to several, and then wrote to the COBs:

> I'm in such an odd spot. I'm bringing a child into the world who'll depend on me for every need. At the same time my two oldest are going out on their own and don't seem to need me for anything—except financial support. It's all good, but it's disconcerting.

That feeling was intensified that evening at supper when Erin heard Mark talking to Vince and Russ about taking flying lessons. She'd given him permission to fly with Vince, hoping it would give them an opportunity for male bonding. She hadn't counted on him falling in love with flying. She hated how it felt when the two men she loved most were in the air.

Two weeks later she dropped onto a kitchen chair with a cry when she heard the evening news anchor say that Minnesota senator Paul Wellstone and his wife and daughter had been killed in a plane crash near Eveleth, which wasn't far from Boulder Lake.

Vince, who was on the deck grilling, was immediately by her side. When she blurted out the news about the Wellstone tragedy and her fears about him and Mark flying, he sat beside her and stroked her back, murmuring words of comfort.

"I don't want you to fly again," she said. "It's too risky."

"So is crossing a street," he said. "And us getting married. And you having a baby at your age."

It was the worst thing he could have said. When Erin started to bawl, he pulled her onto his lap and rocked her like a baby.

"Hey, there. Like it or not, life is full of loss. Bad things happen, people die. But withholding ourselves from life and love out of fear would be the greatest loss."

His words—the most eloquent he'd ever spoken—reminded Erin of what Theresa had said at Kayla's Woman Welcome: "A life lived in fear is a life half lived." She'd always been afraid, she realized. Of love, of lack, of not being good enough no matter how hard she tried. She rested her head on his shoulder, wondering why it was so hard for her to trust in the goodness that life, despite challenges, offered.

WILLADENE

The day Elizabeth arrived home from Romania, Carl called to announce his engagement to Sookie and his plans to bring her to meet the family on Thanksgiving weekend. Deenie hoped Elizabeth would be better by then. Her stateside doctor had said strep and mononucleosis had worn her down. She was so weak and frail, it would take months for her to recuperate.

Brad showed up right after Elizabeth got home, and in the weeks after that came often because he was stateside at his company's head-quarters in Atlanta. Deenie didn't look forward to his visits. In her mind, they kept Elizabeth from the rest she needed. Elizabeth insisted she rested better when he was there.

Evvy took Elizabeth's side. She was wholeheartedly thrilled with the situation. To her it was all so romantic. The way she watched Brad and Elizabeth together convinced Deenie she was picking up pointers for future reference.

Deenie had begun thinking about what the Thanksgiving menu would be when Carl called to say Sookie would be coming alone. "I'll be in Afghanistan," he said. "My commanding officer was called up but has a critically ill child. I was specifically chosen to be his replacement by the overseas commander who's been at Maxwell AFB and knows of my record. It's a real honor."

Deenie was speechless. She'd known Carl could be called overseas at any time, but she'd never believed it would really happen. It took effort to ask calmly, "When will we see you?"

"I'll get a chance for a short visit before I leave, and I should be home by the first of May. Sookie and I want to get married in the Mesa temple then. That's where her dad grew up. Does that sound okay to you?"

"It sounds wonderful, son."

After the call was over, Deenie found a spot in the library to quiet

her spinning thoughts. Thanksgiving was just around the corner, and she
would be having both her future in-laws as guests. She was determined
to do better at accepting Sookie than she had at accepting Brad.

JUNEAU

When Shan had started working full-time the year before, Juneau
invited Serenity to come to their house after school until Shan got
home—and Serenity had moved right into Gideon's life. As time went
on, she'd become almost an appendage to him. At twelve, the girl was so
needy that Juneau didn't have the heart to change the arrangement, even
though Giddy was wanting to spend more time with friends his age.

To Juneau's relief, Giddy handled it very well. When his two best guy
friends, Tanner and Blaik, came over to hang out in the computer room
and Serenity insisted on hanging out with them, he rolled his eyes and
groaned, "Little sisters!" The other boys nodded sagely because they had
sisters, too, and let her stay. Juneau tried to siphon her off frequently to
make cookies or whatever task she could think of. Serenity was coopera-
tive, but as soon as the task was finished, she rejoined Gideon and his
friends.

One day Juneau needed the computer room while the guys were
there, so Gideon asked if they could walk down to the video rental store
in the nearby shopping center. Serenity latched onto Gideon. "I'm going,
too," she said.

"Look, Serenity," Gideon said, "This is just for guys. How about you
staying home and keeping Numbtail company?"

"That's a good idea," Juneau said. "I've got work to do, and it would
help if you'd keep him from getting on my lap while I write."

"I don't want to," Serenity said stubbornly.

"We'll bring back a video for you, too, if you'll stay here," Gideon
offered. "What would you like to see?"

"I want to see the video store!"

"Forget it," Tanner said. "No pesky girls allowed on this trip. Got it?"

Serenity reacted with blinding speed, pounding on Tanner with her
fists, kicking him, biting the arm he put up to defend himself.

"Serenity, stop that!" Juneau ordered. She wrapped her arms around the girl, trying to contain her flailing rage. Gideon grabbed her wrists, restraining her from hitting Juneau.

"Serenity, calm down," Juneau said. "Stop and think what you're doing."

"Yeah," Tanner said, rubbing a bite mark on his arm. "Get a grip."

"Tanner, zip it!" Juneau snapped. She jerked her head toward the door, and Gideon led his friends outside. Then she went back to calming Serenity, her heart heavy.

This was the first time Juneau had seen Serenity lose control. She'd argued with Gideon before, like a sister would argue with a brother. Like she herself had argued at times with Flint when they were young. But this violence was the legacy of her father, Juneau knew. She'd learned it from him.

Serenity was sobbing. "I didn't mean to do that," she said.

"I know. There, now. Shhh. Shhh," Juneau soothed, drawing her close.

"Don't tell my mom," Serenity whispered.

"I have to tell her, hon," Juneau said. "She has to know."

Later that night Juneau wrote to Deenie and Erin, telling them about the day, adding:

> Shan says Dex was an abused child, and violence was a way of life when he was young. Obviously, the pattern's been passed to Serenity. Makes me think about that part in the Bible that talks about the iniquity of the fathers being visited upon the children down through the generations.
>
> Now is the time for intervention. As Deenie says, when a problem arises, you either move toward it or away from it. We're going toward it. After Shan and I discussed what happened with Serenity, we made an appointment with a very sensitive and caring psychologist here in our stake, Dr. Barbara. Pray for us.
>
> Love,
> Juneau

WILLADENE

E-mail, November 29, 2002

Dear Juneau and Erin,

I spent Thanksgiving getting to know my two future in-laws. There is so much about Brad I wasn't aware of. Talking to him one-on-one, something I've never done before, and watching him with Elizabeth has changed my feelings about their marriage. The age difference seems insignificant when compared with their commitment to and love for each other.

As for Sookie, she won us over the minute she walked in. She's a tiny little thing with dark straight hair from her mother, green eyes and freckles from her dad, and enough spunk to fill the Gator Stadium. She says it comes from being a military brat.

Not only do I like her, I admire her. She accepts Carl's absence with such faith. When I asked her how she did it, she said, "The same way I handled my father being gone. I pray often, and I try to live a life he'd be proud of."

That's a lesson for us all. Juneau, I pray for you and Erin and your families all the time.

Deenie

JUNEAU

E-mail, December 2, 2002

Dear Friends,

Deenie, what you wrote about Sookie reminds me of what my brother, Flint, once said about his wife being a major contribution to the success of his military career. It sounds like Carl has chosen well.

Shan and I are concerned about Serenity. She was making good progress with Dr. Barbara until she received a letter from her dad in jail. She's folded up inside herself now, and not even Gideon can reach her. She won't show us the letter.

Even so, we're all preparing for Christmas. We'll have our whole family here, including Shan and Serenity, who are part of it. Our house is missing its roof, but we'll carry on (thank goodness for tarps). Everybody says Christmas would not be the same anywhere else.

I wish you all a blessed season.

Lovence,
Juneau

ERIN

Three weeks before Christmas, Cory called Erin. After a few minutes of talking about the renovations he was making on his new house, an older Mediterranean on the Lake of the Isles near downtown Minneapolis, Cory cleared his throat. "I know we'd talked about getting together at my folks' place for Christmas Day, but I'd like to have just the kids and my parents over here. If that's all right."

"Oh," was all Erin could say. In the year since she married Vince, they'd all been together at birthdays and for dinner at Skipp and Linda's. Cory and Vince had been a little awkward around each other but not enough to prepare Erin for this.

Cory broke the silence. "Vince's family would probably love to have you and him there. Wouldn't they?"

"Yes. Yes, they would."

So after a lovely Christmas Eve with the McGees at Andrew and Brenda's place, Mark, Kayla and Hannah went to Cory's for Christmas Day, and Erin and Vince went to his folks' house. The exuberance of the Gerlach clan kept her mind off wondering what was going on at Cory's, but every so often, she found herself looking for her own children among the cousins.

They came home eager to tell Erin what Cory's house looked like and give her the big news—Skipp was going to retire, and he and Linda hoped to go on a mission soon. "Grandpa Johnson said he wanted to follow in Great-Grandpa Harold's footsteps," Mark said. "And he asked me if I was saving for my mission."

"Are you?" Erin asked.

"Some," Mark said, looking abashed. Between tutoring students in math, giving piano lessons and working as a computer tech, he made good money. "I guess I'd better get serious about it."

When she went to bed that night, Erin couldn't stop thinking about how much life had changed in the last two years. Her marriage and pregnancy. The widening distance between her and Cory. That was understandable but still a bit sad, considering how close they'd been in the early years of the divorce when he'd been her support and confidant. The Johnsons' plans for a mission. Erin was glad for them, but they'd been so much a part of her life that she couldn't imagine how it would be without them.

And her two older children were growing into such interesting, accomplished young people. She was proud of them, although she worried about Kayla, who had no social life. The girl spent all of her time at the university, working at a gift shop, or in the rec room working at her potter's wheel. "She's okay," Vince had said when she asked him how he thought Kayla was doing. The two of them often talked when working on projects, she on her pottery, he on North Woodsy lamps made with birch limbs as a base. "Have a little trust in her."

There was that trust word again. She remembered the words she'd repeated like a mantra at her wedding: Love Vince, trust God, have faith. With all the changes that were happening and a baby on the way, she hoped with all her heart she could do that.

E-mail, December 28, 2002
Dear COBs,

I'm laughing so hard I've got a stitch in my side.

When I was pregnant with my other kids, I remember writing you about how Cory would lie next to me in bed, his hand on my belly, talking to his babies. It was like hearing him give them a blessing.

A few minutes ago, Vince plopped into bed, patted my belly, and said, "Hi, Buddy." Then he went to sleep! That, ladies, is the difference between my two husbands in a nutshell.

I do so love that man. I can't imagine life without him or without this little bambino, a boy, according to the ultrasound. Vince already calls him by name—Anthony, Tony for short. Hannah, who's had to put up with being called Hannah Banana, calls him Tony Baloney! Poor little guy.

Your Erin

Chapter 25

2003

JUNEAU

E-mail, January 1, 2003
Dear Friends,

If you've never had Christmas in a house without a roof, you're lucky! We're looking like a bombed-out zone, and I have to keep going back to the architect's drawing of the way it's going to look eventually (in ten years maybe?) to keep myself upright. Maybe by next Christmas we'll be finished. The work would go a lot faster if Greg didn't want to do some of it himself! (As if he has time!)

Despite the debris, it was a joyful time. Rhiannan (almost four) provided enough enthusiasm to cover any inadequacies of the house. She's such a grandma's girl! Neither of my daughters was ever all that interested in what I was like as a child nor in the things I've kept from those days. But Rhiannan, after all the presents were opened, brought what she calls "Grandma's Box" to the family room and spent the rest of the day going through it, her favorite thing to do here. It's a little cedar chest, about 18"x9"x9," where I keep things that were meaningful to me when I was young.

Both my girls were here. Nicole flew in from Denver for a couple of days. She's going to apply to a hospital in the Los Angeles area for her second year of residency. She's doing well and seemed content, if not exactly cheerful.

Misty arrived with EJ in tow, as often happens. I had a most unexpected conversation with those two after dinner. EJ had read a talk by Sister Chieko Okazaki about young Church members dealing with sexual abuse. Realizing what some girls her age are going through put her own issues into perspective and awakened a sense of purpose—she's planning to major in social work at night school so she can help others.

Shan and Serenity were here, too. I'm happy to report that

Serenity is doing well with Dr. Barbara. The downside of the celebration was an e-mail from Mom asking if I can come to Oregon again for a few days, so I assume Dad is worse.

Hope your Christmas was good all the way.

Love,
Juneau

Juneau sent the e-mail and then walked into her bedroom where she'd put Grandma's Box after everyone left. She ran her hand over the top of it, letting herself think about the item Rhiannan had pulled from the bottom of the box, asking, "What's this?"

Those two words had flung open Juneau's closet of Guilty Secrets and revealed what was in the darkest corner, the guiltiest secret of all, the one that had been festering there since her tenth year. The one that had created the closet in the first place. The one she hadn't thought of in a long, long time, except for the brief flash in Sedona when Erin fell.

"It's paraffin wax," Juneau had told Rhiannan. "My mom used to make blackberry jelly, and she'd melt wax like this to pour over the top of it when she put it into the little jars."

At Rhiannan's look of puzzlement, she suggested, "There still are some pomegranates on our tree. I'll invite you and your mom over next Saturday, and we'll make pomegranate jelly. When we put it in jars, we'll melt this and pour it on top. Would you like that?"

Always eager to come to Grandma's house, Rhiannan had said, "Oh, yes!"

Shaking herself out of the memory, Juneau opened the box and dug down until she found the small oblong block of wax. Removing it from its torn packaging paper, she held it in her hand, examining its worn-down edges. She wondered if Starette's and her fingerprints were on it. She wondered whatever had become of the girl named Brenna Petry.

"We're not pouring this on top of any jelly," she muttered under her breath. Wrapping up the wax again, she went out to the garbage can and buried it deep down in the discarded Christmas gift-wrappings.

She wished she could bury the remembered secret with it, the terrible knowledge that she and Starette had caused injury to a classmate. She hadn't thought of Brenna Petry in decades, and she wasn't going to think of her now. She pushed the secret back into its hiding place, wondering how long she could keep it from oozing out.

WILLADENE

"So did you like Sookie as well after having her with you for Christmas as you did after Thanksgiving?" Delia asked as she stamped the pile of envelopes in front of her.

"Even more," Deenie said. "She knows she gets the newsier letters from Carl, so she calls to read me his latest epistles." Deenie picked up the last of the invitations for the staff appreciation banquet and put them in the outgoing mail basket. "Thanks for your help with these."

"With Ferris on campus working on the board issues, I was glad to have a reason to be close enough to keep an eye on him," Delia said. "He doesn't know when to quit."

"Neither does Roger. It's like he's a yoyo and everything and everyone else has a hand in pulling the string."

"That's the nature of the job, Deenie. How do you think Roger's handling it?"

"I can only guess. With the teacher evaluations coming up, the applications for the new scholarship program, the accreditation review lurking around the corner, and the renovation of the executive suites under way, he's on campus more than he's home."

"Then it must be especially nice to have Elizabeth so improved. One less thing to think about." Delia gave Deenie a quick squeeze. "Do your best to get Roger to let off some steam. Ferris always kept things to himself, too, and I'm sure that's one of the things that landed him in the cardiac unit."

Deenie did her best to run interference for Roger when calls came to the house. She tried to get him to sleep and to eat properly. But by the first week in February, she'd reached the limits of her patience with his strong silent act.

She was holding a paper plate with a breakfast sandwich on it when Roger rushed through the kitchen. "Whoa, boss man," she said. "We need to talk!"

"Not now." Roger grabbed his breakfast and dodged around her. "My new office furniture is coming today. I have to clear my old desk before the janitors move it out."

"Don't move anything by yourself," Deenie hollered after him.

But Roger didn't listen. At three o'clock that afternoon, life as Deenie knew it changed drastically.

E-mail, February 21, 2003
Juneau and Erin,

Roger tried to move a huge mahogany desk on his own and ended up with a herniated lumbar disc. The doctor said it could take six to twelve weeks to heal and might require surgery. Roger says absolutely no to that, no matter how miserable it gets.

And he is miserable—in constant pain. This is the first time since I met him that he's suffered anything worse than the flu or a sprained toe. We're both struggling to find a way to cope.

Deenie

ERIN

Erin was sitting with her feet up and eyes half-closed when she heard the phone ring. Vince answered in his usual pleasant tone. Then he said, "What?" in a voice that brought her upright with a jolt. He handed her the cordless receiver. "Caitlin calling," he said with an expression that boded ill.

Erin took the phone. "It's Sean and Margaret." Caitlin's voice was distorted by grief. "Dad went over to check on them when they didn't answer the phone. Their house was full of carbon monoxide. We're lucky he made it out."

"How?" Erin managed.

"The first responders said maybe that tight construction that's supposed to save on heating. It sometimes causes back drafts of carbon monoxide from a furnace or water heater."

Erin went through the next days in shock. She couldn't imagine The Grandparents McGee gone. She and the children had grown fond of them during evenings spent around the McGees' dining room learning about family history. *If only they'd lived long enough to welcome Tony into the world*, she thought.

Then came another shock when Erin and her children were asked to attend the reading of the will. The family lawyer explained that after the brouhaha following Lindsay's birth, the elder McGees had changed their will to bequeath a sum to Erin equal to that going to Caitlin. Further, they'd revised their trust to state that children born to Caitlin *and to Erin* would be able to request funds for reasons of "health, maintenance, welfare, and education" when they turned eighteen.

"What does that mean?" a bemused Kayla asked Andrew.

Mark answered. "We're rich. We can do what we want to do."

"Excuse me," Andrew said, clearly displeased. "You can *make a request* for funds, but it has to be approved by the trustees—me and the lawyer. I can tell you now we won't approve any frivolous requests."

Erin hoped Mark had taken his grandfather's words to heart, but he started in again on the way home, coming up with wild ideas of what he wanted to do when he turned eighteen in November. "Yeah, I think New York's the place to go. I could get an apartment and maybe go to the New York School of Music. Or maybe just hang out on a beach somewhere."

She was about to say something when Vince pulled the SUV to the side of road and turned to Mark. "I don't know about your mother, but I'm disappointed at your attitude, Mark. Having resources at your disposal isn't a license for irresponsible behavior. And it won't ensure the respect and admiration that really counts—you'll still have to earn those through the kind of man you are."

"I was just having fun," Mark mumbled.

"I know. But remember you'll never have true wealth unless you've developed loving relationships and a testimony of the gospel."

The kids were quiet as Vince pulled back into traffic. Erin touched Vince's shoulder. "Thank you. You said the exactly right things."

Erin didn't blame the kids for not knowing quite how to feel about their new situation. She herself didn't. Even as the realization that she would never want sank in, she still felt the need to earn money and to maintain her secret slush fund. Why was that?

When she told The Jays how she felt, Jake pulled his purple suspenders out with his thumbs and said, "Maybe your fears aren't about money. Like Althea's weren't really about leaving her house."

Erin hadn't thought of it that way before. "I always feel like everything depends on me," she said slowly. "That's dumb, considering how much help and support I've gotten from family. And how willing Vince was to take over some expenses after he sold his house." She sighed. "It doesn't make sense, but I always feel like I have to hedge my bets."

"That's probably because we had it tough when you were growing up," Joanna said. "You had to start working when you were fourteen. And much of what you've accomplished, you've accomplished on your own." She paused. "But you're a long way past that now."

"Why don't I feel it?" Erin said glumly. Then she brightened. "You know what I want to do with some of that money? Give you two that Grand Tour you keep talking about."

They protested it was too much, but she said, "You've done so much for me and my kids. It's time I do something for you."

JUNEAU

Juneau was thinking about Roger's back and Erin's Grandparents McGee when she got a call from her mother saying, "Come now."

She caught the first available flight for Oregon. Her brother, Flint, was already there when she arrived, and the two of them and their mother spent several poignant hours at Paul Paulsen's bedside. When the end drew near, he indicated that he wanted to speak to each of them privately. To say good-bye.

When it was Juneau's turn, she sat in the chair near his head, so she could look into his face. She started to say how much she loved him, but he held up a hand. "I want to apologize to you, Juney." His voice was just a thread, and she had to lean close to hear him. "I never did give you and Flint a firm place to stand. All that moving around . . ."

She folded his hand in hers. "Dad, our firm place was that we knew you loved us."

"More than you know."

"And I love you."

He squeezed her hand. After taking several shallow breaths, he said, "Juney, take your mother home."

"I will, Daddy," she reassured him. "There'll be plenty of room when our house remodeling is . . .

"No." He gripped her hand with sudden strength. "*Home.* To Mink Creek. She needs to go *home.*"

Juneau thought her heart would break from love and sorrow. "I will, Daddy. I promise.

His breathing was shaky. "Unfinished business," he whispered on an exhaled breath. Then, "Tell her I have to go now."

Juneau quickly called her mother and brother to the bedside. Pamela smoothed Paul's hair, whispering in his ear. He died as evening fell on the last day of February.

Juneau, who'd never before watched a person die, found it to be a strangely peaceful moment. He was there, looking up at Pamela, and then he wasn't. As simple as that. But his last words intruded on her grief. She couldn't help but wonder what unfinished business her father had referred to back in Idaho. Were there more secrets to be revealed? Did *everybody* have secrets buried somewhere?

The funeral, a celebration of his life, was held in their Oregon ward. The Relief Society provided lunch for all those who came from out of town, and Juneau was astonished at how many there were. Besides all of her family and Flint's, who came as soon as they were notified, there were at least a dozen people from various cities in the Northwest. One couple even came all the way from Montana to pay their respects.

Listening to the anecdotes people told, Juneau realized that her parents had been far more than just the here-today-gone-tomorrow flitters she'd always thought them to be. They'd taken part in communities, had made friends, had touched people's lives. She hadn't been mature enough to see that when she'd been living with them. If she hadn't made connections herself, it was her own fault.

In honor of Paul Paulsen, and Pamela, too, the local library established a Pillar to Post Mystery shelf, which the family went to see before they flew home. Gideon was the most affected. "Did Grandpa and Grandma really write all those books?" he asked.

At fifteen, Gideon was not easily impressed by authors, especially
since he'd seen his mom, Juneau, writing books all his life. But there in
the library he realized how significant his grandparents (technically great-
grandparents) were. "I wish I'd gotten to know Grandpa better," he said.

"I wish so, too, Giddy," Juneau said. "But we'll have eternity to do
that."

After everything was over, Juneau tried to talk her mother into going
back to Pasadena with them. But Pamela Paulsen refused.

"I need time, Juney," she said. "To say good-bye and to sort out a lifetime of memories. And to figure out who I am, now that I'm not part of a
pair. I'll come down there eventually but not right now."

Juneau had to settle for that.

On the flight home, Gideon, who sat between her and Greg, asked,
"Will I get to see Grandpa again? I mean, in eternity?"

Greg nodded. "Sure, Gideon. He's part of our family."

"But I'm not," Gideon said. "I'm not sealed to our family."

Juneau didn't know whether their mention of eternity had started
him thinking or whether it had been a recent trip the Young Men of their
ward made to the Los Angeles temple to do baptisms for the dead.
Something had alerted him to the truth that he wasn't sealed to anybody.

"We can do something about that," Greg told him. "It's time we got
you sealed to someone."

It was something they'd discussed after Misty first brought him back
to California. Although he'd been too young to see all of the ramifica-
tions of the subject, he'd realized the temple ceremony binding families
together was something so important that he'd need to give it some
thought. "I'll choose who to be sealed to when I'm smart enough," he'd
said.

He was smart enough now. His decision: "I want to be sealed to you
and Mom."

Greg nodded slowly. "We'll have to talk with Trace and Cath."

The thought of that set Juneau's mind to creating various versions of
the scene. Then it went on, digging up all the history that had brought
them to this point. But when it detoured to snag Brenna Petry and what
she and Starette had done, she reined it in. She dug out the novel she'd

purchased to read on the flight home. It wasn't very good, but it kept her from thinking about things best left alone.

Talking to Trace and Cath had to wait until they and Rhiannan came back from a weekend at Sea World in San Diego. The little family arrived at the house full of stories, which they told over dinner. It wasn't until they'd helped clear the table and set up Rhiannan with a kids' movie that Juneau brought up Gideon's desire to be sealed to her and Greg.

Greg cleared his throat. "There are some legalities involved that require difficult choices. Juneau and I would have to legally adopt Gideon, and that means both Misty and you, Trace—" Greg looked directly at Trace, and Juneau saw how pale Trace's face was "—would have to give up parental rights."

"Has Misty agreed to that?" Trace's voice was tight.

"She's willing to do what Gideon wants."

Trace looked from Greg to Gideon and back to Greg. "Do you realize what you're asking? I can't give up my son. Any more than I could give up Rhiannan."

"I'll still be here," Gideon said hopefully. "I'll always know that you're the dad who made me. I'll visit like always and be Rhiannan's big brother. And you and I will still play the guitar and sing together. What would change?"

"You're my boy!" Trace's voice vibrated with emotion. "I've already lost one boy. I can't lose another one."

Juneau exchanged a startled glance with Greg. Trace had never mentioned another boy. He'd never said anything about anyone in his past, except his grandmother.

Cath put her arm around Trace. "Tell them about Dillon, honey. They need to know."

"I guess so." Trace looked at each one of them in turn and then swallowed hard. "Dillon was my little brother. He was the one I wrote 'Little Boy' for."

Juneau had always loved "Little Boy," the poignant song Trace had sung to Gideon that day in 1988 when he'd first come to the house. He hadn't mentioned that he'd written it for anyone particular, a boy who was . . . Juneau felt a foreboding as she realized Trace had used past tense when referring to Dillon.

Gripping Greg's hand, she listened as Trace told them that he'd never met his father, that his mother had been a drug addict. "She loved me, I think," he said, "but she loved her hits and her string of boyfriends more."

He told how his grandmother had tried to get custody of him for years, but his mother, Rita, had managed to paste herself together when necessary in order to keep him. Then, when Trace was eleven, she'd had another baby, Dillon. "He was mine from the very first," Trace said, his face softening. "Except for when I was at school, I was the one who took care of him and loved him. We did okay—until Mom brought Rocky home. He was an angry drunk, violent. I was afraid for Dillon and for myself, so I took him to my grandma's house."

He paused. "I don't know why Rita wanted Dillon, but she and Rocky came and got him one day. When I started to go with them, Rocky said they hadn't come for me." He shrugged helplessly. "I should have gone, no matter what. If I'd been there, I could have stepped in when Rocky went crazy with Dillon's crying."

Trace had told the story in a flat voice, but now it went down to a whisper. "Dillon would still be alive, if I'd been there."

Juneau thought her heart would break as Gideon hugged Trace, and she, Greg, and Cath surrounded them, offering comfort. Little Rhiannan pushed herself into the center of the group and wiped away their tears, saying, "I'll kiss it all better."

There was no kissing such sordidness better, Juneau thought. No wonder Trace would not give up his claim to Gideon.

But then Trace amazed them by doing just that. Pulling himself together, he stood and put one hand on Gideon's shoulder. "There's something I want to say. My life is completely different now from what it was then, and I owe it to all of you—" he grinned slightly "—and to Misty. I fathered Gideon. You accepted me into your family. I met and married Cath. And I learned what a Forever Family is. Without that, I don't know what would have become of me."

Juneau put one arm around Greg and the other around Cath as Trace looked at Gideon and said, "If you want to be adopted by these good people and sealed to them, I'll sign the papers."

As soon as the legalities had been handled, they all went to the temple, and in a lovely, sacred ceremony, the sealing was accomplished.

WILLADENE

Deenie fretted as March went by and Roger didn't seem to be getting any better.

"These things take time and patience, Mrs. Rasmussen," the physical therapist said as Deenie walked with him to the door of Gobb Hill.

Deenie had heard that before when Roger's doctor suggested heat and cold therapy. And again when he changed pain medications and administered two epidural injections in Roger's back—without any appreciable change for the better. Time and patience were two things she and Roger were nearly out of.

A few nights later, Deenie woke to the sound of footsteps overhead. Roger was in the attic again, trying to pace away the pain and the panic that had begun to accompany it.

She slid out of bed, tiptoed up the stairs and slipped quietly into the large space. She'd learned better than to abruptly approach him when he was in such a state.

"Couldn't sleep?" she asked when he finally noticed her.

Roger shook his head. "I keep thinking about some problems Richard Harker brought to my attention. I'll be down in a while. Don't wait up for me."

Deenie lay in bed seething. She'd explicitly asked Harker to refer Academy problems to Marsha while Roger had time off. The man was trying to make himself indispensable to Roger, and his visits sapped Roger of the energy he needed to heal.

She was still awake when Roger finally came down the stairs, but instead of coming into their bedroom, he turned at the end of the hall and went into the apartment, adding physical distance to their growing emotional distance. Her heart fluttered painfully, making her wish she had some of the medications that had made such a difference when she'd suffered the same symptoms after Evvy's birth.

That caught her attention. *There must be something on the market besides pain pills that could help Roger through this rough time,* she thought. *I'll ask the doctor the next time I see him.*

ERIN
>E-mail, March 19, 2003
>Dear Juneau and Deenie,
>
>Wasn't that photo of Tony taken right after his birth funny? He has shoulders like a linebacker, a fringe of brown hair like an old man, and the smallest ears I've ever seen.
>
>It's been two weeks since then, but the combination of long labor, emergency Caesarean, and being forty-five years old has definitely made my recovery time slower. But I'm getting plenty of help from the kids, the adoring grandparents, Caitlin, and Vince's sisters. The Jays have even put off booking the tour I'm giving them so they can get to know their new grandson.
>
>Vince is such a happy daddy. He took a month off from the clinic without my even asking, and we've had some wonderful times with our baby and the kids. I was especially touched at Mark's reaction to Tony. He's very tender with his little brother, very careful. Vince handles Tony as if he were a puppy—I expect to see him pick the little guy up by the scruff of his neck one of these days!
>
>>Your Erin

JUNEAU
>E-mail, March 21, 2003
>Dear Friends,
>
>Erin, congratulations on your little tank. He sounds like a darling boy. We have a new little guy in our family, too! Cath gave birth to a baby boy yesterday. He's so long and skinny that Ira says he can rent himself out as a utility pole in a year or so! His name is Dillon, after Trace's little brother I told you about, who died so tragically. We are all soooo thrilled with him.
>
>I'm trying to ignore the fact that he arrived on the day the war with Iraq started. The reason that bothers me (other than that

I hate war) is it reminds me how vulnerable boys are when war comes along. I pray there are no conflicts when Dillon is old enough to be a soldier (how unrealistic is that?), but then I think that Gideon is fifteen now. What if this war continues, and he goes into the military, like your Carl, Deenie? The Griff thrives.

But I have to think that if these beautiful boys grow up to be missionaries who'll go out to spread the gospel to every tongue and every people, that will help to end all wars.

Loving being Grandma again,
Juneau

Chapter 26

WILLADENE

In early April, the doctor declared Roger ready to return to work—if he took it easy.

The day he went back to work Deenie was encouraged. Roger still moved carefully, but he took time to have breakfast with Evvy and Elizabeth and though he couldn't kneel, he led the family in prayer.

But when he turned to leave, he tripped over Bear, who was sleeping on the doormat. Grabbing his back, he yelled, "Get your stupid dog out of my way!" Then he kicked Bear in the ribs.

Deenie and her girls gaped in shock as Bear yelped and scuttled under the table. "Roger!" Deenie cried.

He raised his hands in silent apology and left the house.

"What's happening to Dad?" Elizabeth asked.

Deenie shook her head. "I don't know."

Things went downhill from there. Despite his doctor's caution, it was clear to Deenie after the first few days that Roger's idea of taking it easy was working as long as he could stand the pain, doping himself, and working some more. Whenever Deenie tried to broach the topic of the amount of medication he was taking, he responded with anger.

As the days passed, Deenie noticed that a growing number of triggers were setting off Roger's temper. The click in the whir of the overhead fan was suddenly offensive. Starch in his shirt collars irritated his neck. He quit shaving on the weekends—it bothered his skin. And woe be to Evvy or Elizabeth if they played their music above a whisper.

When Bear started slinking out of any room Roger appeared in, Deenie cringed for Roger's sake. But as his tension level heightened and his fuse shortened, she and her daughters followed suit.

The morning of Roger's fifth week back at work, Elizabeth stopped her mother in the kitchen. "Mom, I don't think Dad really listens anymore. When I talk to him, he nods his head but nobody's home. It's spooky." And that night Evvy stormed in after a late choir practice saying, "Dad forgot me again, Mom. Miss Winsome had to bring me home. Ugh!" Then Marsha called to express her concern. Roger had missed an important meeting and had left several days' worth of paperwork unsigned.

Determined to confront Roger about his erratic behavior, Deenie approached his Gobb Hill office. He must have heard her coming, Deenie thought when he met her at the door. Before she could speak, he said, "Not now, Deenie." To her amazement he shut the door in her face and turned the key.

Out of deference to her husband, Deenie had kept her fears about his behavior to herself. Now she called Miss B. "Sounds to me like Roger's use of medication is out of control," she said. "Talk to your doctor. Talk to the bishop. If that doesn't help, try one of those intervention things they show on TV."

That seemed too extreme to Deenie, so she put in a conference call to Juneau and Erin to see what they thought. They said the same thing. She spent another night alone—Roger's move into the apartment bedroom was beginning to look permanent—battling against accepting what she knew was true. Roger abusing his prescription drugs? Never! Subject him to an intervention? Unthinkable! It was too public, too humiliating. It would push Roger over the edge, if he weren't already there.

Her resistance to accepting the likelihood that Roger had a drug problem evaporated when Ferris called her early the next morning to say he'd narrowly avoided a catastrophe at a board meeting the night before when Richard Harker reported his suspicion that Roger was addicted to prescription drugs.

"Roger denied it, Deenie," Ferris said, "but the way he's been acting . . ."

Deenie hung up the phone, raced down the hall to the apartment bathroom Roger had been using, and flung open the medicine cabinet. A row of prescription bottles that seemed to have grown exponentially stared back at her. She swept the lot off the shelf, walked into the bedroom without knocking, and dropped them on the bed where Roger was sitting while he dressed.

"What's this?" she asked holding up a half-filled bottle of a prescription she didn't recognize.

"Muscle relaxant. It helps me sleep." Roger grabbed the bottle from her hand and popped it open. Before she could grab it back, he'd downed two of the pills without water.

Appalled at the casual way he'd doped himself, she asked, "And you're taking it now because—?"

"Because my back hurts too much to put on my #!@! pants," he shouted. "Leave me alone and let me do what I have to do."

After Roger left, a heartsick Deenie took the bottles to her office, lined them up on the computer desk, and began researching their uses and cautions. The results were terrifying. Roger had pills for pain. For anxiety. For sleep. For muscle spasms and restless legs. And pills to counteract the side effects of the first pills. With barely a pause to acknowledge the panic rising inside her, Deenie left an urgent message for Roger's doctor.

When he returned her call, Deenie listed the medications on the desk before her. "That's not good," the doctor said. "Half those meds were prescribed to take the place of others that hadn't been effective, not to be piggy-backed on top of them. Have Roger come see me as soon as possible."

When Deenie said Roger probably wouldn't go, the doctor gave her the number of a family intervention specialist named Mitch Jones. Overwhelmed, she hung up and rested her head on the desk. She was afraid of losing Roger if she forced the issue but even more afraid of losing him, literally, if she didn't.

She got to her knees and prayed as she'd never prayed before. Prayed until her heart was filled with the reassurance that she could do what needed to be done. Then she called Mitch Jones.

Deenie shuddered when Jones told her what an effective intervention entailed. She knew how Roger would hate involving people outside the immediate family in their problems, but Jones insisted that the people Roger loved and looked up to most had to be there. Besides family, that meant Ferris and the bishop. She called them after talking to her children and Roger's brothers and sisters.

"Are we celebrating something?" Roger asked when he walked into the living room two days later and found it filled with his family and closest and dearest friends.

The intervention expert stepped forward. "No, Mr. Rasmussen. This is an intervention. I'm Mitch Jones. I'm here to help your wife and the people who care about you tell you some things you need to hear."

"Intervention?" Roger's tone was incredulous.

"Yes," Deenie said. "Roger, you're addicted to your pain pills, and this—

"I'm no addict," Roger spat. He spun away and then grabbed his back in agony.

Deenie started toward him, but Mitch held her back. He talked Roger into sitting down and then said, "Deenie, why don't you start again. Tell Roger what he needs to know."

"Roger, I love you—and you're an addict. You may not think so, but your behavior says so. I won't stand by and let you ruin your life and ours because of it. I'm afraid *for* you, and I'm afraid *of* you. Of your anger and your unpredictability. I won't stay in a house where I'm afraid. The pills go, or I go."

Roger made a furious growl of denial, but Mitch Jones motioned him to silence, saying, "Now your daughters have something to tell you."

Elizabeth took Evvy's hand, and they stood together in front of their father. "Dad, I love you," Elizabeth said. "And I've never been afraid of you until you kicked Bear in the ribs and pushed me when I tried to talk to you. If you don't stop abusing your drugs, Mom will leave and I'll go with her."

"Me too, Daddy," Evvy said. "*You kicked Bear!*" Deenie knew by Evvy's tone that she wouldn't easily get over Roger's violent gesture.

As the girls sat down, Ferris leaned toward Roger. "The board won't put up with an addict at the wheel. I've arranged for you to take a leave of absence to get back on your feet. Take it. Get clean. Or get out."

"I'm no addict!" Roger said again but in a tone of uncertainty.

When the bishop spoke his piece, Roger's resistance finally crumbled, replaced by harsh sobs.

When the grim moment was over, Mitch said, "We've found a spot for you at a rehab center for as long as you need it. Deenie has your bags packed. We need to leave now."

"But Carl's getting married in May . . ."

Deenie remained implacable. "He said to tell you he'd rather have you well than have you at his wedding."

Roger took the suitcase Deenie handed him without responding to her touch or her farewell. After everyone had left, Deenie sent the girls to their rooms and faced the emotional backlash alone. She spent the night pacing and wondering if in an effort to save Roger's health, she had destroyed her marriage.

ERIN

> E-mail, April 23, 2003
> Dear Deenie,
>
> Thanks for calling with a status report. I can't tell you how nervous I was about the intervention. What a wrenching experience for all of you. Fight for your husband and family, dear friend. I know you've got the courage, will, faith, and love to do it.
>
> Your Erin

A month after Tony's birth, Erin invited female friends and relatives to his Baby Welcome. Vince's family had already attended sacrament meeting to see Vince bless Tony, and his mother and sisters accepted this invitation with great curiosity.

But when the Gerlach women walked through the front door, Erin sensed something was up. Her feeling was confirmed when they stayed behind after others had left, lingering in the living room as Vince and Hannah began cleaning up.

"Sit down, dear," Mama Gerlach said, patting the cushion beside her. "We want to talk to you."

Erin sat, and Suzanne gave her an encouraging smile. "Thanks so much for inviting us to the Baby Welcome. It's a tradition we weren't familiar with, and we really enjoyed it."

"But," Mama Gerlach continued, "as a new member of the Gerlach family, you need to accept our traditions, too. Beginning with: Gerlach men always go fishing on the opener, even if it coincides with Mother's Day weekend."

"I—" Erin started to say she'd apologized to Vince months ago after recognizing how much he valued that time with his father and brothers-in-law and the many ways he showed his love for her every day, but Mama Gerlach interrupted.

"You've had many things your way since you and Vince got married, dear," she said. "Can't you grant him this one thing?"

Erin felt her cheeks flush. Was that how her marriage to Vince seemed to others? She must have looked as stricken as she felt, because Vince's sister, Margo, patted her hand and said, "There is a payoff. You can ask for almost anything before that weekend, and he can't refuse you."

After the Gerlach women had left, Vince pulled Erin into a comforting embrace. "You look like you've gone nine rounds."

"Vince, is there anything you want from me that I'm not doing?" she asked. "Just let me know, and I'll do it."

"What brought this on?"

When she told him what his mother had said, he laughed. "I'm so sorry. Don't pay attention to Mom. If there's something I want, I'll tell *you*, not her. That's a promise."

As she lay next to Vince that night, Erin had to admit that despite his reassurance, Mama Gerlach had a point. Vince *had* done more to fit into her life than she had to fit into his. She was ashamed to think how she'd looked on things he liked to do—fishing, lamp-making—with smug indulgence. She really had expected he would morph from a Gerlach into a Johnson, liking what she and the kids liked, doing what they enjoyed doing.

The thought made her ill. He deserved better. She got out of bed and padded into her office. Firing up the computer, she wrote an e-mail to Deenie and Juneau, telling them what had happened and her worries. She finished with "Aargh! I feel like I'm learning how to be married all over again."

JUNEAU
> E-mail, April 30, 2003
> Dear Erin,
>
> Just so you know, even those of us who've been married to the
> same man for thirty-five years periodically have to learn how to
> be married all over again!
>
> > Lovence,
> > Juneau

WILLADENE

Nothing Deenie had ever experienced had prepared her for the
agony of waiting without word while Roger went through his first days at
the rehab center. Mitch had impressed upon her and the girls how important it was for them to take care of themselves and practice stress-relief
techniques. For Deenie, cooking relieved stress. She tried out every recipe
in the Keeping Book. And she tasted them all, more than once.

> E-mail, May 31, 2003
> Dear COBs,
>
> In the midst of this troubled time, we've had occasion to
> rejoice. Carl and Sookie's wedding went off as planned—
> without Roger. After a short honeymoon in Orlando, Carl left
> for Afghanistan and Sookie for Albuquerque, where she has a
> job as an accountant. We all put on brave faces, but parting was
> hard.
>
> Erin, please thank Kayla for the suggestion about tai chi. It's
> right in line with the alternative pain- and stress-reduction
> techniques the girls and I have been learning about at the rehab
> center. Roger's therapist tell us it's as important for us to be
> ready for Roger to come home as it is for him to be ready.
>
> > Deenie

When Roger returned home from rehab, he went straight to the
apartment, saying, "My back's still hurting. I'll sleep better alone." In the
following days, he was present but detached. Although he did respond to
his daughters, the closest he came to Deenie was when he joined her and
the girls for family prayer.

The news that Sookie was pregnant and due in February cheered Deenie immensely. Carl would be home in November, which gave them plenty of time to get settled in a place of their own before the baby was born. Deenie began to count the days—crossing each one off the calendar was the bright spot in her days. She was physically depleted; she couldn't fit into her workout clothes and was badly in need of cheer. Everyone seemed to recognize the fact except Roger, who studiously avoided her.

"Why is that?" she asked Delia during one of their lunches out.

"If he's anything like Ferris, he's embarrassed," Delia said. "Maybe even ashamed. After the heart attack, Ferris couldn't stand to be dependent on me for anything. It went against everything he believed about himself. The doctor warned me men generally don't handle illness well."

"That's what Mitch said. But since Roger hasn't shared his feelings about me in all this, I'm afraid of what they are."

"So ask him about them," Delia said.

Deenie's grin was brief. "Gabby couldn't have said it better."

JUNEAU
E-mail, June 25, 2003
Dear Friends,

What a joy it is to watch all my children—the ones I gave birth to and the ones I've "adopted"—grow into good people and begin to have children of their own. I think loving them through their ups and downs has brought me a long way toward COBhood.

Nicole finished her internship and has obtained a residency in obstetrics here in the area, as she'd hoped. She and Dr. Tim have a lot to talk about when he and Marisol join us for dinner. (He's still hoping he can change Marisol's ideas about marriage.)

Beto writes that he's happy working at Dr. Vasquez's clinic in the Huasteca mountains of Mexico (I finally found out exactly where it is, about two hundred miles from Mexico City). He's become involved in a fledgling organization that brings young doctors to the area for six months. They get lots of experience while helping him and Dr. Vasquez, who are always over-whelmed with patients. Something like Doctors Without Borders, but the doctors sign up for a longer period.

Trace and Cath's baby, Dillon, is thriving and a joy to all of us. Trace is taking over more and more work at Smoketree Systems, so Greg is spending more and more time working on our house. We're having the kitchen remodeled, starting next week. Aargh!

Ira won a much-sought-after post in the English department of Occidental College, just west of Pasadena (he'll still do a pickle commercial now and then). Shoshana has written a movie script from my book *Beyond*. She has great hopes for it. I can't quite take it in that I might have movie credits!

Gideon is taking a driver's training class. Next year he'll be able to get his license. Double aaargh.

That's the news from our part of the world.

Lovence,
Juneau

Juneau sent the e-mail and then began playing a computer game. It was mindless, but it helped her relax. She needed some relaxation. She'd been plagued lately by the secret that had burst out of the guilt closet when Rhiannan discovered the block of wax in the Grandma's Box. It was festering, growing, there in the dark place where she'd pushed it, and it would no longer be contained. Juneau thought frequently now of Brenna Petry. She needed to know what had happened to Brenna as a result of what she and Starette had done.

She closed the game and opened her Internet connection. Palms sweating, she did an Internet search for Starette Heath. Starette would know about Brenna. But she didn't find anything on Starette Heath. *Of course*, Juneau thought. *She's probably married and has a different last name.*

Taking a breath, Juneau did a search for Brenna Petry. It was also unsuccessful. Maybe because she, too, was married. Then a totally differ-ent reason occurred to Juneau. With trembling fingers, she did a search for deaths in 1950 in the county where she, Brenna, and Starette had lived. She went weak with relief when she didn't find Brenna's name listed.

ERIN

E-mail, June 29, 2003
Dear COBs,

With everything going on in your lives, it's good that you both have the joy of children marrying and having babies and traveling to interesting places.

This summer, Duluth seems to be our destination of preference. Kayla's spending the summer there, apprenticing with the Palenskys, a husband-and-wife team of potters, and renting a studio apartment on their property. (She got funds from the McGee trust to pay her costs.) I was uneasy at first, but I like the Palenskys. And Kayla promised she'd call often and go to church every Sunday.

Vince left yesterday for a week by himself at the cabin on Boulder Lake, which is near Duluth. He took Curly Dude and Rascal with him—I'm missing all three of them already! Especially since Hannah's gone, too. She's spending her summer vacation with Cory at a dude ranch in South Dakota and having a ball.

After Hannah gets back next week, she, Mark, Tony, and I will pack up and head north. I'll be dropping Mark off at U of M–Duluth for music camp, but he'll join us when Vince's family gathers at his parents' cabin. You know what? I won't mind having all those people around one bit. In fact, I'm looking forward to it.

Your Erin

P.S. Update: Melina has finished her internship and is working at a nursing home in Hopkins. Tomas told The Jays that he's going to India for a year, so Mom offered Grams's old apartment (where he's been living) to Melina. Althea's caseworker is working on getting her a dog! Not the usual service dog but a pocket dog she can carry with her.

WILLADENE

Deenie put off asking Roger what he was thinking until an evening in August when he seemed less distant than usual. Over the months intimate conversation with Roger had been nonexistent, and she stumbled over the words. "Things haven't been right between us since you got home from rehab. Are you still mad at me?"

Roger answered the question indirectly. "I hate the fact that you talked to everyone else about my situation before you talked to me."

"I tried to talk to you a hundred times."

"I wish you had tried harder."

Deenie wanted to defend herself, but she said only, "I did what I had to do."

"I know that. Now. But having everyone I looked up to and loved tell me I was a failure just about killed me."

"That's not what we were saying. You got hurt, Roger. And then you got hooked. But you faced up to it, and you're on your way to recovery. That's not failure. That's triumph."

Roger shook his head. "That's putting too simple a face on what happened, Deenie. I thought admitting that I was abusing prescription drugs was the hardest thing I'd ever done. But it was nothing compared to rehab. I had to look at places inside myself I didn't even know I had. It changed me in ways I haven't even begun to discover."

Fear clutched Deenie's heart. Had rehab changed the way Roger felt about her, their family, their life together?

Roger reached over and touched her hand voluntarily for the first time since he'd returned home. "Deenie, I love you. I love *us*, and I'm committed to our marriage and our family. But I need time to figure out what all these changes mean. Can you give me that?"

Deenie nodded, hoping their marriage had been granted a reprieve.

ERIN

E-mail, August 7, 2003
Dear COBs,

I really enjoyed being at the cabin this summer. I read a pile of books, laughed a lot with the Gerlach Girls while we watched our children playing, and let Vince paddle me around the lake by moonlight. And I met Kayla's boyfriend, Eddie Beckmann, when we went to church in Duluth!

The look on his face when he called to her from across the church foyer—and the look on hers when she turned to him—told the whole story. They tried to act nonchalant, but the electricity was crackling.

When Eddie introduced us to his parents, Lisa and Frank, they insisted we have lunch with them after church. They're a very nice family. Frank's a coach at a Duluth high school and a volunteer at the Maritime Museum, Lisa is an ICU nurse, and Eddie's working toward a degree in pharmacology at the U of M–Duluth Medical School. His sisters are both married with children. One lives in Bismarck, and the other in Des Moines.

All through the meal I had the strange feeling that I was talking to my daughter's future in-laws. But Kayla came back home right after we did so she could get ready for fall semester at the U of M. She and Eddie probably won't see much of each other until next summer, when she goes back up to work with the Palenskys. If there is something between them, it will need to sustain itself on hope.

Our other news is that Linda and Skipp have sent in their mission papers. Hearing about the Johnsons' plans got Mom and Jake looking for something to do that will make a difference, too. They found a group on the Internet that arranges volunteer vacations. They're leaning toward one in Romania, because of what I told them about Elizabeth's mission. (I'll foot the bill for it, because they never did book the Grand Tour I promised them.)

My dad and Brenda are making changes, too. After working for Andrew for over twenty-five years, Theresa has quit to take care of her ailing parents. Andrew and Brenda are looking for a townhouse they can lock and leave, so they can split their time between here and Brenda's house in Hawaii. Brenda says they can be in Hawaii only two weeks at a time—that's as long as she can stand being away from Caitlin's girls!

It's fascinating to watch these people—my three sets of parents—negotiate this time of life. They're all in transition, all looking for what will bring them joy and a renewed sense of purpose in their later years.

I won't need to look for something to give me purpose for twenty years! Tony is such a treasure. I love sitting in the rocker with his warm little body snuggled on my shoulder. It's really hard to leave him with my mom when I go out on a job. Not that I have that many. My decorating/personal shopping business took a real hit after 9/11. So I'm pretty much a stay-at-home mother these days. Caitlin, too, although she does the occasional contract job.

Tony is making "feed me" sounds, so it's time to sign off.

Your Erin

WILLADENE

E-mail, September 12, 2003
Dear COBs,

Bless you for all your support. Roger is doing a little better each day, and we are slowly making our way toward each other again. We took another big step when Roger moved back into our room.

Elizabeth took a job as a nanny in Atlanta to be closer to Brad whenever he's in town between trips overseas. We expect an announcement any day

As for me, I've felt downright odd the last month. Not depressed, just out of sorts and too tired for words. I suppose that's to be expected—it's been a long haul and it isn't over yet. Maybe I'll try out Delia's masseuse or get my nails done. That should give me a lift.

Deenie

Deenie was feeling encouraged when she sent the e-mail to Juneau and Erin. Then her mother phoned to say Aunt Stella had passed away quietly in her sleep.

"I have to go," Deenie told Roger. "After all Aunt Stella's meant to me, I have to be there for her funeral."

During the flight to Salt Lake City, Deenie was carried along on a wave of memories. Not only of Aunt Stell but also of Deenie's sister Sunny. That night she shared them with her mother and father. As they talked, she realized how important it was for her to be with family, talking about people and events that had formed her life.

After the dedication of Aunt Stell's grave in Logan, Deenie took some flowers she'd set aside for Sunny and walked to her resting place. As she laid the flowers gently on the ground, Deenie felt a rush of warmth as though Sunny were there to comfort her. Then she heard the familiar words whispered in her mind, "Deenie, it's time to come home."

She smiled. Those were the very words that Sunny had often said when she called to ask Deenie to come play with her. It was her way of saying, "I'm here, and I love you."

It wasn't until she was on the flight home, exhausted and achy and feeling not quite right, that Deenie began to wonder if those words were something more than a message of love. Might they have meant that Deenie's time on earth was short, that she would soon be going *home*, where Sunny was?

ERIN

E-mail, September 30, 2003
Dear COBs,

Cory's parents got their call to the Family and Church History Mission. They'll be working in the Family History Library and in the Joseph Smith Memorial Building (the former Hotel Utah), doing anything from restoring old books to helping people research naturalization records. Their specific assignment will come after their initial training.

Linda is excited, but Skipp wonders why he's been called to an assignment that doesn't, it seems to him, better use his skills and abilities. But he's gotten over his disappointment enough to put a deposit on a high-rise apartment north of Temple Square, one with windows showing a fabulous view of the city by night. (They'll be paying their own housing costs, of course.)

Mom and Jake are in Romania and loving it. They spend their days in Tutova Hospital's Failure-to-Thrive Clinic. Mom is assigned to the special needs kids and Jake to the toddlers! His size and booming voice scared them at first, but once he got down on the floor with them, they've been using him as a horse to ride or a mountain to climb. Mom included a charming photo of him almost hidden in a swarm of children vying for a place on his lap.

We've all taken armchair trips around the world, thanks to our families, haven't we? Juneau, you've been to Mexico City, where Nicole was on her mission. I've been to Romania, thanks to The Jays. And you, Deenie, have been to so many places, what with your kids' missions and Carl in Afghanistan and the many trips Elizabeth has taken. Remember back when you hadn't left Utah? What an adventurous woman you've become!

Your Erin

P.S. Vince bought Tony a little billed cap that says Daddy's Boy.

WILLADENE

Deenie was about to answer Erin's e-mail when a huge storm blew in. She disconnected her computer and all the TVs in the house. Even with the surge protectors hooked up, she was concerned about potential damage.

Wind lashed the windows, and Bear paced as he always did in fierce weather. Although he'd been slowed by age, Deenie was tickled to see there was no hesitation or limp in his gait. Since the scare they'd had the year before with his joint pain, a combination of health supplements and doggie massage had restored much of his former strength. She could see the muscles ripple across his shoulders as he followed the storm from window to window.

Deenie was lighting the gas log in the fireplace when the call came from Search and Rescue. "Mrs. Rasmussen," an unfamiliar voice said over the phone, "I see here that Bear is cross-trained to search over water. I know you're listed as retired, but three children are missing from a trailer park in Levy County where there's been severe flooding. Can you lend a hand?"

"I'll get right back to you," Deenie said. She hung up the phone and called Roger at the Academy.

"I'd rather you didn't go, Deenie," Roger said. "But I'll leave it up to you. You're the one who knows your limits. And Bear's."

"I'm good. Bear's good. And the new pickup is great." When Roger didn't respond Deenie added, "There are children missing."

"Then I'll start praying for you and them right now. And Deenie, be safe."

"Always," she said. "I love you."

After a quick call to confirm she was on her way, Deenie whistled for Bear.

"Wanna work? Wanna work?" Deenie caroled the old invitation to search. Bear nearly quivered himself out of his gear in his excitement to be going. "One more time, old fellow," she said and tussled lovingly with the big dog before they ran out into the rain.

The rain lessened as Deenie drove the narrow, refuse-littered road toward the county line as fast as she dared. As she drove, she thought of all the searches she'd shared with the big dog that rode eagerly beside her. Bear had been the symbol of hope to so many in the fourteen years they had been partners. Lost people had been found and wounded souls comforted by his presence. It felt to Deenie as though his life and strength had been extended long beyond his expected years for this task. Extended for the lost children in Levy County waiting for Bear to find them.

Three days later a grieving Deenie sent a copy of the article that appeared in the local newspaper to everyone who had known and loved him.

Good-bye, Bear

Today Gainesville bids farewell to Bear, a big dog with an even bigger heart. The massive fourteen-year-old search-and-rescue dog, who had become a familiar part of our community, came out of retirement Monday afternoon in an heroic effort to find the three missing children of Ernie and Renee Miller. With his handler and lifelong companion, Willadene Rasmussen, by his side, he fought through wind, rain, water, and mud to rescue the three children, who were trapped in an abandoned truck. Later that night, Bear died in Mrs. Rasmussen's arms from heart failure.

Our deep condolences go to the Rasmussen family and all who had taken Bear into their lives and hearts. When asked if she thought she could ever find another dog like Bear, owner Willadene Rasmussen said, "We didn't find Bear. He found us. We'll trust that when the time is right, the good Lord will bring a new dog to our door."

Bear's ashes will be interred next summer on the family property in Utah.

Chapter 27

JUNEAU

Ever since 9/11 Juneau had been aware that a day could start out as perfectly ordinary and then suddenly, without warning, become a before-or-after thing, an incident from which people counted time. "Oh, that happened before the Northridge earthquake," they might say, or "That was after Columbine."

Such a day was October 14, 2003, for Juneau's family. She had just sent Gideon off to school, and Greg was dressing for work. As she opened the door of her little garage office, she heard Greg call, "Juney! I need help!"

His voice sounded odd. She hurried down the hallway and found him standing half dressed in their bedroom, gripping the top of his chest of drawers. Sweat beaded his forehead and his eyes were frightened. He reached out for her. "I'm dizzy and I can't breathe."

Terrified, Juneau supported him with her left arm while she snatched up the cordless phone on the bedside table and punched in the number with her thumb. As the operator answered, "What is your emergency?" Greg's knees buckled. Try as she might, Juneau couldn't hold him, and he thumped to the floor.

Dropping beside him, Juneau described what was happening and where.

"The paramedics are on the way," the voice said. "Stay with me. Do you know CPR?"

"Yes," Juneau said, profoundly grateful she'd passed the course offered by her stake.

She would never remember just what she did then, but when the paramedics came, they said Greg's heart was beating, although irregularly. They did what they needed to and then loaded him onto a gurney and rushed out, asking Juneau if she could get to Huntington Hospital's emergency room.

She nodded, her own chest feeling constricted.

The ambulance was driving away with sirens wailing when Marisol dashed up to her. "Juneau! What happened?"

"Greg. Heart attack. I have to find my keys. I need to get to the hospital."

"I'll drive," Marisol said.

Juneau's head buzzed, and she found it hard to think. "What about your classes?"

"They'll call a sub. Where's your purse? You'll need your medical card."

Marisol got them to the hospital. At the emergency room desk, a nurse told them Greg was being helped and showed them where to wait until a doctor came out to talk to them.

Juneau couldn't sit, so she called her family and then paced. *Is this how it's going to end? Mom at least got to say good-bye to Dad. To say I love you. Oh, dear Lord, don't take him now.*

"Mrs. Caldwell?" A young doctor came from a nearby room, smiling when she saw Juneau. "He's alive. A cardiologist is on the way."

Gideon arrived at the hospital by taxi in time to hear the cardiologist give his report. Sober-faced, he held onto Juneau's hand as the doctor said, "We're going to have to do an emergency bypass. The nurse will tell you where to go to sign the necessary papers." She must have looked stricken because the doctor patted her shoulder. "Was it you who did the CPR?"

She nodded.

"Good job," he said before hurrying away.

"Mom," Gideon said, "you saved Dad's life."

Juneau incongruously noted in the midst of everything that Gideon looked down at her now. When had he grown so tall? "I did what I could. It's up to the doctors and the Lord, now."

Group by group the family assembled in the waiting room of the surgical wing. Ira and Shoshana came, then Misty and Trace and Cath, minus Rhiannan and Dillon, whom they'd left with a neighbor. Nicole was the last to arrive. Juneau was comforted by the presence of all of her family, especially Nicole, who'd had experience fending off death.

A green-garbed nurse came to tell them they could see Greg for just a minute before he went to the operating room. They tiptoed into the room where he lay on a gurney, tubes snaking around his body. He smiled weakly and motioned them closer. "Triple bypass, they tell me." He closed his eyes and took a breath. "Forward pass," he said. "Underpass." Another breath. "And cut-'em-off-at-the-pass."

Juneau had never loved him more than she did at that moment.

"Greg," Trace said, "would you like me to give you a priesthood blessing?"

Greg nodded, and they all gathered closely around as Trace placed his hands on Greg's head. When Trace finished the fervent blessing, Gideon hugged Greg and said, "I love you, Dad." The others murmured the same. Then two orderlies came to take Greg to an operating room.

Struggling with fear, Juneau took his hand and held on tight, walking alongside him as far as she could.

E-mail, October 20, 2003
Dear Erin and Deenie,

Thank you for all the phone calls and cards, especially when things were so iffy for Greg. I was in the clutches of the Griff— what if, what if, what if. And also the Griffly—if only, if only. If only I had been more aware, maybe I could have done something more. But thanks to Trace's blessing, the prayers of family and friends, and Greg's wonderful doctors and nurses, he's going to be fine. Gideon wants me to tell you I kept Greg going with CPR until the paramedics got there. Does that qualify me for a Deenie badge?

Greg's home now. He still looks gray and haggard—I guess that's what a triple bypass does to a person. I'm supposed to help him do a little walking each day. A journey across the room exhausts him, but his spirits are good. "I'm alive," he says.

Our family has been so very supportive, including Misty. There've been times when I've wondered if Misty cares about either of us, but there's no doubt in my mind now that she dearly loves her dad. She was often at his bedside at the hospital when I came to visit him, deep in conversation. But the minute she saw me, she got up and said she had someplace she needed to be.

When Trace (tall and blond) and Ira (short and swarthy) came
in together, insisting they were Greg's sons, the nurses nodded
knowingly and let them in. Another day three college-age guys
who'd been in Greg's Scout troop came in, saying they were his
sons, too. A nurse asked him exactly how many kids he had.
"Haven't counted them lately," Greg said. The nurse laughed
and let them in, too, but for only five minutes.

Gideon has taken over all chores and anything else he can do,
which leaves time for me to help Greg and read to him and talk
with him. And to simply be with him. You remember how I've
always said we didn't speak the same language? We're learning.
Maybe what we needed was time to practice!

Today Gideon received an e-mail from Evvy offering sympathy
about Greg's illness. It meant a lot to him.

> Lovence,
> Juneau

WILLADENE

E-mail, October 22, 2003
Dear Juneau,

I'm sending you a package of all the information I got together
about how men feel when they're forced to face their own mor-
tality. It's quite a journey for them, as I know from watching
Roger. It's hard for him to share his feelings. And on the rare
occasions when he does, I have to remember that he doesn't
need me to fix him; he needs me to hear him. And listening is a
way I can share in his journey.

I hope the information helps. My thoughts and prayers are with
you as always.

> Deenie

ERIN

E-mail, October 29, 2003
Dear COBs,

After all that's happened to us and our loved ones this year, I think we need to have a meeting with the powers that be and tell them, "Enough, already!"

Praying for you both,
Erin

Erin hesitated at the doorway of Kayla's room, her inner sanctum. An exercise mat and some meditation pillows were stacked against one wall. A collection of her best pottery pieces stood on her dresser. Above the dresser hung her favorite painting of Jesus, the one depicting him in red and blue robes. The only link to her skating days was the pile of stuffed animals that admirers tossed onto the ice after she'd skated an exciting program.

Moving quickly, Erin put a pile of freshly laundered whites on the country French dresser. As she did, she noticed something written in faded ink on a piece of pink paper. It looked like a poem.

It's not my business, she told herself, but when she glanced at the first line, she had to read the rest.

> *Some people say that gays are bad,*
> *It makes me cry. It makes me sad.*
> *They say gays can't join God above,*
> *Gays live away from God's dear love.*
> *How can God throw his sons away*
> *When his One Son came here to say*
> *That we can all go home again,*
> *No matter what we've done that's sin?*

"Oh, Kayla." Erin dropped onto Kayla's bed, clasping the poem to her chest. From the condition of the paper, Kayla'd written it long ago, but the feelings were as fresh as ever.

"I didn't mean for you to read that."

Erin's head jerked up to see Kayla standing just inside the doorway. "When did you write it?"

Kayla sat down on a meditation pillow, legs crossed. "Maybe a year after I broke my leg. It was our weekend with Dad, and we were all staying over at Grandma and Grandpa Johnson's house. I woke up in the middle of the night and heard Grandpa going at Dad. "

"I wish you'd told me. I could have comforted you. Maybe talked some sense into Skipp."

"I doubt it." Kayla frowned. "I don't see how he can stand in front of everyone at church like he's so perfect and then slice and dice Dad."

"What are you talking about?"

"The morning I went with Dad to take Grandma and Grandpa to the airport for their mission, Dad said something that made Grandpa suspicious. He asked Dad if he had a partner, and when Dad said yes, he went ballistic. He and Grandma ended up taking a taxi."

Erin drew a sharp breath, and Kayla said, "You didn't know?"

"No, but it shouldn't be a surprise. That's what he's wanted." Erin had noticed Cory seemed happier lately, but she'd been too absorbed with the baby to wonder why. "Did you know before then?"

Kayla nodded. "I guessed from some things Dad's said. And there are signs someone stays in Dad's new house when we're not there. A different brand of toothpaste in the guest bathroom of his new house, a jacket in the closet not his size. Things like that."

"Does Mark know?"

"Why else do you think he won't visit Dad anymore?"

"Hannah?"

"She knows Dad's different. But it doesn't matter. She loves him without reservation, the way she loves Rascal. And Vince, too."

Erin called Cory later that day and invited herself over to his place. "I'd like to see what you've done with your house," she said.

"Come Saturday afternoon," he said.

When she parked in front of the house at the appointed time, Cory came down the front walk to greet her. "Here, let me do that," he said, as she started getting Tony out of the backseat. He tweaked Tony's chin. "This guy's going to be a bruiser."

He was in an expansive mood as he walked Erin, who was carrying Tony, through his home, proudly pointing out the improvements he'd made. "There's a lot to do yet," he said once they were seated back in the living room, "but you can see where I'm going."

"I like the eclectic mix a lot, especially in this room." She paused. "What does your partner think about it?"

His eyes flickered. "So you know."

"Kayla told me what happened the day your parents left."

"Does Mark know?" he asked.

"He must. Cory, the kids need you to be upfront about what's happening in your life. Don't leave it up to them—or me—to guess."

"That's why you came, isn't it? Not to see the house."

"Both. Are you—"

"Happy? Yes."

"I'm glad. I want that for you."

She moved as if to go and then hesitated. "I know you had a testimony of the Church, Cory. When you left us, you left the Church, too. Is your life now—and your new relationship—enough to fill the space in your heart where the Spirit was?"

He leaned against an armoire, eyes downcast. Finally, he said, "I do feel the presence of God's love. I couldn't go on without that. But the Spirit that bears witness to the gospel, which is what I think you're asking about . . ." He paused. "I haven't felt that for a long time."

"You've paid a lot for your choices," Erin said. "Has it been worth it?"

The expression in his eyes was unreadable. "I did what I had to do."

WILLADENE

E-mail, December 14, 2003
Dear COBs,

Carl is home safe and sound from Afghanistan. I'm grateful, but I'm also feeling grief for the mothers whose sons didn't come home. Carl stopped at Gobb Hill briefly on his way to Albuquerque to pick up Sookie. They'll be settled outside San Antonio, near Randolph Air Force Base, where he'll be stationed, in time for the baby to be born.

We are having a quiet Christmas this year. There'll be just the three of us and Leo Flynn, who chose to stay here rather than with the Tuckers over the holidays. When Leo suggested we remember Bear this Christmas by taking treats to the animal shelter, Evvy said we should adopt a new dog while we're there. I'm not ready for that yet.

I'm glad this year is almost over. It's been a hard one for all of our families, despite the good that has come. Blessings of the season on us, every one. I'd say we need them.

Deenie

JUNEAU

E-mail, December 26, 2003
Dear Friends,

Another Christmas in an unfinished house. But who cares? Our great gift is that Greg is almost well again. I told him we should hire out the rest of the work, but he says no way. He loves doing it and is going to leave more of the Smoketree Systems work to Trace so he can hammer nails and paint walls.

I'm with you, Deenie. I wish us all a Happy New Year after this year of disasters.

Lovence,
Juneau

Chapter 28
2004

ERIN

E-mail, January 7, 2004
Dear COBs,

This was one of the best holidays I've ever had. We spent Christmas Eve with Vince's family and had Christmas dinner with The Jays and Andrew and Brenda. On New Year's Eve, Vince and I went out with Sam and Caitlin. It's fun to see the men together—they're like brothers. The Jays and Andrew and Brenda have become a foursome, too. They go to the Guthrie and the St. Paul Opera and are looking to take one of those volunteer vacations together.

My kids miss their Johnson grandparents. They loved watching the home movie Skipp and Linda sent. It was a personal tour of Temple Square, the Family History Center, and their apartment.

After they finished their training, Skipp and Linda were called as one of several teams to train all the couples called to the Family and Church History Mission. Skipp is pleased that he'll be an instructor. Linda says that the training itself isn't as important as making the missionary couples feel comfortable, happy, and loved. She'd be great at that.

Mark got early notification of acceptance from the University of Wisconsin in Madison, where he wants to major in some flavor of engineering. This is definitely his year. He's getting ready to give his senior piano recital—we hear thunderous Beethoven, ethereal Debussy, and rhythmic Hindemith over and over again, sometimes to the accompaniment of George squawking! Then there's his senior prom in April (he's already asked his current crush, Heidi) and graduation in June.

It's tough having a college student, a high school senior, a ten-year-old, and a one-year-old, each one needing and wanting different things from me. Vince doesn't demand much—me sitting across from him when we eat supper and my body next to his when he goes to sleep.

Your Erin

WILLADENE

Deenie sat on a bench outside the Atlanta temple waiting for Roger to dress in his street clothes. They'd come to Georgia to spend some private time together. Attending the temple was an added bonus. It gave them a place to be together without having to talk to each other.

Not that they didn't talk. They both went out of their way to find things to talk about—carefully edited, polite, and mundane things, so as not to upset each other more than they already had.

Ka-thump. Kaaa-thud! Brrrrrrrrrrrrrrrit. Deenie pressed two fingers of her right hand over the spot in her chest where her heart fluttered and held them there until the familiar pressure eased.

"Stress," the doctor had said at her last checkup.

"How can it be stress? My husband has his dream job. I live in a mansion. My whole family is well and happy, and my life is filled with new adventures."

"Stress is stress where the body is concerned," the doctor said, missing her sarcasm. "You need to find a way to get out from under what is burdening you. In the meantime, we'll keep an eye on your blood pressure and heart rate. And if the symptoms increase, we'll run more tests."

Though the symptoms didn't go away, they seemed to lessen on the days Deenie ran. So she ran. Miss B had chided her, saying, "It's good to run, but you need to find the spiritual solution. You need to exercise your soul."

So here she was, doing exactly that, and the flutter was still there. She felt Old Man Griff rear his hoary head and ask, "What if it's something more than stress? What if you died tomorrow?"

Deenie knew the Griff well enough that his questions no longer frightened her; rather, they made her think. What she thought now was, *If I knew I would die tomorrow, what things would I do today? I should make a list.*

When they returned to their hotel and Roger lay down for a rest, Deenie pulled out a sheet of stationery from the desk and did just that. *Tell family and friends that I love them. Say "thank you" more often. Bear my testimony. Write my will.* She paused, pencil poised, and then wrote, *Tell Jenny I'm sorry. And mean it.*

After that, Deenie listed all the things she wanted to do for her daughters, including teaching Evvy everything there was to know about being a wife and mother. That required another list, one that ran the entire alphabet from making an apple pie to setting a zipper.

When she finished she took out a sheet of hotel stationery and addressed a letter to Jenny. She wrote:

Dear Jenny,

Today, while attending a session in the Atlanta temple, I was reminded of how important *Forever Families* are. I thought of NeVae and then I thought of you.

After NeVae's funeral, you said you would accept my apology when I knew what I was apologizing for. I do now.

I'm ashamed to say I didn't realize I was demanding so much of NeVae's time that it left you and your girls without the attention you needed and deserved. I know now how much that must have hurt, and I can't believe I was so caught up in my own life I didn't even see it.

I missed out on something, too. All these years we could have been friends. I hope we can now. Please forgive me.

Deenie

She addressed the envelope with a sense of accomplishment. She didn't know if the increased arrhythmia, fatigue, and headaches she'd been suffering plus Sunny's gentle message after Stella's death added up to the fourth horseman in her life, but she wasn't going to take any chances. Just in case, it was time to get her ducks in a row, chickens home to roost, and her life in order.

JUNEAU

E-mail, January 23, 2004

Dear Friends,

Greg, who's recuperating very well from his October heart attack, has decided there is more to life than work! For Christmas he gave me a travel book of what to see in England and a card he'd created with the quotation from Shakespeare's *King Richard II:*

> *This scepter'd isle . . .*
> *This blessed plot, this earth, this realm, this England.*

Inside the card was an I-owe-you for a trip! That man is learning my language fast.

We're planning to go in a year, April 2005 (as Browning said, "Oh, to be in England / Now that April's here"), when Greg will be up to it. We've already put in a request for two timeshare weeks, one on the Welsh coast and one near Stratford-upon-Avon—brace yourself, Shakespeare. Ask me if I'm excited!

I told Marisol that if she and Dr. Tim were to get married they could go with us! She laughed and said it was a temptation but I shouldn't hold my breath. She enjoys being single and independent, especially now that she's teaching at Pasadena City College (she's been asked to escort a group of college kids to France for a semester). She says marriage wouldn't fit into her life any more.

Church-wise, I've been recycled into working again with the teenage girls in our ward. Our first project is to raise money for girls' camp, so we're planning a mystery dinner. The girls will cook the food and present a show I've written for them, titled *Who Spilled Uncle Will?* (No murders; this involves figuring out who spilled Uncle Will's ashes from the urn containing them and why. I guess I was inspired by Letitia-in-the-Urn.)

So, the busy-ness of our lives continues.

Lovence,

Juneau

Juneau had hoped that staying busy would shove the Guilty Secret back into its closet. But like the troubles released when Pandora opened the box in Greek mythology, the memories released by Rhiannan's innocent question could no longer be contained. Especially now, when Juneau was supposed to be an example for the Young Women.

Sometimes she wished for the confessional, where Marisol used to unload her transgressions when she was a Catholic, or Ira and Shoshana's Yom Kippur, the day of atonement. But even with those, the first thing you had to do was acknowledge the problem. Who should she tell? In the past, she might have unburdened herself to Clyde, but Greg was now her front-line confidant.

She finally got the courage to tell Greg what was pressing on her when they were walking one day, as his doctor had prescribed. "Greg," she began, "I have sinned. A mighty sin."

Alarm crossed his face. "Does it have anything to do with Clyde?"

"Good grief, no."

"I'm sorry, Juney." He gave her a crooked grin. "So what *have* you done? Was the kitchen floor grubby when your visiting teachers came?"

"It's way more serious than that," she said soberly. "Do you remember my telling you about Starette?"

"Your trailer park friend when you were a kid?"

She nodded. "My partner in crime. Back in 1956. We were ten."

She told the story, then, of how the two of them had bonded together to stave off the scorn of some town kids who called them trailer trash. "Brenna Petry, queen of the popular clique, was the worst. She grooved on making our lives miserable. But she was always there when a bunch of us went to play after school at an abandoned house just outside the trailer park."

Juneau described how the house had a steep-pitched roof and an attached, less-steep lean-to, both of which were covered with strips of tin with raised edges between the strips.

"Each one of us claimed our own strip and crayoned our names at the top," Juneau said. "They were great for sliding down—we would go fast on the house part but then slow down on the lean-to part. We had contests to see who dared glide closest to the edge of the eight-foot drop-off."

She walked silently, remembering, and then went on. "The week before my family was to move away, Brenna did something really mean. She said I'd copied answers from her math test, when it was the other way around. I got into real trouble over it, so Starette and I plotted revenge."

It was vivid, there in her mind. The morning before the Paulsens were to pull out of the trailer park en route to their next destination, she and Starette had sneaked over to the old house very early. They'd rubbed paraffin wax on the lower end of Brenna's strip, knowing that when she hit it, she wouldn't be able to stop and she would go right off the lean-to.

They didn't think it was dangerous. Some of the kids daring to slide close to the edge had gone over with only bruised bottoms as a result. They'd laughed in anticipation of the same honor for Brenna.

Only it didn't turn out that way. Brenna had been determined to win the very first contest that afternoon, so she'd pushed off extra hard. That, plus the slick wax, had propelled her over the edge with added momentum.

"She shouldn't have gotten hurt," Juneau said in a low voice. "But somehow she landed wrong. When we saw her lying all crumpled and still, we knew she was hurt bad."

Bad enough to be rushed to the hospital. Bad enough that when Starette came over the next morning to say good-bye to Juneau, she whispered that she'd heard Brenna might not live. And if she did, she probably wouldn't walk again.

"Oh, Juney." Greg put his arm around her. "That's a horrible secret to carry."

"Everybody thought it was an accident," Juneau gulped. "Only Starette and I knew different."

"What happened to Brenna?" Greg asked.

"I don't know. Starette wrote to me in care of general delivery in the town where we went next. She said something in Brenna's spine was messed up and that the old house had been declared a nuisance and torn down."

Juneau kept her eyes on the sidewalk ahead. "I didn't answer. And I didn't even open the next letter. I think I was afraid of what I might learn. When we moved on again, I didn't tell Starette where we were going."

"Isn't there someone you could contact for information? You need to know what happened—no matter how bad."

"I know. But it was close to fifty years ago. I've lost touch with every-body."

"Have you tried searching for Starette and Brenna on the Internet?"

"Yes. I didn't find anything." Juneau walked on for a few paces and then said, "Greg, I'm guilty. I caused harm."

Greg hugged her hard. "Juney, honey. How can I help?"

"Tell me you still love me. And help me find Brenna."

WILLADENE

E-mail, February 12, 2004

Dear Greatly Missed COBs,

We are doing better here, individually and as a family. I was reminded in the temple of how important eternal ties are. That has helped me let go of the resentment toward Roger I didn't even know I had—for his being ill and leaving me alone to cope with the aftermath. He seems to sense a change in me and as a result isn't quite so distant.

Because I've been under the weather lately, Gwen hosted Evvy's sixteenth birthday at her home. Among the presents was a hardbound journal from Miss B titled *Evangeline's Book of Womanly Wisdom*. She had all her friends make entries in it, and Evvy and I have had some wonderful times reading it together. Along with NeVae's Keeping Book we have a whole encyclope-dia of wise advice. Evvy has been blessed with such wonderful women and good friends in her life.

To top off the day, Evvy got a Hallmark snail-mail card from Gideon that made her giggle. Apparently in these days of easy e-cards, going to the store and actually picking one out is a *very* personal thing.

Last but not least, Brad and Elizabeth have announced their engagement! They're planning a June wedding in Orlando. Are there enough tissues in Florida to get me through this next year with Carl and Sookie's baby on the way and a wedding in the offing?

Love,
Deenie

P.S. When I told my doctor I thought I was getting headaches during the day because I wasn't sleeping well at night, he scribbled out a prescription for sleeping pills and was out the door in a blink. I can see why it was so easy for Roger to get those extra pills. Roger says it's time for a new doctor.

After Deenie sent off her e-mails, she gathered three sacks full of recently purchased fabric and hauled them to her sewing corner in the attic. There she put up two long tables and set out piles of cotton fabric sorted according to the artist's color wheel. *Juneau and Erin are going to love this,* she thought, imagining the finished product of appliquéd and embroidered jackets. Then she laid out a series of pictures from southern Utah she had graphed into patterns: Angel Arch, a view of Canyonlands, and a photograph of cactus blossoms by Mexican Hat.

She had begun to match fabric to the pattern pieces when she heard the doorbell ring, followed quickly by Miss B's familiar "Yoo-hoo."

"The door's open. Come on up." Deenie called from the window.

"What's all this?" Miss B asked, still puffing from climbing the stairs.

"When the COBs get together in Moab, Utah, this fall, we're supposed to each bring something that represents what COBhood means to us. Juneau and Erin are keeping notebooks. I thought I'd do jackets.

"Well, let's take a look," Miss B said.

The two women spent some time going over the patterns and fabric choices. "What's this?" Miss B asked, holding up a long list of places and phrases.

"Those are the words that represent COBhood to me," Deenie said. "As soon as I get the appliqués done, I'm going to use the embroidery machine in the home economics department at St. Anne's to put them on the jackets."

Miss B read off some of the words: "*Grace, love, joy, simplicity.*" She paused, searching. "I don't see *peace* or *safety* on this list."

After a pause, Deenie said, "I know they belong there. But I haven't felt safe or at peace since 9/11 and especially not since Roger hurt his back."

"Have you given that burden over to Christ, Deenie dear?"

"I thought I had, but I guess I didn't succeed."

Miss B put down the list and gave Deenie's cheek a soft pat. "Then try again," she said.

E-mail, February 15, 2004
Dear COBs,

Sookie gave birth to a healthy baby boy yesterday morning. Chul Wagner Rasmussen, named for Sookie's grandfathers. Carl, who's every inch the proud papa, sent us photos by e-mail. Roger and I both wept when we saw the picture of our strapping son holding his first child—Carl was dressed in his Air Force uniform and Chul was wearing a tiny Air Force blue T-shirt!

The very next day Paul and Dani announced they are unexpectedly expecting again, in October. Yippee! I love being a grandmother!

Deenie

JUNEAU

E-mail, February 18, 2004
Dear Friends,

Congratulations, Deenie, on the arrival of Chul. Isn't it a joy to see the grandchildren stack up? As one grandmother said, "If I'd known how much fun grandkids are, I'd have had them first!"

We have another one on the way. Shoshana came to our last family gathering wearing a big T-shirt with a yellow sign on the front that proclaimed, "Baby on board." Remember those signs people put in their car windows a few years ago? Like, "Caution, child on board." Or "Child on board, mother-in-law in trunk."

Trace and Ira staged a chest-puffing contest. Trace asked if Ira is going to name the baby Pickle because of the commercials he's in. Serenity got to giggling so hard she literally fell on the floor. By the way, Deenie, I really appreciate that Evvy is so willing to do three-way communication with Serenity as well as Gideon.

Serenity says Evvy is her very first best friend. (I know Gideon thinks of Evvy as his very first girlfriend! He spent a lot of time picking the right Hallmark card for her sixteenth birthday.)

Shan is so pleased with the progress Serenity is making with anger management and all the other baggage she carries from having Dex as a dad. Ray Red Hawk was certainly right about those packages we put together.

Erin, I wish I could attend Mark's recital. When I told Gideon about it, he said, "I'm sure glad guitarists don't have to give recitals." I hate to tell him this, but his guitar teacher is planning just such an event.

Lovence,
Juneau

Juneau sent the e-mail knowing she'd left out the most important information—the Guilty Secret she'd finally admitted to. She'd considered saying something breezy like, "I finally got to the darkest corners of that guilt closet you told me to clean out, Erin, and guess what I found?" But it was too serious to be breezy about.

Greg told her not to be so hard on herself, that she and Starette had been children and hadn't realized what the consequences of their actions could be. But Juneau remembered how Gabby had once said that the consequences are the same whether an action was deliberate or unintended. She needed to know how her childhood mischief had affected Brenna Petry's life. She needed to acknowledge how it had affected her own.

ERIN
E-mail, April 16, 2004
Dear COBs,

How nice it's been to get such good news from you two. A new grandchild, a wedding coming up, a trip to England next April. What a difference a year makes.

My news is that Caitlin and I have gone into the "flipping" business—buying a house, renovating it, and selling it as soon as possible. For a profit, of course. Caitlin got the idea when the hundred-plus-year-old Victorian next to hers went on the market. It was going for a relatively low price because it hadn't been renovated since the 50s. It was structurally sound, though. Perfect for a flip.

Perfect for *us* to flip, Caitlin said. With her experience in renovating and our good taste (!), it was a no-brainer. All we had to
do was talk to our men and buy the house.

The conversation with Sam and Vince was an eye-opener. They
were uneasy that we were moving forward so quickly, even
though we were using our inheritance money to finance the
venture. Caitlin says they want security, comfort, and
consistency—and supper on the table when they come home
after a day at work!

I don't think she's far off. We need to be very careful about taking care of our families before we take care of business.

Your Erin

Chapter 29

WILLADENE

Gobb Hill was full of excitement the second week of April, and despite her physical problems, Deenie was reveling in it. Elizabeth and Brad had arrived to finalize wedding plans, and Evvy was getting ready for the April Match Dance between the Academy and St. Anne's. It was her first grown-up dance, and the ever-present Leo was her escort.

The night of the dance Deenie, Roger, Elizabeth, and Brad all gathered in the living room, waiting for Evvy to appear. She floated down the stairs, looking ethereal in her coral and pink. Her artfully jumbled curls were clipped back from her fresh face with a dragonfly pin in the same colors.

"Can that be my little sister?" Elizabeth said. "You look fantastic."

"You can say that again." Brad let out a long wolf whistle, which turned Evvy's cheeks red. "Who's the lucky guy?"

"Mr. Flynn."

Deenie gave Elizabeth a nudge. "Why don't you and Brad use the library phone to call Brad's parents with a wedding-plan update? It'll be hard enough on Leo to have Roger and me here when he comes to pick Evvy up."

"Of course," Brad said, grinning. He and Elizabeth joined hands as they headed for the library.

After Leo and Evvy were on their way, Roger retired to his office, and Deenie stretched out on their living room couch to rest. She was half dozing, when she heard Brad and Elizabeth come into the room.

"It's all set," Elizabeth said, glowing with pleasure. "We'll be sealed in the temple in Orlando on Friday the twenty-eighth of May. Then we'll have a simple ring exchange in the chapel gardens of the Donaldsons' church and a catered family dinner they insist on paying for. Claire and Matt say they want to do something special to show how grateful they are that Brad is finally getting married!"

"Me, too," Brad said, giving her a squeeze.

"We'll leave for our honeymoon after the open house in Wellsville in June," Elizabeth said with a slight blush.

"Terrific," Deenie said. She was wondering how she would pull it all of with her current lack of energy when they were joined by Roger. Elizabeth repeated what she'd told Deenie, and all four were still poring over notes and ideas for the open house when Evvy arrived at the stroke of midnight, gliding into the room with a look on her face that said she could no longer be ranked among those who were sweet sixteen and never been kissed.

JUNEAU

In early May, the remodeling of Juneau and Greg's house was declared finished. It was time for them to move to the lovely new master suite upstairs with a spectacular view of the San Gabriels. And for Juneau to take over the workroom, a bright, sunny space everyone deemed perfect for a writer.

The whole family—Misty included—came on a Saturday to celebrate and help with the moving. Juneau had everyone sit down to a grilled hamburger lunch on the patio before the work began. The lively mealtime conversation centered on Nicole, who would be finished with her residency in June and had begun interviewing at clinics in the West. Gideon and Serenity were hoping a clinic in Alaska would give her an offer, so they could visit her and establish a sled dog school. Listening to them talk, Juneau was reminded of Nicole and Beto and the endless fantasy projects they'd had when they were kids.

But Juneau heard only snatches of their conversation. Her mind kept returning to that pristine new workroom upstairs and wondering how she could explain that she didn't want to move into it, didn't want to put that old secret she'd confessed to Greg in new closets.

When they were ready to get down to moving, Nicole insisted Greg take a seat in the new addition where he could preside without lifting anything. "I can deliver babies," she said, "but I'm not too swift on cardiology."

With the young people lifting and carrying and Juneau and Greg pointing out where the furniture should go, the new bedroom was set up in record time.

"Now for the workroom," Trace said.

Juneau shook her head. "Not today."

All activity stopped as everyone looked at her. "And that's because . . . ?" Trace queried.

"Because . . ." Juneau began and then hesitated. "Because I've just started a new book and my ideas might dry up if I have to adjust to new surroundings. Let me finish it, and then I'll move upstairs."

There were groans, but Shoshana said, "Reason enough. Don't question the mysterious process of writing!"

Juneau was glad Shoshana had made her excuse seem plausible. Then she noticed Misty gazing at her with questioning eyes.

"What's the title of your new book, Mom?" Misty asked.

Juneau was about to say she didn't know, but then, she did. It came without effort and it was exactly right. "*Closet of Secrets*," she said. Perhaps in exploring the subject by way of fiction, she could lessen her guilt. If not, the lovely new workroom would be unused.

ERIN
> E-mail, May 19, 2004
> Dear COBs,

Things are a little frazzled at the Gerlach house these days. Kayla's getting ready to go up to Duluth, Mark's caught up in pregraduation excitement, and Vince is upset because he's got a couple of touch-and-go cases, dogs from one neighborhood that were purposely poisoned. That's the worst, he says.

I'm happy to say that the flip isn't contributing to the frazzle. It's more than half done, and we've got a prospective buyer! Caitlin and I have managed to balance family and work pretty well. We do a lot of business over the phone, and our contractor is great about getting things done right, if not always on schedule.

Vince and Sam are now our biggest fans. Taking them on walk-throughs and including them in budget reviews (we're over but not excessively so) made the difference. Vince knew I'd been self-employed, but he hadn't realized how knowledgeable I was about the financial side of running a business. After our last meeting, he said to Sam, "We sure married smart women!"

I can't tell you how relieved I am about that. Because I noticed the other day that whenever I'm going somewhere, I'm scouting for another house to flip! I'm hooked!

Your Erin

WILLADENE
E-mail, May 31, 2004
Dear Friends and Family,

Brad and Elizabeth are now linked to a long chain of loving, faithful couples who have covenanted with the Lord to be an eternal family. I get weepy whenever I think of how beautiful the temple ceremony was and how nice the bishop made the ring exchange afterward. Thanks to the Donaldsons' efforts, the family dinner was elegant and romantic. What more could we ask for?

We are enjoying abundant blessings, not the least of which is that Jenny has finally accepted my apology and has offered to pick us up at the airport when we arrive in Salt Lake City on our way to Wellsville. I feel like a line from the song that was sung during the dinner, "I nothing lack."

Love,
Deenie

The gray house on the corner in Wellsville looked sadly asleep when Jenny drove the Roger Rasmussens into the driveway on the last day of May. The lawns were mowed and the bushes trimmed, but the flowerpots were empty and the blinds drawn. If ever a house could be Sleeping Beauty, the gray house was, waiting for the gentle kiss of family to wake it up again.

Deenie didn't have patience for that. In preparation for Brad and Elizabeth's party, she recruited the whole family and shook the house awake in a flurry of washing walls, scrubbing floors, and opening every window in the place. Despite strange aches, pains, and a sometimes fuzzy brain, she didn't stop until every room in the house was stamped with a look that said, "Deenie's home."

Then she started on the yard.

When the garden was in and the orchard had been raked, Deenie called the family together. John and Margaret, Wilford, Roger, and Evvy gathered with Deenie by Rauf's grave and with words of love they interred Bear's ashes. After the little ceremony was over, Deenie groomed the soil over the new grave and scattered forget-me-not seeds across the top, hoping they would grow to match the flowers Dani had planted on Rauf's grave.

Her hand was shaking as she mopped the sweat from her forehead. She was dead tired, and it was more than only physical exhaustion. She'd been in a constant state of unrest since 9/11, Roger's intervention, and feeling Sunny's call home. Some part of her was constantly on the alert, looking for what was around every corner or wondering what was coming next.

ERIN

> E-mail, June 8, 2004
> Dear COBs,

> Mark graduated last night. And today, Melina drove Althea, who now has a darling brown-and-white butterfly dog named Princess, over to congratulate him! It's amazing what having Princess has done for her. If someone drives, she can go to the library, church (Bishop Hardy asked members to treat Princess as a service dog), and the grocery store.

> She has to meet, and keep meeting, certain conditions to keep Princess, but she loves that little piece of fluff, so I know she will.

> Your Erin

JUNEAU

> E-mail, June 20, 2004
> Dear Friends,

> My "new" house is lovely, and it's all ready for my mother to move from Oregon and take over the downstairs master suite.

She's dragging her feet—she says maybe in September, after the three of us return from our week in Moab.

What she *has* agreed to is a trip to Idaho to retrieve Letitia's ashes and scatter them on a mountain near Mink Creek as she requested so many years ago—if she can track down who has them! Misty says she wants to go, too. I don't know what the draw is for her—a trip with Mom and me, retrieving Letitia, or being where she can visit Whitford Morgan, that lawyer she worked for and had the big crush on when she lived in Idaho. She still mentions him once in a while.

Our Young Women mystery dinner, *Who Spilled Uncle Will?* went off very well, and we made almost enough money to pay for girls camp for our eleven active girls (our stake lets the girls earn the money if they have a worthwhile project). We had such fun. I had asked them what kind of character each wanted to be in the show, which features the reading of Uncle Will's will.

So we had Beulah Bankbuster, the richest woman in the world; Tootsie Toodles, a ballet dancer; Anna Rexia, a famous model, and so forth. Serenity was darling as a French maid, OoLaLa LaFitte. The Young Men were in the show, too, and Gideon was a hit as Detective Dudley Dogmeat (his choice of names).

Why do you suppose I so much enjoy doing these things with the young people? Because I've never grown up? Because it's easier to do this fanciful stuff than face real life?

I've saved the most intriguing for last. Guess where Nicole is going to start her obstetrical practice? In that little Mexican village where Beto is! He sent a brochure to Marisol, which told all about that organization he's working with, the one that hosts doctors for a few months. Marisol showed it to Nicole, and that was that. She will leave for Mexico sometime in the fall.

I wasn't sure that was such a good idea, but she says working in that village was as much her dream as Beto's, and this is her chance to realize it. When I asked her, "What about Beto?" she again cited that old movie, *The Nun's Story.* She reminded me that the Audrey Hepburn character and the doctor she worked with in Africa were attracted to each other. But they knew there could be nothing between them, and their feelings didn't affect their ability to work well together. She says it will be the same with her and Beto.

You just never know what turns life will take!

Juneau

WILLADENE

E-mail, June 25, 2004
Dear COBs,

The day after the big open house, which was a lovely success, the newlyweds went with Mom, Dad and me to put flowers on Sunny's grave. It was a way of acknowledging Sunny's part in bringing Brad into all our lives. I know Sunny is happy for them. I could feel it as clearly as if she put her arms around me in a hug.

The next day Brad received a letter from the Department of Homeland Security expressing interest in him for their new overseas attaché program. He was thrilled. Elizabeth, also. They left for their honeymoon in Perth, Australia, looking toward a bright future.

With all these years of bouncing back and forth between Wellsville and Gainesville I've been thinking about home—is it something we find, create, or carry with us? I've decided it's all three. I'm thinking love's like that, too.

Deenie

ERIN

E-mail, June 26, 2004
Dear COBs,

Deenie, you're becoming quite the philosopher. Or the poet.

I'm hoping to create the experience of both love and home at the cabin next month. I invited The Jays, Andrew and Brenda, and Caitlin and Sam for a week of fun. A couple of days later Sam called to ask if there was room for one of his brothers to park his RV, which is big enough for both families. I said yes.

Then Hannah told me she'd invited her dad. He gave her a maybe.

Kayla, who's doing a reprise of last year's self-designed program in Duluth, invited her Eddie. I hope he likes our crew. Kayla told him and his parents the McGee family history—my dad's wives and the schism between me and my grandparents—at dinner one Sunday. She said they could have used weights to pull down their eyebrows.

Your Erin

Erin woke up the second morning of the family gathering with a small warm body snuggled next to hers. She turned to see Hannah looking at her out of solemn blue eyes.

"What is it, Hannah?"

"There's another one waiting to come."

Erin felt goose bumps rise on her arms. "What?"

"I dreamed about him last night. He has red hair, like Grandpa Andy."

"Hannah!"

"He says don't worry, it'll be okay. But you shouldn't wait too long."

Erin gave Hannah a nudge. "Did Vince put you up to this?"

"Noah did."

Erin was almost afraid to ask, but she did. "Who's Noah?"

"*Our baby,* of course."

Later, when Erin carried sixteen-month-old Tony out onto the front porch, the scene before her looked so much like the camp she'd seen around the elder Gerlachs' cabin that she had to laugh. Near the RVs that housed Caitlin and Sam's siblings stood campers rented by The Jays and Andrew. Eddy's tent was pitched nearer the woods. The presence of Cory's car told Erin he'd already driven in from Duluth, where he was staying.

Erin directed Hannah to the long table on the porch where juice, cereal, and milk had been set out. But when Hannah saw the cousins exploring the lakeshore under the watchful eyes of Caitlin's sister-in-law, she dashed off without eating.

Caitlin watched Hannah join the explorers. "I'm so glad the kids are having fun together. And look at the guys. They're loving this."

Erin nodded. On the shore, the men were already playing touch Frisbee. Andrew and Brenda were paddling toward the center of the lake in one canoe; Joanna and Jake paddled in another.

Erin poured some orange juice but put down the glass without drinking. "How did you get the courage to have the twins, Caitlin?"

Caitlin laughed. "Courage comes easy when you have enough desire." Then her eyes went wide. "You're not thinking what I think you're thinking, are you?"

"Maybe."

Caitlin sat down next to Erin, a serious look on her face. "Listen, sis. Courage also came easy because I *knew* my babies would be fine. That's a definite benefit of *in vitro* fertilization. You were very lucky with Tony. If I were you, I wouldn't tempt fate."

Erin rested her head on her hand. Caitlin was right, but what if Hannah was right, too?

"Hi, Mom! Hi, Aunt Caitlin." Kayla bounded up the steps, a bouquet of wildflowers in her hand. She put them in a glass of water and placed them on the table. Then she looked to where the men were playing.

Erin watched her seek out Eddie, saw the flush of love color her cheeks as she waved, catching his attention. Eddie passed the Frisbee off to Sam and spoke a word to Cory. Then the two of them started toward the porch.

Caitlin nudged Erin with her elbow as they approached. "Something's up," she whispered, "and I think I know what it is."

Erin did, too. She held her breath as Kayla joined Eddie, taking his hand.

"Cory, Sister Gerlach," Eddie cleared his throat. "Kayla and I want to get married. We hope you'll give us your blessing."

E-mail, July 22, 2004
Dear COBs,

I drove in to a library in Duluth this morning so I could e-mail you the news—Kayla and Eddie Beckmann are engaged, and they want to get married next month, before the fall semester starts at the U of M in Duluth! (Kayla will transfer and do her senior year there.) Love and youth must make anything seem possible.

Eddie's parents, Frank and Lisa, came to dinner that evening to meet Cory. Everything was fine until Frank asked Eddie and Kayla how they thought they were going to support themselves and go to school at the same time, especially since Eddie has to research and write a thesis for his master's in pharmacology this year.

Before either could answer Hannah piped up with, "What about the money from Grandpa Andy's parents? Kayla can get some of that, can't she?"

You should have seen the looks on the Beckmanns' faces when I told them about the McGee trust. They were taken aback to hear Kayla has access to family money and embarrassed that the most they could offer was help with Eddie's tuition. I hope money—both the having of it and the lack of it—doesn't turn out to be a problem for the kids. I got the feeling that by the time the Beckmanns left they were wondering what kind of family Eddie was marrying into. And I did so want them to like us!

Erin

P.S. Mark will be leaving for Madison right after the wedding. That's a lot of change happening all at once. C'est la vie.

WILLADENE

Deenie sat on the front porch of the house in Wellsville putting the last decorative stitching on Juneau's jacket for the trip to Moab when she heard Roger answer the phone in the house.

"Who was it?" she asked when he came out and sat down next to her.

"Brad called to say he's accepted the job with the Department of Homeland Security. He thinks the DHS will take advantage of all his international experience and train him to be part of a new program that provides DHS attachés for foreign embassies."

"Wow!" Deenie said, putting down the jacket. "I bet Elizabeth's all for that."

"It certainly sounded like it. As soon as they know where they'll be posted, they'll have a moving van pick up their wedding presents and the furniture Elizabeth said she wanted."

Deenie was wondering if that would affect her plans for the Moab trip when Roger picked up the jacket and looked over the decoration. "What's this?" he asked fingering the first two letters of a picked-out word. "P-E . . . ?"

Deenie grimmaced. "That's the first part of *peace*. I'm not feeling that peace or inner safety Miss B talks about these days. So I picked it out."

Roger folded that jacket and put it back in the pile. "I hope you aren't still feeling scared about us."

"Sometimes," Deenie admitted. "I wonder if we'll ever find our way back to where we were."

"Maybe we'll find our way to somewhere better. Someplace where we'll be so close I won't be afraid to tell you how much I hurt."

"I never knew you were afraid to say how you felt. How did we ever get to that point?"

"After Evvy was born and you were so sick, I promised myself never to say anything to worry you again."

"Oh, Roger. We've both hurt each other, haven't we?"

"But we're still standing." He pulled his chair beside Deenie's, and they sat listening to the sounds of the neighborhood as evening settled softly over Wellsville.

Finally Roger spoke. "It's been a good summer, hasn't it? Seeing Paul and Carl as heads of their families and sending off Elizabeth to start her own. Having special time with Chul and Dee. And a new baby on the way."

"Yes, it has. How's your dad settling into his apartment at the assisted living center in Logan?"

"I think he'll adjust fine, especially since Charlotte and Jenny have promised to drive him out to the farmhouse whenever he wants. He wanted me to tell you to feel free to use his new SUV for the trip to Moab. He's keeping it for company use and says a road trip will do it good."

"That's nice."

Roger stood and stretched. Then he gently ruffled Deenie's hair. "By the way, Evvy and I are going on our daddy-daughter date tonight, dinner and a movie. Don't wait up for us. I don't like seeing you so tired."

Me neither, Deenie thought as Evvy and Roger left. *Maybe if I could get my inside stuff together, the spiritual safety and inner peace thing, all the outside changes, the loss of physical strength, wouldn't seem so important.*

That evening after she closed up the house for the night, she sent a quick e-mail to the COBs.

Look for the bright yellow SUV with the smiley faced driver. Ah, good company, a four-wheel drive, all the goodies from the garden I can pick, and the desert. What more could we ask for? See all ya'll soon.

Love,
Deenie

ERIN
E-mail, August 21, 2004
Dear COBs,

My little Kayla is now Mrs. Edward Beckmann, and I couldn't be happier.

It's amazing what can be done in one month when the whole family works together. Cory and Kayla planned the backyard reception, which was at my house. Mom made her wedding dress. And Brenda and Caitlin hosted a bridal shower.

The afternoon before the wedding we had a cookout so the families could get better acquainted. Cory and all of Kayla's grandparents were there, plus Eddie's sisters. Who knew having a private zoo—dogs, parrot, hamsters, turtle, and goldfish— would be such a wonderful icebreaker!

Cory wasn't with us in the temple, of course, but he was very much the proud father at the reception. There was something satisfying about having him on one side of me and Vince on the other as we sent the newlyweds off (they're honeymooning in Branson).

We sat at the kitchen table long after everyone had left and the catering crew had cleaned up, talking about life and love and growing older. Then Tony started wailing, and I remembered— I have a baby. I can't afford to get old!

Tired but happy,
Your Erin

P.S. I'm finally getting around to sending you each a copy of the recital CD.

The day after the wedding, Erin was packing a lunch for Mark's drive to Madison while he said his final good-byes to his girlfriend, Heidi. She wasn't listening to his side of their phone conversation until a snide remark he made about a student he'd tutored caught her attention.

When he hung up, she called him over. "What you said about your student wasn't very nice."

Mark shrugged. "It's true, though."

"Even if it is, why put down someone who has difficulty but is trying his best? You're smart and talented, and you've accomplished a lot, but that doesn't give you the right to demean others."

"I don't talk that way all the time, Mom. Look at me and Ricky. I'm probably the only real friend he has."

"Are you, really?" Erin asked. "You didn't invite him to that Christmas party you had. You never do anything with him unless it's related to family or Scouts."

"What's your point?"

"Sometimes I think you're lacking somewhat in the kindness category. You have little time or patience for those who don't meet your expectations."

"Yeah, yeah." Mark started to leave, but Erin stopped him.

"Listen, you. Accomplishments may become tarnished or be surpassed by others, but the effects of simple kindness go on and on."

"You're talking like the character in that dumb movie you and Grandma Joanna like."

"*Harvey*," Erin supplied.

He held up his hands. "Please, Mom. Don't give me that quote again."

Ignoring him, Erin said, "'In this world, Elwood, you must be oh so smart or oh so pleasant. Well, for years I was smart. I recommend pleasant. You may quote me.'"

Mark huffed, exasperated. "I can't stop being smart, Mom."

"No, but you *can* add 'pleasant' to the quotient," Erin said. "Don't wait until life teaches you the importance of pleasantness and kindness. It can be a hard teacher."

"Are you talking about Dad, now?"

"Your relationship wasn't first in my mind, but it does apply. Think about it, okay?"

WILLADENE

Deenie drew in a deep breath as the three women left the pizza parlor on Moab's Main Street. "There's nothing as delicious as desert air on a warm fall day." She stretched toward the sky and then reached down to touch her toes.

"Show-off," Juneau said.

Deenie groaned as she straightened up. "If only you knew. That horseback ride at Pack Creek Ranch took more out of me than I expected." *And more than I'm ready to share*, she added to herself.

"Me, too," Erin said. "I hate to admit it, but after the ride and all that pizza, I could really use a nap."

"I second the motion," Juneau said.

As they started for Wilford's yellow SUV, which Deenie had driven down, she was grateful someone else had suggested naps. She knew she couldn't handle another activity without a rest, considering how her heart was pounding.

"In earlier days we would have spent the afternoon rafting the Colorado and then gone to a movie," Juneau said.

Erin laughed. "Those days are past. After our nap, I'll be ready for an evening of cocoa and conversation in front of the fireplace. We've got catching up to do."

That evening as they lazed before the crackling fire, Erin said, "I can't get over those jackets you made us, Deenie. They are absolutely fantastic."

"Wearable art," Juneau said.

Erin fetched them from the closet and laid them out in a row on the coffee table. "The picture of Angel Arch you did on the back of my jacket looks just like the photos I've seen of it," Erin said. "It's amazing."

"Mine of Canyonlands and yours of Mexican Hat, too, Deenie." Juneau traced the embroidery on an appliquéd image. "And having the names of the places we've been and words that bring memories to mind was brilliant. Words like 'sacred listening.'"

"Whatever inspired you to make these?" Erin asked.

"Well," Deenie said, "after twenty-four years together, I thought we ought to have something that makes a statement about where we've been and who we are."

The next morning, Deenie didn't want to get out of bed, but she was determined not to miss the adventure of Shaefer Trail.

After breakfast, they met their congenial Jeep driver, Mike, in front of the tour company office. He had them turn around so he could see the appliquéd backs of their jackets. "Cool. Will you make me one?" he asked Deenie.

"Sorry," Deenie said, grinning. "These were a labor of love. You couldn't pay me enough."

"If you ever change your mind . . ."

Deenie shook her head, laughing.

They were excited as Mike drove up to the top of a plateau in Canyonlands. There he stopped and pointed out the pencil-thin dirt road that clung to the side of a cliff as it descended to a lower plateau. "That's our road. It used to be a cattle trail," he said.

"Are we sure we want to do this?" Juneau asked the other women.

"Piece of cake," Mike said. "I've been driving it for a couple of years and haven't lost anyone yet."

"Just in case, you better take our pictures now," Erin said, handing Mike her camera. He had them pose with a view of Canyonlands behind them and then turn around so he could take a photo of the appliqués.

Deenie, who'd always wanted to take her pickup on this kind of adventure, climbed into the front passenger seat so she could see the road ahead. "Everyone fasten your seat belts," she said.

Mike laughed. "If we go off the road, ladies, a seatbelt won't make any difference."

"Maybe we should have written our obituaries last night," Juneau said, only half joking.

ERIN

Erin woke early, about the time when Tony usually yodeled good morning. Neither of the other COBs was up, so she enjoyed a few more minutes in bed, thinking about their adventure of the day before. After the breath-stopping descent from the plateau down to the bank of the Colorado, they'd eaten the lunch provided by the tour company and then gone by boat up the river. The last stretch back to town was by van. Eagles, petrified forests, petroglyphs—Erin filed away all the details to tell Hannah.

That day their goal was Angel Arch Backcountry Trail. It was billed as an easy hike of slightly over a mile, leading to a good view of the arch that Deenie had appliquéd on Erin's jacket. It was a perfect day for a hike, Erin thought as they started out. It was warm but with a slight breeze, and the sky overhead was a gorgeous blue she'd never seen in a Minnesota sky.

Ten minutes into their hike, Erin noticed Deenie was lagging behind. "Do you need to take a break?"

"A short one," Deenie said. "Go on ahead. I'll catch up."

Erin doubted that. Deenie's face was pasty and her expression troubled. Erin hurried to Juneau, who'd gone a short way ahead. "I'm worried about Deenie. Did you notice how pale she is?"

Juneau nodded. "Maybe Deenie-to-the-Rescue needs some rescuing herself."

They joined Deenie on her rock. "Okay, girl," Erin said. "What's wrong? And don't say it's nothing."

"No more secrets," Juneau added.

"It's nothing *new*," Deenie said. "I've been having weird symptoms for some time. I get tired easily, and my legs hurt. Now and then my heart races."

"Have you seen your doctor?" Juneau asked.

Deenie nodded. "He ran some basic tests. The results were all normal, but I know something's wrong. So I'm looking for a new doctor. One who will listen to me."

"This one didn't?" asked Erin.

"No," Deenie said. "That's why I didn't tell him the most important thing." She paused. "Sunny's calling me home."

Erin exchanged a startled glance with Juneau and then listened with concern to Deenie's recital of her experience at Sunny's grave and her interpretation of it.

"Are you sure that's what it meant?" Juneau asked.

"I have to consider the possibility."

They sat in somber silence. Then Erin nudged Deenie's shoulder and said, "You know what I think? I think if Sunny didn't snatch you away on that descent down Shaefer Trail yesterday, you're probably good for another few decades."

During the remaining days, they took it easy. They visited the small town museum, bought matching Kokopelli sweatshirts, and ate a wonderful sweet potato salad at a New Age café-gallery on a side street. And more often than usual, they sat in silence, just enjoying being together.

As they parted ways at the Salt Lake City airport at the end of the trip, Deenie said, "Sorry I gave you a scare back in Moab. I'm counting on us getting together at the Rasmussen family cabin next year on Bear Lake."

"Will you be up to that?" Juneau asked.

Deenie nodded. "I've already claimed a week in September. We can meet in Wellsville and drive up."

Juneau drew them into a group hug. "Can you believe we've actually almost done it? Nothing can stop us now!"

Erin looked at the unhealthy flush on Deenie's cheeks and thought, *I hope you're right.*

WILLADENE

The morning Deenie was to leave Wellsville she took care of last-minute tasks while waiting for Jenny to bring Wilford over to say good-bye.

"I'll drive him out to the farm first," Jenny had said. "He likes to see for himself that everything's fine."

When Deenie heard the van drive up, she hurried to the front porch. The sight of Wilford with his big, work-worn hands cradled against his chest made Deenie long for the days when she'd seen those same hands wield a hammer or gentle a horse.

He reached the top stair, looked at Deenie with watery eyes, and held out a surprise in his hands. "We found him asleep in an old milk dish by the back door of the farm house. Another throwaway. I couldn't leave him there."

Tears sprang to Deenie's eyes when she saw the quivering bunch of butterscotch and brindle fur that Wilford held. She'd told that reporter the year Bear died that she trusted the good Lord to bring a new dog to her door when the time was right—and here it was.

She reached for the quivering puppy, laughing and crying as it licked her face.

"Oh, my goodness," she said. "What will Roger say and how am I ever going to get you back to Gainesville?"

JUNEAU

Juneau had come to question whether Letitia's ash-filled urn actually existed. She was flabbergasted when she received an e-mail from her mother saying she'd located the son of the old friend who'd put the urn in the floor-to-ceiling safe in his Boise store. That was back in 1959, when Letitia had died in the penitentiary before completing her sentence for causing her husband's death.

"She's still there," Pamela wrote. "It's time for you and me and Misty to make the trek to retrieve her. And scatter her ashes on Angel's Roost as she requested."

Juneau and Misty flew to Boise, where they connected with Pamela, who'd flown in from Oregon. They rented a car and drove straight to the store owned by the son of Letitia's old friend. Juneau could feel anxiety and anticipation rising in equal measures as they parked in front of it.

"I was surprised when you called," the friendly man said. "After so many years, I didn't think anyone would ever come for her."

He led them to a large black safe dominating the back office and opened the heavy door. "The story of 'Letitia in the Safe' has been part of our family lore for as long as I can remember," he said, gesturing toward the urn. "We'll miss the old girl."

When Pamela picked it up, the man added, "Don't forget the diaries."

Juneau sucked in a breath when she realized the dusty binders on the shelf were Letitia's diaries. She remembered Pamela telling her about them years ago.

"They're yours," Pamela told Juneau. "Very likely I already know all the secrets in them."

Secrets, Juneau thought, taking them from the shelf. Secrets seemed to be the theme of her life.

When they left the store, Juneau put the binders in the car trunk. The urn rode in the backseat alongside Pamela. "I don't feel right about putting Letitia in the trunk," Pamela had said. "After all, she was my grandmother and the only mother I ever knew."

They arrived in Mink Creek in the midst of a golden autumn twilight. "Oh," Pamela said as Misty drove up the last rise and they could see the church and cemetery and school-become-apartments against a backdrop of mountains aflame with fall colors. "I'd forgotten how beautiful it is."

"It's home," Juneau said, feeling again the call of her ancestors as she had when she and Misty had been there in 1990.

"Yes," Pamela murmured. "Yes. Paul always wanted to come back. I wish we had."

Juneau recalled that when she was saying good-bye to her dying father, he'd requested that she take her mother back to Idaho. "She knows why," he'd said. What had he been referring to?

As if she'd heard Juneau's unspoken question, her mother said, "I want to see Annabelle before we leave."

Annabelle. The girl from whom she'd stolen Paul all those years ago. Juneau was doubtful, but Misty said, "It's about time."

"Yes," Pamela admitted. "I've carried that guilt long enough."

They stayed that night in the old family home where Juneau and

Misty had visited the first time they'd come to Idaho. Adrienne and Clay Ostergaard, relatives of sorts as well as Cath's parents, welcomed them with open arms and a savory pot roast dinner. Clay paid his respects to the ashes in the urn. "Bring it into the house," he said. "Letitia might as well spend one last night in what was once her home."

He carried the urn inside but not to the room Letitia had shared with Orville. Considering what she'd done, that didn't seem right, so it rested overnight on a highly polished mahogany lamp table in the parlor.

Everybody spent the evening looking at the family records Adrienne had so meticulously kept, and Juneau supplied the most recent pictures of and anecdotes about Rhiannan and Dillon, who were Clay and Adrienne's grandchildren as well as her own. Everybody except Misty, who took the car and drove away into the night without saying where she was going.

To see Whitford Morgan, Juneau thought. *That's probably why she wanted to come on this trip.* Misty was still on her mind as she climbed upstairs to bed, taking Letitia's three diaries with her. Sitting propped against her pillows, she began idly flipping through them, first reading snippets and then long stretches. And finally, in disbelief, she spent the entire night reading every word.

The next morning Pamela, Juneau, and Misty, who carried the urn, set off through the alfalfa field they'd gotten permission to cross on their way to the high ground of Angel's Roost, where Letitia had requested that her ashes be scattered.

"Mother," Juneau said, "I read the diaries."

Pamela, still able and agile despite being more than eighty, continued to trudge upward. "So now you know," she said finally.

"Know what?" Misty asked.

"That Orville was a wife-beater," Juneau said. "Just like Dex Beldon." She saw in her mind the ugly words, written in Letitia's neat penmanship. She'd recorded every beating, every bruise.

"Why didn't she use that in her defense at her manslaughter trial?" Misty asked. "It might have justified her hitting Orville with that shovel and shortened her sentence."

Pamela shook her head. "Not in those days. Back then if a wife complained that her husband beat her, the first question asked was, 'What did *you* do to make him angry?' Not just here. Everywhere. So she told no one."

Misty stopped short, turning to face Pamela. "Did *you* know about it?"

Juneau saw the regret in her mother's eyes.

"Yes," Pamela said. "But I was a child. What could I do? I put the knowledge in my . . ." She glanced at Juneau. "What's the name of that new book of yours? *Closet of Secrets?* It's one of the things that drove me—and Paul, too—from one place to the next."

In the silence that followed, Juneau saw secrets leading to other secrets and on to yet more secrets down through the generations, like a connect-the-dots game. She began speaking then, telling about Brenna Petry, letting her own crippling secret out into the crisp, sparkling autumn air.

Pamela hugged her when she finished, a rare instance of connection and comfort. Then she stepped back, businesslike again. "It's time to release Letitia. Maybe that will start us on the way to letting all of this go."

Pamela said a prayer, reminding the Lord that Letitia had been a good mother and neighbor and asking him to forgive her for what she'd done to her husband. When she finished, Misty opened the urn and gently poured out its contents. The slight breeze carried them a short distance and then let them settle to earth like a sigh.

"Rest in peace, Letitia," Juneau whispered.

As they re-crossed the alfalfa field, Juneau saw a tall, spare woman standing in the lane beside their car, watching them approach. Juneau recognized her from when she and Misty had been in Mink Creek before. Annabelle, whose fiancé Pamela had stolen.

"Adrienne told me where to find you," Annabelle said when they were close enough.

"Hello, Annabelle," Pamela said.

Juneau held her breath as she watched the two octogenarians take each other's measure. Finally Annabelle spoke. "So he's dead now."

Pamela nodded. "Yes."

"And you're probably still hauling an elephant-sized bag of guilt."

"Yes," Pamela said again.

"Well, scrap it," Annabelle chided. "I've known for years you were the right one for Paul. I never would have followed him from pillar to post."

Juneau started with surprise at Annabelle's reference—certainly not by chance—to the name of her parents' series.

"You've read our mysteries?" Pamela asked.

"Every one of them. I didn't like the girl in *Perfect for Prison*. Reminded me of me."

Pamela smiled. Then she and Annabelle started to laugh. They laughed so hard they had to hang onto each other for support.

Juneau watched them, wondering if it would be like this when she finally faced Brenna.

ERIN

E-mail, October 2, 2004
Dear COBs,

I'm pregnant again. Vince and I hadn't decided to try for another baby, so we were using protection. But life happens. My gynecologist just shakes her head, as does everyone else we know. Except Hannah, who is tickled pink.

I haven't said this to Vince, but I'm scared. I know more than I'd like to know about all the things that can go wrong. It's a good thing Hannah is certain we're having a boy named Noah and that everything will be okay.

Your Erin

JUNEAU

E-mail, October 5, 2004
Dear Erin and Deenie,

Forgive me, Erin, but I laughed when I read that the stork is flapping your way again. Blame it on those Kokopelli sweatshirts we bought in Moab. Kokopelli is a fertility deity, you know! I'm thrilled about your little surprise package, and I'll pray that all is well.

The big news here is that Shoshana and Ira's little guy arrived safely two days ago. His name is Abraham (they call him Aber), and he's an absolute darling. Shoshana's mother flew out to be with them, so I don't have official grandma duties there yet.

Other news: Misty, my mother, and I flew to Idaho and released Great-Grandma Letitia from the urn where she's been since her death forty-five years ago. Mom even met her old nemesis, Annabelle, and the two of them are friends again.

Mom looked twenty years younger when we left for home. In fact, she felt so frisky that she said she's not moving down to be with us yet. She's signed up for a trip to China organized by a seniors group in Oregon where she lives.

> Lovence,
> Juneau

WILLADENE

E-mail, October 7, 2004
Dear Erin and Juneau,

Erin, you're a mother-to-be; Juneau, you and I are grandmothers again!

Dani gave birth to a baby girl this morning. They've named her Logan Belle. Everyone's ecstatic. Dee is already talking about all the things he wants to teach his Belle right now—like how to jump and how to eat! They are going to have to keep a close eye on that little fellow.

> Love,
> Deenie

ERIN

E-mail, October 24, 2004
Dear Juneau,

Did you know EJ was coming back to Minnesota for a visit? I was lending a hand the first morning of the Big Barn Sale, and there she was, working on last-minute setup. She looked great—the piercings are gone, and she was dressed like a successful young woman. Best of all, she looks comfortable inside her own skin.

I asked her what caused the change. She said one day she suddenly felt the truth of what her mother and I, and you, Juneau, and Flower and Misty and Lucky and many others had all been trying to tell her. That she was unique and had something to offer that no one else could—herself. Her particular insights, understanding, humor, and experience.

Maybe it took all of us telling her all this time to finally make the difference. Moral of the story: Never, ever give up.

Your Erin

JUNEAU

E-mail, October 25, 2004
Dear Erin,

If I helped EJ, it was probably through the conversations we had about some difficult things. Speaking of . . . there's something I need to tell you and Deenie. A story about a ten-year-old who felt hurt and then caused hurt. I'll set up a conference phone call soon.

Lovence,
Juneau

WILLADENE

E-mail, November 5, 2004
Dear Juneau,

Telling us about Brenna was hard, but the hardest part is still ahead. You have to find and face her. As Miss B would say, "Bless you, dearie!"

Love,
Deenie

JUNEAU

E-mail, November 5, 2004
Dear Deenie and Erin,

I know I do. Greg did a sophisticated Internet search, found out Starette's married name, and located her. I've picked up the phone a dozen times to call, but I can't bring myself to do it. I guess I'm afraid of what she might tell me about Brenna.

Juneau

ERIN

E-mail, November 6, 2004
Dear Juneau, Dear Deenie,

Juneau, thank you for trusting us enough to tell us about Starette and Brenna. Give your inner ten-year-old a hug. I got the feeling she's been hiding out for decades, afraid she's unworthy of love or any other good thing. She's not so different from the rest of us, truth be told.

If you two think me being pregnant is funny, imagine me and Kayla being pregnant at the same time! Yep, it's true. We're both due in May.

Kayla and Eddie are thrilled, although they hadn't intended to start a family right away. His parents are less so. Their attitude dampened what should be a joyous occasion. I hope Eddie realizes he needs to talk to his parents. And has the nerve to do it. I think he's the child who tries to make everyone happy in that family.

Your Erin

The first Saturday of December, Erin was watching Vince position a lighted star at the top of the Christmas tree gracing their family room. "Perfect," she said. She picked up Tony, who was pulling low-hanging ornaments off the branches, and stood back. Vince joined her, his arm around her waist.

"Okay, Hannah," he said. "Plug in the lights."

Tony squealed as the tree lit up and the star glowed. "What do you think?" Erin asked Hannah, her ten-going-on-fifteen-year-old.

"It's the prettiest tree yet."

Erin had put Tony in his high chair and started to make cocoa when the phone rang. "It's for you, Erin," Vince said. "Cory."

She took the receiver. "Your timing's perfect, Cory. We've just trimmed the tree, and I'm making cocoa. Wanna come over?"

"Actually, that's why I called," he said. "I'd like to talk to you."

There was something different about his voice, but she couldn't tell what. "Come now, if you like."

When he arrived, she led him up to her home office and pulled two chairs together. When they were seated, he took a letter out of his pocket. "I got this from my dad yesterday. He's had a Road to Damascus experience."

She gave him a questioning glance.

"A man in the training group last week told him he was a master teacher—the only thing missing was love."

"No way."

"He said he was prompted to tell Dad that he needed to search his heart before the next class started. Dad said he wanted to brush the man off, but he couldn't. He knew what the man was talking about."

Cory unfolded the letter and read:

> When I saw myself in the light trained on me by that humble brother, I was ashamed. I realized that when I tried to manipulate you into changing by withholding my love from you, I was also withholding it from others, myself, and even from God.
>
> I ask your forgiveness for that, and for not being someone you could unburden your heart to, no matter what. I love you, son. Whatever happens in the eternities, I promise not to separate us in this life by my actions.

"That's quite the Christmas present," Erin said when she could speak.

"The best ever," Cory said thickly. "For the first time in years, I feel like I can breathe."

WILLADENE

"That's the last of the breakables, Mom," Evvy sighed with satisfaction. She plopped on the couch next to the butterscotch-colored puppy sprawled belly down and snoring. "Everything Chul or Dee could possibly reach has been boxed up and hauled to the attic. Now can we go shopping?"

Deenie laughed. Evvy had been chomping at the bit to go Christmas shopping since Thanksgiving. And considering that the entire family—grandparents included—had announced they were coming for the holidays, there was plenty of incentive.

"We'll go as soon as I confirm a delivery date for the cribs we're renting." Deenie said. "In the meantime, see if you can get that bundle of fluff moving."

"That'll be easy," Evvy said sarcastically as she scooped up the cocker-beagle-poodle-and-possibly-terrier mix that had become part of the family in September. "Honey puts the 'lap' in lap dog!"

Deenie watched Evvy drape the puppy over her shoulder and walk out the door. Honey was the polar opposite of Bear—more Barker Clinic dog than rescue dog. She spent most of her time with her head in Deenie's lap, looking up with a soulful expression in her big dark eyes as if to ask, "Do you need loves? Do you need kisses?"

That was exactly what Deenie did need. A constant warm bit of comfort always available when, no matter how carefully she managed the stress in her life and kept to a strict health regimen, her face tingled and her legs went numb.

Deenie picked up a slip of paper from her desk. It was a phone number for a doctor Delia had given her. A doctor who listened, Delia said. Who didn't write off women's complaints to stress or hypochondria. Deenie had made an appointment with him. It was a long way off, but she felt better knowing she had it.

Despite her worries, there was much to look forward to. Babies in her lap. Presents under the tree. Evvy's clear voice filling the house with holiday music. And shopping!

Chapter 30

2005

ERIN

Erin started out 2005 pregnant and urpy, trying to comfort Kayla, who was pregnant and urpy and bawling her eyes out. It was not the sort of situation a Crusty *Old* Broad was supposed to be dealing with.

Kayla had called early New Year's Day to say she'd overheard her in-laws discussing their "concerns" about her with Eddie—and he hadn't defended her. "I'm driving home as soon as I pack."

At the thought of Kayla driving one hundred and fifty miles in her emotional state—and in wretched January weather—Erin said something she never would have otherwise. "Wait. I'll have Vince fly up to get you."

The minute she arrived, Kayla ran into Erin's arms, crying, "Frank and Lisa hate me."

"I think it's more a case of not understanding you, dear," Erin said. She'd seen how they had reacted upon discovering their future daughter-in-law did tai chi, ate vegetarian, and was a beneficiary of a trust.

That rankled Erin. Kayla had had the benefit of opportunities and resources, even before the trust, but she'd also worked hard for everything she'd achieved, especially after the accident.

"They don't even try, Mom. They actually told Eddie they're not sure if I understand what a stable family is like. There's Grandpa Andy getting Grandma Joanna pregnant but not marrying her. You being born out of wedlock. Him marrying Brenda, having a baby with her, and then divorcing her. Getting back together with her after Lottie died, even though Brenda had been married and divorced all those times."

"But that's not the whole sto—"

Kayla interrupted. "The worst thing is that they're worried about how my having a father who's gay will affect the baby."

Erin took Kayla's face in her hands. "Any negative effect has more to do with how it's handled than the fact he is."

"I know that. I thought Eddie knew it, too. Mom, what if Eddie's decided he doesn't want me or the baby?"

E-mail, January 2, 2005
Dear COBs,

We started out the year with high drama—I think we McGees must have a gene for that! Kayla came home feeling unloved and misunderstood, and Eddie made a mad dash down from Duluth to get her. They're back together, thanks to their love for each other and an intervention of sorts by Vince and Sam.

I didn't know it, but those two have had long talks about what it's like being married to McGees. They were the perfect ones to help Eddie put things into perspective. Dear Vince gave him great advice: Falling in love and choosing to love are two different things. It was time for him to choose to love Kayla.

Vince has a gift for saying the right thing at the right time. Like just now—he just told me it's time to tuck myself in! I love how he takes care of Noah and me.

Love,
Erin

JUNEAU
E-mail, January 3, 2005
Dear COBs,

This is The Year of the Pact! Twenty-five years since we met, come August. *Who'da!* Sorry to hear your New Year's Day was so urpy all around, Erin. And glad that Kayla and Eddie solved their problem.

We had a good Christmas, but without Nicole, who's in Mexico, and Misty, who was out of town. She didn't say where she was going. Back up to Idaho to see Whitford Morgan, I'm guessing. After serving in several county and state elected positions, he's gearing up to make a serious bid for governor next time an election comes around. She can't still entertain fantasies of being the Governor's Lady, can she?

Nicole wrote that she made the right decision to follow her dream of being a doctor in that little Mexican village, although not as *Señora* Sanchez. She said Christmas was a delight. She and Beto, as just friends, attended the Christmas program on the 19th at the little LDS chapel in the next town. All the children call Beto "*Hermano* Doctor." They love him because he sings Primary songs with them, which he remembers from attending Primary with Nicole all those years ago.

On Christmas Eve the two of them attended midnight mass at the Catholic Church on Christmas Eve. They were royally welcomed there, too. Their work has made them much loved among the people of that area.

Poor Gideon. His guitar teacher sprang a recital on his students between Christmas and New Year. Gideon was to do three numbers, one of which would also be a vocal. Even though he's been singing with Trace ever since he could hold a guitar, he went absolutely bloodless at the thought of anything that formal—he even threatened not to go!

Then Serenity offered to join him in a duet arrangement Trace made of his song "Little Boy," the one he sang when he first came to see Gideon. That changed Giddy's whole attitude about the event. He and Serenity captured everyone's hearts. They've been asked to repeat their performance twice in the coming weeks.

Erin, tell Mark that Gideon is wearing out the CD of his recital. Deenie, ditto to what Erin said about taking care of yourself. And tell Roger about Sunny and not feeling safe. Take it from one who knows all about secrets.

Juneau

WILLADENE

E-mail, January 5, 2005
Dear Juneau and Erin,

My holiday was two weeks of pure heaven on Gobb Hill. Family filling the house. Babies to hug. Could anything be more wonderful? I've attached pictures so you get an idea of what it was like.

More good news. I was able to get an appointment with that

doctor I told you about. Roger is relieved. I'll tell him about Sunny after that. In case there is something more to tell, I'd like to get it over with all at once. In the meantime Miss B is joining me in trying out some of Kayla's meditation suggestions for pain control. She says she's open to anything that will make her feet feel better.

What a trouper. Besides, she says, meditation is part of the spiritual path to inner peace.

Deenie

"Is this the place?" Miss B asked as Deenie guided her to the dahlia bed behind the boxwood hedge.

"Yup." Deenie inhaled the scent of the rich earth. The gardeners had tilled for a second time, adding dark, fragrant mulch to the bed and raking it smooth. A garden bench was situated at the foot of the bed where sunshine spilled on the earth and the spring breezes rustled the leaves.

"Sit here," Deenie said.

Miss B placed the cushion she carried on the bench and lowered herself onto it. She allowed a small chortle to escape as she settled back. "Now what?" she asked. "Do we light incense?"

"Not this time." She unlaced Miss B's walking shoes and slid them off. The white anklets followed, revealing the aged and arthritic feet. "Erin said that Kayla said you can feel the energy of the earth best if you're barefoot." Deenie gently massaged the ball and arch of one foot and then the other.

"You foolish girl." Miss B leaned forward and ruffled the curls on Deenie's head. "You're a blessing in my life."

Deenie rested Miss B's feet on the sun-warmed soil. "That goes both ways. You're exactly who I want to be when I grow up. Wise. Kind. Truthful."

Miss B laughed out loud. "Why, Willadene Rasmussen. We're not all that different. In fact, we're two versions of the same thing—women making our way down the same path. I'm a little bit farther along. That's all."

"And glad I am to hear that." Deenie rolled up her pants, kicked off her sandals, and lay spread-eagled on the ground. After a bit she heard Miss B shuffling her feet in the dirt.

"Careful," Deenie teased. "If it's 'dust to dust,' you may be stepping on someone."

"You never know." Miss B paused. "Aren't we supposed to hum or something?"

"You could try the *Om* thing, but I think we're supposed to be still and open and let the earth's energy flow through us."

"You try that, and I'll try the *Om*." Miss B turned her face to the breeze and began. "Aaa-uuuuu-mmmmm. Aaa-uuuuu-mmmm." She followed the sound with a gusty laugh. "That makes my lips tickle."

Deenie smiled and relaxed deeper into the softened dirt until she felt as if her bones were melting. She hoped good earth energy was filling her up, as Erin reported it would.

The minute she closed her eyes, she heard someone run down the path and slide to a halt at the edge of the dahlia bed. "Mom! What are you doing?"

"Getting energized, Evvy," Deenie said without opening her eyes.

"I wanted go to the mall with Christiana, but you said I had to be home right after school. What for? To watch you lolling in the dirt?"

"Aaa-uuu-mmmm," continued Miss B.

"I was going to teach you how to make bread," Deenie said in a lazy voice. "But I'll do it later—I'm too relaxed to move."

Evvy huffed, turned on her heel, and ran back up the path.

Miss B stopped *Om*-ing and said, "You've been pushing that child lately, Deenie."

"I know. But there's so much for her to learn."

"Does she have to learn it all this spring?" Miss B asked.

"Sometimes it seems like it," Deenie said. "Who knows what tomorrow might bring? None of us comes with our life expectancy stamped on our fannies."

"Is there a reason for your sense of urgency that I should know about?" her friend asked.

Deenie sat up and stretched, giving herself time to decide how much she wanted to share. Then she said, "Sometimes I feel like I'm closer to the dead than the living. That if I stretched my hand forward I could touch the veil."

"I feel that way myself some days," Miss B said. "It's not unusual when folks you love cross to the other side. Or maybe it's because you've been putting your heart and soul into getting right with God. The veil is thinner when you do that."

"Then there's my sister, Sunny." Deenie sighed deeply. "I've told you about her. Since Stella's death, she's sometimes been so near I can almost feel her breath on my check. It feels like she's telling me it's time to come home."

"Oh, my. And you think . . . ?"

"I can't come up with any other explanation," Deenie said. "With all the changes in my health . . . That's why I've been working so hard to get my life in order."

Miss B took Deenie's arm. "Have you seen that new doctor yet?"

"Next Tuesday. I'm a little afraid he'll tell me I've slipped a cog and need another visit to the loony bin."

"Would you like me to go with you?" Miss B asked.

"No. But thank you for asking." Deenie gave her friend a hug. "Thank you for everything."

JUNEAU

After weeks of being absent from class, Clyde called Juneau late one afternoon. "Where have you been?" she asked. "We've missed you."

"Sorry." Clyde said. "I retired at the first of the year, and I've been doing a lot of volunteer work with Molly's dog rescue kennel."

"The Barker Clinic," Juneau said.

Clyde chuckled. "Last week I went with Molly to rescue some abandoned dogs up in the mountains. To make a long story short, we brought back six adoptable dogs. They're disoriented and need lots of reassurance. I'm wondering if Gideon might come over and help with them this afternoon. Serenity, too."

"Poor things," Juneau murmured. She had a soft spot for dogs; there'd been an empty place in her heart since Philip Atwater died that even

Numbtail couldn't fill. "Yes, it's fine with me. I'll call Shan at work to see if it's okay with her."

"Great," Clyde said. "I'll pick them up. By the way, how *is* Shan? Is she holding to her resolve to divorce Dex?"

"Yes." Juneau told him what she'd discovered reading Letitia's journals, adding, "Shan's resolve is stronger after she heard about the abuse Letitia suffered—and the final outcome."

"I can imagine. Letitia's story is a cautionary tale," Clyde said. "For both genders."

When Clyde brought Gideon and Serenity home late that afternoon, he also brought a large, skinny brown dog with gentle but bewildered eyes.

"It was my idea." Gideon patted the dog's head. "Don't blame Clyde."

Juneau smiled. "I wasn't blaming anybody. Are you planning to keep him?"

"Can I?" Gideon asked. "He looks just like Philip Atwater, so he must be ours!"

"Please, Sister Caldwell," Serenity pleaded.

Juneau looked at the two of them. Gideon was seventeen now, tall and angular. Serenity, fifteen, was tall for a girl and softly rounded. Nice kids. Kids who had dealt with being disoriented and needy themselves and were now reaching out, wanting to give something back to another needy creature.

"Does he have a name?"

Gideon and Serenity nodded. "Lonesome," they said together.

Lonesome looked up at her, and Juneau's heart melted. Of course, he would stay. "I guess we've got a new dog," she said.

Gideon and Serenity hugged her, gave Clyde high fives, and then headed off to introduce Lonesome to Numbtail.

"There's a story in this somewhere," Juneau said to Clyde. "You should write it."

"If there is," he said with a look of appreciation, "it's about a person who makes good things happen for others. Including the beasts and the children."

WILLADENE

The last Wednesday in February Deenie sat under the live oak on the north crest of Gobb Hill trying to play folk tunes on her harmonica. She'd given it up when Roger was injured because the sound irritated him, but it was back on her Do It Now list. She played a ragged version of a sad song. It suited her melancholy mood.

As she finished, Deenie noticed the afternoon air was getting cooler and smelled of rain, so she pulled her sweater over her shoulders and edged closer to the warmth of Honey. The dog sprawled belly up on the blanket, begging for a tummy scratch.

"How did I end up with the laziest dog in Florida?" Deenie wondered aloud as she gave the butterscotch pooch the attention she craved.

That's where Roger found her a few minutes later. "What's this?" he asked, sitting down beside her. "Another hour of somber meditation?" When Deenie nodded, he said, "You've been having a lot of those lately."

"I've been thinking about Sunny and how close I feel to her. And Aunt Stella, your mom, and Sarah Beth."

"Any special reason?" Roger asked, putting his arm around her, a gesture he made automatically now, and Deenie appreciated it.

In the comfort of his embrace, Deenie let it all spill out. She told him about Aunt Stella's funeral, Sunny's call, and everything that had happened since then. "I've been wondering since then if maybe I don't have much time left."

"Deenie, Deenie." Roger gathered her onto his lap and held her close. "Is that why you've been working so hard to get your life in order?"

Deenie nodded again.

"You went to see your new doctor this morning, didn't you? What did he say?"

"He has some ideas and is running some tests."

"How are you feeling right now?"

"Rotten," Deenie said. She hated the sound of tears and frustration in her voice. "Rotten and worried and afraid."

"I can't tell you how sorry I am for the part I played in that," Roger said. He rocked back and forth as he held her, a motion of comfort.

"I don't think I've told you how profoundly grateful I am for how you stood by me through the whole drug fiasco," he said softly. "How grateful I am that you made me face up to what was happening. And how grateful I am that you are still here with me. Whatever happens, we'll get through it together. You're safe with me, Deenie. Now and always."

Then Roger kissed her gently, deeply. For the first time in months he kissed her the way he had when they'd first fallen in love.

E-mail, March 3, 2005
Dear COBs,

I told my dear husband about my worries. After we talked it over, he asked me if there was anything missing from my life that would make me happier. Walk the Great Wall of China? Sail the Barrier Reef? Move back to Wellsville? I'm pleased to announce none of the above called out to me. I'm where I want to be, doing what I want to do.

Love, hugs, kisses, blessings, and every good thing life has to offer for my dear friends.

Deenie

P.S. Erin, have you had any luck locating that Hull vase I want for Jenny? It's perfect to go with her Roseville urn from NeVae, and I'd love to have it in time for her birthday in June.

ERIN
E-mail, March 7, 2005

Deenie, check the attached photo of the "Sueno" Hull tulip vase Jake found. It's beautiful but rather pricy. Let us know asap if you want it.

Erin

WILLADENE
E-mail, March 7, 2005

Yes, please. Check in the mail. Thanks for your help.

Deenie

JUNEAU

That spring Misty began showing up at family gatherings. She hung around the fringes, often playing with Rhiannan and Dillon and baby Aber, all of whom adored her, and lingering near Gideon, as if she wanted to know him better. One day, Juneau heard her apologizing for not being more involved with him when he was a little boy, the way she was with these new little ones.

"It's okay, Misty," Gideon said. "I'm the age now that you were when you had me. I understand why you had to go."

Juneau was impressed by his mature attitude. Recently he'd started to call his birth parents Misty and Trace. In the past he'd avoided calling them anything unless he absolutely had to, at which times he'd mumble something unintelligibile. Juneau knew he'd come to regard them more as his sister and brother than his parents. That seemed appropriate. In one way or another, she and Greg were parents to all three of them.

One afternoon Misty appeared unexpectedly at the door of Juneau's little writing room in the garage. "Hey, Mom," she said, "mind an interruption?"

Juneau closed down the file on her computer and turned to face her daughter. "I'd love to be interrupted. To what do I owe the pleasure of a mid-day visit?"

"I just wanted to talk with you."

"Have you had lunch?" Juneau asked. "May I get you something?"

"No, thanks. I probably wouldn't eat what you have in your kitchen." A grin took the rudeness out of Misty's statement. She'd recently turned vegan, eating not much more than vegetables and rice. Juneau regarded it as another attempt to find herself.

Misty pulled up a chair and sat, glancing over to where Numbtail and Lonesome snoozed on the floor less than a foot from each other. "Gideon told me about the dog. Did he and Numbtail have adjustment problems?"

Juneau laughed. "No. Numbtail established his seniority right away with a well-aimed swat at Lonesome's nose, and they've been buddies ever since."

Misty chuckled. "I remember using much the same tactics on Nicole when I was five and she was three. She was the 'good girl' and got all the praise and attention. One day I told her I was the oldest and the boss, and she'd better remember that or I'd pinch off her nose and feed it to Philip Atwater."

"You didn't!"

"I did. You know what a sweetie Nicole has always been. She just smiled like an angel and said, 'Okay.'"

Juneau touched Misty's arm. "I didn't know you felt she got all the attention, Misty."

"You should have. Why else do you think I acted the way I did?"

Juneau flinched. How could she not have known that?

Misty saw her reaction, "Don't go storing that in your guilt closet, because it doesn't bother me anymore. In fact, I've realized that whatever my complaints, you and Dad did a good job raising us girls." She leaned forward. "You know I volunteer with a hotline for lost and lonely girls."

Juneau nodded. "That's how you got to know EJ."

"Right." Misty paused. "If I haven't told you before, you were great with her. You took her in with no questions. No demands. No requirements. Like the way you took in Numbtail and Lonesome."

"Why, thank you, Misty. That's nice to hear."

"What I'm getting at is I'd like to bring other girls here occasionally, if it's all right with you." Misty grinned. "The ones I think can use a mother figure."

"Yes, of course," Juneau said. "You can bring anybody you want."

"Thanks, Mom. I think you really could've helped the girl I escorted home over Christmas. Too bad she never got a chance to meet you."

"Oh, that's what you were doing," Juneau said. "You didn't tell us. I thought . . ." She stopped, wishing she hadn't opened her mouth.

"You thought what?" Misty looked at her levelly. "Tell the truth, Mom."

"That you'd gone to Idaho again. To see Whitford Morgan."

Misty leaned back, assessing her. "It's hard for you not to think the worst of me, isn't it?"

"I'm so sorry, Misty. My thoughts go there out of habit, I guess."

"I've given you plenty of reasons." Misty tried on a wavering smile. "I know you don't understand me, Mom. I don't understand myself half the time. I'm thirty-four, the same age you were when you went to BYU Education week, and I'm still searching for . . . I don't know what."

"That's exactly how I felt then."

"I suppose that's why I'm always bouncing off the wall, always trying different things. But no matter how many mistakes I make, I somehow always seem to circle back here. Home. And by the way, Whitford and I are just friends. I do a little consulting work for him via computer. That's all."

"I'm sorry, Misty," Juneau said. "I had this wrong idea in my head. Do you still want to bring girls here under my flawed wings?"

"Yes. So you're not perfect. You're still the best mom I know."

ERIN

E-mail, March 28, 2005
Dear COBs,

On Good Friday, just in time to throw a monkey wrench into my plans for a family dinner on Easter Sunday, Dr. Lamont told me I have preeclampsia. That's blood pressure high enough in a pregnant woman to put her and the baby at risk. The only cure is to give birth, so I have to spend most of my time in bed until Noah comes! That's about five weeks, if he goes to term. Dr. Lamont says that's not likely.

She scared the wits out of me with dire tales of what could happen to Noah and me if I don't follow her instructions exactly. When I stopped by Mom's place to pick up Tony, she called Valerie, who mobilized the Relief Society to help provide meals and bus Hannah to her piano lessons. Mom will watch Tony. (He's in the Terrible Twos. He loves taking things apart, and his favorite line is, "I'm not going to!") The Gerlach Girls are helping on weekends.

My dear Vince is worried sick. Even with all the help, he was ready to take an extended leave from the clinic until I promised him I'd be good. He'd be devastated if anything happens to the baby and me.

The family gathered for Easter dinner as planned, including Kayla and Eddie and Mark, who came for the weekend. Brenda and Mom took over as hostesses. They had the men set up tables and TV trays in my bedroom, so we could all eat dinner together. It was actually quite lovely, despite the incongruous setting.

Before he left for Madison, Mark told Vince and me he was thinking about sending in his mission papers after spring semester's over! I think he's been influenced by letters from Skipp and conversations with Vince, who wishes he'd been able to go on a mission as a young man.

Kayla's doing fine, too. Everything on track for Baby Beckmann to arrive mid-May, and she's getting along better with her in-laws. Which is good, because they're working hard, Eddie on his master's thesis, and Kayla on her senior art project.

Hannah floats along happily. She's finagled Vince into teaching her about "animals' insides," and the two of them take Curly Dude and Rascal to visit a hospital ward or senior center every so often. Her teachers all love her to death.

So much to celebrate, so much to worry about.

Erin

JUNEAU
E-mail, April 6, 2005,
Dear Deenie and Erin,

Erin, if lying abed is what helps with preeclampsia, then you do it. There's nothing that needs to be done that's more important than you and Noah.

As for Greg and me, we're off to London to visit the Queen! Well, to tell the truth, I haven't notified her that we're coming, but I'll wave to her when we visit Buckingham Palace. Our bags are packed and we leave tomorrow.

Misty is staying at our house to keep Gideon company and oversee Numbtail and Lonesome while we're gone. She says she can do her job any place there's a computer and an Internet connection. I think it will be very good for them to spend time together.

Serenity is excited for the chance to get to know Misty better. She still comes here each day after school until Shan gets home from work. Serenity commented to me once that Misty would never allow herself to be hit by anybody, like her mother did. And that made me take a new look at Misty, who (I'm sorry to admit) was right when she said I always thought the worst of her.

All of our accommodations have Internet access for guests (21st century meets merrie auld England), so I'll keep in touch by e-mail.

> Lovence,
> Juneau

WILLADENE

E-mail, April 8, 2005
Dear Erin,

Is chocolate dangerous for the preeclampsic? I hope not. Delia suggested a new brand you have to try. It's on its way.

Roger took the afternoon off, and we made an event of going to the doctor's to get the results of my tests. I'm happy to say none of the big bugaboos we tested for showed up. The heart murmur isn't part of the current problem. Even the irregular heartbeat is of the benign variety.

However, the doctor says all indications point to fibromyalgia. Right now we're concentrating on ways to treat symptoms that don't include lots of pills. It's all about quality of life with this guy.

To celebrate knowing that whatever fibromyalgia is, it isn't fatal, Roger took me to see *Because of Winn Dixie* at the dollar theater. We pigged out on popcorn, Junior Mints, and orange soda. My kind of date!

> Love,
> Deenie

After her visit to the doctor, Deenie began to wonder if she should put away her Just in Case lists. She talked it over with Miss B, who said, "Certainly not. Look at all the good that's come from it. And if it turns out you were wrong about what Sunny meant, you'll have a fine head start on the rest of your life."

So, pacing herself, Deenie wrote her obituary and her will and ordered a new set of temple clothes to hang in the back of the closet, just in case. Each time she took on a new project she prayed intensely to know if doing it would be of benefit to her family and if it would please the Lord. Each time she received a warm confirmation.

As spring went by, she continued on her quest to make up for past mistakes, clear the air with everyone she loved, and keep her heart right with God. But even with all those tasks underway, she was left with a peculiar feeling, like the tickle before a sneeze, that she was leaving something out. That some question she should have voiced in her prayers remained unasked.

Chapter 31

JUNEAU

E-mail, April 10, 2005
Dear Friends,

Greetings from the land where elevators are lifts, car trunks are boots, and everybody drives on the "wrong" side of the road.

We're at our first timeshare condo now. As advertised, it has a computer room for guests, with e-mail access, so I'm taking advantage of it. We're very close to Shakespeare's territory, and we'll tour his home tomorrow.

Today we went to church at a ward nearby. The main speaker in sacrament meeting gave a marvelous talk about eternal families. It was very touching and made me think Nicole's decision not to marry Beto if they couldn't have an eternal family was the right one.

Love from the "scepter'd isle,"
Juneau

E-mail, April 17, 2005
To my Pals across the Pond,

We're at our second condo now, on the Welsh coast where we can walk across the headlands and imagine pirate ships sailing into the cove. Who knows, I might write a pirate book next! (Wanna come when I do research?) Tomorrow we'll drive south to a place called St. Brides and visit sites with quaint names like Haroldston Chins. You can be charmed out of your mind here!

I got an e-mail today from Gideon saying Misty has been cooking foods from different countries every day. I didn't even know she could cook. There are many benefits that come from traveling abroad, including getting a different perspective on a whole lot of things at home. I'm ashamed now that I've had such a narrow view of Misty for so long.

By the way, Misty wrote a P.S. to the e-mail that there was a phone call from a bookstore owner in Oregon asking if I will sign books when I next go to visit Mom, who, I take it, has been talking about "my daughter, the author." That won't be until June, after Mom returns from her China tour.

We're having such a good time!

Lovence,
Juneau

ERIN

Erin had never thought of herself as a control freak, but being unable to do things forced her to realize how much her self-worth was dependent upon producing results, whether it was getting her visiting teaching done, cleaning the house, or taking on a big decorating job. So having Bishop Hardy release her from the Relief Society presidency sent her into a tailspin.

"I've been impressed that this is the right thing to do," he said when he came to tell her. "You need to put all your energy into taking care of yourself and raising your little family."

"I can manage," she protested. "After the baby's born, I'll feel much better."

But Bishop Hardy was adamant. So he took away the one area in which she could still contribute, albeit by phone.

Vince tried to cheer her up, but Erin was desolate. Then one Sunday he came home after sacrament meeting and looked up the poem that a speaker had quoted, On His Blindness by John Milton. He read it to her, putting special emphasis on the last line, which he read twice: "They also serve who only stand and wait."

Erin was touched by his attempt to comfort her. She wiped her eyes and said, "Do you think Milton would mind if I changed it to, 'They also serve who only lie abed?'"

The last day of April, Erin felt rotten. She told Vince that if she didn't feel better in the morning, she was calling Dr. Lamont. When she woke with puffy hands and feet, a splitting headache, and double vision, Vince called an ambulance, and Noah Russell Gerlach was delivered that morning by emergency Cesarean section. Erin felt a huge rush of love for the wet, squalling piece of humanity Dr. Lamont held up for her to see.

E-mail, May 5, 2005
Dear Friends,

When Noah and I came home yesterday, he was wearing the tiny blue *#2 Son* cap Vince brought to the hospital. With his wispy strawberry hair, face red with indignation, and little fists waving, he's definitely a McGee! Hannah took one look at him and said, "Yup, that's the one."

I love him to bits, but he's a challenge. His fussiness wouldn't be so trying if I didn't feel so rotten. I'm still dealing with lingering symptoms from preeclampsia, incision pain, and lack of conditioning from being in bed so long.

Vince is the best. He helps with the kids and rubs my feet at night. Hannah and Tony are great fetchers and carriers. Even the animals are trying to help. Rascal and Curly Dude don't leave my room when I'm resting. And someone has taught George to say, "Where's Erin?!"

In spite of all that, I feel like I've been run over by a truck. Who said it was a good idea to have kids at my age?!

Erin

JUNEAU

E-mail, May 9, 2005
Dear Deenie and Erin,

Erin, who would have imagined that on the year we've reached our goal, you would be the mother of a newborn and a toddler! I'm glad to hear that you and Noah are home. And sorry to hear you've got the baby blues. Cut yourself some slack. Birth—perhaps especially by Caesarean section—takes time to recover from.

We've been back for a couple weeks, and we both agree—it was wonderful to go, and it's even more wonderful to come home. Misty did a fine job of taking care of things here. She and I had a little talk before she went back to her apartment. She said she needed the time here in her old home to set the course for her future. She said she confronted a lot of old ghosts and sent them on their way. I asked if she'd like to tell me about those old ghosts, but she said some other time. Greg says to let her do it her way.

Speaking of Greg, he and I have signed up for a ballroom dance class, which is a lot different from square dancing, we've found. Right now we're learning the tango, which I've decided is a very *sensuous* dance, if you really get into the spirit of things, which Greg did last time. He showed up on the dance floor with a rose in his teeth and a gleam in his eye! I ask you, can you fall in love all over again with a man you've been married to for more than thirty-five years?

Nicole wrote to say we shouldn't expect her home this summer, even though she has finished the six-month "tour of duty" she signed up for in Mexico. I had a moment's concern at her staying longer, but when I read the rest of her letter, I understood why.

She was at Beto's side when he had a very special experience with a critically ill little girl. He'd done everything he knew to do for the child, but she was failing fast. The parents, who are LDS, asked if the *camisas blancas* could come and administer to her.

Beto scoffed that if he, with all his training, couldn't help the child, certainly two twenty-year-old kids would be useless. But Nicole convinced him to let the elders come. Beto watched them administer to the girl—and then watched her get better in a matter of hours! He was humbled and impressed. When he told *Abuelo* Hernandez about it, the old man nodded and said, "The *camisas blancas* do very fine things. It would be good if you listened to them."

When Nicole asked *Abuelo* Hernandez if he listened to the *camisas blancas*, he said, "The old priest and I were boys together. I have to listen to him." Then he grinned and added, "But I have two ears. I hear many things."

Loving the mystery of life,
Juneau

ERIN
>   E-mail, May 25, 2005
>   Dear COBs,
>
>   I'm a grandmother! Tessa Beckmann was born this morning.
>   Going by the photo Eddie took of her with his cell phone cam-
>   era, she's got his black hair and Kayla's straight eyebrows.
>
>   Cory is as ecstatic as I am. We're all driving up for Tessa's bless-
>   ing. Skipp and Linda, who are still on their mission, have
>   requested lots of photos of their first great-grandchild. I'll send
>   you some when we get back.
>
>   I'm draggy and beginning to think the bishop was right. Both
>   my little boys take a lot out of me, but I want to be able to give
>   them my best.
>
>   Erin

WILLADENE
>   E-mail, May 26, 2005
>   Dear Erin,
>
>   How strange, becoming a new mother and a new grandmother
>   in the same month! Tell Kayla congrats from me. Present in the
>   mail. Also please repeat my thanks for the help with the medi-
>   tation for pain control. I do it several times a day. Evvy's made
>   a running joke of the whole thing. If I take too long consider-
>   ing a response, she says, "Mom's having an *Om* moment."
>
>   Love,
>   Deenie

Deenie folded her body into the next yoga position on the chart
propped up on the living room wall. "You said I had to figure it out for
myself, but *if* you were going to tell me how to give my life to God, what
would you say?"

"You get on your knees," Miss B puffed as she stretched out her back,
"and you say, 'Lord, here's my life. Do with it as you will.'" She eased herself down on her mat with a grunt, pulled a towel around her shoulders,
and mumbled, "I'm too old for this."

"And?" Deenie prodded.

"Then you do the best you can to listen and obey whatever directions the good Lord sends along."

Deenie let out a whuff and plopped on the couch. "You make it sound easy."

"It is," Miss B said. "If you're willing to give up control and turn your life over to the Lord. Like I said before, it's all about surrender."

"That doesn't seem so scary. I thought you were going to say submission. I really hate that word," Deenie said, and Miss B laughed.

Email, May 31, 2005
Dear COBs,

I stopped at a local Christian gift store last night with Marsha, looking for a baptismal gift for her niece. I found a stenciled sign that reads, "God, Grace, Gratitude." What a wonderful replacement for our usual Gs—Guilt, Griff, Griffly! I bought one for each of us.

We fly to Salt Lake City June 5—I couldn't face the drive. Honey is too big to carry on, so I am reluctantly sending her with the luggage. She'll probably sleep through the whole trip and never know she left home.

Carl and Paul and their families will be there to greet us. It's going to be a terrific summer.

Love,
Deenie

The day before they were to leave for Wellsville, Evvy marched into Deenie's room announcing Honey was home from the groomers and ready for the trip.

"She looks like she's been in a blender," Deenie said.

"I know." Evvy gave Honey a snuggle. "The groomer said since her hair grows in every direction, unless we wanted her shaved, it was the best she could do. But she's clean, and her claws are clipped, and I love her anyway."

"By the way, Evvy, have I told you today I'm glad you're my daughter?"

"Yes," Evvy sighed dramatically. "And every day for the last two months! I get it, Mom."

"Good."

Later that afternoon Roger hefted the portable kennel into the back-seat of Deenie's truck and then hefted Honey, who was making the flight with them, into the kennel. "When are you going to teach this mutt to get in here under her own steam?"

Deenie wearily leaned her head on the side of the vehicle, thinking of the twenty-seven things on her Just in Case list she hadn't gotten to. "I told you to throw in a treat and she'd follow."

Roger gave her a look of concern. "Are you all right?"

"A headache again, but not one of those wretched migraines. The meds should start working in a few minutes, and then I'll be good to go."

"Are you certain? We can always change our tickets to later in the week if you need to rest."

"Not necessary, but if there's time, I'd appreciate you giving me a blessing."

"It'd be a privilege."

When Roger, Evvy, and Deenie were ready to leave for the airport, Roger had them gather in the living room, where he gave Deenie the requested blessing. When she stood to hug them after it was over, Evvy said, "Have I told you lately that I'm glad you're my mom?"

Deenie grinned. "Yes, but it's always good to hear."

JUNEAU

Juneau flew to Oregon in June to visit her mother and sign books at a local bookstore, as Misty had arranged. Pamela picked her up at the air-port looking remarkably rested for someone who'd just returned from a trip halfway around the world. She'd brought back only one souvenir from her China tour, a large photograph of herself perched atop a camel with the Great Wall in the background.

"That's just like you, Mom," Juneau said, smiling. "You always were out to try everything. But I'm glad you're safely home. I worried about you."

Her mother raised her eyebrows. "Why?"

"Well," Juneau said, "it's a long way for you to go at eighty-one."

Her mother shrugged. "I'd be eighty-one even if I'd stayed home and sat in the corner. You'd better get over worrying, because I've already signed up for a tour of Denmark next spring. I've always wanted to see where our ancestors came from."

"You're amazing, jaunting around the world like that," Juneau said. She regarded herself as lucky. Some of her friends referred to themselves as the sandwich generation, the filling between ailing, aging parents and fractious teenagers. She didn't really have to worry about either age group. Gideon wasn't anything like Misty had been at his age.

Thinking about Misty set off the usual round of second-guessing and wishing that things were different. That Misty would confide in her more, not be so secretive, but how could she be otherwise, with Juneau and Pamela as examples? That she'd come back to the Church, that she'd find whatever it was she was looking for and settle down with a nice husband and some kids. . . .

Juneau sighed. She'd carried her worry about Misty far too long. It was time to get off that carousel. "What time am I supposed to be at the bookstore tomorrow, Mom?" she asked.

Pamela consulted a wall calendar with penciled-in notations. "Lorene—the bookstore manager—said noon to two is best. They have a fair amount of lunchtime traffic on Saturdays."

That day, Juneau slipped behind the table where stacks of books and a pen were laid out, wondering what kind of signing this would be. But Lorene must have advertised the signing well, because right away several teenage girls lined up, giggling, to get what they called their "fave reads" autographed. Juneau was gratified when girl after girl said, "I'm like Catalina, looking for myself," or "That girl in Williamsburg—she could have been me." It was such a satisfaction to know that what she had to say was reaching her readers.

A number of mothers stopped by, too, to examine the books and then buy them for their daughters. It was almost two o'clock when the last person in line, an attractive woman about her own age, approached the table.

"Hello, Juneau," she said.

Juneau smiled. Readers often addressed her by her first name. The woman smiled back, waiting. *Am I supposed to know her?* Juneau wondered. She was about Juneau's height and slender. She wore jeans and a black leather jacket, and her short black hair was streaked with gray and spiked with gel. Nothing familiar so far, but there was something about those eyes, those snapping black eyes. . . .

"Starette!" Juneau cried. Leaping from her chair, she embraced her old trailer park friend. "Oh, dear heaven, how long has it been?"

"Forever." Starette hugged her fiercely and then held her at arm's length. "I see you're still the skinny blonde kid I used to know."

Juneau lifted a lock of her hair. "Blonde from a bottle these days!"

"I used to do the same," Starette said, "until I got too busy."

"Busy with what?"

"Being a bishop's wife. Riding herd on five kids."

"Bishop's wife?" Juneau was startled and knew it showed.

"Don't worry. I haven't changed that much." Starette grinned. "Cameron—he's my husband—and I have matching Hogs. He's known as 'the Biker Bishop,' and everybody in the ward accepts that on Saturday mornings our whole family will be out on the road. Grandkids included."

Juneau grinned at the mental picture of Starette's biker-bishop husband and their family. "I can see we have a lot to talk about," she said. "Beginning with, I didn't even know you'd joined the Church."

"If I'd had your address, I could have told you I joined because of knowing you and Flint and your folks," Starette said. "I kept on going to Primary after you left, and I was baptized when I was a teenager."

Juneau sobered. "Look, have you had lunch? Can we go somewhere and talk? I'm through here now."

Starette waited while Juneau thanked Lorene and shook hands with the young store employees who seemed impressed to have a real live author visiting. Then the two of them went to a quaint little cafe nearby and ordered lunch.

"I can't believe you just showed up at the bookstore like that," Juneau said as they settled back to wait for their food. "It couldn't have been a coincidence. Did you see one of Lorene's flyers or something?"

"Or something. Misty contacted me and told me you were going to be here."

"Misty?"

"She said her dad located me on the computer and gave you a card with all my info. But you didn't call. So she decided to do it for you."

"Oh, my." Juneau felt found out, exposed. "I almost called a hundred times. I was afraid—"

"—to find out what happened to Brenna," Starette finished for her. "So you left me alone to keep our secret for all these years."

Ashamed, Juneau nodded. "Is Brenna . . ."

"Alive? Yes."

"Does she know who hurt her?" Juneau asked.

"I told her."

Juneau twisted her hands together. "Does she hate us?"

Starette dug in her purse and brought out a card. "Here's her phone number," she said. "You can find out for yourself."

Juneau took the card as the food arrived. They spoke of other things and traded grandchildren stories while they ate. "I'll be in touch," Juneau said as they parted.

Starette gave her an appraising look. "I'll be waiting."

That night, back at her mother's little house in the woods, Juneau dialed Brenna's phone number, but she hung up before it rang.

ERIN

The morning in mid-June when Erin woke up rested and pain-free, with no edema in her lower legs, she thought, *I have my life back.*

Joanna was already downstairs with Hannah and Tony, and Noah, who'd had an early feeding, was asleep. So she opened the windows, made the bed with fresh linens, and cleaned the bathroom. After showering and dressing, she put on some makeup and took Noah downstairs.

Joanna, whose graying hair had the odd effect of making her look young, glanced up and smiled. "Why, Erin, don't you look nice? You must be feeling better."

"I am. I thought I'd take Tony and the dogs for a little walk and then make some phone calls."

"I imagine you have a lot of people to thank."

"That, too, but I was thinking of letting my business contacts know I'm back in the saddle."

"Erin, whatever for?" Joanna's worry was in her voice. "You don't need to work. Why don't you enjoy being a stay-at-home mommy?"

"You and Jake are the ones who should be retiring."

"We are."

"That's good news." Erin laid Noah in his carrier and asked, "When?"

"When we sell the store."

"Don't forget, you promised me and Caitlin first refusal a while back."

Joanna gaped. "We didn't think you were serious. You both have young families to care for. You don't need the burden of running the store."

"Let us decide that for ourselves, Mom."

JUNEAU

Five days after she returned home, Juneau finally found the courage to call Brenna Petry. Brenna Roholt now, the card Starette gave her said. She pressed in the number Starette had given her, feeling the way she'd felt just before starting down Shaefer Trail back in Moab. Sometimes you just had to go over the edge of the cliff.

When a cheerful voice answered, "Brenna here," Juneau almost hung up again. But realizing it was now or never, she blurted out who she was.

There was a short silence when she finished. Then Brenna said, "It took about three decades longer for guilt to catch up with you than it did with Starette. She confessed a long time ago."

"I'm sorry, Brenna," Juneau said.

Brenna's response was curt. "You should be."

"What we did was awful. Just thinking about it makes me sick," Juneau stammered. "So I tried not to think about it. I kept it stuffed away for years, but then . . . Will you accept my apologies? Will you forgive me?"

There was a pause, and then Brenna said, "I guess you've had your punishment by now."

"Maybe not enough," Juneau said. "Were you badly hurt?"

"Yes. I still walk with a limp."

"Brenna, I can't tell you . . ."

"You can stop apologizing, Juneau," Brenna said. "I'm not going to hold it over your head. Though I wanted to when Starette first told me. You're lucky she talked to me first—I don't think you would've done very well handling what I dumped on her. I was really mad when she confessed."

"You, can dump it on me now, if you want to."

"No. I'm a long way past that. Hearing how I made life miserable for you and Starette when we were kids helped me look at things differently. I was mean, so you decided to be mean back. We're all to blame."

"You, not so much," Juneau said. "I mean, the limp. . . ."

"Don't think about it. I don't, except on bad days. I've learned how to compensate for my disability." She chuckled slightly. "I even get held up as a great example of courage and determination. How about that!"

Juneau felt ill. Her fears hadn't been baseless. Brenna had suffered because of her actions.

"I've lived a good life, Juneau," Brenna said in a softer tone. "Really. I'm the state director for an organization that does fundraising for spinal injuries. I have a fine husband, two great children, and three grandkids. And an elderly dog and two cats."

"I've got much the same lineup," Juneau said. She told Brenna about her daughters, Gideon, the animals, and her three grandkids. They spent the next half hour sharing family stories. By the time they hung up, Juneau felt the weight of guilt begin to lift from her shoulders.

The next day, she called Erin and Deenie to say she'd cleaned out the last secret from her guilt closet. Then she moved into the bright new upstairs writing room.

WILLADENE
E-mail, July 10, 2005
Dear COBs,

I've spent the last two weeks glorying in grandmotherhood. With Sookie and Dani on the scene to take care of everything else, all I've had to do is play with Dee, Chul, and Belle. Who knew playing with building blocks could be so much fun? As the kids around here say, "Sweeeet!"

My default sitter is Honey. When the grandbabies won't take their naps, I put them in the same room with our lazy dog. They wear themselves out trying to get her to play. In no time all three are asleep cuddled up by her side. Grandpa Wilford claims all the credit. He says he knew Honey was a keeper the moment he saw her. Although he is markedly frail, having his great-grandbabies around has perked him up. Mom and Dad, too.

Love,
Deenie

P.S. Erin, the Hull vase is the perfect companion for Jenny's Roseville. She was thrilled with the choice. The fact I would take the time to get it for her put the seal on our new relationship. Thank you so much for your help.

Chapter 32

ERIN

In July, Erin answered the phone, hoping it was one of her contacts with a lead. "Hey, you," Lucky Brown said. "How come you haven't called me about having a Baby Welcome for Noah? And don't tell me you've been too busy. That would be just plain wrong."

"Okay, I won't," Erin said.

"So when are we going to have it?"

Sighing, Erin checked her calendar. As she marked the agreed-upon date on it, she thought, *One more thing to do.*

Now that she was feeling better, she'd begun taking up all the threads of her life and adding new ones, with the result that she was frazzled and frustrated and exhausted and angry that she couldn't do everything she thought she ought to do.

"You've got to slow down," Vince said one night as he helped straighten the family room. "Your babies miss you. Hannah and I miss you. Mark, too, even if he is always working or with his friends."

"I'm here," she said.

"Here and busy. We *miss* you."

She hugged him, hiding her face on his shoulder so he wouldn't see how ashamed she was. She knew she was never completely present in anything she did with them, always thinking about a phone call or an errand that needed running. That was the way she'd "done" life for most of the past twenty-five years.

It had worked, once, but it wasn't working now, and she knew it. Why had she gotten back on the treadmill again? She wasn't fourteen and without resources. She wasn't a single mother driven to provide the best for her children. Why did she keep herself too busy to enjoy the emotional intimacy she longed for?

On the evening of the Baby Welcome, All the Usual Suspects, as Lucky called the guest list, arrived at the appointed time. Including Linda

Johnson. She and Skipp had been home from their mission several weeks, and they'd stopped by often to spend time with Mark and Hannah. And the boys, whom they treated as grandsons.

The Welcome started out as Erin expected, with conversation and laughter, followed by the bestowing of gifts and then more conversation. But it took a turn when Erin said something about her and Caitlin maybe buying Finishing Touches.

"Hold it," Caitlin said. "I considered doing that—for about five minutes! But I don't want the responsibility. It would take me away from the girls and Sam. In fact—" she paused. "Well, I'm thinking of making this flip our last."

Erin tried to conceal her surprise. Caitlin had been as excited as she when they bought the place they were currently flipping. "Why?" she asked.

"I miss when we used to do things for fun. All we ever do these days is work."

"Not always," Erin protested.

"You do keep yourself very busy, Erin," Brenda said.

"There's a lot to be done." Erin's tone was sharper than she'd intended.

"You don't have to do it all yourself." Joanna touched Erin's arm. "Sit down, dear, and tell me the truth. Has this been an enjoyable evening?"

"Of course!" Erin's cheeks flamed. "Okay, I was put off when Lucky suggested it. I didn't want one more thing on my calendar, even something I wanted to do. Even something I'm glad we did."

"I know what your problem is, girl," Lucky said. "You can't tell the difference between what *has* to be done, what *could* be done, and what *never needs* to be done."

"Probably," Erin said with a little laugh. "Care to enlighten me?"

"It's easy. Ask yourself: *If I don't do this, will it cause young children to die?* If the answer is no, you don't have to do it."

Horrified laughter filled the living room. When it died down, Brenda put an arm around Caitlin. "Learn from my experience, Erin, dear. Whatever you accomplish in your life, if you've done it at the expense of building a relationship with your children and your husband, you'll regret it. And you might not get a second chance, like I did."

E-mail, July 18, 2005
Dear COBs,

You won't believe what I'm going to do today. Nothing—except spend time with my children and my husband. It took a smack upside the head to get me to see I was stuck in old patterns that weren't working, acting as if I were a still single mother struggling to provide for and raise my children.

I'm not. I have a wonderful husband and no financial concerns. All I have to do is learn to enjoy the life I have. I took a big step in that direction when I passed all my clients on to other interior designers and retired!

Tony and Noah are happier now that I'm a more relaxed mother. Hannah and Mark and Kayla, too. They're older, but they still need me, although in different ways. I'm contented in a way I never thought possible, and Vince . . . Well, he just smiles all the time!

The other big news is that Mark's been called to the Mexico Mazatlan mission! All the Spanish he knows is from *The Terminator: No problemo* and *Hasta la vista, Baby.*

Erin

The person most excited about Mark's mission call was Ricky. When the Harringtons came over for supper one night, he could talk of little else. After the meal, when Steve and Vince went down to the rec room to talk merit badges and Hannah took the boys into the great room to play, Ricky said to Mark, "You have to memorize lots of scriptures. And learn hymns in case you have to play."

"How's this?" Mark sat at the piano in the living room and played "We Thank Thee, O God, for a Prophet" with impressive flourishes.

"Neat!" Ricky said. "Show me how to do that. For when I go on my mission."

Mark slid over on the bench and began teaching Ricky the first phrase of the melody. Colleen, sitting beside Erin in the dining room, watched them with a pensive look. Erin knew she must be thinking about

Ricky's future. He had been ordained a deacon when he was fourteen and then a teacher and a priest, and he did most things all the other young men did—with modifications taking his capacities into account. But a mission?

"Maybe there is a way for Ricky to serve," Erin said.

"We've talked to the stake president about it a lot," Colleen said. "He says he'd be glad to call Ricky to a local service mission or ward mission. I don't know what it would look like, but I hope sometime . . ."

She smiled as Ricky played what he'd learned while Mark played the accompanying chords. "Mark's been great with Ricky this summer. It's almost been like old times."

Erin nodded. The talk she'd had with Mark before he went down to Madison last fall seemed to have sunk in. That, and his desire to be ready for his mission seemed to have softened him. He was a nicer person.

Except when it came to Cory.

After the Harringtons left, Erin said, "Your being a friend means a lot to Ricky, Mark." She paused. "It would mean a lot to your dad, too. Can't you give him even a minute or two?"

Mark ran his fingers idly over the piano keys. "I'm not comfortable around him. We don't have anything to say to each other."

"Oh, I imagine you do," Erin said, smoothing Mark's hair.

Mark grunted. "But it wouldn't change anything about who Dad is, would it?"

"No. You have to accept him as he is. Like you do Ricky."

The Sunday Mark was to speak, friends and relatives filled two side pews. All three sets of grandparents were there, plus Kayla, Eddie, and little Tessa, the Harringtons, Melina, Althea and Princess the dog, and Cory. He had slipped into the space Erin had saved for him after the sacrament had been passed.

Before Mark was to give his talk, he went to the piano. To Erin's surprise, instead of beginning the Mozart he'd chosen to play, he motioned Ricky to join him. An ebullient Ricky did so, and together they played a duet of "Come, Come Ye Saints," with Ricky doing the melody. Erin took a tissue from her purse for herself and handed one to Colleen.

After the duet was over, Mark stood at the pulpit. He spoke movingly about his testimony and his desire to serve the Lord. At the conclusion, he began thanking all those who'd made a difference in his life. Erin's eyes filled as he paid tribute to her. Then her heart seized as he said, "I'm also thankful for . . ." And stopped as if something was caught in his throat.

Erin could almost hear the anticipated words, "my dad." But when Mark continued, he said, "my mother's husband, Vince Gerlach. I can go on my mission knowing that my mom and Hannah and my brothers will be fine, because Vince will be there, taking care of them."

Erin's cheeks burned as the family gathered in the foyer after the meeting. She put on a smile when members of the congregation congratulated her on having a fine son, but Mark's obvious snub of his father was devastating to both her and Cory.

When Mark finally made his way to the foyer, Erin took him by the arm and directed him into an empty classroom and shut the door.

Standing arms akimbo, she said, "I never thought I'd be ashamed of you at a time like this. But that deliberate snub of your father when he was sitting in the audience is inexcusable. No matter what you think of the way he lives, you owe him your respect for everything he's done for you."

Mark stiffened. "I didn't do anything different from what Grandpa did in his mission talk."

"He was wrong. He said as much in a letter he wrote to your dad. Surely he told you about it."

"Some."

"Then you know Skipp felt his mission didn't really start until he understood what it means to be compassionate, loving, and forgiving— and reconciled with your dad."

She paused. "Listen, son. You're going to meet all kinds of people on your mission. You aren't being sent to judge them but to love them as God loves them. You won't be able to do that for others if you can't do it for your father."

When Mark ducked his head, Erin gently raised his chin. "You know what I think? I think you love your dad, but you stay angry because you don't want to feel how deeply you miss the relationship you once had. The father you think you've lost."

"I do miss him," Mark choked out, sounding very young.

"You haven't lost him," Erin said. "He's right outside that door. Waiting for his son."

Mark wiped his eyes with the sleeve of his new suit jacket and gave her a little smile. "Are we done here?"

Erin followed him into the foyer and watched as he approached his father. "Dad," he said, hesitantly extending his hand. Cory looked at him with a hopeful yet cautious expression. They gripped hands and shook them for several seconds, as if not sure what to do. Then they hugged, awkwardly patting each other's backs.

Skipp joined them, and the three huddled together. Erin saw Cory's eyes glisten, heard him murmur something to his son and his father. She could discern only the words "sorry" and "forgiveness" but she felt no need to hear more. It was a private moment that belonged to them.

Looking around the table where the family gathered after Mark's farewell, Erin thought how much of her life had been defined by family dinners—the good, the less than memorable, and the definitely ugly. In this joyful, relaxed atmosphere, it was hard to believe that she'd once been at the mercy of the tirades Grams had let loose at family gatherings. Hard to imagine the change Grams had made over the years and the touching relationship she'd developed with her first great-grandchild, Kayla.

Kayla. What a catalyst she had been, naively insisting that people who had avoided each other for years should sit down at the same table because they were *her family*. Because of her, Andrew, Grams, and Joanna had made peace—and Andrew and Lottie had actually come to the wedding of Joanna and Jake. Through Andrew and Caitlin, a tenuous connection with The Grandparents McGee had been made before their passing, and through Caitlin's daughter, Lindsay, that connection had deepened. If none of that had happened, these dear people wouldn't have gathered to celebrate a significant milestone in the life of her son.

She smiled at Cory, who mouthed, "Thank you." Was their marriage a mistake? She couldn't think so. It had put some wonderful gifts in her future. Her beautiful children. Her relationship with Skipp and Linda, which had grown to a deep love and respect. It had also been a stepping-stone to her marriage to Vince and her two little boys.

Her heart was so full, she could hardly breathe. All she had ever wanted was a Forever Family. She'd thought to bind her family together through doing whatever it took to be a good Mormon woman. But now, surrounded by people who meant everything in the world to her, she realized that in the end what bound them together was love.

WILLADENE
E-mail, August 15, 2005
Dear Erin and Juneau,

Erin, I was so glad to hear that Mark has reconciled with his father. After your call, I had a wonderful talk with Pat about unfinished business, family reconciliation, and forgiveness. Until she knocked me for a loop with the question, "Have you forgiven Rod Tulley for trying to kill you?"

Whoa! That wasn't on my list. But she's right. I'll take a first step toward doing that by putting his name on the temple prayer roll. But I'll still keep checking on his parole status.

I'll be there this afternoon for the wedding of Reece Crafton to Miss Rachel Smoot. Having him fall wildly, madly in love with a wonderful girl who feels the same about him is part of the last chapter in the Nicole/Reece/Beto story.

With the grandbabies gone, I'm spending lots of time chauffeuring Wilford and Mom and Dad as we visit the remaining family members of their generation. My sister-in-law Charlotte comes, too, with recorder in hand to take down all the history she can.

Each visit follows the same format. There are hugs and kisses and a few words about the present, but most of the conversations are about the past, deeds done and left undone. They are declaring their lives. I get the feeling that these visits are the last thing on my parents' Just in Case list. One of Mom's cousins, at eighty-nine, says she's not getting older, she's just growing closer to a better life. It is all very poignant. I feel to the very center of my heart their longing to reunite with all the family who have gone on before them.

Tomorrow, I'll help Mom close up the second floor of their house. They've decided the stairs are too much for them and are settling into the guest room on the main floor.

My, what a summer this has been!

Love,
Deenie

Willadene sat down on the kitchen steps with her load of wet sheets. She wanted them line-dried and smelling sweet for the cabin. It was the last thing on her list of things to do to prepare for celebrating the completion of the COBs' twenty-five-year pact. Like the list she had made the first time they'd joined her in Utah, this list contained meals prepared in advance, fresh flowers in the guest rooms, new towels in the bathroom, and chocolates on the pillows at home as well as at the cabin on Bear Lake.

The big difference was that this time Deenie hadn't done it all herself. Roger and Evvy had helped as long as they were in Wellsville. Jenny and Charlotte, who were becoming Deenie's fast friends, stepped in almost daily, and everyone insisted that she take it easy.

"I'm almost as excited about the COBs coming as you are," Charlotte had said one afternoon as they put final touches on the cabin. "Listening to you tell about your adventures together has been as good as any book I've read."

"Me, too," Jenny had said. "Is there a day when we can come up and meet them?"

"Pick the day, and it's yours," Deenie had replied.

Now, she stood and stretched her back. The few minutes' rest had given her a breather but hadn't stopped the ache in her legs or the pressure building behind her right eye. She sighed, hefted the heavy laundry basket to her right hip, and tromped down the garden path to the clothesline.

She'd hung one sheet and was bending to pick up the next when a blinding pain shot through her temple. Her vision darkened from the outside, spiraling inward and closing off the light. A faint breeze whispered by, touching her cheek. A Sunny touch of greeting, of comfort, of love.

Now? Deenie wondered as she fell to her knees and toppled on the grass. There was no answer, and the world faded away.

JUNEAU

Juneau drove the rental car from the Salt Lake City airport to Wellsville. All the way there, she felt the new strength and serenity that Erin, sitting in the passenger seat, radiated. It filled her with both a sense of comfort and of yearning. She glanced at her friend, who was half turned to check on Noah, buckled in his car seat in back. "As Marisol would say, *Que bonito!*"

Erin smiled. "I just love this kid."

Juneau felt the warmth of Erin's contentment. She seemed to have reached the place of completeness that Juneau herself had been striving for but hadn't quite yet reached.

"I think you can declare yourself a COB, my friend," Juneau said.

"I don't know about that." Laughing, Erin retrieved a mini journal from her purse. "I've been writing down all the qualities I thought constituted COBhood. Caitlin says they're like the qualifications a person has to fill to be declared a saint. Going by this list, I'm neither saint nor COB."

When their laughter subsided, Erin asked, "What's the latest from Nicole? Is she happy in Mexico?"

"More than happy," Juneau said. "In her last letter, she reported seeing an open Book of Mormon on the desk in Beto's clinic office. In the past he always declined reading it, but apparently something got to him."

Erin nodded. "Probably the healing of the little girl. Has she talked to Beto about it?"

"Not yet," Juneau said. "She felt it best to wait until he brings it up himself."

"Their story is way more compelling than any of the romances we used to read," Erin said. "I can't wait for the next installment!"

They chatted pleasantly all the way to Cache Valley, their conversation interrupted now and then by a chortle or happy gurgle from Noah. In many ways he reminded Juneau of Gideon when he'd been a baby.

Wellsville sparkled in the bracing autumn air, and Juneau felt excitement rising as she pulled up in front of Deenie's beloved gray house. Deenie had warned them it wouldn't be the same, but despite the changes it still looked warm and welcoming. The orchard, which had been in full bloom when they'd first been there in 1981, was now ready for harvest with red and yellow apples hanging from the trees. Symbolic, Juneau thought, stopping the car and getting out.

"I can't wait to see Deenie," Erin said as she unbuckled Noah from his car seat. "Let's leave the luggage until we give that girl a hug."

"Right," Juneau agreed, eager to see their friend. There was no question in her mind that Deenie qualified for COBhood. She'd seemed almost there twenty-five years ago, with her "be prepared for anything" tote bag.

"You get Noah out of the car seat, and I'll let Deenie know we're here." Juneau hurried along the walk and up the steps. Only then did she see the folded note taped to the door. "It looks like she's going to send us on a treasure hunt or something," she called back over her shoulder. "It's so Deenie!"

"Well, let's get to it," Erin said as she set Noah's car seat on the porch.

Juneau pulled the note from the door, opened it up, and scanned it. "Deenie's in the hospital!" she gasped.

"Oh, no!" Erin cried, peering over Juneau's shoulder.

"The note's from Jenny with a number we're supposed to call."

"Deenie hasn't felt well for some time. And there's Sunny's call. Do you think . . . ?"

Hands shaking, Juneau dug in her purse for her cell phone and punched in the number Jenny had written.

Jenny answered after the first ring. "Hello? Is this Juneau or Erin?"

"It's Juneau," Juneau said, steeling herself to hear the worst. "What happened, Jenny?"

"We don't know," Jenny said. "She passed out cold hanging up sheets to line dry. They've run some tests. We should know more tomorrow."

"Should we come to the hospital?"

"No. She's sleeping now. You and Erin make yourselves at home. She

had everything ready for you, complete with chocolates on your pillows."
Jenny gave a slight laugh. "You know how Deenie is."

Juneau nodded, feeling giddy with relief that Deenie wasn't . . . she
didn't even want to think the word. "Please give her our love when she
wakes up, will you?"

After exchanging a few more words with Jenny, Juneau hung up.
"The door is unlocked," she told Erin. "We're on our own tonight."

The house without Deenie was just a house. Juneau and Erin went
about getting Noah settled in, and then they unpacked, their hearts
heavy with thoughts of The Griff. The Great What If. Despite their concerns about Deenie's health, neither had really believed it would jeop-
ardize keeping The Pact. What if . . . ? They couldn't say it.

Instead, they heated the casserole Deenie had apparently set out on
the counter before she collapsed. Dutifully, they sat down to eat it, but
neither was very hungry. So they watched as Noah gummed his Cheerios.

"I was so glad when you told me you'd cleared out your guilt closet,"
Erin said. "Tell me about your conversation with Brenna."

So Juneau did, finishing up with, "Guess what she said after I'd
whined out all my apologies."

Erin shook her head.

"That I should come off it. It'd happened a long time ago when we
were kids, and we were all partly responsible."

"And to think you've been punishing yourself unnecessarily. You must
be immensely relieved."

"Yes," Juneau said. "There's only one major rock left in my stream,
to use Gabby's words. Misty. If she would only return to the fold."

Erin gave her a quizzical look. "It seems to me that Misty's making
an effort to be part of your family circle again. And from what you've
written and EJ's told me about her, I'd say she's finding her own way.
Making a contribution. And a difference. Look at how she's helped EJ."
Erin paused. "Is it possible that the problem is not entirely with *her*, dear
friend? Maybe what Misty needs is to be significant in your eyes."

Erin's soft statement prodded Juneau into facing what she hadn't
wanted to look at. What kept her from seeing Misty as others saw her, a
significant person, when the evidence of her evolution into a successful

and caring adult was all around? Who did Misty have to be, before she would love her wholeheartedly—another Nicole, good-natured and compliant?

That would never happen, and to be truthful, Juneau wasn't sure she would even want it. Misty was Misty—just as Juneau was Juneau. She seemed to be realizing who she was, more and more, the way Juneau had finally found herself. She thought how Greg and Gabby and the COBs and so many others had loved her, Juneau, without reservation when she had gone through her own search for herself. And how that love had helped her to grow into a woman who now knew and accepted who she was and had built a life and family she loved.

Suddenly, Juneau knew what she had to do. Again she pulled her cell phone from her purse and excused herself. Stepping out onto the porch, she called Misty. When her daughter answered, Juneau said without preliminaries, "Misty, I love you. Unconditionally. Forever and ever. Period."

There was a momentary silence, and then Misty said, "Mom? Do you know what you're saying? I'm still me. Flaky. Off-center. Wandering." She paused and added, "Searching."

"I know." Juneau repeated the words again. "I love you, Misty. Just as you are."

There was a longer silence. Then Misty, her voice uneven, said, "Mom, you don't know how long I've waited for you to say that."

WILLADENE

Deenie woke up refreshed after a sound sleep. The excruciating headache from the night before was gone. In fact, she was embarrassed to feel so good after having caused so much commotion and concern. And she was filled with a warm certainty that everything was going to be all right.

Well, she thought, *that's surprising.* She hadn't conjured the feeling up. After all her striving to create peace in her life, it had presented itself like a gift. It occurred to Deenie as she watched the sun rise through the slats of the hospital window and reveled in the feeling, that this kind of gift was exactly what Miss B had been talking about when she'd given Deenie her farewell advice in Gainesville.

"Remember, Deenie," she'd said. "It's time to let go and let the good Lord do his job."

Have I done that? Deenie wondered.

That jogged another memory. The moment when, as she floated in and out of consciousness in the back of the ambulance, she'd simply released herself into the arms of God. Let go in the most profound way and found herself safe and at peace. And she knew now she would never be the same again.

She slipped out of bed and knelt in a prayer of gratitude. Then, pragmatic as ever, she headed for the shower.

The phone rang as she was dressing. It was Roger. "How's my wife this morning?"

Deenie's voice was bright with all the hope and joy she was feeling. "Roger, sweetheart, I'm fine."

Dressed in her own clothes and waiting to be released from the hospital, Deenie was flipping TV channels when Jenny led Juneau and Erin into her room. Jenny held out her arms to take Noah from Erin, but Deenie, ignoring her friends' astonished faces, said, "Don't take that boy until I've given him a squeeze." She gave Noah a kiss and a tickle, relishing the touch of smooth baby skin. Then Jenny took him from the room.

"What a cutie he is, Erin," Deenie said cheerfully, hugging her and then Juneau. "I'm so glad to see you two! Pull up some chairs so we can talk."

"What's with this miraculous recovery?" Juneau demanded. "Deenie, you scared us witless. We thought you were dying."

Given the extraordinary experiences of her morning, Deenie hadn't thought of how distressed her friends would be. "I'm so sorry I scared you," she said. "I scared myself. I had this terrible pain. I couldn't see, my face went numb, I felt Sunny next to me, and I thought, *So this is what it's like.* That's when I passed out."

"But you're okay now?" Erin asked.

"I just need to take it easy. Doctor's orders."

Juneau's expression changed from consternation to exasperation. "Hey, pal," she said, "what's wrong with this picture? Whenever we come to visit, you end up flat on your face!"

Deenie chuckled. "Guilty as charged. The first time, I fainted because I overdid it trying to be the perfect hostess. This time, it was a migraine crisis." She paused, chagrined. "Looks like I overdid it getting ready to die."

First there was stunned silence, and then they all burst into laughter. They ended up in a clutch on Deenie's bed, holding each other while their merriment broke the tension.

"Honestly," Deenie said, "I really did think I was on my way out. Every time I took on a new project from my Just in Case list, I prayed to see if it would benefit my family and please God. I got a warm confirmation every time."

"Well, duh," Erin said. "It would please God if any one of us did those things."

Juneau leaned into Deenie's face. "Did you really think you were going to put your life in a neat package, tie it with a pink ribbon, and hand it to St. Peter at the gate?"

Deenie laughed at herself. "Sort of."

"There's one thing I've wondered ever since that day on the rock at Angel Arch," Erin said. "Did you ever ask God if he thought it was the end?"

"No. I kept having the feeling I was missing something, and that was it. Asking God, I mean," Deenie said. "I won't make that mistake again! Now, enough of that. Did I tell you how glad I am to see you both?"

"And we're glad to be here, you goofy girl," Erin said affectionately.

"Twenty-five years after we made that Pact," Juneau said. "What do you think? Have we achieved COBhood?"

Erin dug in her purse and held up her mini journal. "I started writing down indications of COBhood after we met at Gabby's house in 2002. I've got pages of them. But you know what? I don't think they're the key."

"Neither is living by a checklist, even a Just in Case list," Deenie said.

"Do you know what I think Gabby would say?" Juneau's voice held conviction. "That there's no great secret, no magical formula. She'd say COBhood is getting up every morning and putting one foot in front of the other, doing our best, and cleaning up our messes and trying again."

"Facing life no matter what it brings," Erin said.

"Loving one another. Trusting God," Deenie said.

In the silence that followed, Deenie felt a deep sense of completion. What an amazing thing that they were here together, after all these years! Their friendship had informed and defined each of their lives in a profound way, changing them, and through them, the lives of those with whom they were connected. Erin and Juneau were feeling the same thing, Deenie knew—it showed in their smiles and the glistening of tears in their eyes.

A clatter in the hall broke the moment, and they gave a collective sigh.

"So what do we do now?" Erin asked.

"You mean besides spending a week at the cabin?" Deenie said.

Juneau's smile was wide. "To quote Gabby, we pull up our socks and then put one foot in front of the other." She paused. "And take the first step into the next twenty-five years of our lives."

Discovery Questions

1. In Latter-day Saint fiction, as in life, there is tension between the ideal that Church members strive for and the realities of life they and their families face. How do the characters and situations in *Surprise Packages* reflect this tension?

2. What issues did Juneau, Deenie, and Erin have when they first met at Education Week in *Almost Sisters*? In what ways do those issues manifest themselves in the second and third books of the series?

3. The holding of guilty secrets, sometimes for generations, affects each woman and her family. Is withholding of information ever justified? Under what circumstances?

4. All of the Crusty Old Broads have blind spots, things they don't realize or refuse to acknowledge about themselves. What are they? How do they trap the women in old, unproductive patterns?

5. How would you describe the relationship each of the COBs has with her husband? (Both husbands, in Erin's case.) What turning points move the women toward deeper levels of trust and love?

6. Using Juneau's interaction with Shan Beldon and Deenie's with Roger as a starting point, discuss if—and when—it's appropriate to intervene in another person's life.

7. In an e-mail Erin asks Juneau and Deenie, "What do men want?" How would you answer that question?

8. When Deenie moves to Florida, she wonders if "a new where requires a new who." How has "place" affected your personal history?

9. Which of the three women do you identify with most strongly in *Surprise Packages*? Why? Is your answer different for the first two books?

10. Erin, Deenie, and Juneau have had many mentors in their quest to become COBs. Who are the women you've looked to as mentors?